Dr. CARTER
Series

CONFIDENTIAL
FILE 101

Dr. CARTER
Series

CONFIDENTIAL FILE 101

Frank Carr & Patrick Sutter

ANGLEHART PRESS
NEW YORK, NEW YORK

Front cover and title page design by M. Richard, Manu Design.
Cover photo © copyright P. Bordes/Explorer/PubliPhoto.
Author photos by G. Ste-Marie, PhotoStop.
Interior and dust jacket design by About Books, Inc.

First printing 2001

ISBN 0-9701583-0-0

LCCN 00-091957

ATTENTION CORPORATIONS, UNIVERSITIES, COLLEGES, AND PROFESSIONAL ORGANIZATIONS: Quantity discounts are available on bulk purchases of this book for educational purposes. Special books or book excerpts can also be created to fit specific needs. For information, please contact Anglehart Press (A Division of MIC USA, Inc.), 244 Fifth Avenue, Suite D243, New York, NY 10001-7604; ph. 1-800-688-9642 or 212-591-0377.

Special thanks are in order to Christina Maria Wolaniuk for sharing with us her time and talent.

The writing of this book is largely due to her choice of words, editing and creative style. It is also very much the result of her tireless effort, professionalism and most noteworthy her loyalty to this project.

ACKNOWLEDGMENTS

The authors have many creative contributors to thank for the final shape and content of this book.

Caty De Sutter's inspired suggestions for plot, scene and character development proved invaluable to our project. Raynold Gideon injected elements of tension and intrigue into the situations, while strengthening clarity in the text. June Alexander applied her considerable intelligence and care to the final proofreading of the manuscript. And Marc Richard produced an alluring internal vision on the cover that beautifully reflects the content and captures the eye.

The accomplished Marilyn and Tom Ross and their About Books, Inc., staff guided our new writing venture to successful completion with perceptive, professional, and prompt follow-through. Sue Collier's editorial input helped build fluid prose and accessible instruction for the reader. Cathy Bowman and Kate Deubert were responsive and resourceful in offering astute advice and implementing production demands.

Finally, we gratefully acknowledge the ingenious Jean-Yves Desjardins. This book is an outgrowth of his innovative teachings in the field of sex therapy and would not exist without his visionary presence in our lives.

This book contains material that could have an impact on your sexual and emotional life. In a preliminary survey conducted in North America and Europe, men and women reported that *Confidential File 101* changed their sexual behavior and attitudes toward sex. They said they are more comfortable with their sexuality, have a greater understanding of their partner, engage in sex more frequently and enjoy sex more than they did previously.

Authors' Note
This is a sex-informative novel. The plot and characters are completely fictional. The names were chosen at random and bear absolutely no relation to real people either in the present or the past. However, all the psychological information, physiological data and sexological descriptions are rigorously exact. They are based on the latest scientific research and numerous case studies drawn from our clinical practices.

My name is Dr. Carter. I've been working in the field of clinical sexology for more than fifteen years. Through my practice, I have had the privilege of helping thousands of people improve their sexual and romantic lives. Today, I am just as fascinated by my job as I was when I first started.

Sexology is a young science. There still remains a lot of untouched ground to explore. Of course, considerable progress has been achieved over the past years. We have reached the point where it's relatively easy to help people obtain an erection, prolong the duration of intercourse or reach orgasm.

But this isn't enough. Far from it! I recall a former patient of mine, a very handsome and elegant man in his forties. He was an engineer for NASA. You can picture the type—intelligent, rational, organized and efficient. At first sight, he seemed to live only for performance. Yet, do you want to know the reason he came to see me?

"Doctor," he said, " I'm not here to be able to accomplish great sexual exploits. Although I wouldn't mind becoming a super lover, I'm looking for something else. My desire is to experience a more harmonious relationship with my wife. I want to really understand her and to satisfy her more fully. In fact what I want is to love her better. Because despite all of my efforts to give her sexual pleasure, I sense her pulling away from me."

His words, along with those of many other patients, dramatically changed how I viewed clinical sexology. I became increasingly interested in the global development of the erotic potential of the men and women who consulted me. My research enabled me to discover new facets of human sexuality. From then on, I began to devise innovative therapeutic techniques.

My university students expressed keen enthusiasm. Professionals who attended my conferences bombarded me with questions. Colleagues and friends urged me to publish material on these findings.

I first went to print with a few scientific articles written in a sterile language, comprehensible only to experts in the field. This didn't satisfy me as I wanted the general public to benefit from my work. So I undertook the huge task of pulling together all of my files and going over my notes. I was now ready to present case studies to illustrate the concepts and sexological techniques I had developed.

At the outset, I simply thought about proceeding as most authors would. I'd explain a new theory and describe a patient therapy to make my point. To protect confidentiality their name, age and profession would be changed as well as any other details that might reveal their real identity. I asked a few of my former clients if I could use their story in this anonymous way.

To my great surprise, one of my patients asked me why I didn't consider publishing his story exactly as it unfolded, in its entirety. Without editing it, without changing his identity, without modifying a single detail. He pointed out that a life experience conveyed with all its true aspects would be a lot more interesting and instructive than the typical watered down versions found in conventional therapeutic manuals.

I pondered this astounding proposition for a long time, debating the pros and the cons. Finally, I told myself that information presented in its unadulterated context would definitely be more accessible, more practical and more useful to the public. The readers could apply what they have read to their own life. And they could also gain knowledge of sexuality by identifying with others and learning through their experiences.

And so was born the series "Dr. Carter."

I asked my patients who had ended their therapy more than two years before if they would consent to have their story told in a book. Why two years? Because I didn't want to impose unfair pressure on them or interfere with the therapeutic process. As you might expect, some refused. And I scrupulously respected their decision. It's not difficult to understand that men and women put an enormous amount of trust in the discretion of their sex therapist. And on my part, I respected this choice. Others, conversely, were very eager about the project and readily agreed to open their confidential file and share their story with you.

The first book in the series is entitled *Confidential File 101*. It recounts the adventures of Michael Lancaster, a well-known Seattle television broadcaster. Women desired him; men envied him. Yet his personal life was shrouded in mystery. He was a longtime bachelor and no one had seen him with a woman for ages. Was he impotent? Was he homosexual? Was he into some sort of perversion? Everybody was dying to find out. This is where the story begins...

CHAPTER 1

M ichael Lancaster lived his life with absolute discretion. Few personal details ever made it into the tabloids. The only things known for sure were that he liked football, French wine and lost causes. And that he had two declared enemies: injustice and corruption. For the first time, he had accepted an offer to guest on a colleague's TV talk show. Already he regretted it.

"You host a public affairs television show popular throughout the United States. We've seen you on the cover of *Newsweek* under the headline: 'The media's defender of justice.' You've received numerous awards of excellence for your show *It Concerns Us*. And yet we know nothing about your private life—"

"I don't think the public would find my private life that interesting."

Kathia Hamilton wasn't going to settle for this answer. She struggled for months to convince the enigmatic Michael Lancaster to appear on her show. It was necessary to get him to lift the veil of secrecy over his personal life. The success of her show depended on it. "You're way too modest. We'd all like to know a little more about a man as seductive as yourself. For example: are you still available?" She then turned toward the studio audience. "What do all of you think?"

Enthusiastic cries erupted and the young women seated in the front row rose to their feet, waving their arms wildly.

Michael had anticipated this question and had prepared an answer that would satisfy the viewers.

"You know, Kathia, there are so many beautiful and intelligent women in this country that I'm finding it extremely difficult to make up my mind. I think I'd prefer not to rush into things and to remain a bachelor for a while longer. Anyway, I think the subject is a very personal one. And I'm of the opinion that everyone has the right to a private life away from the spotlight of the media. For the past three years, my show *It Concerns Us* has been informing the public on the unknown side of political and financial scandals in this country. And let me tell you, friends aren't the only things I've made. But never— I repeat—never have I allowed myself to dig into the intimate lives of the people who were implicated in those affairs."

The interviewer interrupted him with a gesture as authoritarian as it was gracious. Kathia had to regain the upper hand immediately so as not to let her guest take control over the interview, her interview. "Haven't you ever been in love, Michael?"

"Sure, I've been in love before. I'm especially vulnerable when it comes to female charm. And at this very moment, I'm very flattered to be the guest of such an attractive woman as you."

"Thanks for the compliment." Kathia flashed her most enticing smile. The *killer smile*, as her producer liked to call it. When she wore it, nine out of ten men succumbed, spellbound.

But not Michael Lancaster.

Kathia pulled another arrow out of her quiver: "Tell me, Michael, just between us—" There were only two million viewers tuned into the program! "—your outspokenness is what has made your show such a hit. But as soon as we broach the subject of your romantic life, you clam up. Are you hiding a secret?"

Michael wasn't able to hide the tension in his jaw. The arrow had hit its target. For a second he wondered if Kathia Hamilton knew about his situation. But he rejected the possibility immediately.

"The secret is very simple. I strongly believe that to be truly happy in life you must be able to enjoy a sense of privacy. However, rest assured that…" his smile became more natural and his self-confidence returned, "…when I officially announce my wedding, you will be the first to know."

The journalist hauled out the heavy artillery: "Be nice, Michael, promise me you'll answer my questions without beating around the bush. You have the reputation of being fearless. And yet it seems as if you're afraid of a woman entering your private life. Am I wrong?"

2

The camera zoomed in on Michael's face. His features remained impassive but underneath the public mask raged a storm. To everyone's surprise the quick-witted Michael Lancaster struggled to find an answer.

Luckily, he was saved by the bell! It was inaudible and took the form of a red light that the interviewer couldn't ignore: the signal for a commercial break.

Kathia broke in with regret: "We'll get back to our conversation with Michael Lancaster after this brief commercial break."

The journalist disappeared and was replaced on the television screen by a singing box of cereal pouring into a bowl. "All you need is milk! Milk! Milk is all you need...," chanted the cartoon character, to the tune of an old Beatles song whose lyrics had been ridiculously changed.

Vanessa Andressen turned off the DVD and at once her small apartment fell silent. The high definition of the recording she had just viewed was of exceptional quality. Unfortunately, the lighting in the studio made Michael look pale.

"He's a lot better-looking in real life," thought Vanessa each time she went over the recording. "But just as discreet." She put down the remote control on the glass coffee table. "Does he really have a secret? We'll soon find out."

The young woman moved toward her bedroom and stopped in front of the mirror resting above the antique dresser. She stared long at her reflection with a curious combination of confidence and anxiety. At nine o'clock she was going over to Michael's place for dinner. Her womanly instincts told her it was going to happen today. It was more than a feeling, it was a certainty: Tonight was the night they were going to make love together for the first time. This last detail wasn't anticipated in the initial plan. However, she didn't mind this "little extra" at all. What woman would be foolish enough to refuse the chance to spend a romantic evening with a man as sexy as Michael Lancaster?

With all the experience of her twenty-eight years, Vanessa knew she was desirous to men. She also knew that one false move could spoil everything. Not surprisingly, it took her forever to decide what to wear. After considerable deliberation, she settled on subtle makeup, a simple dress and fine lingerie.

The latter selection was made judiciously. Initially, she had slipped into a particularly provocative little number, black panties and a matching pushup bra. But she quickly changed her mind. She didn't want Michael to mistake her for a woman of questionable morals. She continued rummaging through her undergarment drawer. Out came a white cotton bikini brief and matching bra. "Definitely not," she said, wrinkling her nose and shaking her head. "Too sporty."

Vanessa threw the cotton threads back into the drawer and searched anew. She finally pulled out a dark blue satin ensemble. "Perfect," she squealed in delight, slipping her arms inside the thin bra straps. "This is exactly what I was looking for." But when she was forced to struggle with the clasps of the fitted brassiere, she wondered, with a pout, if she had put on weight. "Well, I guess it's better to add some flesh up here instead of down there!" Vanessa sighed, passing a hand over her trim stomach.

She slid into her underwear, scrutinizing her body face-on, and then sideways. "Yup, I'm more curvy all right. But so much the better; men like that. I'm sure Michael will fancy this outfit. It's perfect—sexy, but not too sexy."

* * *

At the other end of Seattle, Michael was just walking into his cellar in search of the right wine to complement his much-awaited dinner with Vanessa. He promptly shut the door behind him, not wanting to disturb the electronically regulated temperature and humidity level inside. He always approached the area with a great deal of respect, as he would a sacred place. When he had worked in France in the Perigord as a reporter, he had discovered the true pleasures of dining. To perpetuate this practice in body and soul he built into his home the best wine cellar money could buy. And tonight, he was more satisfied than ever with his initiative. The mere thought of serving Vanessa, at ideal temperature, one of his amorously conserved bottles of wine was inebriating. He knew she was a woman of discriminating taste, the kind who would certainly appreciate a wine of superior quality.

4

With an expert hand, Michael removed an aged, dusty bottle from the shelf. "There, a Montrachet grand cru 1993. An excellent choice to go with the tarragon chicken. And it has thirteen percent alcohol!" He stared at the bottle. "It would be wonderful if the wine could make me last longer," he wished. Taken by the thought, he no longer looked at the bottle with the eyes of a wine connoisseur. What he now saw was a flask containing a strange magical potion with potent medicinal powers to remedy his sexual problem. "Unfortunately, wine rarely works for me. And if I take in too much alcohol, I risk having no erection at all, which isn't any better." A sharp shiver suddenly shot up Michael's spine. "Brrrr… I'm getting out of here. It's cold," he said, carrying out with him the bottle of wine and a mixed bag of emotions.

* * *

"Mirror, mirror on the wall. Who's the fairest of them all?" challenged Vanessa. The cautious mirror didn't answer. But with her toothpaste smile, long auburn hair and a body that could have been taken directly out of the centerfold of some men's magazine Vanessa felt deliciously desirable. An intelligent liberated woman, she didn't appreciate the sex-symbol-commercial-type exploitation of the female body. But this evening, it suited her fine that she resembled a Victoria's Secret model.

Tonight's dinner for two culminated three months of courtship. Over this time, Vanessa succeeded in gaining the acceptance of this man who was so full of energy and charm. She eventually won his confidence and from then on he opened up to her quite freely. However, she still hadn't managed to dissipate the fog that concealed his private life. But there was no indication that he was having a love affair on the side. Vanessa had kept close track of his daily routine. Michael worked a lot and slept little. He spent what limited free time he had playing sports.

Vanessa, like all the others interested in the illustrious Michael Lancaster, was unable to penetrate the mystery of his bachelorhood. Of course Michael wasn't the only famous guy to shy away from marriage at thirty-six. But all the others lived with a lover or jumped from one woman to the next. Vanessa even considered that he might be a homosexual refusing to "out" himself. When it boiled down to common logic, she found this explanation realistic. But it was actually far from her deepest conviction. In fact, she had to confess that Michael's magnetism had tugged at the heartstrings of her femininity. Vanessa refused to admit that she could have feelings of attraction for someone who was gay. "We'll see for sure tonight...," she concluded, putting an end to her reflections.

* * *

"I have to relax." Michael knew that getting nervous would do him no good. He also knew that he couldn't put off having sex with Vanessa forever. It was tonight or never, he told himself. It was going to work. It just had to. And to boost his confidence, he remembered how well things went with Jennifer.

Two years ago, Michael carried out a majestically revered performance with a young, busty blond from California. They spent one night together and never saw each other again. What he felt for Vanessa, however, was completely different, and this explained his growing uneasiness. He wanted Vanessa to be as much in love with him as he was with her. He would have to totally seduce her. Fortunately, seduction was easy for him. He had the physique of a Greek god, considerable fame and lots of money. Despite all of this, the frank words of his good friend Dave always came back to haunt him: "The best way to drive a woman wild for you is to satisfy her in bed," he had once told him. This was something Michael felt perfectly incapable of doing. Except on the rare occasion, every one of his sexual episodes climaxed disastrously.

To calm himself down, Michael turned on the television.

"Never. That's crazy! It's impossible to legalize drugs without provoking nationwide anarchy. Look at what happened in Holland. They were forced to—"

"Exactly," cut in Senator Davidson, his frustrated face bursting through Michael's TV screen. "They were forced to go backward. But if other countries had adopted the same legislation, we would see drug users escape the vicious cycle of illegality. The criminality linked to trafficking would diminish. My bill is—"

"A joke. That sums up your bill. A disastrous joke!" Captain McDougall shouted back. And then suddenly lowering his voice, he added: "You can't imagine what kind of damage drugs can do to a human being. There was one sixteen-year-old in particular I'll never forget. Her name was Cheryl. She had the biggest blue eyes. And despite the fact that she was terrifyingly thin, she was a lovely child. She worked the streets as a prostitute to buy dope. When the teenager found out she had AIDS, she overdosed. She died right in my arms and I couldn't do a damn thing for her. I've also seen kids kill their parents to pay off a few grams of coke. And I've seen—"

"Exactly," interrupted the senator. "It's to prevent such abuses that I propose drugs be sold in pharmacies and controlled by the state."

"That's insane," the police officer replied, raising his voice. "Absolutely insane. To make drugs freely available? It's completely ludicrous!"

"Not as crazy as wasting millions on a pointless war on drugs. That money could be better spent on information and detox programs. I'm not denying, however, that a couple of police officers might lose their jobs as a result or be required to retrain to deal in drug prevention."

Captain McDougall's face was getting redder by the minute. "All those so-called prevention programs are bull! Take tobacco, for instance. Despite all the anti-smoking campaigns kicked off over the years, more and more young people are smoking cigarettes today. The same thing will happen in the case of illicit drugs. Making drugs available in drugstores will only increase the number of druggies. Young people will adopt a who-cares attitude. They'll indulge in foolish pleasures and, eventually, will degenerate." He paused and added mockingly, "And talking about degeneration, we don't have to search too hard to find an example...."

"I will not allow him to go on," protested the senator. "My private life has nothing to do with my political ideals. And I do have solid ideals. Unlike those who defend the prohibition of drugs and who profit from trafficking."

"What!" exploded the policeman. "How dare you insinuate that I make money off drug traffickers when my best friends have been killed fighting them, when I've received death threats, when—"

"Calm down, gentlemen!" intervened the TV broadcaster. "Please!"

But there was no silencing Captain McDougall. "Drugs are heinous. I intend to fight them 'til my dying day. We're going to prevent you from causing harm!" screamed the policeman. "We're going to stop dangerous individuals like you."

"Gentlemen. Pleasssssse stop!" urged the journalist.

Michael pressed on the remote control, cutting short the debate that had turned into an insult-hurling match. A heavy silence suddenly replaced the cacophony of the television. And almost instantly, Michael returned to his obsessive thoughts. "It has to work this time. It just has to work. I can't fail. I want to satisfy her, to please her, to drive her crazy with pleasure."

* * *

"I'm sure he's a wonderful lover," Vanessa daydreamed. "He's thoughtful, sensitive and strong all at the same time. He's really a great guy."

This thought momentarily flustered Vanessa. Yet she had to stay level-headed. A unique opportunity was being offered to her to plumb the secret depths of the most guarded broadcast celebrity in the United States. There was no way she was going to blow her chance.

Vanessa already had an action plan. She visualized herself behaving both innocently and skillfully, both wild and sensual. She could see herself sometimes surrendering in his arms, sometimes being aggressive and dominatrix-like. Such thoughts filled the hollows of her stomach with warm sensations and a voluptuous wave washed over her entire body. How wonderful it was to imagine being with a man millions of women fantasized over!

All at once, the telephone resounded from the kitchen. Vanessa jumped, her heart beating at an alarming speed. Since her father's death five months ago, she couldn't help herself from panicking every time the phone rang. The tragic news had reached her early one Sunday morning while she peacefully slept. She was stirred from her slumber, only to be informed that her father had died in a hunting accident. And to this day, whenever her phone rang, she relived that moment. She remembered the dinner the evening before, the phone call from the police sergeant, the identification of her father's body at the hospital. The lowering of the casket into the ocher crypt, and the afternoon spent emptying out his apartment—his pipe, waiting to be smoked, had rested against a teacup on the kitchen table. She couldn't seem to erase that image from her mind. He was the person she loved the most in the world.

The phone continued ringing. Vanessa pulled herself together and headed for the kitchen, walking alongside a wall decorated with assorted vacation memorabilia. She was almost by the phone when the answering machine went on. A nasal voice filtered through the machine's speaker: "Good evening, Vanessa. It's Jimmy. I'm not at home right now, but you can call me tomorrow morning. I have something very important to tell you."

Vanessa rushed to pick up the telephone receiver. But it was too late. Jimmy had already hung up. She stood there and wanted badly to kick herself for not answering it when she had the chance. "Boy, am I stupid!" she thought. Frustrated, she turned her anger toward Jimmy: "Why didn't that idiot leave me a number?"

Vanessa walked toward the doorway, all the while thinking: "It couldn't have been that important or he would have left me a way to reach him tonight. I guess it's just another one of his attempts to seduce me. Poor Jimmy, he just doesn't have it when it comes to women."

* * *

"It's going to work. It's going to work," Michael repeated, sitting restlessly on his living room couch. "How will I look if it doesn't work? She'll never fall for me, then. No, I can't let myself fail!" Completely exasperated, he decided to chase away all the terrible thoughts in his head by getting things ready for dinner. He set the table with a romantic touch of fine linen and flowers, selected an eclectic mix of CDs and carefully chose his clothes for the special occasion.

Michael owned only good quality clothing. Yet he didn't bother with the latest trend-setting designers fashioned by other television and movie stars. Although he had the money, he refused to foolishly fork out tens of thousands of dollars just to wear original, often outlandish designs. He preferred the sober elegance of clean, time-honored styles, and dressed in a simple yet refined manner.

The crucial moment when Vanessa would ring the doorbell was approaching. Michael was feeling confident again. He was aware of his charm and knew that a woman—even a very beautiful one—could easily desire a man like him. He imagined Vanessa laughing at his jokes, marveling over his travel adventures and being mesmerized by his intelligent opinions.

Then a dreadful image brutally came to mind. He saw himself stark naked at the end of the bed, searching for excuses to justify his poor sexual performance. "Vanessa, you're such a turn on that I couldn't seem to control myself. This has never happened to me before. It must have been the wine. I guess we're going to have to get used to each other for a while." He could hear Vanessa gently reassuring him: "Don't worry. It's not that bad. We'll try again next time. This sort of thing could happen to anybody." But from the corner of his eye, he could see her lying on her back, her head turned listlessly toward the window. "The great Michael Lancaster, what a letdown," she'd be thinking to herself, completely disillusioned.

Michael was shaken by his destructive thoughts. But he was a strong creature; he was not going to allow himself to be defeated. He took a deep breath and once again felt in top fighting form. He had succeeded with Jennifer and he was going to succeed with Vanessa. "The best thing to do is be myself and everything will go well. Besides, my problem is all in my head," he assured himself. "All I have to do is calm down and think positively."

As Michael took in the opulent surroundings of his living room, a quiet feeling of calm swept over him. The panoramic view of the lighted city created a romantic ambience. And the furnishings, accentuated by authentic art deco pieces spanning from the beginning of the twentieth century, would certainly win him compliments. The patiently selected French wine added a hint of good taste and was the perfect finishing touch to the finely prepared Provençal dinner.

* * *

The door of the liquor store closed abruptly behind Vanessa as she dashed to her red Golf GTI. Next to her, she plunked down a bottle of wine with a screw top that had a label she found pretty. She wasn't much of a drinker and despite her cultural flair, she knew nothing about wine and other spirits. This usually meant that whenever she selected a bottle of wine, the form and color of the bottle won out over the aroma and taste of the enclosed liquid.

Vanessa studied her road map in utter horror. "Oh, no! It's farther than I thought. I'm going to be late. I'd better take Highway 5. At this hour, it'll certainly be free of heavy traffic."

She tossed the map on top of the dashboard and sped away like a bolt of lightning. Catching Vanessa driving off, two teenage skateboarders dressed in oversized clothing who had been executing a series of jumps in the parking lot, stopped to exchange admirable looks and flashed her a thumbs-up sign.

Vanessa drove through the city at vision-blurring speed. She ran two red lights and almost had a collision. Her reckless driving was something to tremble about. Her colleagues teased her at work about her love affair with speed and joked that she was the Rock n' Roll Driving Queen of Seattle. She laughed off their innocent jibes and took great pleasure as she turned their words around to mean that her driving habits were regal and had a royal beat to them.

Vanessa suddenly thought back to Jimmy's call. He might have been serious this time. Maybe there really was something important he had to tell her. Just to make sure, she'd give him a call first thing in the morning.

After driving over the railroad tracks that crossed Garfield Avenue, Vanessa took Magnolia Boulevard and sped up the hill. Once in front of Michael's posh home, she parked in a nervous haste along the sidewalk. The biting February wind forced Vanessa to wrap her long, green coat snugly around her slim figure during the short walk to the villa. As she moved across the manicured lawn, her heart raced. "Tonight we're going to make love. Am I going too far? In fact, all I really wanted to figure out was what his big secret was. Now this adventure is taking a whole new turn."

"Hi, Vanessa. Come in," Michael said as he opened the door. "It's freezing outside! I almost lost a piece of my ear while out jogging this afternoon."

Vanessa responded with an amused giggle. Michael couldn't help feeling great. Everything was going to go well. Vanessa had laughed at his quip—a good omen.

During the meal, Michael politely opened the bottle Vanessa had brought. Even the mediocre wine tasted delectable to him, so in love was he with its exquisite purchaser. He loved Vanessa's long, wavy hair and glamorous smile. He valued her tenderness and sensuality. He devoured her intellectual side and the energetic way she tackled life. He appreciated her company and already imagined what it would be like to spend the rest of his life with her.

The conversation moved along with laughter and friendly smiles. They talked about everything and nothing, cats and trips, the problems the Mariners were having and the corruption of politicians. While they were on the subject of politics, Vanessa took the opportunity to congratulate Michael on the professionalism of his TV show: "I think what you do on television is great. But it must be difficult to put together all those reports."

"Not really," he replied modestly. "I guess when you're passionate about something it makes things that much easier. And I don't think I have to tell you just how much distaste I have for dishonest politicians. I probably hate them almost as much as I despise sensational journalists!" He started to laugh: "I bet you think it's very strange that I have an aversion to journalists, particularly those on television, when I'm in the profession myself. I must say that there are many ways to do this job. Informing the public honestly is one of them. Meddling in people's private lives is another. It's the latter that disgusts me."

Vanessa kept quiet and averted her gaze for a few seconds. Noticing her discomfort, Michael changed the subject. "But enough about me, I would much rather talk about you. It can't be any easier to be the only female architect in the office. With all those men around, you must constantly be having to prove how talented you are, which to me is very obvious just by the tasteful way you dress."

Vanessa lowered her head slightly and didn't answer immediately, flattered by Michael's compliment. She put down her fork and rested her chin on her hand. "You know, I really don't think things would be different for me anywhere else. Women still have a long and rocky path to walk down before they gain the same rights and privileges as men. You don't just change society with the bat of an eye."

CHAPTER 2

S enator Davidson hastily exited the television station and disappeared into the silver Mercedes waiting for him near the door. The swarthy chauffeur pulled away, the tires on the heavy Benz lightly screeching. "Where to, senator?"

"I don't know, John, you lead the way," replied the senator, clearly distracted. "I don't have any energy left in me tonight. I'm getting tired of fighting. Do you think it's worth continuing this battle?"

In his moments of despair, the senator had grown accustomed to confiding in his driver. The chauffeur, although not well educated, possessed good judgment that often helped William Davidson make a decision.

"You could always retire peacefully at the edge of the pool of your California villa. But I know you'd be miserable. You're a fighter. You like challenges."

"You're right, but I'm getting old. This evening's debate infuriated and exhausted me to an extent I have never known before. In the past, I would have easily shut that ignorant police officer up, but tonight, I lacked the strength. The ignoramus even openly threatened me. I have to ask myself if he'd dare to act out his threat. In the good old days, men showed respect toward their elders. But today, it's no longer so..."

The senator rubbed his strained forehead with the back of his hand: "My Lord, you hear me, John? I'm already talking about the past like an old, dilapidated grandfather."

"You're still a young man, Mr. Davidson. A lot of women—"

"Don't talk to me about women! Since the dirty blow Barbara the bitch threw my way, I have cooled down considerably. By the way, my lust for women has waned. I'm no longer the old pig everybody imagines. And this bill I'm supporting will undoubtedly be the last of my career..."

* * *

After the meal, Michael invited Vanessa to sit beside him on his black leather sofa. They looked at pictures from his most recent trip to Nepal. Michael figured this was the ideal time to physically approach Vanessa but a pernicious anxienty infiltrated his body and prevented him from reacting. It was ironic that outside the realm of sexuality, Michael had not endured real panic for twenty years. When he was a young new driver, his car had spun off the road and plunged to the bottom of a ravine. He had experienced profound terror in that crashing moment. But this frightening feeling eventually went away. From then on, in his everyday existence, he never again suffered such fear except when he was about to make love. And Michael knew that if he became intimate with Vanessa tonight, there would be no turning back. He couldn't see himself going on playing the flirt forever like an inexperienced teenager. He would definitely end up making love to her and his problem would be exposed.

Vanessa bent over to get a better look at a photo of Michael swimming. Her voluptuous body pressed against Michael's muscular shoulder. He didn't flinch. She moved back slightly, not wanting to appear too eager. But when Michael cracked a joke, she burst out laughing and grabbed his arm spontaneously. Quickly, she regained control of herself and conscientiously positioned herself beside Michael, making sure to observe a tiny space between their bodies.

Vanessa relished the moment where a man desired her intensely, yet dared not to touch her. It made her feel absolutely irresistible. She also knew the low neckline of her dress was arousing Michael to immeasurable heights. While they were eating, his furtive peeks in the direction of her breasts hadn't escaped Vanessa. Profiting from this asset, she often perched over the photo album so that Michael could plunge his glance into the opening of her dress. She took long, exaggerated breaths allowing her breasts to rise to full advantage. The minute she sensed him getting closer, Vanessa asked Michael to excuse her for a few moments and she slowly got up, pressing her hand against his thigh. As she sauntered toward the bathroom, she could feel his stare penetrate the nape of her neck and slide down to her buttocks.

Michael's blue eyes clung to Vanessa's curvaceous silhouette right up until she vanished behind the cream walls of the corridor. He felt his body grow extremely tense with desire. And Vanessa was playing to this tension like a bow on the strings of a violin.

Her momentary disappearance enabled Michael to catch his breath. He stretched his hand for the glass of cognac sitting at the far end of the coffee table and swallowed a mouthful to relax. He couldn't understand what was happening to him. Vanessa barely grazed his leg and already his sexual excitement level had reached dizzying heights. "I must control myself," he hissed, clenching his teeth. "I absolutely mustn't disappoint her."

In the bathroom, Vanessa touched up her makeup. Michael displayed all the signs of a man entirely under her spell. Yet distressing thoughts typical to women still crept into her head: "Maybe he'll be disappointed in my body. I've gained a bit of weight in the last few months, my breasts aren't as firm as they were when I was twenty and my waist isn't as slender."

She shut her eyes briefly and as they opened, she peered into the mirror above the sink. Staring back at her was a radiant woman wearing a sensual and captivating smile. Instantly, her self-esteem returned. No carnal man could resist such a smile, especially when it accompanied charisma and brains. The hypnotic allure she was able to release on a man as famous and handsome as Michael Lancaster got her extremely excited. She loosened a copper strand of hair from her chignon and let it fall sexily over her forehead. "Mission accomplished," she said to her reflection in the mirror. Vanessa took a deep breath, adjusted her dress and headed into the living room.

"I like the way you've decorated your bathroom, Michael. It's gorgeous. I could spend hours in there."

"You can take a bubble bath," he suggested, "any time you want."

Vanessa blushed softly. Then, to strengthen the impression of coyness she wanted to transmit, she evaded his glance and didn't sit next to him. Instead, with the poise of a princess, she made her way toward the big French windows that opened onto the terrace overlooking Elliot Bay and downtown Seattle. She listened meditatively to the sound of the wind hitting the huge trees planted along Magnolia Boulevard.

"Breathtaking view, isn't it?" Michael approached her. Once again he sensed that this was the right moment for him to get more physical with Vanessa. He could no longer hold back. He stopped at her side and with one hand he gently embraced her shoulders. With the other hand, he pointed at the Space Needle, the King Dome and the lights of the port. Vanessa rested her head softly against Michael's shoulder. With the tips of his fingers, Michael lightly traced the nape of her neck. When his fingers reached the roots of her hair she tilted her head back slightly. She felt Michael's hand massage her shoulders, constricted by emotion. Vanessa closed her eyes and sighed in contentment.

Michael continued to caress Vanessa's arms, shoulders, neck and upper back, at length. Her body quivered with his every touch. He approached his guest's naked neck and placed upon it delicate kisses.

Vanessa's breathing was quick and heavy. Long gone were her worries over what Michael might think of her. All she wanted to do was kiss him. Finally, with irresistible slowness, she turned around and offered him her half-opened lips.

Michael was pleasantly surprised at the fullness and the softness of the lips pressed against his own. He deliciously nibbled at the velvety fruit in between his lips and surrendered fully to the freshness of their first kiss.

Vanessa played at length with the lips of the man she had desired for so long. Her entire body awoke to the most infinitesimal sensation. She shivered with pleasure at the contact of Michael's hands on her hips, pulling her toward him. When she felt her breasts press against his chest, Vanessa wrapped her arms around Michael's shoulders and grabbed him with fervor.

Consumed by pleasure, they both exhaled passionately. Without further delay, they kissed each other more intimately. Their tongues wandered back and forth in mischievous pursuit, eager and greedy. Eventually, their mouths separated and they held each other very hard. Vanessa was confused. What she was feeling inside of her was a lot more intense than she had expected. Michael whispered into her ear, "Vanessa, you are an extraordinary woman." Reciprocating the compliment, Vanessa snuggled a little closer against Michael's chest and closed her eyes.

* * *

The Mercedes-Benz 500 SEL silently halted in front of the senator's sumptuous Washington residence. Curled up in the back seat, Senator Davidson looked hundreds of years old. His voice had always projected the strong stamp of a man of authority, but on this late night it sounded unusually slow and subdued.

"You know, my old John, there are nights when I would like to put an end to all of this. I'd like to walk away from this life-consuming debate like a poker player leaves the table. Not that I'm contemplating suicide, be certain of that. But I don't want to be the Senator Davidson you either admire or abhor. I simply want to be William, the man. I get the idea that I'm not in control of this fight for the legalization of drugs but rather a character I play, an actor of some sort."

"I believe that everybody plays a character—life is like a big movie. You have been excellent in the role of 'senator.' But if you don't like that character anymore, maybe you could choose another one."

"You have a good head on your shoulders, John, and I am inclined to accept your wisdom."

The chauffeur opened the back door, extending his hand to the senator who climbed out wearily.

"Thank you, John. Thank you for listening to me."

"Senator... I admire you..."

"I admire you too, John. Goodnight, my friend."

His chest cramped up with emotion, the chauffeur watched as his boss walked slowly toward his estate. In the darkness, John got the impression that the senator's feet weren't touching the ground anymore, as if he had already left the poker table of life.

17

* * *

Michael shot out a cry of pain. Vanessa while collapsing on the sofa with him had unintentionally scraped his face with one of her rings. She grazed his cheek with her finger only to find a trickle of blood oozing from the abrasion.

"Omigosh, I'm so sorry," Vanessa gasped, sincerely apologetic. "Thank goodness, it isn't deep. Forgive me?"

Michael replied by lightly biting her perfume-scented neck while he went about unbuttoning the dress she had on far too long. Vanessa, sprawled out on the leather divan, relented to Michael's compassionate initiatives, and he fully profited from her surrender. She delivered herself freely into his experienced hands without saying a word. However, the slow and fluid movements of her hips clearly communicated her approbation.

Michael played her body like a musical instrument. He oscillated between sharp and flat notes. He invented melodies and created new rhythms. His hands danced up and down Vanessa's body with the dexterity of a virtuoso.

Vanessa let herself be rocked by the waltz of sensations cradling her. Every inch of her body invited more and more touches and even more caresses. Her dress, already half off, began to get in the way. Her breasts swelled with desire in anticipation of the sweltering stroke of Michael's gentle hands. Her burning thighs slowly parted. Imprisoned by the moist fabric of her satin underwear, her sex sought freedom.

Vanessa's green eyes sparkled as she looked at Michael. Forehead bathed in sweat and face flushed, she undid the chignon that was holding back her long auburn locks and shook her head with feminine grace. It was time to demonstrate exactly what a modern and sensual woman was capable of. Surrender had been delicious, but the desire to bombard Michael with pleasure was even greater. With one hand she opened Michael's shirt—one button at a time— while with the other hand, she stroked his thighs.

Vanessa liked to think of herself as an assertive woman even though she was a little shy. However, tonight, the combination of alcohol and Michael's caresses vanquished most of her fragile inhibitions. Her hand was ready to test its power of seduction on this hunk of male flesh. When her fingers reached Michael's penis, she was totally reassured. She felt the hardness of the member protruding from his pants and feeling a little coquettish and a lot naughty, she sized up the length by caressing it with her fingertips.

Michael felt the veins in his penis swell and his erection become stiff. His entire body was gravitating toward this desirable woman. Absorbed by the sensations Vanessa was stirring within him, he didn't realize the soaring degree to which his sexual excitement had elevated. Everything at this point seemed to be moving too fast and was simply becoming too stimulating. His breathing became shorter and quicker. The muscles in his thighs, buttocks and belly were extremely contracted. Ejaculation was imminent.

Panic-stricken, he instinctively knew that if Vanessa continued in this direction, he would come fast. He had to regain control over the situation at all costs. Already, he had spoiled this extraordinary moment by thinking about other things. Now, there was no other choice except to put an immediate end to all stimulation. He removed Vanessa's hand and placed it on his thigh. "Why don't we go into the bedroom?" he suggested, rising to his feet without waiting for a reply.

More than surprised that a man would abruptly stop such heated action, Vanessa slowly lifted her body off the sofa and, in a sensual voice, asked, "And where is the lion's den hiding?"

"Behind the door, over there, just in front of you, my dear lamb," Michael said, playing along, and pointing in the direction.

"I'll follow you, my good man." Vanessa fluttered her eyelids provocatively and languorously ran her fingers through her hair.

"Absolutely not. Ladies first…" He bowed nobly, legs together and right arm extended widely, reminiscent of a marquis in the royal court of 18th century France.

Vanessa gave him a beautiful smile and walked toward the bedroom, swaying her hips to the rhythm of her steps. This feline-like stride sent out a magnetic allure for it was both stately and wild.

Michael followed at a distance, fascinated by the sensual grace that emanated from this dream girl. But he wasn't dreaming. He knew full well that she desired him intensely and after three long months of waiting, they would finally make love.

Vanessa sat at the edge of the king-size brass bed. She crossed her long legs and tilted her head to one side. Her lovely mouth, with its silky full lips, spilled four enticing words: "Make love to me."

Michael was less than six feet away from Vanessa. Another three steps and she would be all his. The long-awaited moment had ultimately arrived. But suddenly, his old fears crept up inside of him as fantasies do at the hint of dusk. "Will I mess up as usual? Will I be unable to satisfy another woman?" Fright pervaded Michael's being and spread its venom in the most secret hollows of his bones. Finally, he neared the bed like an outlaw mounting the scaffold. Condemned to losing control. Damned to come too quickly.

CHAPTER 3

D espite the frigid cold, Michael continued to run on the marina along Elliot Bay. He wanted to hurt himself. To make his body feel pain. He wanted to punish himself for failing with Vanessa. And by his standards, it was a catastrophic failure. He ached to disappear, to die. But his heart held on strong, and the pain progressively invading his body didn't seem to prevent him from being assailed by thousands of questions: "Why can't I control myself? Is there something that doesn't work inside of me? Why am I incapable of satisfying a woman? For Christ's sake! This is killing me. I'm totally useless whenever I make love."

In reality, Michael wasn't as useless as he tortured himself into believing. Quite the opposite, actually. His charm was ubiquitous and hardly ever went unnoticed. He remembered the evening of the presidential charity gala where the vice president of the United States spoke to him as if he were an old friend: "I would die to be in your shoes," he confided while observing the desirous gaze of two pretty women fixated on Michael. "You must be the most seductive man in the room."

Michael also had the touch of a talented pianist and his body language spoke with patience and gentleness. When he fondled or held a woman in his arms, he made her melt out of pleasure. He became an expert in foreplay and could bring his lovers to multiple orgasms with his combination of caresses refined throughout the years. All these erotic skills allowed him to get by without losing face. Unfortunately, during intercourse, his little tricks no longer worked and his sexual incompetence showed up blatantly. Sadly, a repetition of failures and the disgraceful remarks made by certain women caused him to doubt his sexual capacities. Many times he felt humiliated. Today, he despised himself.

The agony he was experiencing eventually became unbearable and Michael was compelled to capitulate. With calves knotted and chest on fire, he stopped jogging. He turned back and hobbled much of the way home, his body broken by the effort. But after only a few feet, the chill and dampness of the early winter morning submerged him. He felt a stream of cold perspiration trickling down the length of his vertebral column. The sensation was exceptionally unpleasant, but considerably less excruciating than the dreadful feeling of failure tormenting him. Numbed, he began shivering and accelerated his pace.

When he got home, he headed straight for the shower. The steamy water warmed his body and sprayed his morale with comfort. "After all, it's normal for things not to go one-hundred percent well the first time around," he thought, trying to reassure himself. "We hardly know each other. Yet I'm sure she really enjoyed the foreplay. But a man who comes too fast is definitely a loser. If only I could find some way to hold back a little longer. There must be something out there for men like me!" Keeping this in mind, Michael turned off the water and jumped out of the shower.

* * *

Betty Konanski, Vanessa's best friend, was patiently watching a taped recording of the show, *It Concerns Us*. The thirty-one-year-old had a giant screen TV that transformed her modest living room into a movie theatre. Stretched out on a striped sofa, the attractive woman munched on a raw carrot stick. Betty did everything in her control to maintain her slim figure.

Sitting beside her, Vanessa was anxiously watching her friend's every reaction. After a couple of minutes, Betty became impatient. "Vanessa, I don't understand why you want me to watch this."

"Do you know who the host of this show is?"

"Of course, Michael Lancaster... No! It can't be possible," exclaimed Betty, suddenly putting two and two together. "You're going out with Michael Lancaster?"

Vanessa replied with a simple smile.

"You're dating Michael Lancaster?" repeated Betty, wide-eyed. "The mysterious bachelor? The one the tabloids assume is gay?"

"Uh-huh. We've been seeing each other for three months and last night I gained confirmation that he most certainly is not gay."

"You slept with him!"

"Yes. It took me a while to reach that point, but I finally got there. Actually, it could have happened a lot sooner. But if I had given in to him too fast, he might have suspected something."

"Bravo! Job well done, my dear friend."

"I must confess that the work is rather pleasant." Having said that, Vanessa began spouting off a long list of Michael's best qualities. She then went on to describe his property in Magnolia, his collection of art deco objects, his good taste, his great skin and his firm muscles. The adulation dragged on and on, leaving Betty feeling completely nauseous. She was fed up with listening to her friend ramble on like some hyper-hormonal adolescent back from a first date, especially when things between her and her husband Jeff weren't so great.

* * *

"So how is she in bed?" asked Dave, Michael's old college buddy, his ear pressed against the telephone receiver, eager to hear all the juicy details.

But Michael was in no mood for this type of locker room talk today. He was determined to avoid discussing the subject altogether. And he made this point transparent by dryly replying that it was none of his business.

Dave, extremely surprised by this curt reply, answered back: "I've known you to be more explicit, Michael. What's wrong? Are you by any terrestrial chance in love?"

"No!" lashed out Michael. "Sorry, old pal, but at this moment work is the only thing on my mind. I'll tell you about my date later. As for work, do you have that information I needed on Senator Davidson's financial situation for my next show, on his bill to decriminalize drugs? The more I think about it, the more I'm sure it will be a hit."

"Haven't you heard the latest news? Davidson was assassinated last night."

"What! Davidson is dead?"

"Excuse me, but what planet are you living on? That's all the television and radio stations have been talking about this morning."

"Shit, this changes everything. What do the cops think?"

"As usual they're skating around in circles. What else is new? For goodness sakes, it wouldn't surprise me if that fat Captain Foley's offered a lead role in the Ice Capades. By the way, about the information you wanted, we'll discuss that at the sports club. As you know, I have little confidence in the telephone."

"Sounds good to me, Dave. See you tonight." As he hung up, the different elements of the Davidson affair bounced around in Michael's head: It all started when the old senator launched his contentious bill to legalize drugs. Thanks to his intelligent arguments and his great power of persuasion he managed to sway a segment of the population. But little by little as his popularity started to grow, so did the number of his opponents. He received death threats, suffered relentless pressure from ultraconservative lobbyists and was the victim of several defamatory campaigns. He was even the subject of an odious report in which his mistress declared before TV cameras that he was impotent.

* * *

"Stupid computer!" cursed Vanessa, slamming her fist down on the antique desk she had inherited from her father. "The disk is totally empty! My whole document just went up in smoke." This meant she would have to rewrite the entire text and her energy was gradually beginning to ebb. The tortoise-framed glasses Vanessa wore only to watch television and to work on her computer, weighed down heavily on her nose.

She ran her fingers through her hair in exactly the same way Michael had the night before. This gesture made her think back to yesterday's developments. Although the evening had its delicious moments, a strange feeling of "too little" lingered in her memory.

* * *

"I really expected to cream your butt today," Dave groaned, out of breath, his black face dripping with sweat.

"Dream on, Leon!" Michael pointed his finger in mocking fun at his good friend. "But I have to admit you've come a long way since last summer. Your serve is a lot more precise and you keep to the center of the court a lot better than before. In racquetball, both are essential if you want to win."

"True, very true. I've learned a great deal playing against you. One day I'm going to beat you. You just wait and see!"

"Dre-ee-ee-ee-eam, dream, dream, dre-eam..." sang Michael, to the tune of the Everly Brothers. He gave Dave a great big slap on the shoulder. "Come on. Grab your things and let's go to the cafeteria. My treat."

Heading toward the self-serve snack counter located in the sports complex, Michael spotted a row of chocolate cakes. "Those look incredible," he said. "You going to have one, Dave?"

"Are you nuts? I don't want to ruin all that effort that goes into maintaining my body weight at a normal level. I'm no masochist!"

"Get serious," Michael shot back, rolling his eyes. "I don't see why you obsess so much about your weight. You barely have seven percent body fat on you. Everybody says you look like Will Smith."

"Yeah, right, I'm just a foot shorter and twenty pounds heavier."

The friends grabbed their orders and sat down at a square table for two by the window. Dave drank his tomato juice, while Michael devoured his piece of cake.

"There's never enough!" protested Michael, swallowing the last forkful of his chocolate cake. "You see," he explained to Dave, "the portions are diabolically calculated. They serve you just enough to whet your taste buds for this sweet treat so when you polish off the piece, you still have an appetite. This leaves you craving for another piece, but by the time the server brings the second helping, the craving has already curbed and the chocolate taste seems dulled. But despite this keen observation, I can't stop myself from reordering every single time. What can I say, I'm a hopeless chocolate addict."

"Lucky for you, you're happy with chocolate," replied Dave, edging closer to Michael, "because the real drug killed Davidson."

Instantly, the tone of the conversation changed. Michael's facial expression turned serious. "You think his death is connected to the trafficking ring?"

"No, I don't think so, I know so. The police haven't found the murderer and the official spin is that this was some heinous crime committed by an amateur crook. But if you ask me, I think they're way off." Dave paused. Two men had just sat down at the table next to them without saying a word. "Grab your racquet and let's go someplace where we can talk about this more openly."

* * *

Dave took Michael to Bellevue Square, not too far from the sports complex. He pushed open the heavy glass door with disconcerting ease. True, he had an impressive looking set of muscles. Tall and sturdy, Dave was a former Green Wave football player at Tulane University where he had studied international law. Today, despite his young age of thirty-five years, he was senior associate at the renowned law firm Parker and Tucker, which specialized in international taxation. He worked with multinational companies that used his services to reduce their taxes. This made him well aware of the methods, within legal limits, used by his clients.

"It's best we talk in a noisy place," he whispered to Michael. "You can never be too cautious. If what I have to say reaches the wrong ears, the situation could end up being extremely dangerous for both of us."

Intrigued, Michael got closer to his friend. Dave continued. "My team got all the information you asked me about Davidson's finances. Since he's dead, this is of little use to you now. However, I've got some new leads that might interest you quite a bit. As you already know, Davidson had many adversaries. Among the most radical, there are four I have taken an interest in. Senator John Kullinger whose son died of an overdose; Dr. Matthew McKeown of the Department of Epidemiology at the University of Delaware; Reverend William Backford of the Fifth Redemption Church of Cincinnati; and the politician, Jack Kotten. The first three seem to be above suspicion. But I have strong doubts regarding Kotten's integrity."

Michael was only half listening to his friend. He had spotted a woman who resembled Vanessa in the crowded shopping mall. She was a little shorter and her hair seemed darker, but from the back the likeness was striking. She had the same provocative curves that enticed his gaze downward along the small of her back to the roundness of her buttocks. The sight aroused Michael so much that he had a crazy desire to make love to Vanessa.

"Are you listening to me, Michael?" asked Dave, slightly raising his tone.

"Of course!" replied Michael a little embarrassed knowing very well that he was in the wrong for not paying attention. "By the way, you forgot to add Captain McDougall to your list. The man threatened Davidson right on television."

"That's why I don't believe he could have done it. He would have to be completely crazy to carry out his threat the day after the show."

"That doesn't mean a thing, really. And come to think of it, if that's the case, then the childish battle of insults he engaged in on the show would put him above any suspicion. But aside from that, I don't think he's intelligent enough to have had concocted such a scheme. You did mention Jack Kotten. You wouldn't mean Governor Jack Kotten?"

"Absolutely! The very same one whose ambition is to run in the next presidential election as an independent candidate. He talks a rousing talk that pleases certain folks: a return to family values; power to America; an end to immigration; political isolationism; increasing the size of the military; economic protectionism; and a swifter execution of the death penalty. He takes the traditional stand of die-hard populists. The trouble is, he's unassailable. He's never cheated on his wife—an amazing feat in the current world of politics. He's never taken any drugs. He doesn't drink in public. To top things off, although he's filthy rich, he actually pays all of his taxes. This was so hard to believe that it made one of my clients, a commercial competitor of Kotten's, suspect him of cheating the system. So that's when I discovered, even before Davidson was assassinated, several interesting leads indicating that Kotten would have an interest in getting rid of, in one way or another, the poor old senator."

"Not so poor," emphasized Michael. "And not a totally disinterested party either. Do you know what kind of operation Davidson's son-in-law is involved in?"

"I haven't the faintest clue," Dave said, raising his eyebrows.

"He holds a lot of shares in one of the largest pharmaceutical companies in the country, which his cousin happens to own. If the bill to legalize drugs should pass and make it law for cocaine to be sold exclusively in drugstores, then the companies licensed to manufacture the drugs stand to reap a fortune. And the Davidson family will grow richer at the same time."

"I see you're well informed Michael."

"That's not all. I also found out that..."

The two friends continued their conversation for a while, far away from inquisitive ears, right to the exit of the shopping mall. Once outside, they arranged a time for their next game of racquetball and then both went their separate ways, disappearing into the vastness of the parking lot.

CHAPTER 4

"**O**h darn it, not the answering machine again," groaned Vanessa as she listened to Michael's recorded message for the third time that evening. She really felt the urge to talk to him and to hear his voice and not the lousy recording. Despite her disappointment she left a message, making it clear that he could call her back at whatever time. It was late and her stomach noisily reminded her that she had not yet eaten supper. She removed a lemon chicken entree from the freezer and popped it into the microwave. She carefully extracted a plate and fork from a heap of unwashed dishes cluttering the counter and quickly ran them under the tap. Her apartment was a mess. Although she had the means to pay for a cleaning woman, she didn't want any stranger sticking her nose in her "den of disorder." And besides, these past weeks her mind really wasn't on cleaning up.

After she ate, Vanessa decided to stretch out and relax in a nice, warm bubble bath. While the water filled the tub, she got undressed and slipped into an old bathrobe worn out by years of use and a pair of mammoth orange furry slippers shaped like ducks, a gift from her young nephew. She pulled her hair into a careless chignon and smothered her face with a greenish egg-based mixture. The beauty mask wasn't a pretty sight and it smelled dreadful. But Betty had assured her that it worked wonders for wrinkles, crow's feet and dry skin— and even prevented the appearance of age spots.

* * *

A bouquet of pink roses in hand, Michael looked for Vanessa's name on the occupant list posted at the main entrance of her apartment building. He pushed on the buzzer beside the name: V. Andressen. As he read the Scandinavian surname, he slipped into a fantasy. He pictured Vanessa strolling sexily in her apartment, dressed in a sheer black teddy.

Vanessa panicked when she heard Michael's voice through the intercom. She couldn't possibly see him looking like this. She frantically searched for a reasonable excuse not to let him up. But she drew a blank; nothing came to her. Finally, she stuttered: "I'm so sorry... M-Michael, I-I can't invite you up. My mother is here. I'll call you... later.... Have a g-good evening."

Disappointed, Michael didn't insist and turned back toward his black Porsche 911. He opened the door and sank into the leather sports seat. He didn't know exactly what to make of Vanessa's reaction. How could she be so cold tonight after having been so intimate with him the night before? Why did she refuse to see him and why would she not want to introduce him to her mother?

Baffled, he started the motor and went into first gear. The Porsche soared ahead. He usually appreciated the power and the superior features of the recently purchased car, but tonight he missed his old 911. The older model was noisier, more uncomfortable and more difficult to control, but these were the very features that had initially drawn him toward the Porsche: the Spartan style. Today, even drivers of sports cars wanted some comfort.

The more Michael dwelled on what had just happened, the less willing he was to believe the story about her mother's visit. The only other explanation that came to mind was the presence of another man, which would justify Vanessa's embarrassment. "She must have been with one of her former lovers. It's possible that they were even in the middle of making love. She did seem out of breath on the intercom. Maybe she gets more pleasure with him than with me."

To chase away his upsetting thoughts, Michael popped a CD into the compact disc player and pressed down on the gas pedal. The sporty drive of the Porsche and the rhythmic sounds of Herbie Hancock distracted him a bit. He turned onto Highway 5 and headed south, driving aimlessly for more than an hour to settle his turbulent thoughts.

* * *

Betty's tabby cat jumped onto the foot of the bed just as Jeff's burly form rolled underneath the mountain of covers. The petite woman felt her husband's warm hand slide up her thigh. She knew exactly what was about to take place: He would caress her for a short time between her shapely legs, concentrating on her clitoris until she seemed to reach an orgasm. He would then hastily penetrate her, and some pelvic movements later, ejaculate, groaning. After twenty minutes of rest, Jeff would feel obligated to start over to satisfy her. He would attempt another penetration that, again, would not last more than a minute. And then, he would turn over on his side, with a sense of accomplishment and the certitude of being a virile and sexy man.

The scenario played itself out just as predicted. For some reason, however, Betty was having a harder time falling asleep than usual, and her husband's satisfied snores irritated her more than ever. Jeff was a good husband and a better lover than any one of her ex-boyfriends. Still, the orgasmic quiver she experienced after a long and patient clitoral stimulation left her hungry and longing for some kind of human warmth and affection.

When she was in her late teens, Betty had imagined that making love to a man would be an experience of total fusion. She saw herself as being both the possessed and the possessor. Often, she had pressed a pillow really hard against her bosom and became aroused by the thought that an imaginary lover was penetrating her deep inside. She fantasized that with her bare arms around his broad shoulders, she would draw him amorously toward her. She dreamed her vagina was absorbing his entire penis.

Sadly, life experience brought her realities far less exhilarating. Betty's friends, along with the majority of mainstream women's magazines, led her to believe that her fantasies of vaginal penetration originated from antiquated views of feminine submission and that liberated women climaxed from the clitoris. Intercourse served uniquely to make babies and to satiate the domination needs of males indifferent toward feminine pleasures.

Normally, Betty reasoned with and accepted, like millions of other women, the fact that her sex life was less than thrilling. But tonight, not really knowing why, an oppressive sadness overpowered her. Her eyes got watery and warm tears rolled down her cheeks. Betty cried in silence, not wanting to wake up Jeff.

* * *

Calmer and more even-tempered, Michael drove back toward Seattle and headed home. He parked his car in the garage and activated the alarm system by applying pressure on his key chain with his fingers. As soon as he got inside the door, he raced to the old, outdated answering machine whose flashing red light indicated the presence of messages. When he pressed the play button, he heard Vanessa's familiar voice: "Hi, Michael, it's Vanessa. Call me when you get in. I'm home alone tonight and I miss you…"

Michael checked the time that the message was recorded and discovered that it had been left at 8:47 P.M. He had dropped by Vanessa's place around 9:30 P.M. that evening. Therefore, the hypothesis of the sudden visit of a lover between the moment Vanessa called to tell him she was alone and the time he had passed by her place seemed improbable. On the other hand, her mother's unexpected visit became plausible. That is unless Vanessa intentionally led him on by saying she was home alone knowing very well that she'd be seeing another man. But he had to ask himself why she would go through all that trouble when there wasn't any formal commitment between them.

Michael's intelligence and sharp sense of analysis ranked him high on the social hierarchy. But when it came to Vanessa this only messed things up. Tonight, he would have liked to love like a simple idiot, not asking too many questions, not wracking his brain. This exhaustive cross-examination of his only further obscured the truth and made things seem far more perplexing and enigmatic than they probably were. What these thoughts did was just jumble his feelings for Vanessa. In the end, he really didn't know what to think. All he could do was curse himself a million times over for unexpectedly dropping by to see Vanessa.

* * *

Vanessa wanted to kill Michael for dropping by without any warning. If he had only called her in advance, she would have had enough time to get ready and presentably greet him. But he went ahead and screwed everything up. And then she was feeling awfully guilty for using that absurd excuse of hers on Michael. Their history was being built on a dishonest foundation. For starters, she had lied to Michael about her family by consciously choosing not to mention to him that she had a mentally challenged sister. Then, she had lied to him about her true profession. But tonight, her last lie was so stupid that she was ready to call him up and confess everything. However, if she owned up to her lies she was sure he'd leave her. And Vanessa didn't want to lose Michael. But the day he discovered the truth she was sure he'd take off. Caught in her coil of contradictions, Vanessa craved a cigarette, even though it had been some time since she'd quit.

* * *

Michael longed for a tall glass of whiskey. But he knew his worries couldn't be dissolved in alcohol—that was the stuff of B movies. Instead, he turned on the television to drown his mind in a flood of insipid images. Quickly, the movies and commercials—all starring actors who were as beautiful as they were superficial—began to bore him. The shallow images simply reinforced the futility of his existence. He was a celebrity for millions of Americans, made thousands of dollars a day, hundreds of women dreamed of sleeping with him and job offers by the dozens landed on his desk. But on the sexual sphere he was a big zero! His athletic build, his intellect, his chivalrous conduct, his fame—nothing could prevent him from being a premature ejaculator.

And that's exactly what he was. He had to face it. He knew the definitions formed by different researchers on the subject by heart and even though none seemed satisfactory, one constant prevailed: He didn't have control over the rise of his sexual excitement. He ejaculated soon after his penis entered inside the vagina and consequently, his partners never had time to reach orgasm during intercourse.

He had read tons of books on the subject. He sifted through them directly on location at different libraries, sick to his stomach with fear of being found out. Being so famous, he never risked borrowing books on premature ejaculation from the library, or buying such reading material from a bookstore or on the Internet.

He shuddered to imagine what would ensue if an inquisitive journalist learned that Michael Lancaster was reading books on premature ejaculation. With a disgusted tremor he thought back to the ugly scandal raised by the mistress of the late Senator Davidson. Months before he was assassinated, she divulged to the press and television stations, all the gritty, intimate details of their sexual relationship in exchange for a petty sum of money and short-lived fame.

Journalists feasted on the scrumptious details of the senator's sexual difficulties for weeks. In front of TV cameras, with a false air of intimidation, Barbara Rowland had complained despondently of the little sexual satisfaction she derived from the limp embraces of the senator. The sexual weakness of an old man with this woman who was clinging to eternal youth by means of a number of face lifts had something pathetic about it. The whole thing was a farce.

The ridiculed senator defended himself valiantly, but every one of his attempts was received with general hilarity. However, the smear campaign didn't really harm him. Having a mistress was acceptable in the eyes of the public since he had been divorced for over ten years. And to suffer from a sexual disorder was not regarded as morally reprehensible. It wasn't like being a rapist, a pedophile or a pervert. The whole scandal was simply all too funny. Hilariously funny! Everyone joked: "Poor old Davidson, he's just like his bill: he doesn't hold up too well!"

Michael was anguished by the thought of having the same thing happen to him. He could already envision the bold type headlines accompanied by his picture screaming in the tabloids: "The Sexual Problem Plaguing Michael Lancaster" or "Michael's Romantic Setbacks." Not only would his career be compromised, but also he would never again dare to look a woman in the eyes.

That's why he stayed away from muckraking journalists like the plague. From the time he became a TV celebrity, he did everything possible to avoid sexual encounters that risked exposing his weaknesses. He had not had any serious relationships for years. This attitude verged on paranoia, but his show obliged him to always be on his guard.

On every program of *It Concerns Us*, he exposed a political or economic scandal. Business barons were locked behind bars and politicians had been forced to resign because of his show. He gained remarkable popularity but also made deadly enemies. No one dared to attack him directly for fear of appearing suspicious, but many tried to knock him down one way or the other. Consumed by these emotionally draining thoughts, Michael lay down on his bed and fell into an agitated sleep.

CHAPTER 5

Michael woke up to the shrill sound of the telephone. It was eight in the morning. He flicked open the speaker on the phone convinced it was Vanessa. But he was disappointed when he heard the authoritarian voice of his boss who ordered him into work for an emergency *PDS* station meeting. Michael quickly showered and dressed, managing to swallow a piece of toast and a glass of orange juice on his way out.

An hour later, he was in the station's boardroom with the entire *It Concerns Us* team.

"Where do things stand on the March program?" demanded Tony, his boss, staring down each of the members in the room.

"The package is almost complete," mumbled the executive producer.

"You ready, Michael?"

"Yes."

"Perfect, then we'll get started on the next show right away." Tony took off his blazer and flipped it over the gray office chair behind him.

"As you all know, I thought Senator Davidson's bill on the legalization of drugs would be a good subject for our show. But now that the old chap is dead, the story has become a priceless gem. We have what it takes for a successful TV show: an unsolved murder, money, sex and drugs. Furthermore, Davidson wasn't just any regular Joe— former UN ambassador of the United States, former Secretary of State and ex-president of the National Wildlife Fund. We're talking about a resumé that bestowed on him a very high moral authority that conveniently just so happened to cause us to forget his flirtations with the ladies!"

Tony continued haughtily. "His prestigious career gave weight to his intention to legalize drugs. Now there isn't a single politician of such caliber that can sustain his bill. In short, the poor guy was buried with his ideas. It's too bad, we could have at least had six months worth of wild polemics and vitriolic debates with which to work! As for the cops, they're treading water in the kiddie pool. They don't have a clue of what happened. I'm sure we can do a hundred times better than they can on this case.

O.K., here's the rundown. We're going to have to move our butts on this one. My contacts tell me that ABC is coming out with a miniseries on Davidson in June. We need to go to air with this ahead of them. The name of the game is to beat the competition. The other television stations are already talking about this affair on a daily basis. Seeing that nobody knows what really took place, journalists interview just about anybody who is prepared to say just about anything. In brief, up until now we've been ingesting reports that are full of shit. We're going to do things differently, real professional reporting. Everybody clear? Questions?" He put down his pen and once again looked one by one into the eyes of every silent and still individual present.

"I'll take that as a no. Okay, let's get to it: Luis, you're in charge of the old man's family. Crystal, get your hands on every police document available. And check the archives. Mike, I want you to dissect his bill to death. Joan and Robert, snoop into his personal life. Dale, George and Cindy: The three of you are off to New York, Miami and Los Angeles to get the full, gritty details on the criminality and lifestyle of drug users.

"We're going to close the book on this foul affair. I'm prepared to give you more time than usual to work on this package, but I expect you to do an exhaustive job that brings back five star results. It's February twenty-fifth. The show will be broadcast the first Thursday of May. That gives you two months to put together a report that sizzles. I want this to even cause Washington to feel some serious heat up their asses. But remember, I want concrete evidence: names, dates and events. No hearsay. No more, no less. I want solid proof. You know my dogma: facts, nothing but facts.

"You, Michael, you will... are you listening to me, Michael?" he roared, loudly striking the table with his fist. "You seem out of it this morning. Come back to earth and join us. Considering the salary we're paying you, you have no right to fall asleep during meetings."

Michael jumped. He had never been so publicly admonished in his entire career. And he wasn't about to take it, either. As he stared Tony straight in the eyes, the tension in the room seemed to climb a notch. Nobody breathed. Even Dale, known for being chattier than a magpie, remained silent.

Michael knew he was in the wrong, but he was still unwilling to tolerate the reprimand. "Listen, Tony," he replied without raising his voice and continuing to sit comfortably in his chair. "From the time we've worked together, have I ever slacked off in my work or rested on my laurels? No. And you're well aware of this. So don't waste your breath lecturing me. I know what I have to do."

Tony's facial features became strained and he retorted angrily: "I hope that's the case for every one of you in here. Because if it isn't, the station manager will kick my ass, and trust me, I will kick yours right after—and farther!"

Michael let him have the last word and got up with the others to leave the conference room, missing the venomous look Tony had pierced into his back like a murderous dagger.

* * *

The alarm clock signaled eleven o'clock in the morning. Vanessa sluggishly shook her tired body to morning life. It had been a sleepless night, a night disrupted by troubling thoughts and questions without answers. "Everything would be so simple if I just had the courage to tell him the truth." She sat on the edge of her bed. "I guess I'll have to stop acting like the perfect woman and finally start being myself."

Half asleep, she stumbled into the kitchen and made herself a cup of espresso with the machine her mother had bought her for her twenty-fifth birthday. "I'd love to be like all those actresses who appear so strong and sure of themselves," she thought to herself. "Me? I'll die trying. I kill myself at work just so I can afford a bit of luxury. Again last night I went to bed at five in the morning." As for her love life, it was a series of sorry, pathetic flops. Vanessa's ex-boyfriends were so self-centered that after only three months of dating, they would often drop her for another woman with bigger breasts and no brain. And then there were the geeks who had little self-esteem and were so afraid of losing Vanessa that they'd cling to her like submissive dogs.

She stretched out her arm and helped herself to a chocolate cookie from the blue and white checked jar sitting in the middle of the kitchen table.

Vanessa's beauty and elegance intrigued men. Yet a lot of them felt unworthy of such a striking woman and kept their distance for fear of rejection. The bolder men, however—the least loyal and often the most pretentious—didn't hesitate to approach her.

When it came to her profession, Vanessa drove many less successful men to develop an inferiority complex and her exceptional intelligence caused more than one suitable candidate to take flight. But despite her enviable beauty, impressive cultural refinement and wit, Vanessa found herself unattractive and blamed her romantic failures on her slight physical imperfections. And so she did whatever it took to be even more beautiful and even more charming.

She looked at the laminated reproduction of Monet's *Pont d'Argenteuil* hanging above the kitchen cabinet. The print's dreamy quality and soft tranquillity reminded her of Michael. What surprised her most was the gentle way in which Michael had approached her. She remembered their first meeting vividly.

It was a Thursday evening in the middle of November. Vanessa was taking cover from a thunderstorm at the entrance of Sears. It was pouring and she was waiting for a lull in the rain to retrieve her car parked at the far end of the parking lot of South Center Mall. Standing there, she noticed Michael opening up an umbrella on his way out of the store. That's when he looked at her, hesitated a second, and then with a big smile extended his umbrella in her direction and simply said: "Take it."

As soon as Vanessa took hold of the umbrella, Michael darted unprotected into the rain. She stood there in paralyzed amazement for a few seconds. By the time she reacted, it was already too late: prince charming had climbed onto his white horse, or rather, Michael had dashed into his black Porsche.

But fate seemed to be on her side. While leaving the parking lot, she spotted Michael's car being filled up at the *Texaco* gas station across the street. She drove over, making sure to stop her car right next to him beside the gas pumps. After grabbing the umbrella tossed on the back seat, Vanessa rolled down her window and acknowledged Michael with a grateful smile: "Thanks a lot, I'm returning your umbrella. You'll need it again in Seattle."

Pleasantly surprised to again see the pretty stranger who had benefitted from his generosity—and so soon—Michael prolonged the small talk. "So you find it rains a lot here?"

"For a woman who was born in Arizona, I find it never stops in this city!"

Such was the start of a conversation that continued the next evening at the *Szechuan Emperor,* a Chinese restaurant located downtown. An extraordinary opportunity was being presented to her: to be the first woman ever to reveal the secret life of the mysterious Michael Lancaster.

By introducing herself as an architect driven solely by her career, she enabled him to let down his guard. Naturally, Michael still remained incredibly discreet. He rarely spoke of his work and never of his private life. However, with the passing weeks, she eventually ended up winning his trust. And Vanessa quickly developed feelings for this charming man. Despite his undeniable power of seduction, he had not used this to get her quickly into bed—quite the reverse, actually. They spent three months discovering their common interests and differences. Michael always spoke to her in his warm, calm voice while his dark blue eyes penetrated her intensely. He never failed to compliment her on her outfit or comment on the slightest change in her hairstyle. Most importantly, their conversations were always varied and interesting. Vanessa found herself falling for him. She cramped up with guilt when she suddenly remembered that she had not yet called Michael as she had promised to do the night before.

The sound of the telephone traveled into the kitchen from the next room. Vanessa jumped as usual. The brutal news of her father's death on that particular Sunday morning in October always came back to haunt her. But this time, she sprang out of her chair and raced toward the telephone before the answering machine went off.

"Hello?" she answered, hoping it was Michael.

"Hi Vanessa. It's me, Jimmy," replied a familiar nasal voice.

Vanessa's enthusiasm plummeted at once. Then it dawned on her that she had completely forgotten to return his call and so she forced herself to be nice: "What's up Jimmy? And what was so important the other night?"

"The boss is sending me on a photo assignment to Africa. Some country renamed Sambizania after the coup. You know where that is?"

"Of course," Vanessa said exasperated. "But I don't see how this news relates to me."

"Well, the boss told me that this time I could take along the reporter of my choice. So I thought of you…"

"What's up with her? It seems to me that usually it's the journalist who chooses the photographer, right?"

"You know her, she has her caprices. And besides, I'm not just *any* photographer," Jimmy added with pride.

"Sorry Jimmy, but it's just not possible. I have too much work to do at the moment. I have projects to finish and…"

"I don't doubt that. It appears that you're onto some *big* scoop. Top secret, she told me. If you need any sensational photographs tell me. We could arrange things."

"It's quite all right, thanks."

"As far as Sambizania goes, it's still a ways off. The planned departure is not for another few weeks…"

"Please don't insist Jimmy, it's just not going to happen. It's truly impossible." Vanessa's tone was unrelenting.

Jimmy insisted a bit more and then gave up in light of Vanessa's unbending resistance. The last thing he wanted to do was turn her off. He was desperately attracted to his coworker.

Vanessa was well aware of Jimmy's feelings toward her. Jimmy was the magazine's top photographer. Now in his late twenties, he had started off as a student intern during summers in college. His talent landed him a full-time job as soon as he graduated. In the beginning, Vanessa had gone out of her way to make the young, nerdy photographer feel a part of the magazine—friendly telephone calls, gratuitous advice and the odd casual outing for a bite to eat. But she soon realized her bespectacled friend assumed their friendship was leaning more toward a romantic relationship. The shy, maladroit Jimmy started sauntering over to her desk one too many times a day, and his lovesick stares from across the room began making her feel uncomfortable. Vanessa abruptly became distant and very short-fused with him. She wanted to be friends, nothing else, and this was the only way to make him understand. And Jimmy did get the message, but every now and then he slipped and tried his luck.

Although Vanessa wasn't usually curt with people, Jimmy seemed to bring out the worst in her. "Okay, Jimmy. I'm expecting another call. I've got to go. Bye." She dropped the receiver and groaned. "So that was the so-called important news. To think I got all worked up and worried for no reason. That guy is nothing but a headache."

* * *

By the pool of the Splendor Hotel in Miami, two men conversed, isolated from the other guests. Despite the heat from the Florida sun, the older of the two was wearing a buttoned, double-breasted suit and a tightly knotted tie. He had an aloof air of elegance about him, the kind that comes from savvy schmoozing and years of successful public appearances. But this morning, he wanted to maintain a low profile.

The younger man wore a black polo and white slacks. He addressed the older gentleman with deference and spoke hardly moving his lips: "Bad news, sir. The big shit-disturbing Black often sees a friend in Seattle. And the friend's name is Michael Lancaster."

"What exactly does this respectable yet regrettably much too inquisitive African-American know?" inquired Governor Jack Kotten, with a ripple of cynicism.

"He knows a whole lot and if he talks to this Michael Lancaster character it could only spell trouble. You know all about his damn show *It Concerns Us!*"

"It will be up to you then to decide if he knows a lot. And it will also be up to you to act accordingly to ensure that everything falls into place for the better."

"It's hard to say exactly what he knows, but he's been poking around in our affairs for a while now. And over the past two weeks, my men have informed me that he's been spending more time than usual with Lancaster."

"Work things out so we have access to every last detail of their conversations. And I want you to be very clear on this point, they must not talk about me on this show," enunciated Jack Kotten in a calm and sardonic tone generally used by men at the helm of power.

"It's pretty hard to silence Michael Lancaster from saying what he knows or thinks. He's reputed to be an incorruptible man," said the employee.

"Listen to me carefully, my little Christopher. I pay you a stately sum to maintain royal peace." He inched his way closer toward his motionless interlocutor and hissed between clenched teeth: "Do what has to be done. But nothing, I repeat, nothing concerning me must transpire onto this show. I don't want some inopportune revelations to ruin my career. Operate however you feel is best but act with expertise and discretion. Do you understand me?"

"Perfectly, sir."

That was the end of the conversation and with a few quick strides, Christopher Clays disappeared behind the palm trees bordering the hotel's lush gardens. His admiration for Governor Jack Kotten was unconditional. He represented a man America needed—a strong man who made no concessions. He wasn't like other politicians Christopher knew. You would never see him kissing anybody's ass for a few measly extra votes.

Jack Kotten was also a caring and generous man. A hefty chunk of his magnificent fortune went to cancer research. True, his wealth came from drug trafficking, but nobody went around forcing people to become drug addicts. Besides, most druggies were no more worthy than cruddy, disease-infested vermin. Christopher thought it made perfect sense to use the money made killing the vermin on saving those in society who deserved the help.

All these arguments confirmed to Christopher Clays that he had a sacred mission before him. "And outrageously well paid, I must say!" he stated, forming a smile. But the smile didn't last long. This mission was causing him a lot more worries than any others to date. How could he possibly shut this stupid Dave Morton up without resorting to extreme measures, he asked himself, frowning.

The rookie hit man hated blacks and to be officially granted the power to blow the head off of one fueled him with sadistic joy. Unfortunately, the black in question wasn't some panhandling bum from the Bronx but a reputable lawyer from Seattle. This meant there would be a serious inquiry into his death. And Christopher had no desire to spend a precious part of his white life behind bars. He was way too fond of the sun and convertible cars to risk the chance of living in the shade. All of that aside, he had to execute his boss's orders.

CHAPTER 6

Dave turned the key in the lock of the safe under the attentive eye of the bank employee. He pulled out a safety deposit box and disappeared into a spacious compartment. Michael followed him in silence. Away from eyesight, without a word, Dave nervously opened the contents of the metal box and withdrew photocopies of financial statements. He double-checked to see if he had all the documents and then quickly slid the papers into a soft leather briefcase.

Dave slipped Michael a duplicate of the safety deposit box key. As soon as they got outside Michael demanded some answers. The only response he got was the stern instruction to take his car and meet Dave at the country chalet where they had spent numerous weekends the summer before.

Michael wasn't used to taking orders, but the unusual severity and anxious behavior displayed by his friend forced him not to answer back.

Without asking any other questions, he walked to his car parked at the corner of Union Street and 4th Avenue. A quick glance at his watch told him that he would get to the chalet at around four o'clock.

Michael maneuvered his Porsche with confident ease through the dense traffic on Pike Street. His gestures were smooth and his reaction time was quick. He could have been a champion racquetball player or an NHL goalie for he possessed impressive dexterity and great stamina. But to his great disappointment, these abilities were of no help to him during sex. No matter what he did, whether it was holding his breath, sucking in his gut or contracting his rear muscles, he ejaculated too quickly.

Michael steered his car onto Interstate 90 and left Seattle in a hurry. He was driving quite recklessly and soon reached the first slopes of the Cascades. As he approached Snoqualmie Pass, the freeway became more slippery. The road was getting steeper in the midst of a towering forest of snow-covered pine trees. Michael cautiously adjusted his speed and drifted back into thinking about his sexual difficulties. He couldn't grasp the problem. Why had his lovemaking been so heated and flawless with Jennifer and no other woman afterward?

The memory of Jennifer, almost ancient now, was locked in his mind. He met her at Charles de Gaulle Airport in France. At the time, he was a freelancer and had purchased a cheap airline ticket from a chartered company. While waiting for his flight, he had struck up a conversation with a young Californian who was entering the country after traveling around Europe. Jennifer wasn't very pretty. But she looked terribly hot and sexy in her micro-mini that exposed long, bronzed legs. Her delicate limbs conspicuously contrasted the pair of full breasts and large, curvy hips she supported. She had acquired her mother's chunky Dutch body dimensions and natural blond hair. From her American father, of Sicilian descent, she had inherited a small stature and a warm temperament.

Their banal discussion on the beauty and inconveniences of France was interrupted by an announcement from the airline that their plane was going to be delayed indefinitely. Passengers were offered a complimentary evening at a hotel. For the first time in his life Michael delighted over the perpetual delays experienced by chartered flights.

A few hours later, he was sitting at the bar in the restaurant of the Novotel Hotel. Jennifer had changed her outfit and, undoubtedly to magnify her appeal, had applied a darker shade of makeup. She wore a long, off the shoulder tube dress, very much the style that year on the French Riviera. The bright orange dress was extremely clingy and required a perfect body for it not to look vulgar. Jennifer didn't possess such a body, but her sun-kissed shoulders and her full, coral-stained lips diverted attention away from her far too generous hips. And the dress, skimpy on fabric, offered a plunging neckline from which Michael had a hard time freeing his eyes. After they downed the third gin and tonic at the bar, Michael allowed his tongue to tell college day tales laced with graphic detail and sexual innuendo. Jennifer replied with a series of giggles and inviting smiles. By the fourth gin and tonic, Michael rested his left hand on Jennifer's knee. Slowly and gradually she inched open her thighs and, each time, his fingers responded by favorably exploring her further.

There was a long break in the conversation and Michael didn't order a fifth glass of gin and tonic. He knew it was time to leave the overcrowded area. He picked up the tab and led Jennifer to the lobby where they hopped into the first elevator. The doors hadn't even closed when they grabbed each other and began making out. The sexual energy and hungry desire muzzled at the bar were both boundlessly unleashed in a voracious chain of lust. Michael shamelessly groped Jennifer's voluminous buttocks, and she swayed her hips suggestively. Free of inhibitions, Jennifer slid her hand under herself to bring on stronger sensations. And then the blond Californian, her dress now hiked up to the waist, pushed the emergency stop button.

The elevator instantly stood still. Michael was completely turned on by the young woman's sexual forcefulness. Impatiently, he liberated the two golden melons Jennifer's dress had been constricting for too long. He buried his head in their fleshiness and devoured them gluttonously with his mouth and tongue. The Californian moaned audibly. With experienced hands, she massaged Michael between his legs. She wrestled brashly with his belt buckle until finally she tore down the zipper, opened his pants and extracted his erect penis. She then pressed her hands against the mirrored walls of the elevator and arched her back provocatively.

Faced with such an invitation, Michael's sexual excitement soared. He quickly ripped off the silk thong Jennifer was wearing and penetrated her with ease. He was about to initiate rapid in-and-out movements when the Californian grabbed his rear with flaming passion and forced him to stay immobile inside of her. She then began very slowly to move her pelvis in a rhythmic circular motion that both fascinated and aroused Michael. He was about to reach the pinnacle of pleasure when the elevator started to move. Instantly, they released each other and haphazardly whipped their clothes back on.

The elevator stopped on the next floor where a retired couple joined them. Neither one of the senior citizens commented on

Jennifer's flushed cheeks or the fact that she was short of breath, nor did they say anything about Michael's ruffled hair and the steamy mirrors. But their controlled smiles indicated a perfect understanding of exactly what had taken place. Michael got out of the elevator a little embarrassed and quickly led Jennifer into his hotel room.

They made love for the better part of the night. Jennifer had three orgasms—two during penetration—and they fell asleep entangled in each other's arms, both exhausted and sexually ravished. Michael never saw her again, but retained from this naughty episode the self-assurance that it was possible to make love without ejaculating too quickly.

Unfortunately, he was unable to isolate the elements responsible for allowing him to stay under control during this memorable ride. At first he thought that alcohol might have played a role in his ability to hold longer. But subsequent consumption of wine, beer or spirits didn't improve his sexual capacities and caused erection problems if he drank in excess.

He later assumed that not being in love with Jennifer as well as the absence of prolonged foreplay had probably made things easier for him. He had many one-night stands with women for whom he had no feelings and with whom he was able to hasten foreplay to refrain from getting too excited. But this didn't change the situation: In love or not, fancy or scanty foreplay, he couldn't manage to control himself during intercourse.

Finally, he played around with the premise that his penis, being less sensitive that evening, was the source of his superlative performance with Jennifer. With this in mind, he purchased over-the-counter anesthetic creams and jellies aimed at desensitizing the penis and retarding the reflex of ejaculation. These creams sometimes prevented him from ejaculating too quickly but they also neutralized his sensations and annihilated his pleasure. They also required him to use a condom, even in long-term relationships, if he didn't want to anesthetize his partner's sexual organs.

Michael went on to consult various sex manuals. He wasn't exactly thrilled by what he read. Masters and Johnson, along with a swarm of other therapists, swore by nothing but penile compression, a technique whereby the partner squeezes the penis in between her fingers when the male feels he's about to ejaculate. "What sexually sane woman will want to take part in this little game for the rest of her life?" exploded Michael. "And when I eventually meet the woman of my dreams, I can't see myself trying to convince her to consult a sex therapist with me at the start of our relationship. On the other hand, if I don't fix my problem right now, it's hard to say if she'd stick around for any great length of time."

Some time after that, Michael came across a magazine article about penis rings. He bought some in a sex shop and successfully convinced a partner of his that they were a part of foreplay action. The rings had prolonged his erection somewhat after climaxing but had rendered all movement extremely clumsy. In fact, the part of the penis extending from the ring up to the extremity of the gland remained engorged with blood and stayed relatively hard. However, the other part of his penis situated above the ring became limp again. Consequently, the sex organ remained rigid in appearance but no longer held the stable base needed to carry out the in-and-out movements of intercourse. It became difficult to continue having sexual intercourse and satisfy his partner. Of course, Michael had heard talk about Viagra. However, the famous little blue pill was of absolutely no use to him because obtaining good erections was never a problem for him.

He also read about a substance called Prostaglandin E-1, which when injected into the penis could sustain an erection for hours, even after ejaculation. But the idea of sticking a surgical needle into his penis wasn't inviting. And the thought of continuing to receive intense sexual stimulation after an orgasm didn't appeal to him either. He imagined this would be a painful and artificial experience. For Michael—like all men—ejaculation was the end of pleasure and not the beginning.

Then one day while listening to the radio, he heard a psychologist speaking about cognitive distraction, a fancy way to describe the act of thinking of other things during sexual relations. For example, you would play back in your mind the last quarter of the football game, think of your mother-in-law or mentally review your income tax form. Michael couldn't believe his ears. "How insane!" he had said, furious. "What kind of pleasure can you get if you have to think of something else while making love? And a woman would certainly find it frustrating to be with a man who has his head somewhere else! It's the same idea as going to a restaurant with a person who is thinking about something else throughout the meal!"

The only process that helped him a little was to masturbate a short while before making love. After that he felt less sexually aroused, and so he was able to hold on for a bit longer. But this technique had several drawbacks. Primarily, it considerably diminished his desire to make love since a good part of his sexual drive would have dissipated after ejaculation. Then there was the fact that at thirty-six, Michael no longer enjoyed the same sexual stamina of a young man of twenty. This was translated by serious difficulties in getting a new firm erection in the hours that followed the ejaculation. And on top of everything, he was forced to operate with a lot of discretion...

What it boiled down to was that thanks to or because of Jennifer he became truly conscious of his problem. Because prior to their sexual experience he thought, like many of his male friends, that it was perfectly normal for a man to ejaculate after one or two minutes of intercourse. The sexually charged Californian made him painfully aware of the degree of his deficiency. Never, neither before nor afterward, was he able to last as long or bring a woman to such a powerful climax.

* * *

Dave, who knew the route to the chalet by heart, got there first. When Michael finally arrived, Dave greeted him with the following orders: "Come inside, take off your clothes, and put on the ones lying on the bed. Then join me in the car. And by the way, it's cold out there."

Michael knew Dave was afraid that someone might have attached a bug onto a piece of his clothing without him knowing. If you asked him, his dear old buddy was becoming more and more paranoid with age. But he didn't argue and put on the gray track suit and woolen coat neatly arranged on the bedcover.

They drove along several surrounding small roads in Dave's Grand Jeep Cherokee. This vehicle was perfectly adapted to the icy paths of the small ski resort. The narrow roads wound between walls of snow more than nine feet high. Dave stopped close to a parapet from where one could see at a distance any potential intruder. They got out of the jeep and continued on foot.

Dave pulled the collar of his vest high above his ears and threw a glance in Michael's direction. "Now I can talk to you. Sorry for all the precautions, but I don't want to put your life in danger. As long as they don't find out you know anything, you'll be safe. Okay, this is it: Jack Kotten is basically self-financing his future electoral campaign. He quit the Republican Party in which he was a member for over twenty years so that he could run as an independent candidate in the next election. His personal income comes primarily from the fast-food chain, Submarine, of which he's the principal shareholder."

"Wait a minute, I've never heard of Submarine," interrupted Michael.

"That's quite understandable. Out of fifty-four restaurants, only seven are located in the United States. The rest are in Canada. But surprisingly, the Canadian chains are three times more profitable than those located in the States. Actually, I conducted an investigation for one of our clients—a competing fast-food chain that wanted to know why Submarine was making so much money. I don't usually take up cases involving industrial espionage, but Submarine's financial tactics sparked the business lawyer curiosity in me. And let me tell you, I wasn't disappointed.

"All the American branches are well located and make a reasonable profit. I went over the chain's financial books and everything is perfectly legitimate. However, on the other side of the border, the branches are reaping in a lot more profits, even in little lost holes like Baie-Comeau in northern Quebec or Sudbury in Ontario. Upon first glance, everything appears normal. The larger sales are justified by the purchase of loads of sausages, sandwich buns and huge containers of mustard. It could simply be assumed that Canadians like the taste of Submarine's sandwiches more than Americans—there's really nothing suspect about making a hell of a lot of money selling sandwiches. And the Canadian government doesn't have any complaints because Submarine pays all of its taxes.

"However, when I learned that Jack Kotten was thinking about selling his company shares, I found it a bit strange. Who would be so outrageously stupid as to sell out of a business that's running so well? Unless you have your own good reasons, of course, like wanting to rid yourself of a crooked business that would be damaging to a career as the president of the United States. And you could always buy back your shares secretly if you're not elected.

"All of this increased my suspicion and drove me to take a trip to Montreal. I went to a Submarine restaurant and, to my great surprise, there wasn't a soul to be found. I dropped by at different hours of the day and I never had to wait in line to be served. To confirm my initial findings, I sent a team of private detectives to count the number of clients who daily entered a Submarine restaurant in Montreal. It cost a tiny fortune but was all paid for by my client who desperately wanted to figure out what was cooking within the fast-food chain. Another group of experts was paid to gather the details of their business figures from the federal and provincial ministries of revenue.

"I was blown away. According to my calculations, every client had to swallow 12 subs per meal to justify the stupendous profits accumulated at this branch. Which means to say, as you must have already guessed, that the earnings from these restaurants are artificially inflated so as to launder dirty money. But this is very hard to prove because to lend more credibility to the scheme, some restaurants are presented as average profit-makers while others are shown to be making astounding profits. In addition, they construct a round of profits and losses; one month it's one branch that sells a lot, the next month it's another. Since the major purchases are made mostly by the main chain and not the individual branches and supposing that the mother house hands out to each of her daughters according to need, it could be explained that their returns aren't all coming from the visible clientele. In this case, it's almost impossible to find them out.

They even justify their purchases with phony sales bills from fabricated companies. Jack Kotten was bright enough to surround himself with a team of talented accountants and lawyers. Despite all our suspicions, I'm telling you, it would have been impossible to prove one damn thing without the documents we picked up at the bank this afternoon. Don't worry, I'll go over them with you in detail once we get to the chalet. Now back to the story: we then had the major shareholders and directors of Submarine followed by detectives. Here's where luck and perseverance were on our side."

"This is incredible!" exclaimed Michael. "I had no idea commercial competition could grow to such proportions."

"Hell, yes! And you haven't heard the end of it yet. On the one hand, my client is willing to do whatever it takes to destroy his competitor. But on the other hand, he's one of Submarine's many potential buyers. If a scandal erupts, the value of submarine sales will fall considerably and my client will make a killing.

"Keep listening and you'll have a good idea of the methods that high finance uses: We followed every executive director night and day with the hope of finding a discrepancy in their work ethic or a weakness in their character. We discovered that the director of marketing occasionally sniffed a line or two of cocaine and that the director of sales had a mistress in Chicago. Interesting, but nothing incriminating enough to make them betray a man as powerful and dangerous as Jack Kotten. But one of our detectives surprised the chief accountant who was doing some kinky entertaining with young boys in a Bangkok brothel. He even succeeded in snapping some graphic pictures of the threesome and procured a testimony from one of the little victims, which almost cost him his life."

"That's sickening!" Michael said in total contempt and disgust.

"You're right, that's why we had no scruples when it was time to make the guy fess up. It didn't take us very long, mind you, because the slime ball in question is a major wimp. He lives under the complete domination of a tyrannical wife who treats him like a helpless child. The guy's still more afraid of his wife than he is of Jack Kotten. In exchange for our silence and with the promise to let him run into the wild if things should turn out for the worst, he supplied us with copies of the company's financial accounts.

"We now hold copies of phony sales slips; checks made out in the name of fictitious companies and other conclusive proof that you saw in the bank safe. And I'm the only one in possession of all of this evidence. But even if this evidence demonstrates that the fast-food chain launders money, it doesn't prove that Jack Kotten's guilty or that this money comes from drug trafficking.

"Fortunately, thanks to a friend of mine who works at Interpol, I now have the missing pieces to my puzzle. Evidently, Jack Kotten has been under the watchful eye of Interpol for many years. They suspect these guys are buying large quantities of drugs from China, Pakistan and the former Soviet Union."

"Nothing coming from Colombia, Thailand or Burma?" inquired Michael.

"No, nothing. I find this odd, but neither my collaborators nor I have been able to come up with a logical explanation. Maybe you can sniff it out?"

"We'll see. But why hasn't Interpol acted on this yet?"

"It appears Kotten's protected by a high-powered person inside of Interpol, evidently scrapping the idea of any sort of criminal action," replied Dave, pressing his jacket collar closer to his nearly frostbitten cheek.

"By the way, what's the present leader's nationality at Interpol?" asked Michael.

"He's Canadian. You don't think he's involved in—" Dave didn't even have to finish his question. He was already very surprised by his friend's quickness.

"I don't think anything. It could simply be a coincidence, but it would explain the reason behind the success of his Canadian chains. Did you know that the annual business figure from drug trafficking is estimated at close to a thousand billion dollars? You heard me correctly: a thousand billion dollars a year! Faced with such stakes, what could the few miserable policemen who aren't corrupt do?

"But," continued Michael, "what baffles me most about this whole story is why Kotten got himself into a complicated tangle with a chain of fast-food restaurants when most drug traffickers recycle their money without much difficulty. I heard it's very easy to run fraudulent companies in tax havens such as the Cayman Islands or the Bahamas. There are also countless banks in Switzerland and elsewhere, for that matter, that launder money."

"This was true some years ago," corrected Dave. "Back then, large transactions of money could be effectuated by computer. But today, the controls are far more severe and even Swiss banks have had to forego certain concessions for notorious secret banking. It's still easy to stash away ten million bucks in a foreign bank. But it's becoming more and more difficult to retrieve this money to buy that villa in California without having to first justify the origin of this chunk of money. For this, the old system of 'cover' the mafia has used for ages is worth nothing. And besides, Jack Kotten is a very traditional man. He's horrified by modernity. Which explains, without a doubt, his preference for this more complicated yet more secure operation. This didn't stop him however from cooking up a juicy little scheme, which he's been getting away with for the past two years. Get ahold of this! One of Kotten's men put a hundred million dollars in liquid cash originating from the sale of drugs into a bank in the Turks and Caicos Islands, a well-known tax haven. The money was deposited in the name of a new fast-food company with no official connection to the Submarine chain. Up to this point you must be thinking to yourself that this is all very simple and commonplace. The bankers of these tax havens never ask any questions. And since all of this takes place outside of the country, on foreign soil, it doesn't directly interest the DEA or the IRS. A few months later, the offshore company that secretly received the hundred million dollars then launched a television advertising campaign in Canada to promote a new sandwich onto the North American market.

"I want you to listen to this very carefully Michael, because it has to be recognized that this scheme is very well thought out. The offshore company runs a series of advertising spots on TV where it pokes fun at the Submarine logo, which represents a sandwich in the form of a submarine. Cost of the operation: eight million dollars. In reality, this attack is not really that brutal, and far from being damaging to Submarine, it gives the company free advertising. However, as you might suspect, Submarine takes legal action against the rival company. It demands a hundred twenty million dollars in damages and interest for having tarnished its brand image. To avoid the expensive lawsuit, the Turks and Caicos society settles out of court with Submarine for ninety million dollars. Assessment of the operation: ninety million dollars—totally laundered—offered in dividends to the shareholders of the company Submarine, which includes, of course, Jack Kotten."

"Impressive," exclaimed Michael.

55

"Obviously, this is a lot easier said than done. But Kotten has a battalion of lawyers in his pay. This operation was carried out completely unnoticed, and without my informer I would have been totally in the dark about the whole thing. There is, however, even stronger evidence..." But before Dave could further elucidate, wet snow began to spit from the evening sky. And without another word, the two men returned to the chalet.

$$* * *$$

Betty was in exceptionally good form on this particular evening. She was running on the treadmill in the sports complex with surprising ease.

"Would you please slow down. I'm having a hard time talking to you at this ludicrous speed," Vanessa said, huffing and puffing. "You are definitely in great shape, I really don't know how you do it. You're more beautiful today than when you were twenty years old."

True, Betty sported the body of a teenager even though she had just recently celebrated her thirty-first birthday. Her body structure was light and flexible and regular exercise had earned her round and firm muscles. Slowing down the pace, she turned to Vanessa and commented, "You seem distracted. What's wrong?"

Vanessa wiped her sweaty forehead with the sports band holding back her ponytail. "I'm feeling more and more uncomfortable about this dishonest game I'm playing with Michael. He's starting to trust me and gradually open up. And what am I doing? I'm taking advantage of this to ask him personal questions and gather information for the feature I'm writing on him."

"It's your job, right?" exclaimed Betty.

"I know. And my boss is totally counting on me. She knows that this article on Michael Lancaster will boost *Metropolitan*'s dwindling sales. On top of that, she's promised me the job as editor in chief. Just think, Betty, editor-in-chief at twenty-eight years old!"

"Stop worrying, Vanessa. Your career comes before everything else. You can always find another man. For the moment, just enjoy the pleasure of being with him."

Vanessa didn't respond and continued to run, completely absorbed in her thoughts. Betty began to ramble on excitedly about a work colleague. It wasn't the first time she expressed interest in a man other than her husband, but today it seemed a little more serious.

Vanessa, who liked Jeff, Betty's husband, tried to discourage her. But Betty wasn't in the mood to receive moral advice from her friend. Vanessa didn't know all the intimate details of her private life. She wasn't aware that for years Betty tolerated mediocre sex with a husband who was more into football than candlelight dinners. Nor was she aware that Jeff regularly had one-night stands. Even if she was her best friend, Betty had too much pride to share all of this with Vanessa.

* * *

"The best thing to do is take a relaxing bath," Michael thought when he finally got home. His head was pounding, his mind laden with the revelations just disclosed by Dave. He filled the tub with steaming hot water, scented it with a handful of bath salts and soaked his aching body.

His thoughts began to slowly settle. The next show on fraudulent diplomas was all lined up, no worries on that end. As for the Davidson affair, he had two more months to work things out and if, as Dave suggested to him, Jack Kotten were the true instigator of the senator's murder, the show would be sensational. Clearly, the affair was a question of foul play and the risks were high. But the prospect of dragging down a revolting rogue from such a high level incited Michael to the highest degree. Michael could only pull the plug on such a scandal in the United States, and he felt grateful to have been born in this great country of freedom and democracy.

Indisputably, the Davidson affair was one hell of a story and he knew that only shrewd investigative journalism would get him to the kernel of the truth. But he'd have to play a tight game. He'd have to know all the ins and outs of the saga. And despite Dave's considerable legwork, there still remained a significant gray area that demanded clarification. "Why is Jack Kotten waging such a relentless campaign against drugs when he, himself, reaps great profit from this market?" wondered Michael. "Certainly, hypocrisy is second nature among politicians and it's only normal for him not to publicly reveal his support for the drug-trafficking trade. But if the repressive extremes he's proposing in his electoral platform become law, he would be the first one to suffer a loss of profit." Michael was in for a long and detailed study of Kotten's platform. Maybe, he thought to himself, the answer was tucked somewhere in between the fine print.

The telephone's ring resounded but Michael didn't move, leaving the humble job to his answering machine. However when he heard Vanessa's voice, he bounced out of the bathtub and ran naked to the phone, leaving a trail of water behind.

"Oh, you're home, Michael. I see you let your answering machine screen your calls, huh?"

"Not exactly, I was in the tub and I wasn't expecting you to call at this hour," he defended himself, mildly reproachful.

"Sorry for not calling earlier, but I was terribly busy. To make up for it, I have a proposition for you."

"You want to officially introduce me to your mother?" Michael said sarcastically.

"No, I mean, yes…uh, well another time, this isn't about…I called to ask you…I would like to spend some time with you," she stuttered.

Michael would have liked to prolong Vanessa's embarrassment by reminding her that yesterday she was less than eager to see him. But he decided to be tolerant and said, "Sorry about last night. I should have called you before—"

"No," interrupted Vanessa. "I was the idiot. I should have let you up, but…Anyhow, I'm calling to find out what you're doing next weekend."

"Well, I have to go to New York on business…"

"Too bad, I wanted to invite you to the opera."

"Come to New York with me. There's something I must take care of first which won't take long and then we'll have the entire weekend to ourselves."

Vanessa remained silent for a minute and then announced, "Great. When do we leave?"

CHAPTER 7

S tepping out of the taxi, Michael looked around him and declared in an awe-inspired voice: "Wow! The Big Apple is such a fascinating city." His face lit up with a huge smile. Vanessa was by his side and the streets of Manhattan appeared to him as romantic as those in Woody Allen movies.

The wind picked up and the two of them rushed into the hotel. The receptionist at the Sheraton addressed them as Mr. and Mrs. Lancaster since Michael had made the reservations under his name. Vanessa found the misunderstanding cute and momentarily dreamt of marriage with Michael.

They then hopped into an elevator and once inside Michael had trouble keeping his eyes off Vanessa. He smiled and moved closer to her. He took her hand and gave her a long kiss on the lips. He felt so happy. It was much too long since he felt the euphoria of young love.

"I know an excellent restaurant in Manhattan," Michael said as he closed the door to their hotel room. "They serve the best seafood in town. Do you want me to make a reservation?"

"Sure," Vanessa replied, distracted.

"You want to take your shower first?"

Vanessa drew back the curtains hanging in front of the window and stared blankly into space. And then, without turning around, she answered, "No, you go ahead."

Without insisting, Michael disappeared into the luxurious bathroom finished in light gray marble. He sang as he showered, thrilled to be on vacation with Vanessa. For once in his life, he had given himself some freedom, without worry.

He promptly finished getting washed up and stepped back into the room rejuvenated and freshly dressed. He felt wonderful.

Vanessa felt awful.

On the one hand, she was living a fairy tale. What woman wouldn't dream of a romantic getaway with Michael Lancaster? And Michael wasn't like other men who selfishly swore by their personal agendas. He knew how to listen and be tender. But her pleasure was spoiled by the lies she had told him to carry out her journalistic mission to the tee. In the beginning, her role of reporter-spy had been highly exciting; at present, this masquerade was giving her a serious case of nausea.

She had wanted to ensnare him stealthily and now she was the one being stopped in her tracks, trapped in her own game. It was clear that from this point on she had to choose between her story or an honest romantic relationship with him. Her career or Michael, that was the question.

Vanessa refrained from moving as she watched Michael take possession of the room. He was cheerfully unpacking the bags. She kept her eyes on him and didn't budge. For a split second, she thought about turning around and running. It would be easier to leave, she thought, than to crush the confidence and joy radiating off the face of the man she was beginning to fall in love with. But all she did was stand there, in front of the window, silent.

Michael finally became concerned over her impenetrable stillness. "Is something wrong, Vanessa?"

A silence lasting what felt like a thousand years ensued and then Vanessa slowly articulated, "There are things I have to tell you Michael. I lied to you…"

This certainly wasn't what Michael had expected. His brain began to work at full speed: "What could it possibly be?"

Vanessa took a deep breath and declared in a hesitant voice: "I told you I only had a brother. It isn't true. I also have a younger sister in a mental institution for children. I know it's stupid, but I'm just so uncomfortable…."

Michael heaved an immense sigh of relief. He took a few steps toward Vanessa, wanting to comfort her and to tell her that this didn't change anything between them, but she stopped him with the gesture of her hand. "There's something else," her throat constricted and her breathing became more difficult, "and it's a lot worse."

Michael stopped and quickly went back to thinking, "I had my doubts. It was too simple..."

"In fact, Michael, I'm not an architect. I'm a—well, I practice a particular profession you don't appreciate much—"

"Would you just tell me already?" Michael interrupted impatiently.

"All right...I'm a journalist. I work for *Metropolitan* magazine."

Michael withstood the blow without saying a word. "A journalist," he repeated to himself. "That was it!" he thought. "I was trapped like an amateur...I played the good lover in her little romantic charade...and to think I already saw myself married to this liar." Disgusted, he looked away from Vanessa.

Michael had developed an unhealthy hatred against journalists who pried into people's private lives. He was all too aware of the sleazy methods they used. Up to now, thanks to his vigilance, no reporter had been able to dish out any dirt on his personal life. But he knew that the moment a journalist slithered their way into this intimate domain his career would be ruined. And wouldn't you know, the woman of his dreams was none other than one of these wretched journalistic scrolls in quest of a remunerative scoop.

Vanessa remained frozen by the window, her lips trembling with emotion. Michael's surprise abruptly transformed into rage. "Come on," he hissed between clenched teeth, "get your damn interview over and done with quickly. I'm going back to Seattle tonight."

Vanessa was having a hard time suppressing the tears mounting in her throat. Painfully, she began to explain. "No, Michael, there won't be an interview. It's true, I did intend to write an article about you, but—"

"I trusted you!"

"I didn't betray your trust, Michael. I'm not going to write the story. I thought I was doing something for my career. You have to understand the temptation was too great. Anybody else in my place would have done the same thing."

"Not me!"

"I know, Michael. And I was wrong. But believe me everything has changed now. I care about you."

But her words didn't reach Michael who had already closed himself off into a soundproof world of broken dreams. He didn't want to hear another word coming from the mouth of this cursed woman who had lied to him for three months and was now acting out for him the tears and repentance scene. He stormed out of the room without looking at her.

Vanessa thought she was about to faint. She was feeling dizzy. The floor was spinning beneath her feet. Her vision was blurry and her stomach queasy. All of her hopes and dreams were collapsing like a house of cards. Finally, her legs no longer would support her and she slumped onto the edge of the bed.

From the beginning of their relationship, she knew she was in a deceitful position and that when the time came to reveal her true motives it would be difficult and painful. Yet she had not predicted such a reversal in the situation. She was supposed to drop Michael the minute her article was published. And as it turned out he was the one to dump her even after she impulsively renounced her story on him. She tried to get hold of herself, but was no longer able to suppress her emotion and burst into tears.

Michael shivered from the cold. He was walking the slushy streets of New York, dressed too lightly for the season. The walk helped him come to terms with the situation with great lucidity. For the first time in many years he had given a woman access to his heart. But not just any woman: a woman who was just as beautiful as she was intelligent, one who was full of charm and tenderness, and who was also both sensual and spiritual. And today he learned that his trust had been betrayed.

He already imagined what Vanessa would write in her article. She would definitely allude to his sexual problem. He, the popular Michael Lancaster, to be labeled a premature ejaculator. "No way. Impossible! She would never do that to me!" he thought to himself, both worried and revolted. "I know very well she's not the type of person to hurt someone in that way. However, she is making me suffer at this very moment. I wanted things to work out between us. Vanessa is everything I'm looking for in a woman."

Michael was aimlessly walking the streets. He told himself that despite his fierce aversion to journalists who meddled in the personal lives of people, he could accept Vanessa's profession because of how much she loved him. With every dazed step, his anger progressively transformed into sadness. And the sight of snowflakes swirling between the buildings changed his sadness into melancholy. Vanessa's profoundly distressed image when he left the hotel room came back to mind.

* * *

Ever so gently, Vanessa lifted her spirits back to life. Her body that had curled up into a ball of sadness slowly unfolded. Her moistened eyes scanned the silent room. She noticed Michael's laptop on the reading table and his clothes half out of his suitcase. He would have to come back to gather his belongings. There would be one more chance to see him, to talk to him. What she would say to him at that moment could still save their relationship. But none of the reasons or lines she came up with satisfied her.

There was one thing she was sure of: She would maintain her dignity. She would neither beg, nor attempt to justify her actions. She would simply tell him that he was someone very special to her and his leaving pained her enormously.

Vanessa got up slowly, feeling both drained and sore, like after a long and strenuous aerobic workout. She went into the bathroom and washed her tear-stained faced. Just as the tepid water began rejuvenating her weary face, she heard a knock on the door. She quickly paled and her breathing stopped. Was it Michael? What kind of state would he be in? Furious, certainly. Would he insult her? No, he's not the type to do that. Would he collect his things without a word? Yes, that sounds more like him." Vanessa could not move, even as another knock resounded at the door.

As if in a movie in slow motion, the young woman walked toward the front of the room and opened the door. It was Michael.

"I'm sorry, Vanessa, I overreacted," he said, handing her a dozen red roses.

Vanessa stayed still, incapable of uttering a single word, amazed by Michael's unexpected return. She didn't know what to think any more and simply rode the wave of emotions she was feeling. She fell into his arms and burst into tears. Michael tried to talk but Vanessa stopped him by placing upon his lips tiny, soft kisses soaked with tears. She pressed her body tightly against his and locked her arms securely around his shoulders, afraid that he would leave again. Her kisses intensified and Michael was inundated by Vanessa's gush of passion and her sweet scent. Her urgency became so intense that he soon found himself pinned to the wall. She pressed herself harder and closer against his body and stayed stuck to him like this for several long minutes. Michael didn't move and surrendered to the passionate love radiating from his companion.

Vanessa slowly slid her hands on Michael's chest and unbuttoned his shirt with agile fingers. She covered his muscular thorax with tiny kisses and nibbles, making him quiver with pleasure. Vanessa was on a high, her entire body trembling with ecstasy. She felt as if she was floating on air, light-hearted and weightless, hovering in euphoria. She thought she had lost Michael forever. And now that she felt him hard against her, there was nothing left for her to do but totally and selfishly possess him. She wanted him all to herself, to completely devour him.

Michael was extremely aroused by this generous demonstration of ardor. He slid his hands under Vanessa's red angora sweater and started caressing her back. But this form of arousal was apparently not enough for Vanessa who was on the verge of losing control. She pulled off her sweater impulsively, freeing her breasts from the mesh of underwire and black lace and pressed them against Michael's pounding chest. Vanessa let out a long, exhilarated moan. She then began swaying her bust and rubbing her erect nipples against him. She breathed in his masculinity as she showered his neck with moist kisses. Michael groaned with pleasure and leaned in closer, wanting to completely savour the sensual fervor escaping from this woman he loved so much.

Burning with desire, Vanessa ripped open Michael's pants and pulled out his erect phallus. She grabbed it in her hands, appreciative of its virile firmness, and slid her fingers slowly toward the base. With exquisite slowness, she brought it up close to her face and amorously pressed it against her cheek.

Vanessa lightly grazed the full length of Michael's hard penis with her wet lips. She then began stimulating its extremity with tiny, rapid flicks of the tongue. Next, with a firm hand, she directed it into her partially opened mouth. She fused her lips around the hot, pulsating penis and pushed it deeper and deeper into the cave of her mouth. She closed her eyes and concentrated on the pleasure she was bringing to her lover. Vanessa wrapped her fingers tightly around Michael's penis. Her head, mouth and tongue were moving in synchronized speed. As the movements got faster, she could feel his penis swell, ready to burst.

Michael's pleasure was quickly becoming uncontrollable. He was going to ejaculate any second now. He clenched his teeth, pulled in his stomach, held back his breathing and contracted every muscle in his body hoping to prevent ejaculation that was coming too early. But without delay, his penis jolted with unyielding bliss and he shot his semen out with force.

Caught off guard by how fast Michael had ejaculated, Vanessa got up slowly and snuggled next to her partner. Michael was embarrassed for ejaculating so quickly. Since his sexual excitement had dissipated, he was left with nothing but a painful feeling of failure and discomfort. He couldn't even share his pleasure with Vanessa. All he really wanted to do was to take her in his arms and pamper her with love and affection. But he knew very well that Vanessa was far from being sexually satiated and that it wasn't time yet for the tenderness and decline of after-play. He was going to have to make up for his shortcoming by stimulating her in another way now that his penis had lost all of its rigidity.

Michael scooped Vanessa in his arms and carried her to the bed. He walked his fingers up to her black underwear and slid the flimsy piece of lace down her long, tapering legs. Vanessa languorously spread apart her thighs, moaning audibly. Her sex opened involuntarily. She fully savoured this delicious moment of liberty and sensuality.

Michael began by kissing Vanessa's feet and ankles, patiently working his way up the length of her legs. Sometimes he bit her body lightly and, each time, she would respond with a craving cry for more.

But he took his time, approaching with infinite slowness the insides of her smooth thighs.

All the while, Michael was thinking to himself: "She has such a fantastic body and she smells so good. I could ravish her. If only I had not ejaculated so stupidly quick. I really can't enjoy this now. I'm so drained; all I want to do is sleep. Besides, she must suspect how I feel. She must consider me a lousy lover."

Vanessa didn't have the faintest clue of the kind of sinister thoughts that were floating around in Michael's mind. She had completely let herself go to the masterful kisses of a man who was such an expert in oral sex. Michael's tongue traveled with ease into the mysterious regions of her mons veneris. After numerous unexpected detours, he reached her clitoris. He gently outlined it with the tip of his tongue. And then with the precision of a watchmaker, he took it between his lips and sucked it delicately.

Vanessa dug her nails into the bedsheets. Her thigh and stomach muscles stiffened. Michael intensified the movements of his tongue. He sensed an intense excitement growing in her clitoris. Vanessa's back arched suddenly and her breathing stopped, she was ready to explode. Her face twisted into a painful grin. As she breathed in a little, her tension rose to extreme heights. At once, a series of spasms emanated from her genitalia and shook every inch of her drenched body. Her head tilted backwards and, exhausted, she succumbed to an orgasm.

Michael slowly came up from under her and moved to her side. Vanessa was spread out on the bed, void of all energy. After a few minutes, she finally caught her breath and lay washed up in her lover's arms by the ocean of pleasure that had swept her.

CHAPTER 8

A pale morning sun shone down on Manhattan's giant skyscrapers, the edges of their windows amply covered in glistening snow. The streets, however, were already dirty from the heavy city traffic. A dingy yellow taxi dropped Michael and Vanessa off at the entrance to Central Park where the snow was still immaculate. After a couple of paces, the happy duo felt as if they were in another world. The city traffic came to a hum and the bustling of the street lulled. The deafening noise of the city transformed gradually into a murmur and they heard the chirp of a sparrow perched high on the ornate iron of a lamppost.

Michael wrapped his left arm around Vanessa's shoulders and pulled her close to him. She responded with a smile. They both felt wonderful and happy. The two of them stopped on top of a little bridge overlooking a frozen pond. Michael kissed Vanessa's chilled lips, reddened by the cold. She reciprocated with ardent passion and whispered into his ear: "You know, Michael, I still haven't confessed to you the stupidest lie. I swear it's the last one and it's quite funny."

Michael smiled. So in a shy rush of words Vanessa recounted the anecdote of her mother's pretend visit. They both laughed heartily, thinking back to the funny incident. A beautiful bond was formed between the two lovers and Michael ended up finding New York to be nothing short of marvelous. In this unique and absurd city, the spectacle of life unraveled without modesty: misery went hand in hand with wealth, folly collided with reason and ugliness united with beauty.

The couple ended their stroll in a fast-food joint where they even found their half-dry mustard and relish hamburgers delicious. They discovered more things they had in common with each other and got a kick out of listing children's names they liked and disliked.

* * *

When they were leaving the restaurant, Michael said to Vanessa, "I don't know where the time has gone and I have a lot of things to do. You'll be doing me a great favor if you run an errand for me. One of my colleagues has a contact in Manhattan who is supposed to hand me an envelope containing very important information. All you have to do is swing by his office and he'll give it to you personally. That's it."

"Is it dangerous?"

"No, no! Just ask for Allen Alper. He's a former police officer, turned private detective. It'll save us time if we want to eat out and catch a Broadway show. Here's the address. Are you okay with this?"

"No problem, I'll take care of it."

"We'll meet at five o'clock at Columbus Circle."

Vanessa left Michael with much regret on the corner of 58th and Broadway. She took a cab and was dropped off at the indicated address. Getting out of the old yellow Chevrolet, Vanessa stomped over a snowdrift alongside the sidewalk. Feet covered in snow, she rushed into the gray and black building occupying the offices of the New York contact.

Allen Alper always had topnotch tips, which he sold for a handsome price. No one knew for sure how he got his hands on this information, but it didn't bother them. He had promised over the phone the inside details surrounding Senator Davidson's death, material he obtained directly from one of the FBI investigators.

When Vanessa got to the twenty-eighth floor, a hyperactive secretary made her sit in the waiting room. A few minutes later, the woman articulated in a shrill voice: "Vanessa Andressen, room twenty-three, left corridor, fifth door to your right."

Allen Alper appeared to be just as nervous as his secretary was. He spoke through his teeth at incredible speed, making it hard for her to decipher just what he was saying. He smoked his cigarette with rapid, impatient puffs and coughed loudly without covering his mouth.

"Mr. Lancaster sent you in his place. He has good taste," Alper said, eyeballing Vanessa's body. "The documents he requested are on the desk. Everything is to be found in this manila folder. Would you be interested to know what it's about?"

The proposition tweaked Vanessa's curiosity. However, she held back and politely refused. "No, just give me the envelope, please."

"Does the one who sent you trust you?"

"Of course!"

"All right then, I'm going to share a few interesting elements with you." Alper, first-class voyeur, wanted to keep this beautiful woman in his office for as long as possible. "Here are the facts: Senator Davidson was killed by gunshots released from a Colt 45, model 1911 A1, belonging to a World War II veteran. Whatever may come of this, we can say Colt makes weapons that last a long time.

"The weapon was retrieved in a garbage bag not far from the site of the crime by a former high school professor turned homeless who being an obsessive compulsive brought it back to the police. For obvious reasons, the gun had no fingerprints on it. However, we were able to track down its first owner by the serial number. The distinguished veteran has been dead for a long time, but his son sold the weapon two years ago when he was in desperate need of some fast cash to buy his drugs. Ironically, it could be concluded that Davidson—the great knight of drug legalization—died indirectly as the result of drugs," he said, with a sardonic smile.

Vanessa felt uncomfortable with this creepy character. His slimy eyes were casually roaming up and down her body. His shabby presence and rude gestures reminded her of the old, greasy, sleazy gas attendant from the service station in her native town. She couldn't wait to get out of this office that reeked of cigarettes and the male animal in heat.

Alper cleared his throat and rubbed his bony hands together as if in delirious glee. "The ballistic analysis indisputably proves that the seven bullets which killed the senator came from this weapon. And moreover, after analyzing the impact of the bullets, the experts came up with the following two assumptions: The killer is either someone with little experience or someone very uncoordinated. The shots were either fired grouped together or aimed directly at the vital organs. Considering the destructive capabilities of the Colt 45, a professional would have been able to kill Davidson with a single, direct bullet. This means that the person could have gained time and made less noise.

"As for the noise, the neighbors have declared hearing a dozen or so gunshots. And in fact, we found the impact of two shots in the walls that surrounded the senator. The distance between the shots has been estimated at between ten feet for the first impact and three inches for the last two, which blew off the senator's head."

The New Yorker paused and drew in a puff of smoke. He looked at Vanessa from the corner of his eye, hoping that he had somewhat shaken her with the last gruesome detail.

But the young journalist remained impassive: "So what you're getting at is that to have missed a sick and barely mobile man like the senator by 10 feet, with a Colt 45, you definitely have to be somewhat of a one-handed idiot."

"Unless the trigger was pulled by a woman," he laughed.

That was it! Vanessa couldn't tolerate this jerk for one second longer. On top of vulgarly staring at her as though she were a piece of raw meat, he had the gall to denigrate women. Vanessa took a deep breath and hit back with the ferocity of a lightning bolt: "For all the woman I am, with a Colt 45, I could put you down without hesitation or a tremor. And despite your skinny hide, I could easily lodge five bullets into your boney chest from 15 feet away. And I've only been training for two years."

Struck dumb by this unexpected reply from a woman, Allen Alper couldn't come up with a response. He stuck his cigarette safely between his lips, took a long, comforting drag and continued nervously. "In any case, what I know is that the weapon was sold to a woman matching the description of the senator's former lover. What I also know, is that the bitch was sleeping on his will. And whores who only kiss for money, I know many myself," he hissed, looking Vanessa straight in the eyes.

Vanessa didn't want to listen to him anymore. Besides, this didn't concern her. She took the manila folder and placed a check on the edge of the desk, just as Michael had asked her to do.

With a rapid gesture, Alper grabbed the check like a spider rushing to its prey.

Vanessa left the office without a second glance.

* * *

While Vanessa was picking up the envelope, Michael dropped by a mafia repentant he knew who supplied him with precious information on his former relations. Don Pasquale Giamorcaro had at one time belonged to a powerful *cosche* (or family) of the Sicilian mafia, the *Cosa Nostra*. He now went by the name of Matthew Casey, maintained a low profile and lived in a small house in Greenwich Village. He tried hard to forget his past by devoting himself to numismatics and talking to no one. Except for Michael and only in private, alone together.

Michael had caught up with him during the course of one of his investigations on the theft of containers in the maritime ports on the eastern coast of the United States. Following revelations incriminating the mafia of Palermo, the head organization behind this huge operation, Michael had protected Don Pasquale. He had kept him clear from traps set by the police and away from the deadly clutches of the mafiosi. In appreciation, the former *uomo qualificato*—influential member—had agreed to blow the whistle on the key players and schemes of the underworld.

Michael's visit with Don Pasquale was very brief. Neither Davidson nor Kotten had any ties to the *Cosa Nostra* during the period when the ex-mafioso was a part of it. This came from the repentant, making it clear that his information went back more than two years. Because he had distanced himself from that time on far away from the milieu, he couldn't say any more. Michael knew, however, that serious bonds with the mafia aren't formed overnight. It was highly unlikely that Kotten or Davidson had colluded with the New York Sicilians.

Since Michael spent less time than he expected with Giamorcaro, he had some time to kill and decided to hook up with a few of his old buddies from Tulane University. He knew of at least two who settled down in New York following graduation. After a couple of phone calls, he managed to connect with Isaac Kalechman, a Jewish lawyer specializing in criminal law.

In less than ten minutes, Michael reached the office of his old college friend. As with every one of their meetings—unfortunately, all too rare—Isaac displayed his proverbial good humor. "Michael, you haven't changed a bit!" he exclaimed, leading him into his office.

Isaac, on the other hand, had changed. He was completely bald and his glasses seemed even thicker than beforehand. "And you, Isaac, business must be rolling along pretty well—an office on Fifth Avenue, not bad. I can tell you aren't having to make too many sacrifices."

"I guess I can't complain," the lawyer responded modestly. "But I'm not as famous as you are. I watch your show every week. It's very good. You haven't lost your old bite."

"Talking about the show, I'm working on one of the hottest subjects of the day."

"Wait, wait! I'll serve you a glass of bourbon first and then you can tell me all about your latest passion just like old times." Isaac bent over and removed a large, half-empty bottle from underneath his desk. "It's the best!" he said, laughing. He poured two glasses, inspected them at great length, and handed the fuller of the two to Michael.

"Thanks, old friend." Michael took a quick mouthful of the corn-based liquid and placed his glass on a huge desk cluttered with piles of files. "It has to do with the late Senator Davidson—"

"I should have bet on it!" exclaimed Isaac. "Tell me everything you know. I'm interested in the story myself."

"Sure. But first tell me what you think."

"Holy cow, Michael, still a good tactician, I see. All the same, I'll give you my legal opinion. I have a feeling that there's a political connection to this filthy ordeal—a conspiracy disguised as a sick murder."

"Could it not have been a crime of passion?" probed Michael.

"Don't tell me you believe in the guilt of the senator's former mistress!" cried out Isaac, practically downing his whisky. "She has a solid alibi: Her neighbors heard her voice through the walls."

"Witnesses could be bought off. You know that, Isaac."

"True, but when I saw this woman, Barbara Rowland, on television, she didn't come across as a cold-blooded killer."

"You shouldn't go by impressions," pursued Michael, quite enjoying this intellectual joust. "To tell you the truth, I don't buy the guilt of the woman either. I'm also convinced that the whole mess is effectively part of a conspiracy orchestrated by people who wanted to silence the senator and to get rid of his contentious bill. I believe we're talking about powerful people here, people who are dangerous to attack."

"And, of course, you're going to attack them. Honestly, Michael, you haven't changed a bit. Always that hunger for risk, that desire for a good fight."

Michael fell back into the soft leather tan armchair. "No, that's not it, Isaac. I don't have the desire to fight. But I feel that underneath this affair is a dirty coverup. And my job is to expose this type of criminal impropriety. To get there, I'm forced to confront certain dangers. I do take risks. Lots of them! But you have to remember, it doesn't necessarily mean I like what I have to do."

"I'd love to be like you," admitted Isaac, replacing his heavy eyeglasses. "Unfortunately, I have four children and I can't allow myself to get too adventurous. On the subject of children, you still not married?"

"No," Michael answered, pensive. "Maybe one day. Who knows?"

"Yes, one of these days. Anyway, to get back to the Davidson affair," pursued Isaac, a man who was more passionate about politics than his feelings, "you should pay particular attention to those who were hoping that his bill would die. Like General Kulliger, to name just one..."

"The one who is part of Governor Kotten's campaign?" Michael asked, with skepticism. "What could possibly be his motive?"

"Since the end of the Soviet regime, a lot of people have wanted to see military spending shrink drastically to receive what we call peace dividends. Few citizens want the United States to play the great protector of the world and intervene in every single local war. But General Kulliger has very good friends among the big magnets of the American industrial military. He has also found new enemies for the country, justifying the pursuit of additional military spending. These same enemies also happen to be cocaine and heroin producing countries. Consequently, a law legalizing the consumption of drugs would ruin his plans."

Michael was listening to his old buddy with a cautious ear. He couldn't help having some reservations. "You don't think your hypothesis is a bit…how should I put this…farfetched?"

"I could be wrong," replied the lawyer. "It's but one possible hypothesis among a mountain of others. But I assure you, there are astronomical sums of money at stake here and the senator's life didn't count for much."

"This certainly warrants some consideration. But listen, I don't want to chew up your time; I'll leave you to your paying clients. It was great seeing you again, old chap, and remember if you're ever in Seattle, give me a call. We'll have to do some serious reminiscing. Don't forget to say hello to your wife on my behalf."

"I wouldn't pass your offer up for the world. And you're always welcome, you hear me? The next time you're in New York, drop by the house. Myriam would be thrilled to see you in body and soul. She's crazy about your TV show."

* * *

Michael left the elegant building where Isaac had his office and decided to take on the streets of Manhattan by foot. Naturally, his thoughts drifted to Vanessa. She was heavenly and his happiness was consummate. Well almost, because there was one doubt in particular that always darkened his thoughts. And Michael knew exactly how to torture himself. He reverted back to his last sexual experience with Vanessa. Once again during last night's steamy reunion, he was unable to control himself and ejaculated soon after Vanessa intensified stimulation with her hand. Following thirty minutes of recovery, during which time he was totally engrossed in pleasuring Vanessa, he had succeeded to hold back long enough to proceed to penetration.

But after that, all it took was a few pelvic movements to make him lose complete control. The third time around, which took place in the middle of the night, he prolonged intercourse a little longer. But his erection suffered serious weakness and he had to give in, totally exhausted.

He was comforted by thinking back to the fact that Vanessa had several orgasms after his oral and finger caresses. Even more reassuring was the fact that she had clearly expressed her great satisfaction and appeared completely satiated. The memory of her satisfied words actually destroyed the nagging doubts he was having and at that very moment, life seemed marvelous to him.

Although not very religious, as Michael passed by a church, he felt the need to kneel down and thank the Creator for all his happiness and good fortune. He walked through the portico and took a seat in the last pew. The impressive silence inside the sanctuary reminded him of his fragile existence. When it came down to the nuts and bolts of humanity, who was he really, if not a poor mortal like all the rest? Sure, he had fame and money. But wasn't all that was truly important above that? Didn't the importance lie in vanquishing the misery and injustice in the world? Wasn't it all about spreading around the love he had within him? All these spiritual reflections confirmed just how lucky he was to know such happiness and love with Vanessa. Immersed in his thoughts and engulfed by the celestial calm that reigned in this sanctified place, Michael lost track of time.

Vanessa was waiting at Columbus Circle where she had arranged to meet Michael. Despite the cold, the area was as lively as an anthill. And Vanessa felt like an ant stranded on the endless surface of the globe. She realized all of a sudden just how much Michael meant to her. Michael's presence reassured her and gave her the necessary courage to respond so viciously to the chauvinist comments made by Allen Alper. In the past, she would have defended herself with a lot more restraint. But today, she felt a lot stronger and wasn't afraid to forcefully put those men who lacked respect for women in their rightful place—which was, evidently, under the unmerciful bite of her sharp tongue.

The throng of tourists and busy folk swerving and bustling on the sidewalks of Manhattan was making Vanessa lightheaded. And

Michael's tardiness was starting to worry her. Her thoughts started conjuring up car accidents and muggings. Originally from Arizona, she grew up with the notion that New York was a dangerous city where you put your life at risk on every street corner. These melodramatic scenarios made her realize just how deep her feelings were for Michael. She had to be very attached to him already if she was making herself sick with worry when he was only ten minutes late.

A taxi came to a screeching halt close to the curb. Michael sprang out and Vanessa raced into his arms. He apologized profusely, blaming his tardiness on absent-mindedness. But Vanessa really didn't care what the reason was. The main point was that he was once again securely by her side. Michael suggested they catch a bite to eat some place nice and the happy lovers strolled the streets of the Upper West Side hand-in-hand, in search of a cozy restaurant.

CHAPTER 9

T wo young waiters inside the restaurant Le Parisien, located on Columbus Avenue, discreetly exchanged comments about Vanessa. She was glowing with happiness and her beauty seemed to light up the room. She had on a sweater made of fine Scottish wool, in a rich shade of green that went perfectly with her auburn hair. The cinnamon mane was pulled back in a French twist, a few loose strands falling in waves around her temple. The hairstyle accentuated her lean, milky-white neck.

Michael looked at Vanessa admiringly. He appreciated every moment spent in the presence of this exceptional woman. From the interior right pocket of his navy blazer he removed a thin velvet box. He held it out to Vanessa who took it nervously and opened it without saying a word, so great was her surprise and excitement. Against the black case glittered a striking emerald and diamond necklace. She sat there unmoving, eyes welling up with tears, unable to utter a single syllable.

Michael took the necklace between his fingers and fastened it around her neck. Vanessa's entire body tingled as her lover's fingers grazed the nape of her neck. She leaned over the table and wet his lips with a moist kiss. "I've never received such a beautiful gift in my whole life. It's gorgeous."

Michael smiled and explained. "I chose emeralds because the color matches your eyes."

Vanessa looked at him and sighed. The restaurant's dim lighting and the soft music enveloping them encouraged her to disclose her innermost feelings. "You're a remarkable man. You have been so kind and generous to me. You blow me away." She paused and with a flirtatious smile, added, "You also have the body of an athlete, which I like a lot, and a very nice mouth, which you know how to use very well."

Flattered by the avalanche of compliments, Michael leaned forward and replied softly, "You're the most amazing and the most attractive woman I've ever met. Not only are you beautiful and intelligent but you're also extremely sexy." He lowered his voice some more and let the following words spill over his lips and into his lover's ears: "You have magnificent breasts—so firm and beautiful that for a minute I didn't think they were real."

"They are too!" asserted Vanessa, blushing a little. "And they're far from perfect. Did you notice that the right one is bigger than the left?"

"No," replied Michael, not the least bit concerned. "I think they're perfect. But I did notice something else…" He paused, moving in closer toward Vanessa until their foreheads were almost touching: "You've trimmed the fine fuzz of your pubic area in such an adorable manner. This cute tiny rectangle with red highlights resembles a French garden. It makes me want to become a gardener."

Vanessa blushed even more. The poetic description embarrassed her but at the same time, she felt a tingle of excitement rising from the very depths of the private area so eloquently described. She wanted Michael to go on seducing her with his erotic talk.

And from Michael's point of view, the conversation was getting more and more interesting. "I imagine the charming rectangular cut is justified by wearing particularly high-cut bathing suits. I'm sure you would look exquisite on the beach in a tiny bikini. I'm visualizing you right now on an exotic white sand beach under the blazing Mexican sun. You're wearing a black and gold two-piece, exposing a lot of caramel flesh. Your body is glistening with protective sun oils smelling of cocoa butter and almonds. As you walk, toes sinking into the sand, the undulating waves wet your ankles and the gentle ocean breeze rustles your auburn tresses. With each footfall, your perfectly rounded buttocks peak out of their skimpy sheath enhancing the sway of your hips. You are a golden image of beauty."

Vanessa closed her eyes to better visualize the scene. Picturing herself in Michael's fantasy, she murmured slowly: "Mmmm...that sounds nice. But I know what I'd like a whole lot better...to be on a deserted beach, wearing no bathing suit at all."

Her titillating alternative drove Michael's libido wild and he felt himself getting aroused. Vanessa continued in a smooth voice, "It's true, when you're close to me, my clothes feel suffocating. And I feel but one need...that you strip them off quickly."

The sexual audacity of her own words excited Vanessa. Every part of her body had suddenly become more sensitive. She could feel a delicate tingling in between her legs. Her sex was alive and begging to be caressed. A tropical mugginess swept over her. Vanessa squeezed her thighs together, hoping to reduce the sensation but this did nothing except swell her growing desire.

Michael could hardly contain his excitement. "Since your clothes feel so constricting when you're around me, I think you should take them off...at least partly. I bet you're wearing little black lace panties. Would you dare to take them off and show me?"

"What, here?" Vanessa asked, both shocked and turned on by Michael's indecent proposition. He nodded in silence. She glanced around the restaurant and figured that sitting with her back to the wall if the deed was done discreetly enough, nobody would notice. She recalled such a scene in a film she had seen once and for a split second she saw herself in the place of the actress.

So with extreme slowness and trying her damnedest to avoid any excessive movements, she pulled her long woolen skirt above the dark lacy trim of her stockings and then slowly up to her thighs. Still holding the glass of wine in her left hand, and after some twisting and wriggling, she finally freed the panty that had been clinging to her rear. She bent down to pick up the napkin that had slipped off the table just as she retrieved the little bit of lace that glided down her long, lean legs. Vanessa crumpled the tiny white panty into Michael's palm and with a triumphant smile said, "I guess you lose your bet."

Michael's face formed a huge smile and turned a bright shade of red. Embarrassment wasn't responsible for this sudden change of color, but rather the flame of desire that burned within him. He displayed no sign of surprise and deftly stuffed the little white underwear into the exterior pocket of his jacket. From afar, it would pass for a decorative handkerchief made of fine lace from Bruges!

* * *

Stretched out on the couch in the hotel room, Michael was trying to watch the news. But he kept coming back to that afternoon's unexpected little adventure. He never would have guessed Vanessa to be so bold, so sexually mischievous. And he was also surprised by his own actions. Normally, his sexual problem curbed his imagination considerably because each time an erotic thought crossed his mind, the horrible memories of his failures crept into his head. He also avoided carrying out his most risqué fantasies for fear of precipitating ejaculation. But with Vanessa, everything was different. She showered him with so much love that he felt confident and despite his persistent difficulty, he let himself go to more sexual creativity.

However, again last night he came too quickly. But Vanessa was nonchalant about it. And when he tried to explain himself, she confirmed otherwise, saying such eagerness flattered her. She appreciated seeing him become so excited so quickly and it made her feel very beautiful and desirable.

This way of looking at their lovemaking suited Michael fine. He would have been perfectly convinced if Vanessa had not said, "It's nothing, it's very normal in the beginning. In a few weeks, I'm sure you'll be able to make love to me for as long as you wish, right?"

Michael didn't answer. He already knew the answer. From the time he became sexually active, he ejaculated too fast. Things weren't going to get better in a few weeks. Unless…unless this newly found love would somehow bring about the much hoped for transformations within him…

CHAPTER 10

T he plane took off from John F. Kennedy Airport and made its way out of the cluttered New York skies without any prob lems. A little after takeoff, Vanessa confided to Michael that Allen Alper had disclosed to her some of the contents of the envelope: "Be wary of that informer of yours. He talks too much."

"You're right. I'm not going to deal with him anymore."

"Don't you find it odd that the police haven't suspected Davidson's mistress?"

"Of course they suspected her," replied Michael. "But she had a solid alibi. At the time of the crime, she was spending the night with her new lover, some guy named Johnny Silver. He confirmed her whereabouts and the neighbors apparently heard her moaning for hours. You could just imagine what the two of them were up to. Luckily, the neighbors formally recognized her voice or she would have found herself in a fine mess. You've got to figure that after the scandal erupted, the senator obviously wanted her stripped from his will. This would have given Barbara Rowland one hell of a motive to have him done away with as soon as possible."

"I don't think she's guilty," stated Vanessa.

"Me neither. I've analyzed enough criminal cases to know that we're not dealing here with an act committed by an amateur but by someone highly organized. The official line is that this was a sick, cold-blooded murder. However, according to the information team at *It Concerns Us,* the senator's wallet, two paintings of little value and a brass candlestick were actually stolen. Yet the alarm system never went off, which is to say that the perpetrator either knew the access code or was equipped with some pretty sophisticated technology. This means it wasn't carried out by an opportunist, but by a professional who had planned the murder."

The plane passed through some turbulence and Vanessa grabbed onto Michael's arm. Unfazed, he continued. "The alarm system didn't go off, so the thief had lots of time on his hands to scope out the mansion. He could have taken only the most expensive items, exactly the way a professional burglar works. If he didn't do this, it was because he wasn't there to steal but to kill.

"It wasn't some young punk drug user either, like the police are trying to make us believe. A druggie desperate for a fix settles for money and jewelry that he could quickly resell on the black market in exchange for some instant, cold cash. He wouldn't waste his time on items that are hard to sell like paintings and antiques. Besides, they found the senator's dead body with a priceless signet ring on his finger and an eighteen-karat gold chain around his neck. The killer was just trying to make the murder look like it had been committed by a thief who got the hell out of there as fast as he could."

"Your reasoning makes sense. It wasn't just a senseless murder or a case of botched robbery. But we can't dismiss the fact that the senator's mistress could have been behind the killing. She would have certainly known the alarm system's access code," pointed out Vanessa, playing devil's advocate.

"You're right, we can't eliminate that possibility. But I'm still convinced it wasn't her," Michael insisted with a pensive air.

Exhausted, Vanessa looked at Michael with her big emerald green eyes and smiled tenderly. She nuzzled closer to him and rested her head on his shoulder. This demonstration of affection melted his heart. He rested his head against the seat and gently took her hand in his.

* * *

The plane landed smoothly in Seattle where the temperature was milder than it had been in New York. An enormous pile of work awaited the two of them, yet it was still hard for them to part upon their arrival. Vanessa thanked Michael for taking her to New York and kissed him passionately. Then she hopped into a cab and blew him one more kiss. Delighted, Michael responded with a great big smile.

* * *

Michael was glad to be home. He walked into the living room lit up by the sun's last pinkish-red rays and propped his suitcase against the foot of a table made of Italian glass. He moved toward the answering machine to check his messages. First he heard the harsh voice of his boss and next the more conciliatory voices of his coworkers. Then he heard Dave's wife's voice.

"Michael!" Audrey was crying. "Dave is…Dave had a car accident…. He is…He's dead…." Her voice broke with emotion. "Dave is dead, Michael. Dave is dead," she sobbed again and again.

The machine fell silent.

Time came to a brutal halt.

"No, it can't be!" cried out Michael. He felt the floor underneath his feet giving out. Time and space became unreal. The objects in his apartment appeared faraway and translucent. The memories of Dave and then the unknown circumstances surrounding his death bounced around his head at a crazy speed. He couldn't believe it. It was over. His best friend was dead.

He feverishly replayed the recording, praying that somehow he had heard wrong. But it was no use. Every time Michael released the play button, the answering machine played back the same ugly message: "Dave is dead." He picked up the phone and quickly dialed Dave's home phone number. Audrey answered the line, but her voice immediately broke into heavy crying, making it impossible for her to talk.

When she could finally speak, her voice was so frail that Michael could barely make out what she was saying: "A car accident…the road was slippery…the brakes, they are saying…. We don't know anything else…. He died on the way to the hospital…."

"Stay where you are. I'm coming right over," Michael said into the phone, his heart strangled with emotion and his hands shaking. Despite the disjointed conversation, there was little doubt in Michael's mind that Dave's death was not an accident.

* * *

Night had fallen by the time Michael headed back from his friends' home. He drove like a robot, detached from the world. As he opened his front door, he was overcome by a feeling of profound sorrow. Once inside, he sank gloomily into the easy chair facing the large French windows. Before him, the colorful lights of Seattle were putting on a bedazzling show, but he didn't see a thing. His grief was too great. He had just lost his best friend. His eyes filled with tears. In the great book of life, a chapter was to be closed forever.

He mentally flipped through the pages holding the precious memories of his younger days. He saw Dave and himself playing on the football team. He remembered their macho horseplay, their teasing, their chronic girl chasing and their fight against every type of racism. He recalled the enormous efforts they made in hopes of striking it rich and finding their place in the sun. He remembered the evening his buddy asked him to be the best man at his wedding and the happiness he felt as he witnessed Dave's marriage to Audrey. He thought about the three small children Dave left behind. His friend's death appeared unjust. Dave was a good and honest man.

Michael's pain turned into anger. His friend's assassins had to be punished. He would avenge Dave's death himself. With his own weapons. Meanwhile, he was left alone with his sorrow and all the rage within him did nothing to ease his pain.

* * *

"Hi, Vanessa. You'll never believe what happened!" Betty squealed with enthusiasm into the phone. She paused for effect. "I was just offered an awesome contract. I'm going to be the personal physiotherapist for tennis pro Valerie Custer!"

"Wow! That's fantastic! I'm so happy for you! You work so hard. After all those years of toil, you really deserve this."

Betty was a reputed physiotherapist and many high-ranking athletes already used her services. But this was beyond her wildest dreams. On top of the perks and prestige attached to working with a world champion, her new job offered a much more attractive salary.

"The catch is that I have to travel with her to all her matches. But to tell you the truth, it's exactly what I need. This will definitely allow me to distance myself from Jeff."

"Are things going that bad?"

"Well, let's just say they aren't getting better. You know, Vanessa, Jeff is a good guy but…"

Actually, deep inside the pit of his soul Jeff wasn't bad—or anywhere close to being a monster. He was even making an effort to please her lately. Every now and then, he'd surprise her with a bouquet of flowers or call her when he was running late. But Betty was positively no longer physically attracted to this man. She thought of him more like an old friend instead of as a lover. Consequently, she did everything in her power to avoid any sexual contact with him. She made up two-week menstrual cycles, insupportable migraines or chronic stomach cramps. But there were times when she felt obliged to give in to her husband's advances.

She tried to make the act less dreadful by concentrating on sexual fantasies. While Jeff was making love to her, she would close her eyes and imagine herself locked in the arms of another man. But for the past few weeks, not even the most erotic fantasies had been able to render sexual relations with her husband bearable.

This sexual dissatisfaction polluted all other aspects of their married life. In the past, she used to enjoy taking long walks in the park with Jeff, holding his hand lovingly and talking to him about everything and nothing. Today, the mere presence of her matrimonial companion irritated her. This upset Betty because she had always had so much in common with her husband. They had the same ambitions and shared the same tastes. She even suggested to Jeff that they consult a sex therapist to correct their sexual problems, the real source of their marital setbacks.

Jeff went berserk. The way he saw things, sex therapists were reserved for the impotent, the perverts, the obsessed and all other such degenerates. And of course, he didn't see a problem on his part. He enjoyed making love and had good, strong erections. It wasn't his fault if his wife always had a headache. He tried his damnedest to give her pleasure and he couldn't do much if she was never in the mood.

Betty was going through all of this in her head but refrained from talking about it with her friend. Instead, she said, "To tell you the truth, I feel better when I'm away from him." And then in a tone of dismay, she added, "I feel like my marriage is going down like a ship in distress."

Vanessa didn't know what to say. She generally wasn't the type of person to shrug off difficult matters. But with Betty she knew that it was no use trying to get to the bottom of things. She changed the subject to distract her friend and began asking questions about her new job. "When do you start?"

"In two weeks. We're going to Europe. She wants to be well pre-pared for her matches at Roland Garros by playing in diverse competitions on a hard court. I can't wait to visit Paris," she said enthusiastically. "Hey, talking about trips—your friend Jimmy McFarlane called me."

"Don't talk to me about him," Vanessa replied. "He has such a hard head. He's always expecting a miracle…that eventually I'll fall in love with him!"

"He told me you turned down a reporting job with him in Africa on behalf of the *Metropolitan*."

"Yup, that's right. The prospect of spending two months in his company and particularly two months away from Michael didn't ap-peal to me at all."

"What does it involve exactly?" asked Betty, whose curiosity knew no limits.

"A CNN television crew will be heading to southern Sambizania to produce a televised report on the raging civil war there. My boss suggested I accompany them."

"You did the right thing by refusing. It would have been terribly dangerous. And besides, no one is interested in Sambizania. Inter-ethnic wars in Africa? They rage year-round."

Vanessa shook her head. "It wouldn't be that dangerous. We would be under the protection of peacekeepers from the United Nations. Sambizania is one of the largest countries in Africa but also one of the poorest. It's also one of the countries in the world with the worst conditions for women. This is something our readers would be inter-ested in. Did you know that excision and infibulation are still commonly practiced there?"

"Infibulation? What's that?" asked Betty.

"It's part of an ancient custom which obligates every little girl to have her clitoris sliced off and the lips scraped and sewn together, leaving only a little orifice for menstruation. This is performed without any anesthetics. Neither are anesthetics used on the wedding night when the young groom brutally opens his wife's vaginal entry."

"That's appalling!" shrieked Betty, completely horrified.

"Yes, and to think it takes place in this day and age on this very planet and only a plane ride away from here. And that's not all. Since the usurping of power in Sambizania by the General Sibouar El Tabernasti, the conditions for women have only deteriorated further. A husband practically has the right over the life and death of his wife. He may beat her liberally and adultery by the woman is punished by stoning."

"Listening to you speak, Africa is hell for women!"

"No," objected Vanessa. "You shouldn't generalize like that. Most African countries respect women's rights. But Sambizania is a religious extremist state that sanctions the domination of men. This explains the cruelty and the deplorable treatment women suffer in this region."

"This is powerful stuff. You'd better think it over, Vanessa. I think you should go. And who knows? This could land you a shot at the Pulitzer Prize."

"I don't want to leave Seattle right now."

"Seattle or Michael?" badgered Betty. "You're not going to throw away your career for a man, I hope?"

"Too late," Vanessa admitted. "I already told Michael everything."

"You didn't!"

"Yes, Betty. And I'm not writing my story on him."

"Are you crazy?"

"No, in love."

"What about the editor-in-chief position? Are you just going to give that up?"

"Let's not talk about this. Anyway, I have to let you go. I have errands to run. We'll talk tonight." Vanessa hung up and made herself a cup of mint tea, wishing she could get her hands on Jimmy for opening his big mouth.

CHAPTER 11

Barbara Rowland was seated on an old brass chair facing Special Agent Toriani. He was a man of an indefinable age and his face showed no sign of emotion. Perpetual confrontation with everything vile and despicable imaginable to mankind had formed a cold, hard shell around him. He resembled a turtle with his stooped back, short limbs and hooked nose and spoke without aggression and without compassion. But every now and again a hint of cynicism crept into his sentences.

"Barbara, you don't seem to bring any luck to the men you sleep with. Davidson was shot to death a month ago, and now we find the lover who replaced him with a rope around his neck. If you invite me to your place for a drink tonight, I have to ask myself what kind of a state they'll find me in!"

Barbara was in no mood to laugh. She didn't regret what happened to Davidson. He even left at the right moment. When she met Johnny, the old senator no longer compared as a lover. That's why, although they were still officially an item, she had not hesitated to make her famous scandalous revelations about Davidson's lovemaking. But Johnny's death came as a major shock to her. Discovering the body of her young lover suspended from the bathroom ceiling had profoundly upset her. And since the tragic incident, she began to fear for her life.

The police investigator interrupted her thoughts. "When you were questioned regarding the senator's assassination, you swore you had been with Johnny the night of the murder. He and neighbors corroborated your testimony, which is lucky for you. But now, what have you found as an alibi? A third lover, maybe?"

Barbara didn't flinch. She didn't want to break down in front of such a cruel and heartless monster. But she couldn't stop from asking herself why Johnny hanged himself. Or rather, *who* hanged him?

Toriani was asking himself the exact same question. According to the information he got from the pathologist, it was a suicide. But he also knew it was improbable that Barbara could have overpowered and hanged a man weighing 200 pounds on her own. His twenty-two years of experience told him that Barbara did not kill Johnny. But she was the primary suspect in the senator's murder.

The policeman planned to take full advantage of her state of bewilderment to come back to the Davidson affair and set a trap for her. "We recovered the weapon used to kill Davidson. A Colt 45. We found your pretty fingerprints on it," he bluffed.

Barbara cried out, "That can't be true, it wasn't me! Yes, you're right, I did have a handgun and it's possible that it has my fingerprints on it. But I was mugged on the street and it was stolen with my purse two weeks before the crime. I even reported the incident to the police."

"But you forgot to mention the loss of your pistol," he reminded her, laughing. And then with cruel pleasure he slammed his fist violently onto the table and screamed into Barbara's face, "Are you playing games with us here? Are you seriously trying to make me believe some pathetic purse-snatcher found a gun in your bag and said to himself, 'Hey look, a gun. Gee, I think I'm going to shoot Senator Davidson'?" he mocked. "You take me for some kind of a fool, lady?"

"All my personal documents were in my purse along with Davidson's phone number and address," roared Barbara, just as loud. "His house keys were also in there. That explains why the door had not been forced open—"

"You just gave yourself away, lady. No one apart from us knew that the door had not been forced open. It wasn't reported in the papers. You're finished. You're going down."

The merciless policeman said nothing for a few seconds and then continued more calmly: "I'll tell you what happened. You were sick of the old senator. And on top of that, he didn't even screw well. You're the one who told all of America! That little kiss-and-tell got you some money but nothing in comparison to what the senator was leaving you in inheritance. You had no idea before you opened your trap to the world that he had left such a large sum of money to you in his will. Eight million dollars. Not bad. But only after your scandal—I suppose to get you to choke on your own words—did he reveal to you what his intentions had been. And then he added that he was going to cut you out of his will. That's when you realized the high price of your stupidity. You panicked, killed him before he had time to do it, and then asked that idiot Johnny and your dishonest neighbors to testify in your favor in exchange for a few thousand dollars." He paused. Then he threw the final blow: "You don't even have to confess, you know. We already have enough proof to send you to the slammer for life."

The special agent got up and gave the place over to his female colleague who had been standing silently beside him throughout the interview. Policy stated that all women accused of a crime must be interrogated in the presence of a female police officer. As he left, he murmured to his coworker, "The bad cop routine is finished. Your turn."

The new police officer gently closed the door behind Toriani. She looked very young and seemed to be just fresh out of the police academy. The kindness of her smile and the nonthreatening ease of her gestures gave her the advantageous air of a social worker rather than a cop. After a few seconds of silence, she introduced herself: "My name is Janet White. Would you like a cup of coffee?"

Barbara didn't reply.

Janet put a cup down next to her. "Listen," she said, "I'm new on this force and yet I've already seen a steady stream of all sorts of criminals come through these doors. Eighty percent of the cases we deal with are drug-related. Six months ago, my partner on the job was gunned down by drug traffickers. He graduated from the same class as me, a great guy, always smiling…. He was godfather to my first child."

Janet paused and looked away for a second before continuing. "He was killed while trying to intercept twenty pathetic kilos of coke whereas tons of the stuff is smuggled into the United States daily.

"You see, Barbara, as a mom, I find drugs to be the worst of all evils. But as a cop, I'm sick of risking my life to give the impression that we're stopping a drug trade that has completely surpassed us. Let me tell you a good one: In the twenties, the infamous mobster Al Capone was the first supplier of bootlegged alcohol in the country. At that time, alcohol was illegal, just as drugs are today. It was also believed that by prohibiting it, all problems related to alcoholism would be solved. And yet, Al Capone was only charged with tax evasion even though the whole world was aware of his crimes. But big-shot politicians protected him.

"I believe the same thing goes on today. I'm pretty sure you were nothing but a pawn in the plot against Senator Davidson. True, his infamous bill made him a lot of enemies. Among these, drug traffickers and corrupt politicians who protect these very losers but not without something in it for them. And with the decriminalization of drugs, they stood to lose everything.

"If it's any consolation to you, when you have your day in court the jury might also think like me. If they believe you're nothing but a greedy piece of filth that murdered for money, they'll send you to prison for life. However, if they see you as the poor victim of an odious political conspiracy, chances are you'll get off lightly, maybe even be acquitted. But for that to happen, I need solid proof. And I can't get the proof I need if you don't start talking."

Barbara Rowland remained stone cold.

The young policewoman took a sip of coffee and then began again in a soft voice, almost maternal. "Look, I understand that men could drive us to do things we disapprove of. Sometimes we may feel we don't have a choice. Life for us women is like that. Maybe if I went through what you've gone through, I would be in your place right now. Maybe you simply didn't have a chance."

Janet delicately placed her fingers on Barbara's icy hand. "But there's an opportunity to seize here. The chance to lead a new life. The first real chance of your life. Your chance." She hesitated before going on, as if she were about to reveal a big secret: "Special Agent

Toriani is tough. Yet with your cooperation, I could maybe convince him to let you benefit from the same advantages as those of the mafia repentant: freedom and a new identity."

No matter what she said or how hard she tried, Janet White got nowhere. Barbara Rowland was totally mute. She was locked in silence. And all the police officer's efforts to break through this silence proved to be in vain.

* * *

Betty was sweating. And the effort seemed more excruciating than usual because Vanessa wasn't there to encourage her. She had to cancel their weekly meeting at the gym to meet with Michael. Betty was left alone to slowly work herself to death on the body toning machines and the stationary bike.

She didn't go unnoticed. Her flashy pink body suit and mauve tights enhanced her natural thinness. Her black hair, pulled back in a ponytail that fell to the middle of her back, revealed a finely sculpted profile. All her movements exhibited refinement and feminine grace.

She abandoned the bike and moved toward the bench press. Her quick and lithe walk resembled that of a gazelle. She turned on her Walkman, since she wasn't in the mood to make conversation with the sub-humanoids who populated the gym.

The men at the club really didn't look like the seducing type. Some strutted such pumped-up muscles that their heads looked like tiny buds above their massive shoulders. A few, dressed in tiny briefs in order to enhance their hyperinflated physique, paraded proudly in front of the wall of mirrors. Others heaved prehistoric animal grunts while lifting enormous weights or slammed the barbells down noisily to attract the attention of the women. But Betty was not impressed in the least by these modern-day brontosaurs.

And then there were the others, the newcomers. They were built like bus tickets and had the round belly of the driver. They wore oversized sports garb to hide the muscles they didn't have. They moved timidly from one piece of equipment to the next and suffered in silence on the machines, hoping that one day they'd parade in the king's court.

"Are you still using this machine?" a man asked Betty politely.

She removed her earphones and answered, "I'm almost finished."

Betty couldn't believe her eyes. The person in front of her actually looked human. He had the appearance of neither a dinosaur nor a starved cat. His body was well proportioned and his warm, animated voice denoted the confidence of a mature man.

"Would you like me to sing you something? It'll be a change from what you've been listening to on your Walkman," he said, smiling.

"What did you have in mind?" Betty laughed along good-heartedly and happily took part in casual conversation with him. He was easy to talk to. Finally, Betty reluctantly brought herself to leave. She let him know, for whatever it was worth, that she trained every Tuesday, Thursday and Saturday, "same time, same place." And as Betty waved to her new-found friend on her way out of Jurassic Park, she realized she was attracted to him.

CHAPTER 12

I t was time to head off to the station for his weekly *It Concerns Us* production meeting and Michael really didn't want to show up. It was now a month since Dave had died and everything seemed to be going wrong. The last program had rolled off without a hitch, but the one on the Davidson affair was far from coming together. The file was frozen. Michael's team had not come up with any new leads and the police investigation was at a virtual standstill. The senator's ex-mistress was still waiting for her day in court since no one wanted to pay her bail. Michael, for his part, had initiated his own investigation, but there remained many ambiguities. Even if Governor Jack Kotten was at the head of a major drug trafficking operation, as Dave had suspected, there was nothing to prove that he was the one who had ordered Davidson's assassination. And Michael knew from experience that this type of proof was practically impossible to confirm. His search had reached an impasse.

To make matters worse, things with Vanessa just weren't the same. Michael had a sick sense that she was losing interest. He was starting to believe that it might have to do with his problem of premature ejaculation. Vanessa slept at his place regularly and they made love almost every time. She never made the slightest reference to the fact that he systematically ejaculated less than two minutes after the start of penetration. On the other hand, he sensed that she was less passionate, more distant. He was worried she was getting bored. Furthermore, whenever she was in a bad mood or angry with him, he couldn't help thinking it was because of his problem.

After the euphoria from their trip to New York wore off, Michael was forced to deal with reality: He still had the same sexual limitations. To apologize, he showered Vanessa with extravagant gifts. The first few times Vanessa couldn't contain her excitement. Now, she no longer seemed thrilled by the floral bouquets and expensive jewelry. Michael had the awful feeling Vanessa's attraction toward him was slipping through his fingers like a fistful of sand.

There was a time when Michael was convinced that a healthy sex life was an essential ingredient for a balanced relationship. Today, the simple thought of participating in romantic frolics caused him more anxiety than joy. When they made love, he prevented Vanessa from touching him too much even though he knew she desired to do so. He preferred keeping his sexual excitement level down and concentrating on what he did best: manual and oral sex. He saw himself as a paraplegic: perfectly in charge of his upper body, but having no control whatsoever over the lower half. Whenever Vanessa fondled his body a little too much or as soon as he penetrated her, he felt the irrepressible need to ejaculate. He bit his lips, squeezed his rear, held back his breathing or tried to think about something else, but nothing worked. Ejaculation always came too quickly. Michael truly despised this penis of his that worked so badly. He knew full well that other men faired far better in bed than he did and he felt more and more sexually unfit as his failures accumulated.

* * *

Curled up in her favorite recliner, Vanessa put down the sex therapy book she had purchased earlier at the bookstore. She was profoundly disturbed. She couldn't make sense of the strange incident that took place on her last visit to her lover's place.

Vanessa had been stretched out on the sofa with her head resting on Michael's knees. The two of them were relaxing, quietly listening to classical music. Michael was playing with her hair and she loved that. He was also gently caressing her shoulders and arms. She felt wonderful and wished that the moment would last forever. Then Michael began lightly touching her breasts. She felt herself getting excited. Her breathing got heavier and a wave of heat washed over her stomach. It felt as if the sensitive tips of her breasts were connected directly by some mysterious internal channel to the very depths of her genitalia. Vanessa took pleasure in squeezing her thighs one against the other to intensify the delicious sensations germinating between her legs. She could feel the million nerve endings of her sex come alive like the buds of a tree in spring. Swollen with life and desire, the lips of her vulva gently opened to let some of its intimate sap seep out. Right then and there, Vanessa yearned to feel stronger sensations. So in sensual supplication she murmured, "I want you, Michael. I want to feel you inside of me."

But instead, Michael pulled away from Vanessa. He told her he wanted to take a shower and got up and left the room in a hurry. The storm of desire raging within Vanessa at once calmed down, leaving a monstrous void in the pit of her being. Vanessa approved of Michael's concern for hygiene. But why did he always have to wait until the last minute to wash up and why did he need to shower that very moment when he had already had a bath two hours earlier?

Left alone on the sofa, Vanessa had felt angry, her hot sex screaming for relief. It was the same feeling she experienced every time Michael ejaculated after only tens of seconds. Since the flame of her desire had not been completely snuffed out, Vanessa squelched her anger and decided to surprise Michael. She crept into the bathroom. The noise from the shower prevented Michael from hearing her and he couldn't see her either. But Vanessa was able to see him clearly through the translucent glass. He was masturbating! Vanessa couldn't believe her eyes: rather than make love to her, he preferred to masturbate! Disturbed by what she saw, Vanessa took two steps back and closed the door discreetly. She returned to the living room and tried her best to maintain her composure.

Still curled up in her recliner, Vanessa opened her eyes. Every single detail from that awful episode was perfectly engraved in her mind and just thinking about it again got her all upset. She shook her head in an attempt to bring herself back to reality and picked up the sex therapy book she had been reading. She flipped to the chapter on masturbation, but an explanation for Michael's curious behavior was nowhere to be found. "So much for that," she muttered in exasperation and closed the book. She decided to talk to Betty about what had happened. She was, after all, her best friend and was the one person in the world she could trust and confide in.

* * *

"I caught Michael masturbating before he was going to make love to me. It's crazy. I can't even put it into words... I find it completely abnormal, weird. And frankly, it's humiliating for me. Why would he do that? Was he thinking of another woman? Am I a lousy lover? Maybe he no longer finds me beautiful. Or perhaps I simply don't turn him on anymore. I shouldn't have told him I wanted him."

Betty responded reassuringly. "Stop blaming yourself; it has nothing to do with you. Jeff did the same thing. Men who come too fast sometimes use this method. They ejaculate a first time to diminish their excitement and hope that they'll then be able to last longer."

Vanessa appeared suddenly deeply crushed. "So you think premature ejaculation is Michael's problem?"

"It happens to something like one out of three men. It isn't something worth getting all worked up over. With Jeff, I thought for a long time that it was normal. But now with Bob, I see the difference!"

"Bob? The guy you met at the gym?" Vanessa said in surprise. "You're sleeping with him?"

"Yes," replied Betty, casually. "It's my right!"

"I know you're separated from Jeff but I didn't expect you to find a new lover this fast."

"Why wait? I've been sexually frustrated for years. So now I'm making up for it. And besides, Bob is such a charming man and he's so—"

But Vanessa had already tuned Betty out. She couldn't admit to herself that Michael was a premature ejaculator. Her heart simply rejected this painful thought. But reason forced her to come to terms with the facts. She knew very well that every time they made love, ejaculation occurred less than two minutes after the beginning of intercourse. She never timed their lovemaking but the end always came too soon. It was very true that outside of intercourse, Michael took all of his time and was always very attentive to her needs. And when it came to oral sex, he made her feel things she never felt before. He fondled, nibbled and played with her body with a kind of tenderness and passion she never knew existed. It was no wonder that Vanessa never paid very close attention to his sexual weaknesses. She attributed these shortcomings to the newness of their relationship and on the stress he was under at work. However, today, she finally opened her eyes. They had been sleeping together for two months and the situation was deteriorating. Nonetheless, Vanessa was still unable to admit that the man in her life was a premature ejaculator.

Betty seemed to be reading her mind: "Listen, Vanessa, you have to see things the way they are. For ten long years I believed Jeff would get better. I even thought it was my fault until the day when I made love to Bob. In one night, Bob convinced me that not only did I not have a problem, but that Jeff was simply a so-so lover. I know now that my husband was always a premature ejaculator and that he'll always be one. And I must tell you I'm not too optimistic concerning your handsome Michael. He's already thirty-six. He's probably had this problem for twenty years. This kind of thing doesn't get better overnight. I think it's time for you to find yourself another man, my poor darling."

* * *

"Just what I needed! Things can't get any worse than this."

Michael shook his head incredulously as he looked at the registered letter he had just received from the government. It was a notice from the IRS to pay his overdue income taxes. As if he didn't already have enough worries without the fiscal vampires biting into his life! He slammed the letter onto the table and went into the living room. Michael was in no mood to get tangled up in accounting.

His thoughts continually drifted back to Vanessa. Slowly but inexorably, he noticed she was distancing herself from him. Of course, she was neither mean nor aggressive about it, but there was clearly a frosty air to her. One day Vanessa couldn't see him because of too much work: "I hope you understand, Michael, I'm just too busy right now. Maybe tomorrow?"

On another occasion she deliberately shortened a telephone conversation. "I'm really tired, Michael." And then there were a zillion other little details, seemingly insignificant, but which gave away the fact that her interest in Michael was dwindling. She began showing up late for their dates more often. She didn't go out of her way to try to please him anymore. She cuddled less with him. She no longer spoke of the future in terms of "us," but "I." He got the feeling she was about to leave him and had tried many times to revive their love. Unfortunately, this hadn't changed Vanessa's attitude at all.

Right now Michael couldn't see a solution. Torturing himself wasn't helping matters. So for the umpteenth time, he plunged into the Jack Kotten file, trying to discover the precise motive that would have pushed the governor to assassinate the old senator. Despite the evident lack of proof, Michael's instinct incited him to persevere in this direction. He wanted to solve the Davidson affair at whatever cost. It was absolutely necessary for justice to be rendered and society protected.

When Michael was a little boy, he dreamt of becoming a great defender of justice just like his superhero Clark Kent. But since there wasn't a course on how to become a defender of justice, he became a lawyer. It didn't take him long, unfortunately, to figure out that the law had little to do with justice. It was a business like any other. The client with the means to pay for the best lawyer was also the one who had the better chance of winning his or her case. To combat these inequities, Michael realized that television constituted a powerful and fearsome weapon. An accurately informed public carried incredible weight and could be used to alter, through honest means, the outcome of certain events. As a TV journalist, Michael became the so-called defender of justice he had always wanted to be.

The telephone rang. It was his boss. However, his voice seemed far less authoritarian than before. "How are you doing, Michael? Good? That's great. Me, the rain is pissing me off. I keep asking myself if Seattle will ever see the sun again!" Tony continued to ramble on about this and that. And then suddenly he went mute. After several seconds of worrisome silence, he declared in a hoarse voice: "Michael, we're dropping the Davidson affair!"

* * *

"No-o-o-o-o," protested Betty, "I didn't tell you to dump Michael. I know it's none of my business. I'm really sorry if I was a bit too blunt with you earlier. I didn't mean to hurt you. All I wanted to do was share my own experience with you."

On the telephone line, Betty's voice was a lot calmer than usual. Vanessa, sitting on the edge of her chair, elbows plunked on the kitchen table and telephone receiver stuck to her ear, was listening to her attentively: "It wasn't easy for me to leave Jeff. I still have feelings for him. It's just that his problem of premature ejaculation gnawed at our sex life like a colony of termites chewing away at a wooden house. The foundation of our marriage was just about ready to collapse, eroded by mutual dissatisfaction," she said dramatically. "Behind his public display of machismo, Jeff had lost complete confidence in himself. He confessed to having numerous one-night stands. He told me it was to make up for the lack of attention he got from me. But I believe it was also a way to confirm his virility and charm. I must admit that with time, I avoided any type of physical contact with him rather than being constantly frustrated by too little too soon."

"I understand. But it's different in my case," insisted Vanessa. "Michael satisfies me in other ways. Penetration isn't all there is to love and sex! There are a thousand other things men could do to give us pleasure."

Betty continued calmly, "Yup, that's true, you're right. They can always give us oral sex, stimulate us with their fingers or use a vibrator. But trust me, when you find a man you can make love to for as long as you like, you'll realize what you've been missing. I remember with Jeff, I would crawl into bed completely stressed. I was afraid of touching him, I avoided moving, I even tried not to show him how turned on I was because he would get so excited so quickly. I couldn't do a thing. It became unbearable. With Bob, I let myself go. I'm experiencing incredible moments with a man who's able to share sexual intimacy with me. I no longer take part in a spectacle put on by an individual who during foreplay is trying to compensate for his incompetence with a thousand caresses and who during intercourse struggles like a shipwrecked person at the surface of the water hoping not to drown."

Vanessa played nervously with the telephone cord. "I don't know what to tell you. It's more complicated than that. Obviously, I wish he could last longer. I'd also like him to be less stiff when we make love, more natural. I'd like to be able to touch him, I'd like him to stop masturbating, I'd like him to…Ahhhh !!! I'm far too demanding, Betty. That's my problem. Anyway, I'm ashamed for talking like this. I really shouldn't be disclosing these intimate details to you. And besides, I feel behind the times for liking intercourse so much and for absolutely adoring to be taken. On the other hand, I've read stacks of books on male domination and I often ask myself if as a modern woman I shouldn't gain my sexual autonomy and stop depending on a man's penis."

Betty interjected violently. "What kind of a stupid theory is that? Good heavens, don't you dare mix sex with politics! I, for one, don't give a damn what all the frustrated sex therapists and neurotic psychologists out there think. It's the least of my worries to know how a modern woman should be screwing! All I know is that I like to feel a man penetrating me deep inside. I am not interested solely in having my clitoris fingered by a sorry fellow trying desperately to make me orgasm so he can forget what a lousy fuck he is. Trust me on this one, Vanessa. Fifteen minutes are better than fifteen seconds! And don't let them tell me vaginal orgasms don't exist. With Bob, I've had many electrifying ones!"

"I believe you, but I also think a sexual problem could get better if you both talk it through."

"You think so?" scoffed Betty. "And what will you tell him? Something along the lines of, 'My handsome, Michael, I find you ejaculate too fast and it frustrates the fuck out of me!'?"

"Obviously not!" retorted Vanessa. "I'd approach it more delicately. A couple should be able to talk about everything and anything, especially things intimate in nature."

"That's what I believed. And I brought the matter up with Jeff, I can assure you of that. But it didn't help. The more I attempted to bring up the subject, the more uncomfortable he became and the more defensive he got. Tell me honestly," added Betty, "has Michael ever tried to talk to you about it?"

A long silence ensued.

"Vanessa, are you still there?"

"I'm still here," she said. "No…no, Michael has never opened up on the matter."

"It doesn't surprise me a bit. Men are all the same. They place their pride above everything else. You could try talking to him all you want; he won't want to hear anything on the subject. And even if he does listen to you, it won't change a thing concerning his sexual problem."

"I don't know. I'm going to think it over," maintained Vanessa with a hint of uncertainty. She paused momentarily, and tired of talking about her problems, changed the subject: "So when are you leaving on vacation?"

"After I come back from Europe for work, I'm heading to Canada on vacation. In exactly a week from now. I'm taking a ski trip in the Rockies with Bob. We're going to Whistler in British Columbia."

The two women exchanged a few more trivial tidbits and ended the conversation with the promise to call each other the following day.

Vanessa went back into the living room, cheerless. An uncomfortable doubt lingered inside her mind. The chance that Betty could be remotely right troubled her terribly. She had imagined the possibility of marrying Michael. But she now asked herself if she was prepared to spend the rest of her life with a premature ejaculator.

At the same time, she heard the telephone ring in the kitchen. Like a poor, conditioned animal, Vanessa winced, images of her dead father jumping back into her memory. After momentarily thinking about her dad, she ran to answer the phone.

"It's Jimmy. How's it going?"

"Listen, Jimmy, my mind is not—"

"I just wanted to invite you to my photo exposition, Vanessa. You know the beach scenes I took while on assignment in Venezuela? The gallery, *Opened Eyes*, has agreed to exhibit them for a week. I blew up the photo of a super fat woman in a bikini waddling in front of a stunned ape. It's hilarious. I'm going to mount it on the back wall so that people will see it as soon as they walk into the gallery. What do you think?"

"Great idea, Jimmy. But I'm saying goodbye. I'll call you back later."

Vanessa hung up and gritted her teeth. "What a pain in the neck that idiot Jimmy is, with his stories about obese women and other stomach-turning stupidities. He'll never change. I can't stand him anymore!"

CHAPTER 13

"I've heard enough of your wild fabrications," roared Michael's boss. "Your version of the Davidson affair is completely off base. The whole world is convinced that his ex-mistress, Barbara Rowland, killed him. Besides, nobody cares about this crazy affair anymore. I've already told you: We're dropping it."

Michael raised his voice. "We're not dropping it. There are too many disturbing elements, too many missing pieces. Haven't you ever wondered why Barbara's new lover would suddenly commit suicide when he was supposedly madly in love?"

"I don't have the slightest idea. Anyway, it doesn't surprise me at all. The guy was a serious junkie, a manic coke-head. Who knows? It happens all the time to guys who abuse powder. There's nothing newsworthy about a drug user who commits suicide. And besides, the unscrupulous mistress hypothesis holds a hundred times stronger than the so-called political conspiracy theory you've dreamt up and have no proof to support. Get this into your head, Michael: The Davidson affair is over."

Michael was not about to back off. "No, Tony! The Davidson affair is not over! I have evidence that will dramatically turn public opinion around."

"What's wrong with you? Why are you going on like this?" Tony yelled back. "This story is making you nuts!" Suddenly, he changed his tone. His voice got softer and he began to speak more slowly. "Listen, Michael, we've done excellent work together for years. I want this to continue in the future. Take a vacation with your pretty redhead and come back to us in a week when you're in shape. In the meantime, I'm putting Julian in charge of finding a topic for our next show. Don't panic about this, it will not be the first time we throw something together at the last minute. I'll see you next Monday. Goodbye, Michael."

Michael left the room both stunned and frustrated. There was something strange about the way his boss handled the situation. Usually, Tony dug right to the bottom of things. Controversy didn't scare him off when he had solid proof in his hands. "This time he didn't even want to see the documents I have," thought Michael. "But he'll be forced to change his mind when I stick them under his nose. Even if it was impossible to establish a direct link between Kotten's frauds and Davidson's murder, this was at least something concrete for his boss to take into consideration." And then his thoughts turned to Vanessa. "Will she be at the restaurant tonight? Or is she going to come up with another excuse to back out?" He still hoped the magic they had shared in New York would be rekindled.

Suddenly he remembered something Tony had said. He had never discussed Vanessa with Tony, so how had he known she was a redhead? He didn't discuss his personal life at work. Dave was the only one who had known about her, and he didn't know anyone from the show.

* * *

The atmosphere in the restaurant was heavy. The soft music seemed syrupy to both of them and the candlelight sparked an undesired glow of old-fashioned romance. They exchanged brief glances without saying a word. Michael crumpled his table napkin and Vanessa nervously played with her necklace.

Vanessa ran her fingers through her hair and was first to break the silence: "Michael, I'm leaving for Africa tomorrow. You remember the assignment in Sambizania that I turned down? Well, Judith Gerald, the journalist who was suppose to replace me just found out she has breast cancer. She has to undergo chemotherapy. I'm taking her place."

Michael looked at her in silence, accepting with difficulty what he had just heard.

CHAPTER 14

V anessa tried without success to fall asleep on the plane to Nairobi, capital city of Kenya. Bothered by the events of the previous evening, she had not slept a wink at night. She admired the dignified way in which Michael had accepted the breakup, but it wasn't exactly how she had pictured it in her mind. She would have liked for him to demand an explanation from her, to somehow restrain her and declare his undying love. Under such circumstances, she would have without a doubt broken down and thrown herself into his arms.

But the more she thought about their sex life, the more certain she was of having made the right decision. She fully understood that Michael's masturbation was used as a method to get him to last longer. But the brevity of penetration wasn't the only thing that annoyed her. It was how Michael made love on the whole. He was very stressed. He always followed a set pattern to stimulate her. All his attention went into trying to make her orgasm. Yet, he never allowed himself to enjoy the simple pleasure of being there with her. He wasn't spontaneous. He constantly observed her to make sure that he was exciting her. And after sex, he would ask her with insistence if she had an orgasm so as to reassure himself of his own performance.

Michael was clearly very good with his hands. He worked every part of her body with his fingers like the finest baker kneads a piece of dough. His fingers walked, danced, tickled and surprised. They made her tingle. They made her moan. They often didn't stop exploring until they found their way deep inside of her. And that's when she would scream. Loudly! God, she loved his hands. But as for his body—it was rigid, barely sensual, and not at all receptive to what she was doing to it. The atmosphere after their sexual encounters wasn't exactly romantic, either. Michael always seemed withdrawn and moody. And lately, he started getting angry and putting himself down. This, along with the usual foreplay and brief lovemaking, added further to their strained sex life. She, who liked the sharing and complicity, the fusion of their bodies and the communion of their souls, couldn't help feeling more and more resentful.

Following her talk with Betty, she read up on what different sex manuals had to say about premature ejaculation. The treatments out there didn't exactly thrill her. In some way or the other, they were all versions of the therapy developed by Masters and Johnson. Within this approach, both partners had to disclose to each other their sexual preferences in terms of type, speed and location to receive adequate stimulation.

She couldn't see herself having to tell her partner where and how he should fondle her in order to bring her to orgasm. Neither could she conceive of him doing the same and continually dictating to her his own preferences. This type of sexuality—by alternation— simply doesn't work in real life. Your turn, my turn—it's not natural. Sex is interacting and sharing, not servicing. As for the method of control, it consisted of the woman squeezing the man's penis to prevent him from coming. She didn't like the idea of suddenly stopping intercourse to compress his organ so that he could control his ejaculation. This would just mean trading one complicated, mechanical and frustrating system—Michael's—for another complicated, mechanical and frustrating system—that of dehumanized sex therapists. That wasn't at all what she imagined when she dreamt of sex. During those slumber-filled escapes, she conjured up in her mind scenarios full of passion, pleasure, romance, discovery, spontaneity, affection, fusion and love. She most certainly never imagined sex sessions by alternation paired with therapeutic interludes on prescription.

She really would have liked to talk things over with Michael. But the more she thought about it, the more convinced she was that it was impossible to alter Michael's sexual ways. Everything had to be changed. And she couldn't conceive of the notion of living the rest of her life like this. Sexual compatibility was for Vanessa an essential dimension of conjugal happiness. Yet the quality of their erotic encounters was quickly and steadily diminishing. She didn't have much trouble imagining what their sex life would amount to after a few years together. Vanessa was too complete and passionate a woman to settle for quick and stiff romantic embraces. It was better to put an end now to a relationship that would lead in the future nowhere but toward failure.

Jimmy, sitting next to her, interrupted her train of thought: "Are you okay, Vanessa? You look worried. You don't have to be. You know the region isn't that dangerous. UN soldiers have been there for five months and they have not yet had any serious incidents."

Vanessa really wasn't in the mood to talk to him. "No, Jimmy. I'm not worried. I'm just tired. I think I'm going to rest a bit." And then, much to Jimmy's disappointment, she turned toward the window and pretended to fall asleep. But her mind was fully awake. Michael shouldn't have left so brusquely, she thought. Unless he was the one who wanted to break up with her all along. Come to think of it, he had been less attentive lately. Maybe he jumped at the opportunity she had presented him with to slip away on good terms. The situation suddenly seemed to be reversed. She was no longer the one responsible, he was. If he really loved her, he would have tried everything in his power to keep her from leaving him. Maybe there was another woman in the picture. The mere thought of this sparked Vanessa's jealousy. And if she was jealous at this point, could this mean she was still in love with him?

She had to admit the answer was yes. But she had to ask herself, "Do I love him for who he is or for what he could be?" And the answer came up both instantaneously and spontaneously directly from the pit of her being: "I adore him, I love him. But I just don't want to have to sacrifice myself, I don't want to have to alienate my romantic side or my sexuality."

She opened her eyes. Jimmy was quick to react: "Vanessa, the flight attendant just passed by. I didn't want to wake you. But if you want something to drink, I can get it for you."

"Sure. I'll take a bottle of mineral water," replied Vanessa, hoping he'd take his time getting it.

* * *

Michael didn't want to admit the loss of Vanessa. In retrospect, he realized he should have demanded some kind of explanation or at least tried to have stopped her from leaving him instead of playing the role of a man perfectly in control of the situation. She never did answer his questions. He was convinced this breakup was tied to his problem. If that was the case, then Vanessa wasn't worthy of him. If she wasn't willing to go beyond the sexual dimension, it wasn't worth investing in this relationship. Anyway, it was better that they split up now, before he became too attached to her.

But it was too late. Michael was terribly hung up on this woman. No amount of reasoning could ease the pain gnawing at his gut. He turned his eyes toward the window in his living room and caught a glimpse of two birds pursuing each other. Oddly enough, this bucolic sight, instead of intensifying his sorrow, caused him to snap out of it. He had a busy day ahead of him. His first stop was the bank. After retrieving the documents, he would make copies of them and hand them over in a sealed envelope to his notary, William Smith. He trusted the man with his life. Smith had taken care of the details concerning his father's estate when he passed away and had proven himself very reliable.

Michael hurried to his car. He turned the key in the ignition. He heard the comforting roar of the motor. He exited the garage and drove his sports car to the bank where the safety deposit box was stored. The employee, a short, thin man wearing the inevitable navy jacket with white shirt and gray pants, produced his key, turned it in the lock and took two steps back. Michael used his own key to extract the metal box containing the documents. It seemed lighter than it had the last time. He rushed into the adjacent room and quickly opened the box. It was completely empty.

* * *

There wasn't much legroom on the plane. Vanessa was definitely planning to hold a grudge against her boss who was stingy when it came to airfare and always made her fly charter. This flight was terribly long. There had been a stopover in New York and then another one in London. She was beginning to wonder if she'd ever get to Kenya.

Sweltering heat welcomed Vanessa and Jimmy to Nairobi. At the airport, a CNN television agent greeted them warmly. The two other journalists accompanying them weren't on their first assignment. They had already covered the Gulf War, the ethnic cleansing in Kosovo and the guerrilla warfare of the Congo for CNN. This time, they were hoping to bring back shocking images of the war in Sambizania.

The guide drove them downtown and Vanessa couldn't help feeling somewhat disappointed. When she was a child, Africa had always been described to her as a wild kingdom full of ferocious animals. She grew up believing all Africans lived in huts under the domination of mysterious sorcerers, speaking an incomprehensible tongue. Here she was in Africa and it looked like any metropolitan area in United States. The locals spoke English, dressed like the French and became excitable in traffic jams blocked with Japanese cars.

They finally arrived at the Africana Plaza, a hotel that could have passed for any Holiday Inn across North America. The group was told they had two days to relax since the journey to Sambizania would be a long and tiring one. Jimmy asked Vanessa to dinner, but she politely refused, explaining to him that she needed to rest more than eat. She went up to her room and promptly fell into a deep sleep.

* * *

The telephone woke Vanessa up. It was Jimmy wondering if she wanted to have breakfast. It was already nine-thirty in the morning and the complimentary breakfast service was ending in half an hour. Vanessa was starving, so she accepted the invitation.

Jimmy was waiting for her at the entrance of the dining room. A bright, Hawaiian-type flowered shirt fell loosely over his narrow shoulders. He was short, on the skinny side and very high strung. He was an excellent photographer and a devoted collaborator. While socially awkward, he had an amazing memory and a vast literary knowledge. He was also mad about history and geography and could go on for hours about the different socio-political climates that prevailed around the world.

Vanessa dipped her croissant into a mediocre cup of coffee as Jimmy earnestly explained the situation in Sambizania to her. "What you have to understand, Vanessa, is that the country has been at war for years and things are generally a mess. This war between the southerners and the northerners is centuries old. The conflict is currently raging in the south. Since the Brits left, several serious confrontations have taken place between the different ethnic groups. It's estimated that close to half a million people have been killed during the course of the hostilities and more than three million have taken refuge in neighboring countries. Five years ago, a military group from the north gained power and turned Sambizania into a religious fundamentalist republic. The government even sided with Saddam Hussein during the Gulf War. This gives you an idea why American journalists aren't welcomed with open arms in this country."

Vanessa was trying hard at this point not to miss a word of what Jimmy was saying. She had to pull together as much information as she could to write her article. She had been waiting for an opportunity like this for years. And finally, here she was on her way to realize one of her greatest dreams—a feature report carried out by a woman in a high-risk area of the world. She switched off her thoughts and turned her full attention to Jimmy's verbal incontinence.

"Lucky for us, the area we're going to is under UN control. It's a tiny enclave south of Sambizania, situated in the province of Jonguru, not far from the border. The mission is humanitarian in nature and has the support of neighboring countries that are sick and tired of the flood of Sambizanian refugees driven out by the war. The trouble is that the Sambizanian government considers the UN protected enclave within its borders to be a violation of its territory."

"What do the locals think?" asked Vanessa.

"They have obviously welcomed the UN troops as liberators. Mainly because these guys bring with them enormous quantities of food and first aid supplies and their presence safeguards the status quo in the region. You should know that the populations of the south territories have religious beliefs rooted essentially in animism. As for the northern government, it's trying hard to impose its religious laws on the entire country. Which is to say, for example, that a Sambizanian woman from the south who commits adultery would consequently be judged in a language she doesn't understand, and then immediately stoned to death in accordance with a tradition that isn't even her own. By the way, I hope you brought along long, black clothing and a veil. Because from now on we'll be living under new precepts! You will also have to walk behind me and carry my bags. And don't forget to have your clitoris cut off!" Jimmy burst out laughing.

"I don't find that funny at all," Vanessa answered back. "This appalling excision of the clitoris has nothing to do with religion. It stems from some cruel tribal custom."

"Don't get angry, Vanessa. I was joking. In reality, the majority of Sambizanian women are not veiled. And you're right about the excision. But only half right. Because even though it may be true that this custom is disappearing in the more westernized social classes, it still remains common practice in the other strata of society. And since the time when Sambizania dismissed all western values as satanic, this custom has once again become prevalent. But you'll see, no one will want to talk to you about it."

All this talk about the ritual mutilation of women's bodies reminded Vanessa of how lucky she was to be a North American woman—free to eat herself to death, free to control her body, free to go wherever she pleased and free to change partners whenever she decided. And then again, all of this freedom brought her no happiness, for at this moment she was particularly unhappy. She had only just left Michael and already she was missing him terribly. Vanessa tuned out Jimmy and slipped into daydreaming mode as she looked at the partly dried leaves on the palm trees lightly swaying under the hot breeze of the Kenyan capital.

* * *

The cold wind was ripping right through the red maple tree planted in front of Dave's home. Michael stood in front of the large window in the living room and watched as the spring leaves on the young tree rustled wildly. After a long silence, he turned to his friend's widow and spoke to her in a kind but firm tone: "Please, Audrey, stop denying it. I went to the bank yesterday and the safety deposit box was empty. Dave and I were the only ones who had that key and you were the only person he told. You were also the last person to have signed into it, five days after his death. You're the only one who could have withdrawn those documents. Why are you pretending not to know anything?"

Audrey, curled up in a corner of the couch where she had spent many hours in her husband's arms, replied hesitantly, "Dave did tell me about the documents at the bank. But I never saw them."

Michael sat down next to her and took her hands in his. "These documents are extremely important. Audrey, please. Where can I find them?"

The bereaved widow burst into tears. "Dave is dead because of this slimy Davidson affair. I don't believe it was an accident. Dave was a notoriously cautious driver. They killed him." And then stoned-faced, she added, "I burned all the documents. I didn't want the same thing to happen to you. I didn't want people to…"

"What!?" screamed Michael. "You *destroyed* the documents? Tell me you didn't. Please, Audrey. Tell me you didn't," he looked searchingly into her eyes, but Audrey didn't flinch. "What happened then?" he demanded. "Did they threaten you? Did they try to—"

"No, no! I destroyed them so they wouldn't make anyone else suffer."

"But don't you see, those documents would have put an end to this mess. What can we do now? We have no more proof. They'll keep on going about as they see fit. We no longer have a way to stop them!"

Michael got up and paced back and forth in the living room to calm himself down. Audrey had meant well in doing what she did. He put a reassuring hand on the young widow's shoulder. "Don't worry, Audrey. I'll find another way." Michael once again stared out the window at the little maple tree that was still taking a beating from the wind and the cold. It was now very important for him to recall his past conversations with Dave. Maybe he'd find a clue that would help him continue with his investigation. A sparrow landed transiently on one of the thin branches of the tree.

"That's it!" Michael suddenly cried out. "I remember Dave telling me about a contact in Canada. It's our only hope. We have to find him!"

Audrey, collecting her thoughts, offered to help him. "I think I know the person you're talking about. Dave spoke to me about that contact. He didn't like him too much. He called him the Iguana. It seems he has the profile of a lizard. Yes, I remember now. He lives in Montreal. His name is Beatlow, I think. No, that doesn't sound French. Beelow...Bilo...Bilo...deau...Yes, that's it! Bilodeau...Mario Bilodeau," she cried out triumphantly. "I'm sure I could find his phone number in Dave's address book."

Michael thanked Audrey. He held her tightly in his arms in a gesture of comfort and whispered, "Just remember that Dave is still with us. He is watching us from above."

* * *

Michael opened the door to his Porsche and got in. He turned the key in the ignition and the engine started immediately with a contented purr. To get to Seattle he had to cross over Washington Lake. He drove toward Evergreen Pt. Floating Bridge taking highway 520 going west.

At the last minute, he changed his mind and decided to turn south toward Renton. He figured the detour would get him to Seattle-Tacoma International Airport a lot faster. He quickly turned his wheel to make the exit. He cut off a few drivers in the process who, in a show of disapproval, honked their horns. As he checked the flow of traffic in his rearview mirror, he caught a glimpse of a red Toyota executing the exact same dangerous maneuver. He immediately got the feeling he was being followed. When he decelerated his speed little by little, the Toyota did the same. He then accelerated sharply. The Toyota picked up its speed. He pressed down heavily on the gas pedal and within seconds his Porsche surpassed the speed limit. But the Toyota didn't let up.

Michael shifted down and floored the gas pedal. The Porsche's back tires spun, leaving a bluish cloud of smoke on the road behind. His back was pressed up against the seat and his hands clutched the steering wheel. The car zoomed forward and reached 110 mph. He shot a glance into his rearview mirror and saw his pursuers were still on his tail. He kept his foot firmly down on the gas pedal, his car continued to accelerate. His driving was getting more and more per-ilous. The speed of his Porsche was such that the other cars appeared to be standing still on the highway. He felt as if he was manipulating a high-powered racing car inside a video game. But in this case, there was no second try if he made a false move. The slightest error could cost him his life.

There was a long right lane ahead of him free of cars. It was exactly the break he needed. The red Toyota was nowhere to be spot-ted. Michael heaved a great sigh of relief and progressively slowed down.

The breather was short-lived. Five miles later, a police car, with lights on and sirens blaring, forced him to pull over. The cop ap-proached him with a big smile: "My congratulations, sir, you just broke a new speeding record between exits 7 and 9. You managed to hit 153 mph."

Michael, still shaky, replied without thinking, "Listen, I was be-ing followed by—"

"And your name is Bond, James Bond, I suppose?" scoffed the police officer. "At 153 miles per hour, you not only put your life at risk, but the lives of all the other drivers on the road! Could I see your driver's license, please?"

Michael opened his wallet only to realize that his license wasn't there anymore. "Shit, I must have forgotten it at the bank. That was the last time I used it. But wait..." He searched his jacket and handed over his passport. "This should be enough."

"Sorry, sir, a passport is not a driver's license. It's against the law to drive without one. I'll have to confiscate your car."

Michael replied calmly. "I'm trusting a man of your intelligence will be able to understand me. I most certainly am not James Bond, but my name is Michael Lancaster. Have you ever heard of the show *It Concerns Us*?"

"Yes, Mr. Lancaster, I recognize you," said the officer. "But your fame doesn't give you the right to break the law and drive without a license."

"You're right," said Michael, with a hint of a smile. "But if I broke the speed limit, it was for a good reason. Look at me. Do I look like a delinquent who drives fast for kicks?"

"No, Mr. Lancaster, but it's impossible for me to let you off like this. The law is the same for everybody."

It was no use. Michael knew he wasn't going to get anywhere with this incorruptible cop. He felt, however, that the officer held nothing against him. So, he made him the following proposition: "I understand your point of view and I respect it. But I'm right in the middle of an extremely important assignment. Could you not apprehend my car until we reach Sea-Tac Airport? I have to get to Montreal as soon as possible. It's urgent. You don't have to worry; I'll drive behind you. And I won't go over the speed limit. You have my word," he smiled.

The police officer hesitated a second and then replied with a concurring smile: "Okay, follow me."

* * *

Michael was trying hard to keep his calm in front of the airport employee who was telling him there were no direct flights between Seattle and Montreal. "Sir, you could always fly to New York and then make a transfer to Montreal. Or you could fly to Vancouver and then take a direct flight to Montreal. But since the next flight to Vancouver doesn't take off for another seven hours, I suggest you drive there directly. It will take you only about three hours, even less if you don't stick to the speed limit, and at the same time you'll save yourself the cost of a plane ticket."

Michael was close to losing it, but instead he cracked a joke. "Since the speed limit doesn't seem to concern you too much, lend me your car because they just confiscated mine for speeding."

The lanky employee stared at him wide-eyed, at a loss for words.

"That's fine, don't worry about it. I'll just take that ticket to Montreal via New York." Michael removed his credit card from a black calfskin leather wallet and handed it to the speechless employee. But already his thoughts were elsewhere. He had to find Mario Bilodeau. He positively needed to gather enough proof to put Jack Kotten behind bars forever. The outcome of the Davidson affair depended on it.

* * *

117

Michael finally arrived at Dorval Airport, on the outskirts of Montreal, looking awful. He had the bloodshot eyes of an insomniac, the stubble of a beggar and the pasty complexion of a corpse. When his turn came to pass through Canadian customs, the agent behind the counter took one look at him and asked suspiciously, "What brings you to Canada, sir?"

Michael simply said he was here for a vacation, knowing well that the less one said to a customs agent, the better.

The officer looked him in the eyes for a long time and, relishing the only brief moments in his life where he held considerable power, he continued his interrogation. "Where do you live?"

"Seattle."

"Occupation?"

"Journalist."

"For a newspaper?"

"Television."

"What television station?"

"For the PDS network. I host the program *It Concerns Us*. And I'm debating if I should do a documentary on Canadian hospitality soon."

The agent, who by this time was out of questions, felt quite sheepish. He automatically turned friendlier and let Michael pass through the border, wishing him a pleasant stay in Canada.

A cold, damp wind greeted Michael into the metropolis of Quebec. He wondered why anyone would want to live in a city where even in April huge piles of snow still bordered the sidewalks. After stopping at a store to buy himself a warm jacket, he took a taxi to the address written on the scrap of paper Audrey had given him: 540 Laurier Street West. But when he got there, no one answered the door. For a split second he wanted to kick himself for not calling Bilodeau first, but he quickly remembered Dave's prudent advice. It would have been risky phoning from Seattle. Iguana's telephone line could have been tapped. Jack Kotten's men would have had no problems following him here. Thanks to this hasty departure, no one knew where to find him.

* * *

Vanessa had called Michael before leaving for Nairobi. But despite the late hour, she got his answering machine. She wondered what Michael was doing out in the middle of the night. Maybe after hearing her voice on the answering machine, he chose not to answer the phone. Or maybe he was spending the night with another woman. Vanessa couldn't bear to even consider that.

A pocket of turbulence on the plane pulled Vanessa from her thoughts. Jimmy was in the midst of one of his rambling sessions about the geography and political situation in Sambizania: "Shortly, we'll be flying over Lake Turkana, historically called Lake Rudolph. We'll be landing close to the Sambizanian border where a UN convoy will take us to the interior of the country. Once we get there, multinational armed forces soldiers will receive the four of us. This force consists of no American, Russian, British or even any French troops. They didn't want to get involved in this messy civil war."

Vanessa was looking outside the window of the Cessna that was flying at low altitude. The landscape below was breathtaking. She really felt like she was in Africa now. Faced with such imposing scenery, her spirits lifted and she felt fortunate to be able to share in the magnificence of such a beautiful universe.

CHAPTER 15

T he small twin-engine propeller plane landed on a deteriorated runway marked by old oil barrels. Not far from the airstrip, two Mercedes Unimog military trucks painted in white waited for the American journalists under the blaring sun. Vanessa grabbed the huge knapsack containing her personal necessities and walked confidently toward the vehicles. She climbed briskly into the first truck in line and Jimmy quickly followed suit. The CNN cameramen got into the truck behind.

In the overheated front seat, Vanessa and Jimmy took a seat sandwiched between the driver, a sinister-looking European soldier, and the expedition guide, a tall beaming African man. The driver was wearing a two-week old beard and a shabby uniform. A lit cigarette dangled precariously from his thin lips. He wore a dirty T-shirt covered with cold ashes and traces of his last meal clung to his sweaty skin. With a sticky hand bearing pudgy fingers, he handed Vanessa a brownish bulletproof jacket.

Jimmy tried to make conversation with the driver who didn't answer him, mutely keeping his eyes on the road. The African guide roared with laughter as he observed the photographer's futile attempts. "The driver is a corporal in the Belgian army. He doesn't speak English. He only speaks French!"

The convoy drove off in a cloud of dust. They left the somewhat primitive aviation site and began a long drive along a rugged dirt road. Jimmy, nose buried in a map of the region, once again picked up the conversation: "From here, we should reach the border in about three hours. If we drive all night, we should make it to the Sambizanian camp by daybreak."

Vanessa barely heard him. The rhythmic rocking motion of the vehicle compounded with the suffocating heat had lulled her to sleep. "If you want," Jimmy suggested hopefully, "you could rest your head on my shoulder."

An abrupt stop made by the truck propelled the passengers on board mere inches away from the windshield. A group of agitated and armed Africans stood blocking the road. The guide stepped out of the truck and quickly became embroiled in a heated exchange with them. Vanessa couldn't understand what they were saying, but the conversation appeared very strained. Everyone was ordered off of the trucks and forced to produce their passports and identification papers. After many minutes of verbal combat and hostile gestures, the African guide explained to the journalists that they had trespassed on the territory of the tribal group, Mokenge, and that the "border" soldiers weren't going to let them pass through unless they were paid.

Jimmy angrily protested that there was no way a UN convoy should have to give money to a so-called tribal band who claimed to enforce the law. Vanessa calmly reminded him that the tribesmen were armed, UN headquarters was nowhere in sight and getting out of there alive was worth far more than a few dollars. The convoy got on its way while Jimmy, slumped in his seat, continued to grumble about these pirates of savannah.

Night had fallen and the convoy progressed slowly through the thick bush, guided only by the glow of headlights. At times, wild animals jumped in front of the truck along the trail. Even though Vanessa admired the driver's skill, the trip seemed interminable with all the frequent stops. At ten o'clock at night, the path had to be cleared of a fallen tree. Later, the jeep's front axle broke. Three hours after that, there was another discussion with a tribe of indigenous people who had popped out of nowhere. At dawn, a large herd of gnus on the way to their water source cleared a path by knocking against the trucks.

The sun was already high in the sky and they had not yet reached their destination. Jimmy grumbled and complained endlessly about the shoddy organization of the trip. He crabbed about the driver's offensive body odor, the absence of air conditioning in the truck and the lamentable state of the trail.

By mid-afternoon, the sky clouded over and a violent storm broke. The rain fell with incredible force. The trucks were forced to pull over and stop because it was impossible to see anything two feet ahead. Vanessa asked the guide if Sambizania was still far away.

"We've been here for hours," he chuckled.

"I thought Sambizania was desert."

"The north of Sambizania is pretty much all desert right down to the sand and camels, but the south is wet. During the rainy season, it could pour every day. Besides, for me, the south is the Republic of Tounga."

Vanessa wasn't sure what the African guide meant by that, but Jimmy had caught on immediately. "The southern provinces of Sambizania are in revolt against central power. They want independence since their culture and religion are different from those of the northern provinces. Ever since the military coup that brought the religious extremists to power, the situation has steadily declined. The northerners want to impose their customs on the southern population, that of the Toungalians, whereas the 'southerners' as they are called, refuse to accept this. To ease its conscience, the UN decided to intervene in this never-ending war so humanitarian convoys could circulate more freely. But considering the lengthy delay we're experiencing, I don't believe things are running smoothly yet."

The day was almost over when the convoy finally arrived at the UN encampment. The terrain was covered with tents aligned as far as the eye could see. The tents were crammed with refugees chased away by the war and famine. The trucks were greeted by naked children and despite their frightening state of malnutrition they cheered loudly and smiled joyfully. When they got close enough to the military camp, everyone had to get out of the trucks and walk to the checkpoint. The guide explained the reason for this to Vanessa: "The colonel is afraid of terrorist attacks. He hasn't dismissed the fact that Sambizania has terrorist training centers."

The checkpoint soldier, his face reddened by the sun, had the blond hair of a Scandinavian. He addressed Vanessa in English with a trace of a Germanic accent. "Are you the American journalists? Wait here, I'll call the duty officer."

A swarm of local flies took advantage of the motionless new arrivals, giving them each a warm and buzzing welcome. Jimmy seemed to be the insects' favorite victim, although they were hardly impressed by his hysterical gesticulations.

A young officer approached them smiling. He had on camouflage military garb and the light blue beret worn by UN soldiers. In a thick French accent, he said, "Welcome to Sambizania, I am Lieutenant Edouard Demat, Marine Infantry, Belgium. I have been assigned your liaison officer. I am in charge of your needs during your stay. Follow me, I'll drive you to your palace."

The so-called palace was nothing more than three khaki military tents coated in ochre dust. "This is the men's section," the lieutenant said to the three American males, referring to the two tents on his right. "And this here," he added, pointing to the third tent, "is madam's suite. You have one hour to get washed up and changed. There's no shower, but you'll find a pail of clean water in your tent. Your presence is requested at the officers' mess at precisely eighteen hundred hours. A soldier will pick you up. Any questions?"

They all had questions but were too exhausted to ask them. And so, the weary journalists entered their new homes in silence. The heat inside Vanessa's tent was oppressive, and there were just as many flies inside as there were outside. The furniture was limited to a cot, a table, a folding chair and a metal chest equipped with a lock and key. Vanessa noticed, however, that the Belgian soldiers had put some effort into improving her comfort. On her bed, there lay a series of objects indispensable to any soldier. Some of them would come in quite handy, she supposed, like the flask, net and insect repellent, water purifier and toothbrush. The other things seemed less necessary, such as the five tiny boxes of black polish, the firearms cleaning kit, the three bottles of shaving cream and the combat shovel.

At exactly eighteen hundred hours, a soldier rounded up the journalists and led them to the officers' mess. In reality, it was simply a tent a little larger than the other ones. But much to Vanessa's surprise, the food being served was actually very edible and the presentation was quite elegant. Colonel Robert Tellier oversaw the culinary gathering. The man impressed Vanessa a lot. He was sturdy as an oak tree and had a deep baritone voice. Visibly, he was born to command. Nonetheless, behind this imposing facade was a man full of gentleness and kindness. The colonel politely asked the journalists if they required anything in particular to make their stay more comfortable.

Jimmy was quick to take the floor. "First of all, I must say the trip over here was poorly organized. And—" He suddenly doubled over as a sharp pain struck his stomach. Every eye in the place focused on him. A heavy silence hung in the tent. Even the stewards stopped what they were doing. Jimmy clutched his stomach and articulated in agony: "Could somebody tell me where I could find the…toilets?"

The colonel called over one of the service soldiers. "Pirotte! Would you please drive Mr. McFarlane to the desired destination. I believe it's urgent."

The soldier held back a smirk and headed for the exit followed by Jimmy. The officers had a hard time containing their laughter. Even the colonel's eyes gleamed with malice. He reassured Vanessa, who was worried about Jimmy's medical state, with the following advice: "I don't think Mr. Mc Farlane will be drinking the water in the camp anymore without purifying it first. If not, he's going to be spending a good part of his stay in the toilet. It's not serious, but just to be on the safe side I'm going to request that a doctor look him over tonight."

The discussion turned to the sanitary conditions in Africa. The subject concerned Colonel Tellier a great deal. An engineering officer, he had greatly contributed to the improvements of the living conditions in the camp. Vanessa was barely following the conversation; her eyes were fixed on Lieutenant Demat. For the occasion, he had on his white marine officer's uniform. She couldn't help herself from admiring the young soldier's imposing presence and natural elegance. More hostile than not toward those in uniform, Vanessa had to admit Edouard was unquestionably charming with his tanned face and dark eyes. She secretly wondered what kind of an impression she was making on him. But she wouldn't get her answer tonight. As soon as dinner ended, she headed back to her tent, beat from the long trip they had made during the day. Vanessa crashed down on her mattress and despite the sweltering heat that reigned inside her humble quarters, she was overcome by sleep within minutes.

* * *

It was bone-chilling cold in Montreal and Michael was trying to find a comfortable hotel so he could take a good hot bath and unwind. He finally checked into Hotel du Parc, which offered a magnificent view of Mont Royal.

The release brought on by the warmth of the water enabled Michael to assess the situation at hand. In less than a week, he lost the chance to do a program on the Davidson affair, lost Dave's documents, lost his driver's license and lost Vanessa. His fighting spirit had taken a mighty blow. Nonetheless, he was confident that a swift turnaround of luck was hiding in the wings. If he just managed to get his hands on some information surrounding the Davidson affair that could be used to incriminate Kotten, everything would fall into place. No matter what, he had to get a hold of Mario Bilodeau, the mystery man who had helped Dave during his investigation. Tonight was virtually shot. Since Bilodeau wasn't at home, there was nothing else he could do. But tomorrow, he would try to contact him at work.

* * *

Michael's nervous tension kept him from falling asleep. He gave up tossing and turning to no end and decided to clear his mind with a walk. As he roamed the streets of downtown, he felt a rush of fresh blood flow to his brain. On St. Catherine Street a huge neon sign for a strip joint named *Chez Aphrodite* grabbed his attention. Michael had stepped into such a place only once before in his life and that was at the university, with a gang of guys, to celebrate the end of final exams. But tonight, having just arrived in a strange city, loneliness and his male curiosity lured him through the doors of this lewd place.

A huge bouncer dressed in a black tuxedo escorted him to a table next to the show stage. But Michael opted for a table in the back, in a darker corner of the club. Actually, the place wasn't as sleazy as he had imagined. The clients were for the most part young tourists drawn by the tantalizing spectacle of feminine curves. Michael was sur-

125

prised to discover that in Quebec dancers were allowed to get fully undressed at a client's table. He watched as a completely naked girl swayed her buttocks languorously a few inches away from the nose of a client who sat motionless, totally hypnotized by the erotic oscillating movement.

Michael was, despite himself, turned on by what he saw. The show was sexy and raw. And after polishing off a few bottles of Boréal, a local beer, he accepted one dancer's proposition to perform for him at his table. The young naked woman moving inside of his personal space was causing him more embarrassment than pleasure. She was so close to him that he could smell her skin's natural perfume and at times her long chestnut brown hair would lightly graze his face. But this sudden and artificial intimacy annoyed him and he regretted his alcohol-induced initiative.

Sensing that she was bothering Michael, the pretty woman stopped dancing and asked him in a soft voice, "You don't like this?"

Michael politely replied, "You're very beautiful and you dance well, but I'm afraid my mind is somewhere else at the moment."

The dancer smiled at him and answered back with a delicious Quebec accent: "It's very kind of you to say I dance well because, honestly, my mind was somewhere else too."

This time Michael smiled. "It can't always be easy to dance in front of men who are thinking of something else."

The woman, somewhere in her early twenties, was quick to reply. "It's better than dancing in front of men who are only thinking of *one* thing. Sometimes I get the feeling their eyes are going to pop out of their head!"

Michael laughed and introduced himself. She shook his hand, saying, "My name is Nathalie."

The trivial nature of their conversation distracted Michael from his worries. He offered to pay Nathalie for more table dances on the condition that she didn't dance for him. The striking stripper accepted and spent the rest of the evening in his company. From time to time, she got up to perform her dance number. This way, she didn't pile her responsibility on the other girls with whom she was supposed to rotate on the dance stage.

Now that Michael had established a human bond with Nathalie, he appreciated her striptease a lot more. The Montreal dancer was amazingly lithe. Her long hair twirled about provocatively in perfect rhythm with the music. A lively pair of dark brown eyes lit up her youthful features. Her breathtaking body bore no traces of fat and her breasts were surprisingly round and firm, given their generous proportion.

Nathalie danced suggestively and threw long, lascivious looks in Michael's direction. He liked the attention. He felt somewhat special, even though he was well aware that the sexy stripper's smiles were meant more for his wallet than for him. Still, he couldn't seem to repress the obvious physical attraction he had for this stunning creature. Sadly, the desire screaming from his sex also painfully reminded him of his limitations. He knew this seductive dancer was inaccessible. Even if the occasion to sleep with her did arise, he knew he wouldn't be able to satisfy her sexually. Not her any more than the others. Not her any more than Vanessa.

Michael got the sudden urge to escape from this place which reminded him in a haunting way of his own handicap. He realized then, that his problem had grown to such an extent that it risked transforming into a real phobia of women. He had always been attracted to pretty women. But for years, with the exception of Vanessa, he avoided most of them because of the crippling fear of failure and humiliation. Tonight, the presence of all these naked beauties was making him terribly miserable.

Nathalie returned swaying to Michael's table, running her right hand through the back of her hair which further projected her breasts forward. She sat down languorously, then leaned toward Michael and declared with the spontaneity of a child, "I'm hungry. Starving, actually. I have this sudden urge to eat lots and lots. Invite me to a restaurant!"

Michael, caught off guard by the invitation, sat there without answering. Nathalie teased him in a suave voice. "Don't worry, I'm not going to rape you!"

The off-the-cuff remark was a sharp jab to Michael's male pride. Had his sexual malaise become that apparent that even a complete stranger could sense it after only a brief conversation? Embarrassed, he said the first thing that came to his mind, "To be raped by such a charming person as yourself would be a most pleasant torture..."

Nathalie placed her hand gently on his shoulder and whispered into his ear, "Listen, I don't sleep with my clients. It's my last day in Montreal. I leave tomorrow for Toronto. I just wanted to grab a bite to eat with someone friendly. Are we clear on this?"

Michael nodded.

"I'm going to get dressed and you find your way out on your own. We'll meet in fifteen minutes in front of the club, on the other side of the street, just outside of the Bay's department store."

And without another word, Nathalie pranced back to her dressing room.

* * *

Michael and Nathalie stopped at a Submarine restaurant situated further east of St. Catherine Street. They ordered two subs, fries and an orange soda and sat down at a table by the window. Michael had gallantly proposed a ritzy restaurant, but the young dancer had preferred the casual simplicity of a fast-food joint. The choice of Submarine presented the perfect opportunity for Michael to confirm Dave's information. The decor was kept to the barest minimum. Pale yellow walls, bright red tables and cushiony plastic seats in faded orange. Besides a street hobo warming up in front of a cup of coffee, they were the only other clients in the place. Dave's idea that this chain was nothing more than a cover to camouflage illicit activities seemed more and more plausible. But without documents, proof or witnesses, Jack Kotten could sleep in peace and continue on with his election campaign undisturbed. If justice was to be served, Michael had one last hope: Mario Bilodeau. And he had to find him. Fast.

Nathalie, who had practically devoured her food in silence, was now determined to grasp Michael's attention. "Normally I don't get involved with my clients. No contact. It's an important rule in my profession. Well, that's if you could call showing off your ass a profession. I don't intend to do this for the rest of my life, you know. I'm not so sure this sort of thing will work at sixty. I want to be a cameraman, or rather a camerawoman. I'm enrolled in an arts and communications program. I hope I can do well but I am so afraid of failing...."

Michael, far away from the constraints and inhibitions troubling his corner of the world, felt he could also be open with her. "I'm in the midst of failing myself. I have many problems at the moment. Things have been rough lately. Fortunately, I'm a fighter and I don't give up easily. If not, I would have already sunk."

Nathalie put her delicate hand atop Michael's and asked, "What's your biggest problem? The one that worries you the most?"

Michael knew the answer to that one very well, but he wasn't ready to talk about it. He stared at the bottom of the table and a long silence ensued.

Nathalie picked up the conversation. "Things are bad for me too. My life is full of shit! I know I'm pretty, they tell me every night, but I'm never satisfied with my appearance. I work out like crazy to keep my body toned. I spend hours on makeup. I even had my breasts enlarged. And still, I always feel ugly. A lot of people say I'm smart, but I think I'm stupid. I work like a dog and I never seem to have any money. It doesn't help that my boy friend snorts my hard-earned money up his nose. I don't do much coke. Maybe a line or two once in a while to stay slim and to give me courage when I need it. I really want to stop, but it's so hard. I told you I'm good for nothing." She turned her head and looked out the dirty window.

Michael was touched by the dancer's sincerity. He looked at her and spoke compassionately. "Don't say that, Nathalie, it's not true. You blew me away tonight. Not with your great body, but with the gracefulness of your movements and the gentleness of your words. I was discouraged when I stepped into the club and now I feel better. That's where your true beauty lies—in the small pleasures you give to others." He took a gulp of his soft drink and continued quietly. "And since you told me about your problems with such frankness, it's only fair that I share mine." Michael took another sip, this time for strength. "I'm in love with a wonderful woman and I think she loves me too. Unfortunately, we had a problem. I should say I had a problem, or to be exact, I have a problem. It's something extremely personal. It's a sexual problem. Nothing kinky, I promise you. I'm no pervert."

Michael was already uncomfortable and the last thing he wanted was for Natalie to make an erroneous judgment about his sex life. He tried explaining the situation by detaching himself from his problem, but it didn't work. "It's simply that I don't have any control. It's real stupid, but I can't last long." Michael's throat clamped up, as if to prevent the truth from coming out. His emotions were getting the better of him. He grabbed the napkin lying on the table and crumpled it. After an interminable pause, at which point he gathered up his courage, he took a deep breath and then in one gulp blurted out, "I think I suffer from premature ejaculation."

Nathalie replied firmly. "Stop sulking. It's nothing! Nothing at all! I've known loads of men who've had this problem. It should get better."

"Maybe," replied Michael, "but my case is more serious. I'm thirty-six and I've lost all confidence in myself."

"Trust me. It can be treated," she reassured him, running her fingers through her dark mane. "My older sister is a doctor and she may know a specialist who could help you."

"Thanks, but no thanks," Michael stated firmly. "I really don't have the time. I'm only here for a short while. I'm really not even sure why I told you. Somehow, I just trust you."

"I'm really happy that you feel you could trust me, because you're about the only person who does. I stole prescription drugs from my sister. I swiped money from my parents. I slept with guys for a quarter of a gram of coke. You can't imagine all the foolish things one does for some dope. I'm sure there would be less crime if we would be able to buy drugs in a pharmacy at a reasonable price."

"That's what the late Senator Davidson was proposing in his bill," Michael said, nodding his head.

"Ya, I know, I heard them talking about him on television. He was an extraordinary man. Too bad the bastards had him killed. At least with such a law in place, junkies wouldn't steal from the good people in this world to pay for their trip. Have you ever seen a boozer kill for a bottle of beer?"

"It's not that simple, Nathalie. It's true that by making alcohol legal, crime associated with trafficking was eliminated. However, it still hasn't prevented other disasters from occurring. Certain hospitals estimate that fifty percent of their emergency room cases are victims of alcohol-related incidents. This includes accidents caused by drunk drivers, women battered by their hammered partners and people suffering from alcohol poisoning. You see, legalizing a drug doesn't solve all problems. What's needed is to get people to feel happy without the help of any sort of substance. But you and I both know how difficult that is to do."

Nathalie wasn't really interested in the subject. She nodded nonchalantly and went back to talking about her life. Michael couldn't take his eyes off of her. The dancer was even sexier with her clothes on than she was with them off. She had a tiny, sulky-looking mouth like that of a whimsical schoolgirl. But her long fingers and blood-red nails gave her the allure of a *femme fatale*. She looked at him, her head lazily resting on her left hand, without saying a word. And then she started the conversation again, running her fingers through her wavy hair. Quite often Nathalie's feet would brush up against his, as if by accident. And every time her story got intense, she grabbed hold of Michael's hand and only let go very slowly, letting her fingers slide through his own.

Michael didn't know what to make of the young woman's flirtations. He couldn't understand why she would try to seduce him after his sad sexual revelation. Whatever the case, Michael became hopeful again. Maybe with a stranger like Nathalie he could replay the sexual exploit he had with Jennifer?

* * *

Comfortably installed in the presidential suite at the Lakeshore Hotel in Chicago, Jack Kotten, surrounded by the key members of his electoral team, was watching the ten o'clock news. A pretty Asian broadcaster was announcing the latest presidential election poll results: "Results indicate that Governor Jack Kotten's popularity is rising at a steady rate. He trails only eight points behind the Republican frontrunner. His speech last night in Boston had a resounding effect among voters. Now for the key highlights of the speech...."

At the same moment, Jack Kotten's good-natured face appeared on the screen. He didn't have John F. Kennedy's playboy good looks, but neither did he personify Richard Nixon's gangster image. His round features mirrored the joviality and serenity of an all-around nice guy. He spoke in a tone that denoted not the slightest hint of aggression. Only his creased eyes betrayed his fierce will.

"I ask you honestly," he said on the news clip, "what difference, what real difference has any one of you here tonight perceived between the Carter, Reagan, Bush or Clinton administrations? One was softer, the other tougher? One wanted to save humanity—the other wanted to play war games? But fundamentally, what kind of improvements did they bring to your life? Believe me, I tell you this knowing all the facts: Republicans, Democrats—they're interchangeable. Not one of these presidents did a thing to stop the decline of America. Not one among them reduced the rate of violence in our cities. Not one of them came close to winning the war on drugs."

Kotten paused, then smiled pleasantly. "I don't think they were terrible men," he said, not wanting to offend the senior citizens who had elected these very men into power. "But they were prisoners of their party, prisoners of all the lobbyists who attempt to paralyze the progress of our country. These men were political puppets without any real power. By voting for the Republican or Democratic candidate, you will do nothing but perpetuate this absurd system. As an independent candidate, I am the prisoner of no interest group and no party. I am only the prisoner to the commitments I make to you, the electorate. These commitments are simple: Lower taxes and greater security for American citizens. No more drugs! No more violence! Peace and prosperity for all! The ways I plan to meet these objectives are clearly outlined in my political election platform."

Jack Kotten turned off the television. His handpicked men clapped and cheered triumphantly as if they had just won the election. Their no-nonsense boss brought them quickly back to reality: "The campaign is going well, but it's not yet in the bag. Calm down." He plunged his hand into a small box of electronic chips. "Ted, did you check on our electronic protective equipment?"

"Yes sir, everything is in order," replied a thin man in his fifties.

Jack Kotten had a phobia about tapping devices, which being more and more minuscule in size could now be slipped in almost anywhere. He himself used the most sophisticated electronic spying

and scrambling countermeasures that destroyed all attempts at recording his conversations. Feeling safe from now on only with his
right-hand men, he spoke freely for the first time in a week. "Men, I
need money to win this lousy election. Lots of money! This campaign has already swallowed up almost all of my personal fortune
and it's too late to back out of the race. As each of you here well
know it's the huge drug traffickers who possess the most liquid money
on this planet. They manage to launder a good portion of this, but at
the end of the day there's always a tiny fortune of dollars left over
which they don't know what to do with it. The true trafficker is a
poker player in spirit. Those who aren't get involved in clean activities until they have amassed a few million dollars. The others, the
real drug barons, always want more and don't know how to stop. I
know of one who's prepared to give me all the money my greedy
heart desires under the cover of a series of umbrella companies and
charitable organizations. He likes the game and is ready to gamble
on my victory, even if this could end up costing him a fortune."

Ted interrupted. "I don't see what a man so rich and powerful
could hope to gain from a president of the United States who, as we
know, will always remain limited in his actions."

"You're absolutely right, the president of the United States possesses limited power. But with a well-televised campaign and the full
support of the population, the future president I will be could under-
take an anti-drug crusade. Congress would have difficulty opposing
such a noble campaign. And since my associates know all the underground networks of distribution in America, we could give a hand to
the DEA and carry out an enormous cleanup operation on U.S. soil.
With the collaboration of the army headed by my good friend General Kullinger, we would get the job done in no time. I can even see
destroying the production zones in Columbia, Burma and Thailand,
with or without the consent of their government. There's no way one
of these helpless countries would be able to stop the U.S. Army. Our
soldiers are motivated to fight for a good cause. And you could all
rest assured, no one would criticize my actions for fear of being accused of collaborating with the traffickers. It would be a true
international crusade."

There was stunned astonishment written all over Ted Bradburry's face, while the other team players smiled knowingly. With the exception of Ted, they had all understood their boss's clever ploy. Kotten licked his lips in anticipation and continued. "This crusade will evidently lead to a momentous shortage within the drug trade in the United States and the world. The price of a quarter gram of coke or heroin will multiply by five or ten. However, my drug trafficker and generous benefactor would have been smart enough to develop an impregnable network. Consequently, he would become the exclusive holder of the international drug trafficking monopoly—a position that would probably make him the richest man in the universe. But for this to become reality, he needs a president of the United States like me!" chuckled Kotten, with a malicious smile. And then in utter disgust, he added, "And to think that imbecile Davidson was ready to take this all away from us with his stupid bill to legalize drugs. We took care of him nicely!"

CHAPTER 16

T he sound of an army bugle startled Vanessa out of a deep sleep. She cursed the obsessive military gurus who made it a point to wake up at six o'clock in the morning even when they were stationed somewhere in the middle of Africa. She tried to fall asleep again but as soon as her head hit the pillow, a sergeant with a deep baritone voice began to hurl orders in French and Flemish. At once, the men stomped into a rhythmic run and began bellowing army chants. Vanessa decided to make the best of the situation and get up for breakfast. She slipped on a pair of shorts and a tank top and headed toward the tent where the officers ate their breakfast. She wasn't even halfway to the mess when Lieutenant Demat stopped her. "Excuse me, Miss Andressen, but would you be so kind as to find something less provocative to wear?"

Still feeling somewhat annoyed at her abrupt wake-up call, Vanessa said sarcastically, "I thought the French fancied their women prancing around half-naked on beaches. You must have changed!" And then in an even drier tone, she added, "Besides, I don't believe I'm under any obligation to take orders from anyone here. I am a free woman and I do as I please when it pleases me!"

The lieutenant stared her straight in the eyes and replied firmly: "First of all, I am not French but Belgian. Second, I should remind you that you are on a military base and not some Mediterranean resort. And finally, if you do not want to conform to my orders then yes, you are free...that is, to leave. You either pass by the clothing depot and get yourself something decent to wear along with a pair of shoes more suitable for the African terrain than your white sandals or leave the base on the next convoy. Have I made myself understood, Miss Andressen?"

Vanessa was furious. Without a word, she turned around and walked back to her tent. She could feel her anti-military sentiments intensifying. "I hate everyone in uniform. They make me sick," she grumbled under her breath, "especially that picky lieutenant." Once inside her tent, she fell onto her cot and thought through the situation at hand. After careful consideration, Vanessa got a grip on herself. She realized that her news report would have to take precedence over her pride. And if she had any inkling of getting her work done, it was time to buckle down and start making some personal sacrifices.

On her way to the uniform depot, Vanessa bumped into Jimmy. He had on a huge pair of black combat boots and a used military uniform a few sizes too big for him. He looked like a cross between a penguin and a beggar. Vanessa couldn't keep herself from laughing and her bad mood lifted.

Inside the uniform depot, Vanessa greeted Chief Corporal Vandenbroeck, who was in charge of the distribution of uniforms, with a friendly salute. Like all the other corporals, Vandenbroeck liked beer, Friday night outings and beautiful women. Vanessa was the perfect candidate for his latter weakness, especially in the male-dominated military environment. It took no time at all for the short corporal to get chatty and kind-hearted with the pretty journalist. Not surprisingly, she left the supply store with brand-new clothes in her size.

Dressed as a soldier, Vanessa walked over to the lieutenant who was cleaning his rifle under the shade of an acacia tree. "I believe I have conformed to your demands. In return for my speedy cooperation, I hoped you would be able to introduce me to an African woman from the refugee camp."

Edouard, glad for the chance to make amends with Vanessa, replied with his customary cordiality. "Certainly. I have a friend who's a nurse in the UN camp. She's African but speaks very good English since she was raised in the United States. Her name is Yasmine."

* * *

The sight of Yasmine impressed Vanessa. A pair of sparkling black eyes lit up an exceptionally beautiful face the color of ebony. Tall and slender, the young nurse carried herself confidently, moving with the grace of a Nubian princess.

The two women hit it off wonderfully, and a warm bond was instantly formed between them. Yasmine was absolutely delighted to talk to an American. The two of them walked beside the tents on their way to the main infirmary. Along the way, refugees—with faces prematurely aged by the hardships of the war—called out to Yasmine. With each shout, the sought-after nurse took a moment or two to answer questions and encourage them as best as she could.

Yasmine expressed how angry and sad she was over the fratricidal war that was violently splitting her people apart. She had been born in the northern part of the country and practiced the religion of her parents. This, she said, didn't stop her from medically treating people from the south of the country or from respecting their beliefs. She felt that tolerance was one of the greatest virtues. "I'm very interested in your report on the condition of women in Sambizania," she commented. "And I've decided that I'm going to do whatever it takes to help you with your article."

"Thanks. I really appreciate your help."

The new friends spent the whole day together. Regrettably, they were forced to part in order to meet the camp's evening curfew.

On the way back to her tent, Vanessa spotted Jimmy sitting on a fallen tree trunk. He was soaking his feet in a basin of water and fussing with his face, which was the crimson color of a lobster.

"I took part in a reconnaissance patrol in the bush," groaned Jimmy. "Now my feet are all bloody and killing me. And take a look at my face—it's on fire! Damn country! They don't even have a place around here where I can buy something to soothe the pain." The badly burned photographer persisted to whine and whimper to no relief. "I'm counting the days until my return to civilization!"

Vanessa gently put her hand on his shoulder. "Really, Jimmy. No one has ever died from a little exercise," she teased.

"Damn this godforsaken place," he continued to grumble, patting his gashed and blistered skin.

Vanessa burst out laughing and left him to sit there in misery. She caught sight of Lieutenant Demat sitting at the foot of the same acacia tree, still intensely preoccupied with the cleaning of his rifle. "Hey, lieutenant," she called out, "still in love with your M 249?"

"What M 249?"

"Come on, your M 249 SAW, Squad Automatic Weapon," insisted Vanessa pointing to the machine-gun resting on the lieutenant's knees.

"Ah, yes, I forgot, M 249 is the American name of my machine gun. But originally it was a weapon conceived and manufactured in Belgium," Edouard indicated with a degree of patriotism. "We call it a MINIMI. With all the dust flying around here, if I didn't maintain my weapon it would jam up on me the moment I'd need it most. So you know a thing or two about weapons?"

Vanessa answered with pride. "Although I may be just a weak woman, I know my weapons pretty well. I'm even a member of a shooting club in Seattle. But I must say, something baffles me, lieutenant. Why do you, an officer, carry a machine gun instead of a handgun like all the others?"

Edouard commended the young woman for her keen sense of observation and added, "I must admit that it has a lot to do with personal preference. I'm a lousy shot with a pistol and the MINIMI handles with more precision. And besides, with my special 200-shot magazine, I could afford to waste a few bullets. On the other hand, the snipers always fire first at the officers on sight to create chaos among the adversary. The officers are easily identified from afar because they are only armed with a pistol. While as for myself, with my MINIMI and without my rank plastered on my shoulders, I could pass for a simple soldier in the eyes of the enemy. Despite everything, this doesn't stop me from keeping a pistol in my backpack."

Vanessa smiled broadly: "For a serviceman you're not so stupid!"

"And you're not so stupid for a journalist!"

They both laughed.

The ice was broken.

* * *

When night fell, the soldiers built a fire in the middle of the camp. Edouard spotted Vanessa sitting alone and sat down next to her. "Life in the tropics isn't depressing you too much, I hope?" he asked.

"I think I'll survive. To be honest, it's both difficult and fascinating. The sweltering heat, the hectic pace of things, the people, the scenery, the vegetation, the colors and not to mention, the military...I don't think I have anything to complain about," she laughed. "I'm only kidding. I'm fine, thank you. But I must say, very homesick for the comforts of North America. I miss my cozy apartment, ample food in the fridge, air conditioning, a shower and television. This may come across as stupid or perhaps somewhat smug, but take these things away and they suddenly become a necessity."

"You know," Edouard said, feeding a branch to the fire, "I'm beginning to miss Europe. I've been in Africa for three months now, and time is starting to drag. There's not much action happening. My men and I are under strict orders to remain in noncombat mode when only some kilometers away from here there are heinous massacres and inhumane atrocities taking place daily. It makes me seriously question the role and effectiveness of peacekeepers. And I am constantly reminded of what took place in the former Yugoslavia, Rwanda and Somalia."

Vanessa empathized with the lieutenant but her mind had already drifted from the depressing realities of the military. The beauty of the starry African sky commanded her full attention. The air must be purer in this corner of the world, she thought to herself. Everything around her felt bigger—as if the landscape had no beginning or end. Vanessa was hit with a heavy pang of nostalgia and found herself asking the lieutenant what he thought was the most important thing in existence.

Completely caught off guard, Edouard pondered the enormity of her question. "Love, I think."

Vanessa couldn't resist pressing him for specifics: "Physical love or spiritual love?"

"Between a man and a woman who love each other, the two are complementary. The mind is nothing without the body and the body is nothing without the mind. A healthy sex life enriches the love between a man and a woman. But sex without love doesn't mean much."

Vanessa thought about her experience with Michael. She was sure she loved him. But her love for him was more spiritual than physical.

A light breeze had lifted, making the air around the camp slightly more bearable. Sergeant Hermans, seated on the other side of the fire, picked up his guitar and started strumming softly. He played Flemish songs to which the men sang in unison. Even the French-speaking soldiers attempted to sing along, although they were clearly having a hard time following the lyrics. Noticing this, the sergeant stopped playing. He looked around the fire at the American visitors among the troops and within a matter of seconds switched over to tunes by Simon and Garfunkel.

The romantic ambience created by the fire and the mellow music moved Edouard to open up to Vanessa. "I know we don't know each other that well, but I have a feeling I could talk to you. I'm in love with Yasmine, the nurse I introduced to you this afternoon. We love each other and plan to get married at the end of my mission in Sambizania. Whenever possible, we meet in secret and make passionate love. These are exceptionally special moments where our bodies and minds come together and become one with the universe. Yasmine's religion forbids such carnal acts but we believe God prefers our love to the crimes and hate destroying humanity. I must confess, I never saw things in quite this way before I met her."

"How beautiful. What you both have is very special. I even envy you. Sad to say, my love life isn't nearly as wonderful. Before coming to Africa I broke up with a good and intelligent man over a silly problem. It really wasn't all that serious but it wrecked our relationship. I must say, I did love him. And even as we speak, I can't help wondering if I made the right decision. I'm really not sure any more."

Vanessa became quiet and the two of them turned toward Sergeant Hermans, who was playing *One More Night* by Phil Collins. Listening to the words, Vanessa couldn't help feeling sick with emotion. The song made her think of Michael. She remembered all the good times they shared: how they met at the gas station, their first supper at home, and their trip to New York.

The evening slowly wound down and the soldiers retired to their tents. Vanessa returned to her canvas palace, escorted by the lieutenant who, sensing how she felt, remained silent.

* * *

Michael found his way back to Hotel du Parc with Nathalie holding him snugly at the waist. The young dancer's bouncy step was turning him on incredibly. She was clinging to him so tightly that despite the night's chill, he could feel the heat from her body. They walked into the hotel without the sleepy night-duty receptionist even noticing them.

Inside the hotel room, Michael wrapped his arms around Nathalie's shoulders and she rested her head on his chest. Nathalie lifted her head languorously, her lips searching longingly for those belonging to Michael. A shiver of desire rippled through his entire body. A beautiful young woman was embracing him and offering him her parted lips hungry with desire. All he had to do was plant the desired kiss on her lips and she would be his—dream body and all.

But Michael wavered. The alcohol consumed over the course of the evening combined with the spellbinding scent of the cute Quebecer's perfume made his head spin. "We're both looking for some comfort and affection tonight," he whispered into Nathalie's ear. "You know as well as I do where things will lead if I kiss you and we'll both be disappointed. You're extremely desirable, but…"

Nathalie didn't move for a minute. Finally, she placed a simple kiss on Michael's cheek. "This is the first time a man has refused to sleep with me. I can't explain it, I should be furious. But it sucks that you rejected me, because I do find you attractive. However, I'm also very touched. I think you're the first guy who respects me."

Michael couldn't bring himself to respond. A storm of contradictory feelings raged within him. Tired from thinking and worn out from the day's long drama, he threw himself on the bed without saying a word. Nathalie took off her clothes, leaving on only her tiny white lace panties and her body-hugging cotton T-shirt. She snuggled up against him and feeling safe in his arms, fell asleep quickly.

Michael had a little more trouble falling asleep. Pressed against his body was a warm, desirable woman. Nathalie's presence was driving him nuts. He wanted to touch her so badly. He couldn't help regretting his noble gesture. His mind kept on taking him back a few hours to Nathalie's erotic dance number. He visualized her big breasts bouncing up and down, her tight round buttocks lifted in the air and her long legs wrapped sexily around the fluorescent shaft on the stage. He felt his penis getting rock hard. All he wanted to do was make love to her. Michael moved away from the hot, young flesh. How could he possibly take back his hasty words now? But after many minutes of restless consideration, fatigue got the better of him and at the same time presented him with a sensible solution to his sexual dilemma.

When Michael woke up, Nathalie was no longer by his side. He thought for a second that she might be in the washroom. But a quick glance at the carpet confirmed otherwise: her jeans, bra and socks were gone. The mysterious dancer had bolted without saying a word. "Too bad. I would like to have at least said goodbye to her," he thought to himself. He had to admit she was an awfully nice girl.

There was no point in dwelling on it. Michael jumped out of bed, took a shower and began getting dressed. When he pulled his pants up to zip them, they felt noticeably lighter than they did the night before: "My wallet!" He fumbled through his pockets in vain. They were all empty. He scanned the room and eventually spotted his wallet on the floor, very close to the door. All his identification and credit cards were in place, but the paper money was gone. Stuffed inside the dollar compartment was a hastily scribbled note. "I need money, you need help! Here's the phone number of my sister, Dr. Carole Bérubé: 286-1486."

Michael was furious. What he really wanted to do was find the dancer and tell her exactly what was on his mind. She had betrayed his trust and that revolted him. He slammed his fist onto the night table, overturning a glass of water. His blood was boiling, but he knew that getting all worked up over something he couldn't change was a waste of time.

As he calmed down, Michael thought about his brief encounter with Nathalie. He came to the conclusion that the time he spent with the young dancer wasn't negative in all respects. For once in his life, he had worked up the courage to talk about his sexual problem with someone else. It felt good to get it off of his chest. And moreover, he was being offered another chance. The phone number Nathalie left him might hold the answer to his problem. Maybe they developed some new treatment he could try, he thought. It wouldn't hurt to get informed. Michael decided he would call Nathalie's sister.

He picked up the phone and quickly dialed the number. The receptionist told him the doctor was busy with a patient. She offered to set up an appointment for him, but Michael insisted he wanted to talk directly to Dr. Bérubé. So he left his phone number and asked the woman to have the doctor call him back at the hotel.

With the phone still in his hand, Michael decided to give Mario Bilodeau a call at work.

"I'm sorry sir," the secretary replied, "but Mr. Bilodeau is on vacation for three weeks."

"Could you tell me where I may reach him?"

"Excuse me, sir, but who are you? I'm afraid I don't recognize your voice. I'm not at liberty to give that sort of information."

Michael cleared his throat and gave it his best shot. "Oh, pardon me, madam. I'm Dr. Schwartz from the Montreal General," he said, hoping to God that Montreal had a hospital by that name. And, not giving her any time to think about it, he quickly added, "We just received Mr. Bilodeau's test results and I must get in touch with him immediately."

Michael held his breath. He couldn't be sure if the snappy woman on the other end of the line had swallowed his lies. Did she fall for it? Would she divulge the information he needed to pursue his investigation? The seconds that followed seemed like an eternity.

"I could have Mr. Bilodeau return your phone call as soon as he arrives in town," she suggested more pleasantly.

"No, no, no! That won't be good. It could be too late by then," replied the make-believe doctor. "Mr. Bilodeau's health—his very life—is at stake. I must get in touch with him at once!"

"Oh, my!" exclaimed the secretary. "I'm very sorry, doctor. I had no idea how serious—"

Michael heaved a sigh in victorious relief and carried on with his act. "Yes, it is very unfortunate," he said melodramatically.

"Mr. Bilodeau left for Miami by car. And I'm afraid I don't know what hotel he's staying in," she panicked.

Michael cursed under his breath as he put down the telephone receiver after thanking the receptionist for her help. "Just what am I supposed to do now? The whole thing is awful. I don't have enough time to find him." Michael set his mind into motion until he finally came up with an idea. "That's it! I'm going to get George and Cindy in on the action. They'll be able to track down Bilodeau's whereabouts in no time. And frankly, I don't give a damn what Tony's going to think about this."

The telephone rang.

"Mr. Lancaster?" asked a female voice.

"Speaking."

"Dr. Bérubé."

Michael, a little ill at ease, briefly explained his situation to her.

When he finished, she replied compassionately. "I'm sorry, sir, but I don't treat this type of problem. I could, however, refer you to the leading specialist in premature ejaculation in all of North America. He recently presented his method at a sex therapy conference in Spain. And since you are currently without a partner, his approach is perfect for you. In fact, his method was specifically developed for men seeking treatment on their own. He practices in West Palm Beach, Florida. His name is Dr. Carter. I don't have his number, but you'll have no problem finding him in the phone book."

Michael could hardly believe his ears. For the first time in his life, he actually believed there was real hope of dealing with his problem. And going to Florida would allow him to kill two birds with one stone: He would consult the sex therapist and have a chance to meet with Bilodeau.

As soon as he got off the phone, he packed his bags and made his way to the airport. He landed a seat on an Air Transat plane that was leaving in an hour and a half. And on top of that, it was a direct flight to Fort Lauderdale, less than a half-hour drive to West Palm Beach! He thanked the heavens that Florida was a favorite winter destination among Quebecers.

Six hours later, Michael was booked into a comfortable ocean front hotel room in Palm Beach, a small town located between West Palm Beach and the Atlantic Ocean. Even before unpacking his bags, he called Dr. Carter's office. The doctor's secretary answered the phone. It was close to five o'clock and she was anxious to go home.

He was told that the sex therapist couldn't talk to him at the moment. Disappointed, Michael left his number and put down the phone.

He dropped his bags haphazardly on the bed and stepped outside onto the patio. It was a beautiful evening. Michael breathed in the invigorating ocean breeze. The salty air filled his nostrils, almost making him dizzy. He took a couple of deep breaths and exhaled. The surface of the water glittered under the sun's last golden rays. He listened to the rhythmic crashing of the waves hitting the shore. But instead of calming him down, the hypnotic flow struck him with a strange sensation. The rise and fall of the waves reminded him of his sexuality. He wondered how he would ever be able to successfully hold back all the sexual energy surging within him when it came to making love. It was a mystery that both troubled and intrigued him. When he got excited, an overwhelming force grabbed hold of his being and carried him like an uncontrollable tidal wave. Swept by the storm of pleasure raging within him, he sunk miserably inside of his disillusioned lovers.

The hotel receptionist pulled him away from his thoughts. "Mr. Lancaster, you have a phone call."

Michael returned to his room and picked up the phone.

"Hi, Michael. How are you doing?" It was Cindy, the researcher from *It Concerns Us*. "We found what you were looking for. Mario Bilodeau is staying at the Atlantic Waves Hotel. We tracked down the information quite fast. But it wasn't that easy. We had to come up with some creative excuses to prevent Tony from becoming suspicious. He doesn't suspect a thing, don't worry." Cindy gave Michael the phone number to the hotel where Bilodeau was staying and wished him good luck.

"This is so great. You guys are fabulous. I never expected you to work so quickly. Thank George for me, okay? And I'll make sure to keep you both posted. Talk to you soon." Michael hung up and immediately called the hotel in Miami.

"I'm sorry, sir," replied the receptionist, "but Mr. Bilodeau was rushed to the hospital by ambulance late this afternoon."

Michael put down the receiver in complete disbelief. Was this drama ever going to end? He threw himself onto the sofa and shook his head slowly from side-to-side as if hoping that eventually the entire affair would erase itself. He slapped open the telephone directory over his knees and systematically began calling every hospital in Miami. It took six calls to track down Bilodeau at Mount Sinai Hospital. He was in intensive care. Michael couldn't help wondering what had happened. "I hope he makes it," he worried.

Lying on the sofa, Michael continued to speculate about what could have happened to Bilodeau: He was too young to have a medical problem. An overdose? A car accident? Possibly. An attack? Probably. "It wouldn't surprise me at all," he concluded. "We are dealing with Kotten."

Michael was exhausted from thinking too much. "It's time to put an end to this," he thought to himself. Jack Kotten was involved with drug traffickers and they were financing his election campaign. This was a given. His right-hand man General Kulliger, for his part, had the support of the military-industrial lobby. This was another known fact. But what was the link between these two men? And why did they absolutely have to kill off Senator Davidson?

Unable to make sense out of things, Michael turned on the television. He desperately needed some brain candy. An African-American journalist was commenting on images from a riot taking place on the streets of Washington: "A delegation of Green Peace activists are protesting in front of the Chinese Embassy against nuclear testing being carried out in that country," reported the news anchor. "Our correspondent is standing by."

"That's it," cried out Michael, springing off of the sofa. "That's the key to the mystery." Ever since Dave had told him that Kotten dealt only with drugs coming from Pakistan, the former Soviet Union and China, he had been racking his brain trying to understand why this was the case. But now he had the answer: The common thread among these three countries was the fact that they each possessed nuclear arms. General Kulliger would never be able to intervene militarily in these countries without exposing himself to incredible risks. If, however, he managed to destroy the production zones in Colombia, Thailand and Burma, the traffickers in the other three countries would rake in a fortune. And since Kotten continues to maintain close ties with these countries, it would be no surprise at all if they were financing his election campaign. The U.S. presidency in exchange for eliminating their rivals in South America and the Far East. This was the deal Kotten had struck with the traffickers in Asia. But if his plan was to work, there was no way Davidson's bill could ever pass. For the sale in pharmacies of drugs legally manufactured and imported into the United States would have caused his entire plan to go up in smoke. Davidson, therefore, was Kotten's worst enemy.

Michael felt relieved. He had finally figured out the motive of the crime. But he still had to scrape together the evidence needed to incriminate Jack Kotten. And there wasn't any time to waste. His show was going to air in two weeks and Vanessa would be back in less than two months. Michael was prepared to take on what had turned into the Davidson-Kotten affair, head-on. He was not in the least bit daunted by the potential danger involved. But on the other hand, winning back Vanessa depended on the results of the therapy and he had no idea how long that would take. And this scared him.

The phone rang and Michael got up quickly. It was Dr. Carter. The two men spoke for about ten minutes. Michael finally asked him if he could set up an appointment.

"I'll check my scheduling book," replied the sex therapist. "Let's see, the earliest I could fit you in is sometime in the month of September. The eighth, to be exact. Two o'clock okay with you?"

"What?" Michael exclaimed. "That's four months from now. I'm going to lose her, doctor. I'm going to lose the woman I love. Don't you have anything sooner?"

"I'm sorry, Mr. Lancaster. I'm booked right up to that date."

"What am I supposed to do until then? This is very serious. My girlfriend left me because of my sexual problem and if I don't get help soon, I'll never get her back."

Dr. Carter could sense Michael's desperation. He flipped vainly through the filled pages of his appointment book and after a long pause, said, "Listen, there's no way I can get you in before then. I have no room. I can't do much.... Wait a minute, it might be possible...that is unless you object to meeting late at night. I could make an exception and see you in the evening, after my regular office hours—"

"That's great!" exploded Michael, raising his arm high in the air in victory, as he used to do when he played football.

"All right then, tomorrow night at ten. We'll go over the approach I use and then you can decide if the method suits you or not."

Michael was on a fantastic high. He couldn't contain his happiness. He finally felt a glimmer of hope. At last, he told himself, he might be able to remedy his sexual problem. And despite the fatigue that had accumulated over the past few days, he felt a surge of energy. He threw on his sneakers and went running along the beach.

The light breeze hitting the back of his neck and the salty ocean mist filling his nostrils felt awesome. The ocean rose and fell with fury dumping seaweed and seashells along the shore. Michael's strong strides mirrored his courage and bravery. He was thirsty for a fight and for victory. More than anything else in the world he wanted to avenge his friend's death. He promised himself that he would punish Senator Davidson's assassins. He also dreamed of winning back Vanessa. A wild fire was burning within him, a passionate desire to hold and possess her. And for this, Michael was prepared to beat all odds.

* * *

The next morning, Michael called his boss in Seattle. Tony was his usual arrogant self: "Where the hell have you been? Abducted by aliens, perhaps?" He laughed at his own joke and continued sternly, "Never mind that. I want to know how the next show is coming along. I hope you're aware that there are only fourteen days to air time. Where are you, anyway?"

"I'm in West Palm Beach, Florida, gathering proof on the Davidson case."

"What?" raged Tony. "Didn't you understand me the first time? I told you—we are *through* with that story."

"No, we're not," Michael replied. "And just to let you know, I've discovered the motive behind Davidson's murder. It was a political assassination."

"Have you completely lost it? You're really dense, you know. The police searched Barbara Rowland's apartment and found the chandelier and the two paintings that were stolen from the old senator's mansion. The Davidson affair has not a single shred of interest to us anymore. The cloud of doubt hovering over the case has once and for all been lifted. The senator's ex-mistress is indeed the murderer."

The new revelation took Michael by surprise. For a second he said nothing, but he quickly pulled himself together and held his ground. "Listen Tony, I'm convinced the cops are on the wrong track. There are too many loose ends, too many disturbing elements. We have to follow this through."

"I always knew you were stubborn," Tony said, flaring up, "but never to this outrageous degree. I want you to get this through your thick skull, okay? Listen to me very closely: The Davidson affair is history! Finished! No more! Did you hear that? Over!"

Michael raised his voice: "No! It's not over! I'm not going on air with any other story. It's Davidson or nothing."

"All right then, it's going to have to be nothing!" snapped Tony, "Because you, mister, are fired! Go ahead—waste your time on the Davidson affair. But as far as PDS goes, you're fired!" And he slammed the phone down noisily.

CHAPTER 17

V anessa was starting to appreciate the daily routine inside the military camp. Plunked in the middle of Africa, in an environment totally foreign to her, there was something comforting in the way the Belgian army worked. Wake-up time, drill call, meals, exercise, rest time and lights out were all carried out daily at the same time, in the same order and in the same place.

The two CNN journalists accompanying Jimmy and Vanessa wore brand spanking new U.S. Army uniforms devoid of any rank or insignia. Their new uniforms made the Belgian troops burn with jealousy. The soldiers were forced to make do with old-fashioned, stuffy uniforms resembling those worn by the U.S. Army thirty years ago. Their jackets were made of a dark forest green fabric that provided them with little camouflage in the African bush. Even more unbearable was the way the fabric locked in perspiration. In the scorching heat, the soldiers were literally swimming inside their uniforms. When it rained, the same fabric absorbed liquid like a sponge and made moving around a difficult exercise.

A thousand other details revealed the inadequacies of this modest army that stemmed from a country far too small to successfully participate in distant expeditions. Yet this western European kingdom had since participated in numerous missions and sent peacekeepers into the former Yugoslavia, Cambodia, Angola and Somalia. In general, Belgium was actually very well suited for UN missions because it was a peaceful country and held a long, democratic tradition. But when it came to this particular mission in Sambizania, it was felt that the UN had made a bad choice in recruiting the Belgian army. The sorry reality was that even though other

NATO countries backed it, the means of defense at its disposal was largely insufficient. In the face of the growing intensity of the conflict, the Belgian soldiers could no longer effectively control the large sector assigned to them. The Sambizanian government openly criticized and attacked the peacekeepers for being white, European and Christian. And to make matters worse, it suspected them of taking sides with the population of the southern countries.

The country's dictator, General Sibouar El Tabernasti, vowed to kill every last UN soldier if even a single one among them dared to set foot on Sambizanian territory. Yet the threat didn't stop the peacekeepers who, in the name of humanitarian intervention, set both feet and even left track marks on the ground from their armored personnel carriers. The southern population to which they brought food, protection and life-saving medical services and supplies looked at them as freedom fighters and great liberators. In the meantime, a number of terrorist acts had taken place in Brussels and it was believed that General El Tabernasti's iron fist was behind the attacks. As it had previously done in the case of Rwanda, Belgium would have liked to pull its troops quickly out of Sambizania. But this time, it was forced to respect its UN peacekeeping commitments and support Pakistan, Senegal, Italy and Norway who were positioned in other sectors. Consequently, the tension onsite had mounted and the Belgian soldiers no longer felt safe.

The CNN journalists were hoping to put a spotlight on the crisis. If things ran smoothly, they would break the story to the rest of the world. CNN would be the first station to broadcast the facts and images coming out of the conflict in Sambizania. To make this possible the cameramen were equipped with the latest technology. Thanks to a high-powered transmitter, people around the globe would be receiving the images live via satellite.

Vanessa marveled at the speed and efficiency of the sleek technology. She used it several times to call her mother so as to reassure her that everything was fine. But she had not been successful when trying to reach Michael. She had landed repeatedly on his answering machine and had not wanted to leave a message. Not being able to connect with him was extremely frustrating. The more she thought about it, the more she regretted leaving Michael and taking off to Africa. She would have liked to try to find a solution to his sexual problem, to have talked about it, instead of leaving on such an impulsive whim.

* * *

"Hi, Vanessa," Yasmine said, plunking a heavy metal case containing first-aid supplies down on the ground. The young nurse had just returned from the refugee camp where she had been treating the latest arrivals. "Phew," she said, pulling the long sleeves of her dress up above her elbows. "It's hot today!"

"It's hot here every day," complained Vanessa, wiping the sweat off her brow with the back of her hand. "I admire you for working in such conditions."

"The children's smiles keep me going. And what about you? How's that report of yours coming along?"

"It's coming along, but slowly. I bet if you'd give me a hand it would go a lot faster."

"Sure. But what can I do to help?"

"Come with me," beckoned Vanessa. "I'll explain everything."

Vanessa grabbed one end of the medical chest and the two women carried it into the journalist's tent. Vanessa motioned Yasmine to take a seat on the cot as she prepared a pot of tea on the imposing gas burner sitting on a wooden table in the middle of her tent.

"I'd like to know more about how the women in Sambizania live. Are they aware of their rights?"

"For women like you and me who come from the States, the living conditions here appear appalling. But for women born in Africa, they seem very normal. And before the war, most of the women would have told you that they were happy to live in Sambizania."

"And how do they feel about female excision?"

Yasmine replied in a hushed voice, "It's a taboo subject around here. No one likes to talk about it, certainly not me."

The journalist in Vanessa couldn't help asking her for an immediate explanation. "Why not?"

Yasmine moved closer to Vanessa. "Promise me first that neither my name nor anything that could identify me will find its way into your article."

Vanessa took the pale ebony hand into hers. "I want you to know that I admire you very much and there's nothing in the world that would make me want something bad to happen to you. I'll be changing all the sources and locations in my report. You have my word that no one will ever be able to trace what I have written back to you."

Yasmine withdrew her hand, hesitated a little, and then cautiously began sharing her story. "When I was three, my family emigrated to the United States from Africa. I was raised like every other little American girl. At least that's what I thought. But when I hit the age of eight my mother took me to see a distant aunt who also lived in New Jersey. She told me that I'd soon be a woman and that I would have to undergo an operation. It was going to be painful, but it was the only solution if I was ever to find a husband when I was older. I remember panicking. I was led down a narrow corridor and into a small room filled with women. They were speaking in a dialect I couldn't understand. I had no idea what was about to take place."

Yasmine's throat constricted around her remaining words and her eyes filled with tears. And then the words began to flow from her lips. "The women laid me down on a cold table and spread open my legs. I resisted with all my strength. I begged my mother for her help. I pleaded with her to make them stop. I screamed savagely for her to take me home. But my mother didn't react. She didn't even move. I will never forget the look on her face: profound resignation. It was the expression worn by a woman who was doing her duty. She was sad and upset over what was being done to me, but she didn't want to show it to the others."

The young African woman took in a breath of strength and continued. "An old woman was reciting prayers the whole time. Another one came toward me and slid her fingers into my vulva. A sick shiver of terror shot through my small, innocent body. And with her other hand, she seized a large knife with a straight blade. I felt the cold metal touch my skin. I no longer dared to move. My eyes stung from my tears. I swallowed hard. And then like a butcher burdened with the execution of an unjust yet necessary slaughter, the nameless woman made a swift movement with her wrist. I felt an atrocious pain. And then everything went black. I can't remember anything that happened after that. But never again did I feel like all the other little girls.

"From that day on I set out to hate my parents, their customs and their religion. Only when I became a teenager did I learn just how lucky I had been on that chilling day when I was eight years old.

They had performed the slightest form of excision on me and had used sterile instruments. Here in Africa, a lot of little girls die shortly after from infections. At least in America they survive."

Vanessa's body shook with violent indignation. "You mean to tell me that genital mutilation is still being performed on children in the States?"

Yasmine shook her head affirmatively.

"But it's against the law!" raged the female journalist.

"Exactly, but the secret is kept within the family and the little girls feel so guilty and are so submissive that they don't talk to anybody about it. Since the mutilation usually takes place when they are underage, these girls have no legitimate way to defend themselves. As for me, I grew up loathing the people who were allowed to mutilate my body and impose their laws on me. I wanted so badly to be an American like all the others. But as a result of what happened to me, that was no longer possible. When I became a teenager, I was ashamed of myself. I felt different and I was convinced that no boy would ever be interested in me."

"How did you deal with that?"

"In the first place, my parents prevented me from going out and didn't want me to date an American. Anyhow, guys scared me. When I left home at eighteen, I tried living the life of a normal, modern woman. My romantic relationships were across the board and every single one of them ended in shambles. Men treated me like I was an exotic bird and were interested in me solely for sex. I was also having serious problems integrating socially. I felt comfortable neither with whites nor with blacks. I wasn't a true Westerner. When I finished nursing school, I decided to return to my roots by coming back to Africa. That's why I'm here now. In the States, I grew up in fear, hatred and with a spirit of vengeance. Here in Africa, I've learned about self-sacrifice, respect and love. Africans are beautiful and extraordinary people. They live in squalid misery and meet death face-to-face daily. And despite all of this, they always have a smile on their face and share what little they have with others."

Vanessa hesitated momentarily, and then asked Yasmine a question she was dying to have answered. "Excuse my curiosity, but how is your relationship going with Lieutenant Demat?"

"You know about that too!" gasped the young nurse. "All of Sambizania will know about it before long!"

"I'm so sorry, I didn't mean to be rude. And please, don't feel obliged to answer," added Vanessa, clearly uncomfortable.

"No, no, it doesn't bother me at all. And don't be silly, you shouldn't feel bad for asking," assured Yasmine. Then, like any woman about to share the details of her romantic life with a good friend, the young nurse got all flushed and excited. She sat down cross-legged and placed her hands on her ankles. "Edouard is a wonderful, wonderful man. He was incredibly patient and gentle with me when I first met him. You see I had rather unfavorable preconceived notions toward men and particularly, men in the military. But Edouard changed all of that and slowly brought down my defensive barriers. He treated me with respect and affection."

"Have you made love?" Vanessa couldn't help from asking.

"I was the one who made the first move. Edouard didn't need any persuading, but he approached me with a lot of tenderness. And the tenderness turned into passion. He allowed me to discover my body. He made me feel in control. I had my first orgasms with him," she paused. "The reason I'm revealing these very personal details of my life to you is that I believe my experience could help a lot of women. Before, I was convinced that without a clitoris I would never be able to reach orgasm. Boy was I wrong! During intercourse, I'm very aware of Edouard inside of me and I feed off of his powerful presence. He carries me and I belong to him both in body and soul. I know very well that I will never be able to experience the clitoral pleasures enjoyed by other women. However, this doesn't stop me from totally letting myself go and having an orgasm when we are together. I love feeling like a woman in his arms. I love feeling desired. I love being possessed. And I love being showered by his love. The ultimate testimony of our love will be our marriage in the near future." And then as if reality had struck her in the face, Yasmine sat up straight and declared in a self-admonishing tone: "My goodness! Just listen to me talk about the future when the turbulent present worries me greatly. The latest wave of refugees at the camp told us that the northern troops are less than thirty miles away from here and that there's going to be a deadly massacre."

CHAPTER 18

T he taxi dropped Michael off in front of Dr. Carter's clinic. The fairly new building was situated on a quiet avenue lo cated on the outskirts of West Palm Beach. Michael walked in and took a seat in the simple yet elegantly decorated waiting room. The receptionist was long gone, given the lateness of the hour. Even though the room was empty of patients, Michael couldn't help feeling slightly self-conscious. To distract himself, he walked over to the wooden bookshelf, grabbed a magazine and flipped through it.

A few minutes later, Michael heard a male client thanking Dr. Carter and leaving by the back door. It was his turn. He wondered if this was such a good idea after all. Despite his respect for profession-als in the field of mental health, he wasn't exactly thrilled about the prospect of sharing his sexual setbacks with someone he didn't even know.

But before Michael could bail out, a tall, thin man in his forties was standing in front of him. "Michael?" the well-dressed doctor smiled, extending his hand. "I'm Dr. Carter."

"Pleased to meet you," replied Michael, jumping to his feet.

The two men shook hands and the sex therapist led Michael into his office.

"I'd like to thank you once again for seeing me at this late hour. I'm sure you know just how important this is to me."

When they entered the consulting room, Dr. Carter gestured for Michael to take a seat on a pale blue upholstered armchair. The muted lighting, the salmon-colored walls, the painting depicting a small fishing village in Maine and the healthy ficus tree, created a reassuring ambience.

As Michael eyed the room, he began to relax. To his relief, the famous couch used by most psychoanalysts was missing from the surroundings. Another pleasant surprise was the simple fact that the desk was placed against the wall and not between the therapist and the client. The arrangement created an informal and warm atmosphere.

The men exchanged a few polite pleasantries on Florida, the presidential election campaign, Michael's job and then Dr. Carter eased into the real subject. "You told me this was important to you. I'd like you to tell me more about that."

Michael described in detail the evolution of his relationship with Vanessa, the sexual difficulties he encountered along the way and the doubts he was having regarding the reason for her departure.

"You know," said the sex therapist, "we could only presume her motives for leaving you. And you'll probably never know for sure, unless you raise the subject with her one of these days. What is clear, however, is that you suffer from premature ejaculation. And at your age, if you don't do anything to control it, it is highly probable that your condition won't improve. But to help you, I'm going to need some more information. Tell me, have you experienced these problems the same way since the beginning of your sex life?"

Dr. Carter continued to probe in this manner. He asked Michael questions on his health, his consumption of alcohol, his personal habits and his pastimes. He questioned him on how he handled his sexual excitement during sex and masturbation. He inquired about the quality of Michael's erections, his behavior during foreplay and intercourse, his emotions, and more.

Through this line of questioning, the therapist was able to determine that Michael possessed several characteristics of the classic premature ejaculator. He was a man of action. He moved quickly, ate in a hurry, enjoyed fast driving and participated in powerful sports like racquetball and football. On the sexual level, he had good, healthy morning erections. When he was young, he fell into the habit of masturbating quickly, interested in experiencing the strongest sensations of ejaculation instead of savoring the subtleties associated with excitement. Even today, if he took his time during foreplay, it was to bring his partner to orgasm rather than to indulge in the intimate moments spent with her. In reality, as soon as he was with a woman, strong sexual impulses surged within him, settling for nothing less than spurting their way directly to discharge. In spite of this, Michael was patient and he knew how and when to enjoy the good times in life.

Dr. Carter presented his diagnosis to Michael using colorful imagery. "Like most men who ejaculate sooner than they desire, you do not suffer from any physical or psychological disease. Quite the opposite, you're a vigorous man and you are in great physical shape. You could be compared to a rushing torrent on a warm spring day in the snowy mountains or a wild horse running freely in the open fields. The program you'll follow isn't going to cure or transform you. This is not the goal. It will simply allow you to discover and exploit another aspect of yourself."

"You mean to tell me it's not a disease?" Michael asked, raising his eyebrows in sheer amazement.

"No. Premature ejaculation is certainly a handicap for those suffering from it, but we cannot call it an illness. To shed light on this point, allow me to explain the causes of premature ejaculation. However, before starting, I'd like to give you some basic information about the neurophysiology of ejaculation. First of all, it's extremely important for you to understand that ejaculation is a reflex process. And secondly, this reflex process is triggered by sexual excitement when it becomes intense enough. It's simple, actually. The ejaculatory reflex works exactly like the reflex in your knee. If you hit the patellar tendon hard enough, the reflex is kicked into action and your leg jerks automatically.

"If a man ejaculates earlier than he wants to, it's because he hasn't maintained his sexual excitation at levels below the level of excitement that sets off the ejaculatory reflex. You see, it's somewhat like the phenomenon of boiling water. Water only boils at 212° Fahrenheit. When this temperature is reached, it's too late. The pot boils over. However, if the heat is maintained at a temperature below the boiling point, the water will never boil over from its receptacle. In other words, if a man ejaculates quickly, it's because he is unable to keep his sexual excitation under control. Basically, his sexual excitement gets too intense too fast and provokes the ejaculatory reflex. Consequently, premature ejaculation isn't due to an absence of control over ejaculation as Helen Kaplan wrote in 1989 in her book, *Premature Ejaculation*. It's caused by a lack of control over sexual excitement.

"It's important you understand the following: A man cannot in any way control his ejaculation. And why can't he? For the simple reason that ejaculation is a reflex process and reflexes are beyond voluntary control. Therefore, if a man wants to prolong the length of intercourse, he must pay absolute attention to his sexual excitation level, not his ejaculation. He has to maintain his sexual excitation below a certain level. In other words, he has to refrain from getting too excited. For it is sexual excitement, when it becomes too high, that provokes ejaculation.

"It's also completely useless for a man to attempt to hold back his ejaculation once the ejaculatory reflex has been triggered. The reason being that nothing can deflect reflexes from following their course once they've been set into motion. It's like sneezing. Once a sneeze has started, it's impossible to hold it back. We can reduce its intensity somewhat, but we can't stop it from happening.

"The program is based on the comprehension of these basic phenomena. I will explain them to you in further detail because it's fundamental that you grasp all of the subtleties. When a man becomes sufficiently sexually aroused, the well-known neurophysiological process of ejaculation occurs. This process comprises two phases. The first—called the emission phase—is characterized by a succession of contractions taking place at the level of the accessory sexual organs. These contractions start in the testicles and continue down the vas deferens, the seminal vesicles and the prostate. They have the effect of bringing into the prostatic ureter—situated at the base of the penis—the diverse substances which have been secreted and which make up the sperm. The second phase of ejaculation—named the expulsion phase—consists of the propulsion of sperm from the prostatic ureter all the way to the exterior of the penis. The expulsion is carried out through a series of contractions from the urethral bulb and the bulbospongious and ischiocavernous muscles. The emission phase and the expulsion phase are both reflexes. A man can't control either of these by will, effort or determination.

"The moment where the emission phase begins is called 'point of no return.' We use that expression because once the emission phase is set off, you can no longer turn back. The two phases take place one after the other and ejaculation occurs without your being able to prevent it or slow it down. The only way you can control the moment of arrival of your ejaculation is to remain at sexual excitation levels inferior to those that provoke the ejaculatory reflex. In other words, you must keep yourself at excitement levels below the point of no return.

"To keep your distance from the point of no return, you must first identify the sensations that arise at this precise moment in your body. Certain men describe these sensations with phrases such as 'I'm coming,' or 'It's gone' or 'I can't control myself any longer.'

"After this you must recognize the signs that appear just before the point of no return and which indicate its imminence. These include heightening of pleasure, increase of muscular tension, quickening of respiratory rhythm, increase of the speed of movements, the nearing of the testicles against the body and the inrush of particular sensations at the level of the genital organs. The last sensations are the most specific and the most important ones to detect. For example, most men say they feel swelling and increased rigidity of the penis at that very moment. A large number report the presence of a 'current' or of 'shivers' running right through their penis. The knowledge and perception of these reactions will allow you to identify what level of sexual excitation you could reach during sex without prompting ejaculation."

"So how do you prevent sexual excitation from rising out of control?" Michael asked eagerly.

"Well, there are three ways to go about this. The first consists of controlling the amount of stimulation a man receives. In this way, he doesn't get too excited and could keep his excitation level under the threshold that sets off the ejaculatory reflex. This is the approach that was made popular by Masters and Johnson in their book *Human Sexual Inadequacies* published in 1970. These two therapists invented the 'squeeze technique.' This procedure consists of a woman stimulating the penis and then compressing it when the man signals to her that he is getting very aroused. Like this, the man's sexual excitation is interrupted and doesn't reach the necessary level required to release the ejaculatory reflex. The couple then carries on with intercourse and when the male once again becomes too excited, the woman squeezes the penis another time. They continue like this to the point of mutual satisfaction, or until the man is no longer able to control himself. You will find a more detailed description of this therapy in their book.

"Although this technique is very effective in slowing down the arrival of ejaculation, it has several drawbacks. The most serious being that it interrupts the natural flow of sexual activity. Because of its mechanical nature, it counteracts the romantic ambience that most people try to create during their sexual relations and harms the progression of erotic exchanges.

"Another major disadvantage is that the technique literally entrusts a man's means of controlling his sexual excitement in the hands of a woman. This comprises a number of disadvantages. First of all, the man doesn't learn to deal with his internal processes. He doesn't learn how to handle his sexual excitement by himself. He simply learns to rely on his partner. Then, if they should separate, he has to start all over again with his new partner. This leaves him with no other choice but to explain to his new partner what premature ejaculation is all about, to convince her to follow a treatment, to motivate her to participate in the exercises.... I'm sure you can imagine all the difficulties he risks encountering.

"Finally, the therapy by Masters and Johnson could only be followed as a couple. Bachelors and men who aren't in the position to go in for therapy with their partner cannot benefit from this approach. This excludes a large segment of the population.

"There exist more simple ways than penile compression to limit the quantity of stimulation that a male receives. The couple could, for example, take breaks, alternate the rhythms of intercourse, vary the speed of their movements, change positions and so on. I will explain to you later how it's possible to make these moments pleasurable for both you and your partner.

"To sum up, the first concrete approach aims to control the amount of stimulation a man receives to prevent his sexual excitation level from rising too high and consequently from releasing the ejaculatory reflex."

"And the other approaches?" asked Michael, leaning forward in his armchair. He wanted to know more. Never in his life did he expect a therapist to provide a client with so much information. For the first time, someone was making him understand what was going on inside of him.

"We're getting to that. We will now move on to the second approach. This approach consists of reversing the physical reactions caused by sexual excitation. We know that a number of different reactions are produced in a man's body when he becomes aroused. His heart beats faster, his pupils dilate, the vasocongestion of his genital organs provokes an erection, his muscle tension increases, et cetera. What he must do then is to reverse these reactions, which is to say he must reduce their intensity and his sexual excitement level will drop accordingly. However, we all know it's extremely difficult to intervene directly in the number of times the heart beats, the dilation of pupils or the vasocongestion of the genitals. It's much easier to control our muscular tension. Therefore, these are the reactions a man must monitor.

"I'll explain. When we become aroused, most of the muscles in our body, and in particular the gluteus muscles, the crotch muscles, the inner thigh muscles, the abdominal muscles and the thoracic muscles, contract. If a man decides during sexual relations to reverse these reactions, that is to say reduce the tension of these muscles, he will lower his sexual excitement. And by decreasing his sexual excitement, he stays away from the ejaculatory reflex.

"Sexual arousal is intimately interconnected with muscular tension. When sexual excitation rises, so does muscular tension. As soon as muscular tension diminishes, sexual excitation lessens. This is amazing because it teaches us that by modulating our muscular tension—which is to say by relaxing certain muscles—we can modulate the course of our excitement. We are, therefore, in control of slowing down the arrival of ejaculation and prolonging our pleasure."

"So what's the difference between this program and a course in relaxation?" Michael asked, intrigued.

"A relaxation course teaches you how to relax when you aren't moving. Within this program, you learn how to relax when you are active. This is very important because during sexual relations you are not immobile but active, you're moving and you have to be able to control the degree of tension in your muscles at this particular time. The approach differs greatly from traditional relaxation. Here's an example: If you want to learn how to swim, draw or drive a car, you won't enroll in a relaxation course. You'll take swimming, drawing or driving classes. The same thing applies for sexuality. There are specific skills you must get to know and this program is designed to teach them to you.

"Let's move along to our third point: sensuality. The more sensual a man is, the greater his chances are of lasting longer."

Michael raised his eyebrows questioningly.

"I'll explain," continued the sex therapist. "To act in a sensual manner requires you to take the time during sexual activities to feel your partner, touch her, savour her, taste her and enjoy her. It means slowing down, breathing and letting yourself go. It's about loving and allowing yourself to be loved. Metaphorically speaking, it's like appreciating the journey you're on and not only the destination to which you are heading.

"And from a technical point of view, when we're sensual and take our time everything goes more slowly and more gently. We don't anxiously seek stimulation. The muscles in our body are less tense. Our sexual excitement remains at a lower level. And we stay further away from the ejaculatory reflex.

"If we just take a few minutes to think about this, we realize that a sensual man is an individual who moves slowly and with a minimum degree of muscular tension. He can't be sensual and at the same time move along at a feverish speed. He can't savour an erotic experience and at the same time act as stiff as a slab of iron. We know that a febrile emotional state combined with extreme muscular tension quickly leads to ejaculation. But slower movements and less muscular tension produce the contrary effect. Sensuality, therefore, simply because of the slowness of movements and the little muscular tension it induces, gives a man the means to control himself. It naturally leads a man to behave in the technically appropriate manner needed for him not to ejaculate too early.

"In another respect, when a man goes slowly, alternates the rhythm of penetration, varies the speed of his movements, relaxes his muscles and breathes more deeply, by force of circumstance he becomes sensual.

"You can see how in the end technique and sensuality come together. That's why the program you're going to follow incorporates the three approaches I just spoke to you about. As a result of the training you will receive, you'll be able to control the amount of stimulation you receive. You will know how to reverse the physical reactions caused by sexual excitement. And you'll acquire new attitudes that will cause you to become a more sensual man. Thus, your excitement level will become more manageable and your sex life will become more satisfying. Finally, your partner will appreciate you not only because you'll be able to last longer but because you'll be a much better lover."

Michael was hanging onto every one of Dr. Carter's words. He had to admit that what the therapist was saying made sense. However, he wondered about the program's actual effectiveness and what the chances were that it would work for him. And he doubted if all of this could be applied in reality. Michael had zillions of questions, but he decided to let the doctor finish with his explanations before asking them.

"On the other hand, I should tell you that there's a good chance that you'll need therapy. We could work on treating certain anxieties or certain ways you behave with women, for example. But we'll see about this when the time comes."

"How long does this take in all?"

"The program necessitates twelve separate appointments and because of my heavy schedule, we'll only be able to do one a day. As for the therapeutic interventions, they rarely require more than five sessions."

Michael did some quick math. There wasn't much time before his TV show and Vanessa was coming back in less than two months. "Would it be possible to get through the program any quicker, since I have to get back to Seattle very soon? Could we skip over some of the less important lessons, perhaps?"

"I understand your eagerness, but unfortunately, that isn't possible. The elements in this program are all connected. And they are learned in a progressive manner. You have to tackle the first step to move along to the second, and then once you succeed you are fully prepared to master the third stage. This approach was clinically tested on several hundred men and proven in an experimental study within a university setting. It's based on sex therapy, physiology and psychological knowledge, and its effectiveness has been confirmed by scientific research. In the past, people spent two to four years in psychoanalysis to obtain results that were more than disappointing. During the age of Masters and Johnson, it took about a dozen two-hour sessions. Now, a dozen half-hour sessions will do. Maybe one day we'll find a faster procedure. But we haven't quite gotten there yet."

"And if we do two back-to-back sessions every time we meet...will this affect the treatment?"

"No, it won't change a thing. Gee, you're a tough one! I had not anticipated this, let me think.... That means we'll finish at eleven o'clock. That's really very late..."

Michael kept quiet.

"Well, all right. I'll rearrange my schedule considering the urgency of the matter. However, it won't be possible to get through the program in six consecutive days. I already made commitments this weekend. We'll meet for two half-hour sessions on the following days. How does that sound to you?"

"Perfect. You're very conciliatory and I appreciate that a lot. Before I go, I'd like to ask you one last question: The fact that I have no partner—will this create any problems?"

"No. This program was specifically designed for men who don't have a partner or for those whose partner isn't participating in the treatment. And clinical research has demonstrated that it is as effective as the program for couples."

"Great! So when do we meet next?"

"Tomorrow evening, at ten?"

"Okay, doctor. And thank you once again for taking me in at this late hour."

Michael returned to his hotel room full of optimism. He had been won over by Dr. Carter's professionalism and friendly nature. His explanations gained his confidence and his laid-back style made the atmosphere a lot more comfortable. All that was left now was to wait and see if this therapy would work for him.

CHAPTER 19

T ension was mounting in the UN camp. Terrorized refugees, arriving in endless droves, recounted stories of appalling atroci ties, one more stomach-wrenching than the next. The medical staff was swamped with casualties of all sorts and extremes. Certain survivors of the massacres perpetrated by General El Tabernasti's government soldiers reported terrifying incidents of beatings and dismemberment.

The insurgents from the south of Sambizania withdrew in chaotic disorder and their retreat was transformed into bloody defeat. The rebel villages fell one after the other into the hands of the northern troops. Under their control, civilians were subjected to the worst conceivable cruelty. The women were brutally raped and the villages were torched after being systematically looted. The survivors were forced to flee to other regions for, with their crops burned, they were facing famine. The destruction was ordered with the goal of regrouping the people in villages controlled by the army. There, the government proceeded with religious conversions more or less freely consented to in exchange for food and safety.

One part of the southern population refused to convert despite all of this forced integration and sought refuge with the peacekeepers. The camp headed by the UN couldn't accommodate this new wave of refugees. Consequently, the majority of them ended up in Kiboyo, one of the last villages of the south that had not been destroyed by the government troops.

Colonel Robert Tellier, who was in charge of the UN detachment, was a brilliant soldier and a good-hearted man. He suffered inwardly knowing his armed soldiers were on orders to stand by while more and more innocent people were going to be massacred. When he received word that the village of Kiboyo was going to fall into the hands of the Sambizanian government troops, he implored UN headquarters to let him freely intervene. After interminable procrastination, he was reminded that his UN mandate prohibited him from taking any offensive action. However, they gave him permission to extend the civilian protection zone by fifty kilometers. Normally, UN decisions were made incredibly slowly so that once granted they no longer corresponded to the reality of the area where they were to be applied. This time around was no exception to the rule. And that's why the colonel decided to secure the protection of the village of Kiboyo, despite the fact that as far as reinforcements went he had not yet received any more men or equipment.

The moment they were brought up-to-date, the CNN journalists requested permission to cover the operation. Jimmy equally expressed his desire to accompany them. As for Vanessa, before making up her mind, she decided to get Lieutenant Demat's opinion. She found him busy reading a military map.

"What do you think of this operation, lieutenant?" the journalist asked him.

He raised his eyes and replied: "I see you already know about it. There are no longer any secrets here. The enemy must also be aware of this!" He folded up his map and stuffed it into his bag. "Sit down, I'll tell you what I think. According to me, it's completely foolish! On the one hand, I admit that it revolts me to let women and children get slaughtered at our doorstep. What's more, our men are very motivated, they want to fight. But on the other hand, we also have to be realistic; the human and material resources at our disposal are totally insufficient. The colonel wants to send me out with my marine infantry platoon and Lieutenant Burton's four armored vehicles. That brings us up to around sixty men. And the Sambizanian troops in question, how many do you think they are?"

Vanessa had no idea, but the lieutenant's remarks worried her. "How many?" she asked, faintly.

"In reality, we don't know a thing," replied Edouard. "And that's the problem, we don't know a damn thing! There could be a hundred, a thousand or ten thousand of them for all we know! The colonel maintains that they don't have any heavy artillery and that our light-weight tanks should cause them to retreat. Pictures furnished by Helios, the European observation satellite, indicate no traces of any heavy artillery, assault tank, or combat helicopter in the vicinity of Kiboyo. The photos also don't reveal any heavy concentrations of trucks or other types of vehicles. Unfortunately, the European satellite's resolution is limited to one meter. It's impossible to know if the government troops possess any machine guns, mortars, bazoo-kas, portable missiles or any other light arms. The American military satellite Kennan could give us more details. It possesses a resolution of only fifteen centimeters! But unfortunately, for reasons of military secrecy, they don't want to provide us with these images.

"The colonel has my utmost confidence, he's an intelligent man. He has promised us reinforcements in case of any problems. What does worry me is that the chief of the operations is Captain Muller. He's the most incompetent officer I know. He only came here so he could buy a new car with the risk premium. For my first real difficult mission, it's nauseating to find myself once again under his orders. I'm really unlucky. If I was in your place, I'd leave tomorrow on the first convoy heading to Kenya."

That's exactly what Vanessa wanted to do. But her pride was at stake. Greg Bryan and William Honneker, the CNN reporters, and Jimmy all wanted to participate in the action. It was too late—there was no turning back for her.

* * *

A flock of pelicans flew gracefully above the Atlantic Ocean. Stretched out on the sandy shore of West Palm Beach, Michael was sifting through a series of photos given to him by Mario Bilodeau. He finally tracked down the mystery man in a Miami hospital. A stranger had jumped him and snatched his wallet. He had also beaten him with a baseball bat with brutish violence. After several days in a coma, Iguana miraculously came to life, sustaining, however, a bad case of aphasia caused by the multiple blows he had received to the head during the attack. Incapable of speaking, he had communicated with Michael through writing. He confirmed then that Jack Kotten was involved in laundering money coming from the drug trade.

Dave had skillfully collected all the proof exposing Kotten's implication in the recycling of dirty money. He hadn't been able to glean a single trace of information supporting the hypothesis that the U.S. presidential candidate had ordered the assassination of Senator Davidson. Then, just before Dave's death, a notorious drug trafficker, a rival to Jack Kotten, had contacted him. They called him *Muerte Blanca*—white death in Spanish—giving a pretty good idea of the guy's character. He gave Dave a videocassette showing Jack Kotten asking Christopher Clays to kill the old senator. For months, Muerte Blanca monitored Kotten closely to eliminate him from the market— legally.

Mario Bilodeau had serious doubts regarding the authenticity of the tape. It's not hard today to tamper with a videocassette to make it look like something it isn't. On the one hand, it would be very easy to validate the authenticity of the videocassette by bringing it in to specialists in the field; on the other hand, it was disturbing to note that Christopher Clays took a flight to Washington the day of Davidson's assassination. But whatever the case might be, Mario Bilodeau had no idea where the video could now be found and he didn't know how to get in touch with Muerte Blanca. The Davidson affair had thus reached an impasse.

Michael took a second look at the photographs he got from Bilodeau. In some, Jack Kotten was photographed alone. In others, he stood in the company of diverse personalities as well as influential political figures such as Norman Gordon and Jesse Smith. Michael's gaze rested on a picture of a man dressed in black pants and a polo shirt. According to Bilodeau, the young man in the picture was Christopher Clays—the thug who took care of Kotten's dirty work. Unfortunately, the face said absolutely nothing to him. In the end, the pictures proved to be of little use and Michael couldn't help feel that his investigation was going nowhere.

Thirsty, Michael left the beach and went to have a tall glass of grapefruit juice at Café Australian Wind located near the hotel. Contrary to the opinion of the tanned server who suggested a table on the patio in the sun, Michael opted for a shady place to go over his notes on the Davidson affair.

To add some Australian ambience to his establishment, the owner replaced the classic cocktail stick with miniature-shaped boomerangs. The gadget proved to be more original than practical. Michael ended up spilling the fruit juice over his documents. A cute redhead sitting at the table in front of him noted his clumsiness with a smile that basically said, "It's nothing, look on the bright side of life." Michael reciprocated with a facial expression that could have been translated as, "You're right, this little incident won't spoil such a beautiful day." And then he went back to his paperwork.

This momentary exchange of smiles had revealed to him a young woman with a friendly face. She was chatting with two girlfriends and everything seemed to amuse her. Although her face was speckled with too many freckles, her infectious smile made her almost pretty. Michael raised his eyes several times to get a better look at the young woman. A long curly mane of hair cascaded over her narrow shoulders, which were so thin that she appeared fragile. A tight baby blue T-shirt hugged two small, perky breasts. She radiated *joie de vivre* and her spontaneous gestures were marked with grace and youthfulness.

Michael and the young woman exchanged glances more and more frequently. A connection was forming between them. When he dove back into his documents, he could no longer read. His mind was already wandering in the company of his ravishing table neighbor. As does often happen under similar circumstances, the more he looked at her, the prettier he found her. He told himself that maybe this was the right time to put into practice Dr. Carter's techniques.

Suddenly she stood up with her two friends: one, a sandy-haired blond who was a little on the plump side and the other, a brunette who wore too much makeup. Michael was caught off guard. They were leaving before he even had a chance to make contact with the young woman.

However, after a few seconds of hesitation and much to Michael's surprise, the brunette walked up to him. She pointed to the redhead and said, "My friend wants to know if you're Michael Lancaster from the show *It Concerns Us?*"

Michael didn't reply. His facial features stiffened like that of an ice sculpture.

"Do you mind if we take a picture of you beside Sandra?" added the brunette, batting her eyelashes, which were thickly coated with mascara.

Without waiting for an answer, she whipped out a tiny disposable camera from her backpack, stepped back three paces and framed Michael in the lens. The frail redhead slid by his side. She giggled nervously then gave Michael a kiss on the cheek and took off with her friends.

* * *

Michael was taking refuge at the West Palm Beach municipal library. Here, he hoped to enjoy the tranquillity and the anonymity needed to pursue his investigation.

Sitting in a far corner of the reading room facing a wall, Michael limited the risk of distraction by an admirer. He folded his hands under his chin and thought back to this latest incident. The young redhead would have followed him into a hotel room without much persuasion. She seemed perfectly open to the possibility. She would probably even have bragged about the whole thing with her friends. And that's exactly what stalled Michael. Knowing that a woman would sleep with him just because of his celebrity status made his stomach turn. It corresponded too closely to prostitution or to the abuse of power. He wanted no part of that.

He couldn't avoid women for the rest of his life. Obviously, there was Vanessa. But right now she was a world away. Was there only one chance in existence to win her back? Perhaps. But he would try to, no matter what. In any case, supposing Dr. Carter's method was actually effective, wouldn't it be better to play it safe and first test things out a few times with another woman before trying his fate again with Vanessa? Under these conditions, it would be okay to have a fling with a stranger.

He had to be careful, though. His own safety was at stake. It was best that Kotten's gang remain unaware that he was in Florida investigating. What Michael didn't know, however, was that they already knew his exact whereabouts in West Palm Beach.

*** * * ***

The last golden-red rays of the sun were quickly setting on the African savannah. While heading back to her tent, Vanessa spotted the two CNN reporters cooking hamburgers on an open fire.

"You want one?" Greg called out to her. "I even have some mustard and relish!"

Vanessa's mouth was already watering at the mere thought of eating a real American hamburger.

"And I managed to get six cans of Coke too! " Greg boasted happily. "The cook gave them to me in exchange for a Zippo. Come and join us in our feast!"

Vanessa sat beside the journalists and devoured two medium-rare hamburgers. "That was the best meal I've had in a long time," she said, smacking her lips together.

Greg flashed her a gracious smile, showing off a perfect set of teeth. He had a square face and his blond brush cut accentuated his features. He was from Georgia and spoke with a Southern drawl. "It's a lot harder this time around than in the Gulf War. Over there, we had the entire infrastructure of the American army at our disposal. Here, I get the feeling I'm in a scout camp. On the up side, the heat is a lot more bearable than it was in Saudi Arabia."

"Really?" Vanessa said, surprised. "I'm dying of heat. I'd give anything to take a long shower in my apartment back in Seattle."

"You're from Seattle?" William asked, in his deep voice. "I'm from Tulsa, Oklahoma. I haven't been back there since I got married."

"You married?" Vanessa took a huge gulp of her cola.

"Six years, two children. My wife wants me to stop covering these foreign events. She's afraid I'm going to get hurt one of these days and of course, she'd like us to spend more time together."

"Women! They're all the same!" Greg joked. "They dream of a wild adventurer and as soon as they get married, he's expected to transform into a family man."

"That's not true," retorted Vanessa. "What we want is a man who assumes his responsibilities."

Greg got serious all of a sudden and explained his point of view: "Like William, I have two children and I'd love to see them more often. But we don't have a choice. It's not easy to find a job that pays as well as this one does. I have to secure their future. I also know myself well enough to realize that I'd be miserable working as a public servant. It's true that my family misses me. My oldest son turned nine years old yesterday and I wasn't there to celebrate his birthday. In three days, my wife and I will be celebrating our ten-year anniversary. I would have loved to arrange something special for her, you know, maybe a weekend in Las Vegas or a week in Florida. But I'm going to miss that occasion as well."

"You could always do that when you get back," suggested William.

"I know, but it's not the same thing. When I was little, we always celebrated my birthday on another day. My father was a traveling salesman so we always took advantage of his rare stopovers at home to organize parties and celebrate holidays. It really bugged me having to receive my gifts a month in advance or one week late. My mother always complained of being left alone in the house. I realize, that in fact, I'm repeating the same scenario as my father." Greg turned his gaze toward the fire. A long silence followed.

William got the conversation rolling again. "I would sure like to be on the other side of the Atlantic surrounded by my family at this very moment. But I believe that I'm providing an indispensable service over here. I think that the world, to become a better place, needs journalists like us who sacrifice a part of their comfort and their family life to inform people. We must expose all types of oppression that humanity suffers. Suppose no one cared about foreign events; the dictators in this world would do and act however they pleased with complete impunity. If the horrors of Nazi concentration camps still haunt our memories today, it's in part because of the images the journalists of that time brought back to us. We are the eyes of America. And also its conscience."

Greg interjected in a weary voice: "We know all of this, William. But what is the greatest ideal in the world worth when faced with the sad look in the eyes of your son who asks you, 'Dad, why are you leaving again?'"

CHAPTER 20

M ichael returned to the library, which was full of retirees consulting the computer files and surfing the Internet. He planned
to access newspapers from previous years and find out more about
the careers of Jack Kotten and General Kulliger. This would complement the information obtained by Dave.

The computers providing access to execute the bibliographical
research were too few in number and often out of order. It was necessary to wait in line to use one. When Michael finally got a terminal,
he dug up references on the main national dailies. After that, he attempted to find articles in each of them, which during the last four
years referred to either Kotten or Kulliger, and print them out.

Regrettably, his research traced only two articles and the findings
turned out to be unexceptional. He headed from there to the information desk. An elegant librarian with an oval face and a fair complexion
was tending amiably to the queries of the various visitors. When
Michael came around, however, she was already dealing with someone and he had to settle for her colleague who appeared less
personable.

The man had almost no hair and wore a tiny pair of glasses atop
a nose the size of an anteater's. The right flap of his bifocal spec-
tacles had been roughly stuck back together with model glue. He
raised his heavy eyelids when Michael addressed him with a friendly,
"Good afternoon."

"Afternoon," grunted the old man.

"Can you show me how I could find information on these two public figures in the following newspapers?" Michael held out his list of references.

The bald-headed librarian drew the piece of paper from him with the tips of his fingers as if it were a glob of used chewing gum from a tuberculosis patient.

"Our computers are not equipped with the programs needed for this type of research," muttered the employee without lifting his eyes.

"Do you know where I could go?"

"No, I don't."

A feminine hand suddenly snatched Michael's reference list. The pretty librarian had come to his rescue. Janice Spalding signaled for Michael to come with her. "I'll see what I can do for you," she offered.

Michael followed her all the way to the other end of the large room of periodicals. He took advantage of this time to admire the graceful movement of her hips, which swayed in rhythm to her gait that was both supple and determined. Janice was wearing dark, conservative clothing that muted the shapely curves of her body. However, the somber pair of navy blue pants couldn't completely conceal the splendor of her behind. The image that spontaneously jumped into Michael's mind was that of a delicious ripe peach. He would have liked to sink his teeth into it.

They headed toward a small office in a remote corner of the vast building. The room, reserved for library staff, contained just enough space for a dilapidated desk recovered from a former elementary school. The polished wood of this outdated piece of furniture glistened under the yellowish light of an electric bulb. The cramped area was windowless and smelled stale. Ironically, the compact office was enriched with a brand new powerful computer.

Janice rested her round bottom on a rickety chair as ancient as the desk and started up the computer. Her slender fingers, with nails cut short like a sportswoman's, tapped away on the keyboard.

"With this computer here, we'll be able to find what you need," said Janice, throwing a quick sidelong glance at Michael.

While she scrutinized the screen, Michael observed Janice's facial features. She was actually quite attractive. The small scar across her upper lip, far from disfiguring her, drew attention to a delectably full mouth. Michael imagined the lush contact these beautiful velvet-smooth lips would bring to his own.

Janice frowned. A small vertical wrinkle formed between her large dark eyes, which shone with metallic brilliance from the light of the terminal. She couldn't find the information she was looking for. At the same time she jotted down multiple coordinates on a scrap envelope, she lightly bit her bottom lip. Even though this action was obviously done out of annoyance, it in fact emitted a raw sexiness. The pretty employee's white teeth delicately grabbed the rim of her mouth and then let it go with a really sensual slowness.

A second later, still staring straight at the screen, Janice seized the rounded extremity of the pencil between her incisors. She tapped the keyboard a few times and then her fingers stroked the writing instrument planted in her mouth. Finally, she withdrew the pencil, which slid languidly down the shiny mucous membrane of her lip before landing against her chin.

The lovely librarian's gestures were so natural that they would have simply passed for involuntary mannerisms. However, Michael interpreted them as a terribly erotic invitation. He felt the beginning of an erection in his pants.

"Here we go; I found the articles you were looking for," Janice declared, cutting short Michael's thoughts. "I'm printing them off right now on the central printer."

"Fine!" Michael heard himself say in a huskier voice than he would have liked.

Janice got up quickly and went toward the door, whereas Michael would have liked to prolong the conversation.

"Thanks for your kindness. The identical search would have taken me hours."

"It's just a matter of habit."

"You seem to know your way around the computer."

"It's a favorite hobby of mine."

"That surprises me, I would have thought you were the sporty type."

"What makes you think that?" inquired Janice, giving him a look that was more amused than interrogative.

Michael displayed an affable smile. He had finally reached his objective: a conversation tinged with seduction had begun. He continued on in the same tone, "Just by the way you walk. Your steps are flexible and strong. Furthermore, your nails are short, and I'd be surprised if you bite them. And, well, you seem to be in fantastic physical shape."

Janice stretched out her hand and looked at her fingernails.

"You're very observant. I do indeed regularly play beach volleyball. Are you a police officer?"

"No. I work in television."

Michael rejoiced inside. She didn't seem to recognize him. Could she be one of the odd people who didn't know his show?

"I must confess to you that I never watch television. Between work, volleyball, exercise and my passion for computers, I don't have much time for it."

Michael extended his hand. "My name is Michael."

* * *

A few hours later, Michael was sitting on the edge of his seat in the sex therapist's office. He was listening attentively to Dr. Carter's explanations. The therapist, his features creased by the day's fatigue, was speaking more slowly than usual. "As I explained yesterday, each session of the program is divided into two parts. In the first part, I will give you information on sexuality. With this material, you'll be able to maintain better control over your excitation and enjoy a more satisfying sex life. The second part consists of practical exercises. These exercises are easy to learn and with time, will become second nature. The best part is that they won't seem artificial at all. They'll become easily integrated in your lovemaking style and your partner will not be able to tell that you've gone through therapy. And trust me, you won't be mistaken for a machine. Your companion will only notice the improvement in your lovemaking and that you've become a better lover."

"A better lover...really?" Michael said, giving the sex therapist a funny side-glance. His facial expression denoted a hint of suspicion like on the day when his friend Dave showed him with his hands the impressive size of the last pike he had caught.

"Yes, really," replied Dr. Carter without the least bit of hesitation.

Michael had heard too many wild propositions that didn't hold up to their promises to take the therapist's words at face value. He said nothing, but his entire body expressed the reservations of his thoughts.

Dr. Carter discovered a long time ago that it was no use trying to convince a client verbally. He preferred the patient to recognize and admit the effectiveness of the technique on his own. So, like a pianist cutting into Beethoven's Ninth Symphony, he plunged into the heart of the subject without further delay. He took a deep breath and declared in a no-nonsense voice, "We will now start our first session. If I understood you correctly, your primary reason for being here is to learn how to sustain intercourse long enough to satisfy your partner?"

"Exactly."

"Your goal is laudable, I must admit. However, it's essential for you to know that just being inside her vagina a long time doesn't necessarily give a woman more pleasure. And it could produce the opposite effect. In order for a lengthy intercourse to be enjoyable, it must be carried out with a clear understanding of the nature of feminine eroticism. I can't begin to tell you how many women have confessed to me in therapy of having their mind on something else while making love. They think of how they're going to dress the kids for school in the morning or what they're going to make for the next meal. There's nothing erotic about that!

"Forced to reflect on the reasons behind this disinterest, I discovered that the way in which a man approaches his wife plays a primary role. This is how most men lead into sexual contact: They kiss their partner a little, linger around her chest area, stimulate her clitoris at length and then move quickly to intromission. So even if intercourse lasts a long time, these women quickly switch off because they've been led along a path that doesn't really mean much to them. In fact, these men come onto their mate the way they like to be approached— through the genitals."

Michael didn't have a hard time identifying himself as one of those men. In fact, to compensate for his sexual shortcomings, he had read dozens of books on lovemaking techniques and on the thousands of ways to make a woman orgasm. But this didn't seem to be what the sex therapist wanted to talk to him about.

"What's important, is not the quantity of stimulation but the quality of the sexual encounter. It is in your best interest to remember that in general women like to experience their sexuality in a romantic ambience. This ambience breaks away from the daily routine and is characterized by the presence of affection, tenderness and emotions. It rests on elements such as sharing, creativity and spontaneity.

"Creating a romantic atmosphere doesn't mean to say that you always have to watch a sunset on a beach in Mexico, visit the castles of the Loire or travel by gondola in Venice. In other words, you don't have to spend a fortune or invest a lot of time whenever you want to ignite some sort of a romantic spark. Going out to a movie, taking a drive in the country, eating at a restaurant, walking around your neighborhood in the evening, having supper by candlelight, talking or simply watching television sitting beside each other on the sofa are all activities that draw couples closer together and induce loving feelings. Such a setting is beneficial to a woman because it awakens her sensitivity and creates a mood conducive to kindle her sensuality.

"As I mentioned a moment ago, tenderness, emotions and affection play significant roles in a woman's sexuality. In fact, they are so important they could be considered the front door to her sexuality. In what regions of the body do you think tenderness, emotions and affection reside?"

Michael suddenly felt stupid. He couldn't believe that he—who had successfully completed a university degree in law and whose profession as a journalist kept him informed on everything that went on in the world—didn't know how to respond. A good sport, he admitted his ignorance: "I have absolutely no idea," he replied laughing. "But I'll take a guess and say everywhere! Affection and love could be experienced throughout the body. A man could touch a woman tenderly all over the body."

"You're partially right: A man can touch a woman anywhere with tenderness. However, her body won't always perceive this touch to be romantic; it all depends on the area you are touching. For example, the same caress will be interpreted as affectionate on the shoulder whereas if rendered on the butt, it will carry a sexual connotation. There exists a geographical map of the human body. The area that corresponds to tenderness, affection and love—called sentimental polarity—is situated in the upper part of the body. It encompasses the top of the hands, forearms and arms, the shoulders, the upper back, the back of the neck, the head and the forehead. It's clearly distinguishable from the 'genital polarity' that is found in the center of the body and comprises the inner thigh, the stomach, the breasts, the buttocks and the genital area. From the sentimental polarity, the insides of the hands, forearms and arms, the sides and front of the neck, the top of the chest, the cheeks and the mouth are also excluded, as they already constitute erogenous zones."

"But, of course! And the sentimental polarity corresponds as well to the region we touch when we comfort or make someone feel safe and secure, right?"

"That's correct. Consequently, when you caress your mate, it's preferable that you begin at the top of the body and not at the center. Very few women like to continually start sexual relations by having their breasts or genitals fondled. Most of the time a focused approach on the genital organs antagonizes women more than anything else and they don't get turned on. Women prefer to start off by holding hands, being held in your arms or having you play with their hair. They then become receptive to kisses and more sexual touches. Afterward you can extend caresses throughout the body: the sides, belly, breasts, hips, legs, buttocks and the genitals.

"One method of fondling the genital area is to start by the pubis. After that, you move to the large lips, to the small lips and then to the clitoris. The clitoris could be approached a thousand different ways: in and out movements along the shaft, pinching, rolling and pushes on the pubis all constitute appropriate forms of stimulation. It's best to avoid direct contact with the gland for in the majority of cases it is a hypersensitive organ.

"Finally, you prepare the vagina for the coming act of penetration. The vagina responds favorably to different forms of pressure as opposed to light touches. That's why it's preferable to exercise pressure with your fingers against the vagina's wall instead of carrying out in and out movements along it. The pushes should be applied slowly and with force. They facilitate the awakening of the woman's deep sensitivity and favor access to her interiority.

"The procedure I just described to you isn't immutable. It is recommended you vary your approach. You should diversify the way you fondle, kiss and embrace your partner. If you always follow the same routine, it's very likely that your partner will get bored quickly. Using the method of progression I taught you—stimulating the upper part of the body before the lower part of the body—really works. And moreover, it contributes to countering the tendency among men to race toward a woman's breasts and genital organs at the start of sexual relations.

"Clearly, this all takes place interactively with your companion. The woman participates as much as a man does in sexual exchanges. She is neither passive nor overly aggressive. A man has only to approach a woman in a manner suitable to the feminine psyche and physiology. Besides, women also have guidelines to respect if they desire to be in harmony with their partner. Women should always keep in mind, for example, that the departure point for male sexuality is situated in the center of the body and not the upper part of the body like it is for them."

"I agree with you completely. It's very important for a woman to get involved in and participate in sexual exchanges. But this notion of differences between women and men doesn't exactly concur with the thrust of most feminist theories, right?" asked Michael, with a bit of humor.

The overly tired sex therapist perked up and burst out laughing: "No, I don't think it does! And I will tell you that although I adhere entirely to the principles of equality and respect between the sexes, I do not share some of their more extreme views. You know, with all the politically correct people in this world who go around distorting our remarks, the field isn't always easy. A colleague of mine, who's a professor, was accused of sexism by some of his female university students. He mentioned in his course that receptivity constituted one of the fundamental characteristics of female sexuality. The students reproached him for devaluing the woman by forcing her into passivity. All of this sparked because they associated receptivity, the act of a woman welcoming a man inside of her, with passivity, the fact of being submissive and inactive. It's very sad and unfortunate because in our society, we confuse equality with resemblance: To be equal, you have to be the same. In order for a woman to enjoy the same rights as a man, she must be similar to him, hold the same occupation, share the same pastimes and get excited in the same way. We deny our differences for fear of sinking into inequality. And yet, what sets us apart holds incommensurable richness."

Michael shot a quick glance at the large black watch wrapped around his left wrist.

Catching him, Dr. Carter commented, "I've been intrigued by your watch for some time now. Its unusual form makes me think of a miniature transmitter-receiver I once saw in a sci-fi movie."

Michael smiled. "You have a wild imagination, doctor! Sorry to disappoint you, but it's merely a watch equipped with a monitoring device that indicates my heartbeat when I train."

"I have one of those too, but I guess mine is a more conventional model. Okay, let's go on with our session. But before beginning our exercises I would like to mention the following principles. It's recommended the next time you engage in sexual relations that you apply the techniques of control from the start of sexual activity—meaning from the first caress and the first kiss. At this time, your sexual excitation will not be too high and it will be easier for you to learn how to modulate your sexual excitement. It will be important to apply these techniques before, during and after the intromission of the penis into the vagina. The reason being that these moments are very sexually arousing and they risk provoking ejaculation without your knowledge. Finally, it will be advantageous to apply these techniques during intercourse when sexual excitation generally soars to very high levels. And the same goes even if you're still far away from the point of no return. Actually, waiting until you get close to the point of no return to employ the techniques is always very risky. And what is more, is that it puts you in a very urgent situation, which can in the end hinder the erotic nature of your sexual encounters. Everything okay so far?"

"Yes, it's very clear. Now, it's just a matter of doing it!"

"All right, to help you out, we're going to move right along to our exercises. We'll start with breathing. I want you to sit comfortably in the chair; arms opened and legs apart. You will keep your eyes open and breathe with your mouth half-open. To have better control over the moment of the arrival of your ejaculation, it's best to keep your limbs open, unfolded, away from your body.

"Now let me explain the reason for all of this. When we have our eyes closed, we have a tendency to concentrate more on the penile sensations and curl oneself up. What this does is converge the sexual tension in the pelvic region and thus spur ejaculation.

"As far as the mouth goes, it's preferable to keep it half-open so that air could enter and escape from it. When the mouth is half open, air escapes more freely from the thoracic cage than when we breathe from the nose. Consequently, the pressure inside of the thoracic cage diminishes more rapidly. When there is less pressure inside of the thoracic cage, it is easier to lower muscular tension. In addition, when the mouth is half open, the jaw muscles are relaxed and this is helpful in decreasing tension in all of the muscles of the body.

"As for the legs, the natural reaction is for them to come together when a person becomes sexually aroused. The muscles that contract are the thigh adductors. Keeping the legs spaced apart goes against this natural tendency and increases the capacity to delay ejaculation.

"Concentrate on your body…. Slowly, breathe in…feel the movement of your belly as it expands when the air penetrates inside of you…."

* * *

Right from the break of dawn, an ever-growing feverishness seized the military camp. Every soldier was carrying out his assigned task with a nervousness that was hard to disguise. The most stressed among them were the mechanics working on the maintenance of the assault vehicles.

A small but sturdy corporal-mechanic checked the engines on the tanks. His hands and arms were tattooed with gritty oil and dirt, and he grumbled loudly, "Damn dust is everywhere! Pass me wrench number seven, would you, Bruwier?"

Bruwier could count to seven, but probably not much higher. Yet when assigned to the role of worker's assistant, he carried out the tasks with paramount perfection. He went around affectionately mothering all of the tanks. Not surprisingly, everyone called him the mother hen. Bruwier's most cherished chickadees weren't the massive assault tanks, but the small troop carriers equipped with a .50 machine gun or a 20mm rapid fire canon. Each vehicle carried six men along with equipment and was armed with enough armor plating to stop small caliber bullets.

Jimmy, who was a cautious man by nature, managed to convince Lieutenant Burton to have him drive along in the command vehicle. Greg and William, who were both in good physical shape, decided they would accompany the marine infantry platoon by foot.

The men manifested their nervousness in different ways. Corporal Van Gyseghem wrote a long and tender letter to his mother while compulsively smoothing his thin mustache. Soldier Henrotte, for his part, scribbled a quick, optimistic note to his fiancée. Blondiau, nicknamed the "legionnaire" because of his filthy mouth and his firebrand spirit, sat chain-smoking while cleaning his weapon over and over again with the help of a cottonball.

Vanessa couldn't help thinking of Michael as she watched these young men, some barely eighteen years old, bravely trying to hide their fear behind a wall of false strength. He too possessed a fragile little boy side to him that he masked behind his serious public figure persona. She tried to reach him by telephone again, but either he wasn't home or simply didn't feel like answering. She left a message on his machine: "Michael...it's me. I miss you a lot. I want to see you again...soon, I hope."

The agitation in the military camp made the day pass by quickly. Vanessa, utterly exhausted, plunked herself down on a rusty vat resembling a giant beer can and closed her eyes. The pervasive odor of oil and gasoline emanating from the abandoned jerrycans lined up along the fence filled her nostrils. This acrid essence blended with the smoke coming from the cooking fires that were burning between the refugee tents in the neighboring camp. A young soldier, not yet showing any sign of facial hair, passed by her. Vanessa immediately picked up another scent—finer, more acute, more penetrating: the sweat of a man. But not simply the odor given off by perspiration triggered by toiling laboriously in tropical conditions. No, it was definitely another smell. It was the same scent Vanessa whiffed the day she accompanied her father hunting. The odor of an animal that's being tracked down, the offensive stench of someone who knows death is imminent. A nauseating wave washed over Vanessa and she forced open her eyes.

The soldier disappeared behind a jeep. Jimmy appeared from the other side of the vehicle. The spindly photographer spotted Vanessa and approached her at double speed. He was more nervous than usual and expressed himself using exaggerated hand gestures: "I managed to get you a seat on one of the armored vehicles. Come with me, we'll be safe. The Sambizanians don't have any cannons."

It was a sensible proposition. And really, although she loved walking, the prospect of being hit by a stray bullet wasn't all that attractive. It didn't require any serious contemplation on her part to accept the photographer's offer.

Happy with her choice, Jimmy flashed Vanessa a huge smile and his tiny eyes shone with an unusual sparkle. He moved closer to Vanessa and took her hand awkwardly. "I'm worried. I don't like what's about to take place. I can't stop myself from thinking about all those peacekeepers killed in Somalia, Rwanda, Bosnia and elsewhere. I wouldn't want that to happen to you.... I—"

Jimmy squeezed her hand a little harder. Vanessa pulled away her hand, but more brusquely than she would have liked. Jimmy froze, disconcerted. Then he gathered up his courage and uttered: "Vanessa, I-I-I have feelings for you.... I'm in love with you.... I'm wondering if..."

Vanessa stared at him in stunned astonishment, her eyes opened as wide as they could get.

This second reaction destroyed Jimmy. He understood clearly that he had no chance of ever conquering Vanessa. His hopes collapsed instantly, like a dynamited tenement building crumbling to the ground. He now looked even smaller, even punier, and his eyes swelled with tears.

"I'm sorry, Vanessa.... I'm sorry.... I feel so stupid.... I'm not good enough for you...."

Vanessa wanted to protest, but Jimmy didn't give her the chance. "I know what you're going to tell me, but I'd rather not hear it."

Extremely uncomfortable, Vanessa once again parted her lips to say something but a flood of words coming from the young photographer's mouth left her unable to speak for the second time. "I've thought about you so much over the years. You're always on my mind. I see you everywhere—on my vacations, in the fashion shows I shoot, in my apartment that I've been keeping clean especially for you. I have had many wild dreams about you: We would go to baseball games together and pig out on jumbo hot dogs. On Saturdays we'd rummage through local garage sales. And on Sundays we'd wash the car in the sunshine...."

Jimmy's eyes glistened like two fireflies in the African night. "I thought that one day you could love a man like me, that you would eventually have seen all the good inside of me. And that you would have found me attractive. I thought you would have been the first woman to tell me I was handsome.

"I would have taken pictures of our children at every stage in their lives, and I would have also photographed you. You would have been my personal model, my muse, my fairy princess...my dream mermaid. They would have been the most beautiful pictures in the world. Pictures of an angel—captured through the lenses of love, processed on the paper of passion. That would have been...that would have been...if only..."

The flood of words faded into the dense and humid air surrounding the camp. Jimmy finally gave up, letting his arms drop to his sides in dejected defeat. And then, with a detached look on his face, he whispered, "Tonight, I have a bad feeling that just won't go away. This mission scares me.... I...I think I'm going to die. It's stupid, I know. But I really have a premonition that tomorrow...I will see you for the last time...."

Vanessa replied gently, "There's no reason to worry, Jimmy. First of all, they would never dare to fire on UN soldiers. And we'll be sheltered inside the tanks."

But Jimmy didn't seem reassured at all. Always so chatty, he suddenly locked himself up into an eerie and disquieting silence. Vanessa had no idea what else to say. This delicate situation was making her very uncomfortable. Finally, the greatly distressed and heartbroken photographer wished her a good night and left. His shoulders bent forward and his gait shaky, he traveled the dirt road leading to his shelter without ever looking back.

Vanessa crawled under the mosquito netting draped over her bed and spread out fully clothed on the khaki sheets. The anxiety that had been stealthily suffocating her mind transformed into real confusion. To hell with her article, she thought. She didn't want to write it any more. All she wanted to do was go away—somewhere very far. Far away from pathetic Jimmy and his contagious worries. Far away from this cruel war. Far away from Africa and its miseries. All she really wanted was to be in Seattle, safe in Michael's arms.

* * *

Relaxing on a warm bed of sand, Michael went over the main points from his meeting the evening before with Dr. Carter. The sex therapist had talked to him about the technique that most premature ejaculators use at the time of sexual relations: "These men, fearing rejection, try to make up for their deficiencies by bringing their part-ner to orgasm before intercourse. They tell themselves that if they don't manage to last long, they would in the very least have made their partner climax and that despite everything else she would have been sexually satisfied. Their intention is commendable, if you take their limits into consideration. But understand me well, since you'll be having much longer intercourse in the future, it's important that you alter this approach to avoid the pitfalls that it comprises. Know-ing the following will help you.

Actually, women differ as to the frequency and intensity of the orgasms that they can obtain during a single sexual encounter. Some women only have one orgasm and they are completely satisfied. Oth-ers have many, the first being the most sexually gratifying, the others less. For these two types of women, it's not a good idea to bring them to orgasm before penetration. In fact, if they have an orgasm during foreplay and they are satiated, they will have neither the energy nor the desire to participate in a lengthy, enduring intercourse. On the other hand, for women who have several orgasms and the last one is the one that is the most satiating, it doesn't create a problem if you give them one or several orgasms prior to intercourse."

Michael spotted a young woman with blond hair, most likely dyed, heading for the ocean. She was wearing a neon yellow string bikini, too small by about two sizes—unless it was a matter of her breasts being too voluminous for her small frame. Her enormous bosom was literally spilling over the skimpy bikini top. The rest of her body didn't exactly display much more dainty elegance: her hips were exaggeratedly large while her buttocks, a little on the flat side, rested on legs that were way too stubby. However, her slow and very leisurely saunter released a raw sex appeal that did not escape Michael. He couldn't stop himself from wondering if this buxom girl was the multiple or single orgasm type. His thoughts drifted back to his session with Dr. Carter.

"It's very important that in all cases neither you nor your partner begin intercourse in a hyper-excited state. Actually, it's quite common to find among premature ejaculators, men who stimulate their partner very intensely just before intromission. They hope that by doing this, their partner will become sexually aroused enough to be able to have an orgasm during the very brief time that intercourse lasts. To reach their goal, they generally focus all their effort on their mate's clitoris. They stimulate the clitoris continuously right up until their partner reaches very high levels of excitation immediately prior to intromission of the penis into the vagina.

"This method of proceeding is inappropriate for a number of reasons. First of all, when a woman is very sexually excited, she has a tendency to move her pelvis quickly right at the start of intercourse. This increases the amount of stimulation on your penis and favors the arrival of ejaculation. In fact, the start of intercourse is a critical moment for the man.

"To begin with, the heat of the vagina is very arousing. Then, if the woman's vagina is a little tight—this places pressure on the gland, provoking a reflex contraction of the muscles at the base of the penis and this contraction invites the arrival of ejaculation. In addition, if the man is on top of the woman, he must exert a certain amount of effort to support the weight of his body when the penis is introduced into the vagina. This effort requires the contraction of different muscles—that adds to the muscular contractions caused by the excitation—and this, of course, has the effect of inducing ejaculation. Finally, the threshold reaction of the ejaculatory reflex is usually lower at the beginning of intercourse. This means that the man has a harder time handling an intense stimulation at the beginning of intercourse rather than later on. It's very important for you not to be too stimulated at the start of intercourse. If your partner is very sexually turned on at this moment, she risks being a determining factor in your premature ejaculation—simply by the speed of her pelvic movements.

"Second, if your sex companion has been very excited during foreplay and she is then forced to quickly refrain from moving at the start of intercourse so as not to provoke your ejaculation, she will likely be frustrated having to bridle her passion in this way. And since a man needs things to go quite slowly at the beginning of intercourse, it's definitely not the best idea for you to stimulate your partner in such an intense manner just before intromission. In fact, to her great displeasure, she will be obliged to restrain herself during the first minutes of intercourse so as not to make you ejaculate.

"Third, focusing intensely on your partner's clitoris just before intercourse involves major disadvantages. To start off, a woman who has had her clitoris concentrated on during the time leading up to intromission will be inclined to keep this stimulation going during intercourse. When she is centered on her clitoris, she generally affects short and rapid movements from her pelvis as a way to stimulate this organ and reach an orgasm. And, obviously, these quick movements favor a man's ejaculation. Next, when her attention is turned toward her clitoris, she tends to uniquely concentrate on the sensations emanating from this organ and the other elements of the romantic relationship become distracting. That is to say, if you kiss her, alternate the type of caresses or stop moving to express your passion, you will interfere with the progression of her excitation. In addition, it's more difficult for her to feel the sensations in her vagina. And by paying less attention to her vagina, she ends up not developing her vaginal erotism. When a woman is in tune with the sensations in her vagina, she doesn't move in the same way. The movements from her pelvis tend to be slower and more ample. This manner of moving stimulates the man less and, by consequence, helps him to better control his excitation. This also gives the woman access to her inner world where she can cultivate all the symbols associated with her femininity and her sexual union with the man."

Michael once again became distracted by his present surroundings. The bleach blond was getting out of the ocean and water was running down from her colossal breasts like a waterfall pouring into an Arizona canyon. Despite her very stylish micro-bathing suit, its garish color, her fifties hairstyle and loud makeup emitted a romantic aura of an era gone by. As he stared at the dripping water nymph, he wondered if perhaps she was from Russia or another republic of the former Soviet Union. When she turned around toward the ocean and bent over to dip her hands in the water, her seemingly flattish rear rounded out, gaining an unexpected shapely curve. Michael suddenly wanted her. A surprising sexual urge washed over him: He imagined penetrating her vigorously from behind. This desire, paradoxically, drew him back to Dr. Carter's wisdom.

"It's more advantageous for you and your partner to approach intercourse as a sequel to foreplay and not as the beginning of the run up to an orgasm. You could very well stimulate her clitoris and bring her to high levels of sexual excitement and even an orgasm during foreplay. However, when you both head toward intercourse, it will be important that she effectuates the transition from her clitoris to her vagina. To realize this passage, what she could do is breathe from her belly, decrease the tension in her muscles, move her pelvis and feel the sensations coming from her internal genital organs. For your part, you could stimulate her either through pushes on the anterior and posterior walls of her vagina or through external pressure on the lower abdomen. This approach will cause her to become conscious of her interior. Like this, she will naturally opt for slow and deep movements during intercourse. This will not only help you to modulate your sexual excitation but at the same time it will encourage even more expansion of her receptivity.

"As for you, you could also experiment with very high levels of excitation during foreplay. However, because of the surplus of stimulation that is provoked by the intromission of the penis inside of the vagina, it will be in your best interest to lower your sexual tension before initiating intercourse so that you may stay under control."

Following the theoretical portion of the session, they moved on to the instruction of practical techniques. Dr. Carter had explained to Michael in greater detail the role breathing plays in sex. "Breathing is one of the most important tools to modulate sexual excitation and, consequently, slow down the arrival of ejaculation. When a man is relaxed," emphasized the sex therapist, "he breathes from his diaphragm and his abdomen moves. As soon as he gets sexually excited, his breathing becomes thoracic and his muscular tension increases. The strategy I recommend consists of reversing this process and returning to diaphragmatic breathing. This will help reduce the normal muscular tensions caused by sexual excitation and consequently decrease the degree of sexual arousal. Moreover, this type of breathing puts you in contact with yourself, your emotions and your sensations—and this on the whole, benefits the emergence of your sensuality."

Still lying in the sand, Michael yanked his baseball cap over his face to shield himself from the blistering rays of the sun. He then made himself comfortable, his arms resting at his sides. He began going over the exercises Dr. Carter had taught him. He breathed in deeply—right to the bottom of his belly. And then, he breathed out. Gently. He relaxed his muscles. Once again, he breathed in. Slowly. His lips parted. His belly swelled. The salty air penetrated him and sailed right down to his genital organs. And when he exhaled, his entire body surrendered, exulted by a wave of sensual pleasure. He felt the warm breeze of the Atlantic Ocean caressing his male body. He listened to the waves as they knelt down at the sandy shoreline. He was actually taking the time to feel what was happening inside of him. All of his life, he fought hard to find himself a place in the sun, and to banish the injustices on earth. His outlook, thoughts and energy were always turned outwards. Of himself, he knew little. Now, he was taking the time to listen and to feel. He let go of the fighter in him. He was no longer trying to conquer the universe. The universe was coming and going within him, in rhythm with his breathing.

Moved by the contact he had established with his own sensitivity, Michael lay on the sand for a few, long minutes without moving. Finally, he opened his eyes and slowly stretched himself out. He sat up on his sand-covered beach towel and looked at the ocean that was shimmering before him, joyful as a schoolyard of carefree children. He looked beyond into the distance, and imagined the coast of Africa being rocked by the trade winds. And then he thought of Vanessa. "Where is she? What is she doing? Does she still love me? Did she ever love me? And if she loves me, but doesn't want to see me again, what use is this therapy?" He was quietly drifting—like a ship lost at sea; he floated aimlessly, carried away by the current of his cynical interrogations.

"Ice cream! Ice cream! Vanilla! Chocolate! Pistachio! It's the best ice cream in the world!" A stocky vendor was hollering at the top of his lungs, walking down the half-deserted beach, trying to gain his livelihood for that day.

Michael suddenly snapped out of his mental wandering. "Whoa! What am I thinking? I can definitely forget about smooth sailing if I keep up with this rotten attitude. Get a grip on yourself, Michael!" He gathered up his belongings, stuffed them into the sports bag Vanessa had given him as a gift and left the beach, a chocolate ice cream cone in hand.

* * *

Michael walked confidently into the main lecture room an hour before closing. He was anxious to see the pretty librarian again. He didn't have any doubts about his power of seduction. There did however exist one tiny glitch, a certain fly in the ointment as the expression goes: He still loved Vanessa.

Michael wasn't the type to spin yarns. He knew perfectly well that Janice could never take Vanessa's place in his heart. It was purely a physical attraction. And the prospect of a long, drawn-out affair with Janice wasn't what he wanted. There was no time for that.

"Good day," Michael called out to the group of employees at the library.

"Day," grumbled the bald man.

Janice didn't reply. She was talking with a client and ignored him completely. Operation seduction was starting off badly.

"That's women for you," Michael thought to himself. "In the evening they put on their seductress act. The next morning they play it cool." He didn't take offense and sat down in the reading room.

After about twenty minutes, Janice appeared at his side. "Hello, Michael," she murmured in a hushed voiced to avoid breaking the studious silence inside the library.

"Hi, Janice, nice to see you again. By the way, I have some more information to ask you about. Could you help me to—"

The librarian didn't let him finish his sentence. "Sure, let's go back to the computer."

Janice was dressed more femininely today. Light pumps had replaced the sad-looking black shoes of the day before. An elegant skirt had taken the place of the dull blue pants. A blouse of bridal whiteness offered a glimpse of a sexy lace bra. Her long glossy hair was coiffed by the professional hands of a hairdresser. A subtle shade of lipstick accentuated the plump fullness of her lips.

They both went back into the small office accommodating the powerful research computer. "Why don't you sit here," Janice suggested, pointing to the chair facing the screen of the terminal. "I'm going to show you how to access the documents you're interested in."

Michael sat down in front of the computer and the pretty librarian remained standing by his side. She leaned over his shoulder several times to show him which windows to open on the screen. Each time, Janice's long hair brushed his cheek.

Whereas the conversation remained purely professional, their bodies moved closer together, their shoulders touched and their hands made light contact as they worked on the keyboard. Traces of the young woman's soft perfume reached Michael's nostrils every time she whispered an instruction into his ear. Charm was working its magic.

The library's loudspeaker brutally upset the flow of their exchanges. The building was closing in a few minutes and visitors were asked to finish up what they were doing. Michael ignored the call and continued to ask the beautiful employee questions. At one point, Janice bent down some more to pick up a dictionary resting on top of the terminal. Michael felt the light pressure of the young woman's breasts pressing against his back. He also extended his hand toward the document, and they grabbed hold of it at the same time. Their fingers met.

A second of hesitation followed.

Michael took advantage of this juncture to take Janice's hand.

He then looked at her. The pretty librarian's face displayed a mix of surprise and interest. Without uttering the slightest word and keeping Janice's hand prisoner, Michael got up to face her.

Their lips met simultaneously and they exchanged a first kiss at the same instant as the loudspeaker diffused its final closing call.

Janice's reciprocation was so intense that one would have said that she had been waiting for this moment all of her life. In a matter of minutes, the polite municipal employee transformed into a passionate lover. She pressed her body against that of Michael, slipping her thighs in between his legs.

His male libido responded willingly to the female provocations. Soon Michael was unbuttoning his partner's silk blouse only to discover two inviting mounds draped in white lace. His mouth didn't delay to delight in the perfumed taste of a chest that was both firm and tender. His lips locked around her nipples, which hardened under the caress of his tongue.

Janice responded to the gourmand kisses on her breasts put forward by even more audacious caresses. It didn't take her any time at all to find the path to Michael's boxers. With surprising rapidity, she turned the key in the lock of the only door and extracted a condom from inside the purse she had placed next to the computer.

Michael understood then that the moment had come to put into practice Dr. Carter's techniques. He was caught a little off guard, not having expected things to unfold like this. However, the idea of making love to this incredibly sexy creature inside of this small quaint room turned him on enormously.

Seconds later, he felt Janice's fingers making up and down movements along the length of his erect penis. His hand slid into the fine feminine fuzz covered by a delicate little panty. The librarian, very aroused, moaned in pleasure and moved her hips in fervor. She pushed Michael into the wooden chair, back against the wall. She wrapped her arms around him and rode him swiftly. She began rubbing her moist sex against that of Michael's. And then with agile fingers, she moved away her little damp panty, slid the condom on his virile member and drove onto it.

Michael's excitement was propelled to such terrific heights that it was becoming hard to control. It wasn't going to be long before he'd ejaculate. Fortunately, he remembered Dr. Carter's advice and immobilized his partner by grabbing her by the hips. The time was right because she was wriggling all over the place. He equally forced himself to breathe deeply from the bottom of his belly.

Janice did not become offended by her partner's sudden stillness. On the contrary, she closed her eyes and contracted her vagina to better feel the man who was inside of her. This pause allowed her to fully appreciate the thrill of the situation. She was making love to a handsome stranger where she worked. An old fantasy of hers was finally being realized. This good-looking stranger seemed to know exactly how to handle women. Instead of immediately carrying on like a sex-craved maniac, he appeared to fully savor the magical moment where she had welcomed him inside her. This short pause deliciously slowed down the arrival of other sensations.

For his part, Michael was trying hard to calm himself down. He tried to expand his stomach to the rhythm of his breathing, but his arousal didn't want to diminish. Fearing disappointing Janice, he decided despite everything to move a little. Each one of his movements precipitated a long erotic moan from his partner. The cries of feminine pleasure aroused him to the maximum and his penis contracted even harder. Ejaculation was imminent. He attempted to relax his muscles, but at the same moment he felt the jolt of his penis which was ready to explode. In a last effort, he curled up against himself and held back his breathing to stop from ejaculating. But it was useless. His phallus projected his semen once again too soon. Cold shivers ran up and down his body, which was shaken by a bitter pleasure.

His orgasm had the taste of ashes.

Another try in Janice's room was just as unsuccessful.

* * *

Michael's features were drawn and he bore a bleak look on his face when he walked into Dr. Carter's office.

"I met a woman and this method of yours doesn't work, doctor."

"Explain it to me," said the sex therapist not in the least surprised by his client's discouraged declaration.

"I tried everything: pausing, breathing from the belly, relaxing the muscles, but it doesn't work."

"If you will, I would like you to go over the details with me. It was somebody you just met, I suppose?

"Yes. I don't know anybody in Florida."

"You found her immensely desirable, highly stimulating?"

"Of course, she's a very beautiful and very provocative woman."

"There's a first sign: It's normal to ejaculate quickly during the first encounter with a new partner whom we desire intensely."

"But doctor, I tried again later and it didn't work any better."

"Give me more details about the circumstances in which these sexual episodes took place."

Michael recounted without detours all the specifics of his failed attempts.

"I understand," said Dr. Carter. "Under these conditions, it couldn't be anything otherwise. Premature ejaculation was inevitable."

"Really?"

"You were with a new partner who in your own words, demonstrated an unparalleled lust. From the beginning, you had jumped into a sexual encounter under particularly stressful and steamy conditions. Afterward you were under the impression that you failed and thus committed a second mistake by wanting at all costs to succeed. True?"

"Exactly," acknowledged Michael.

"From that point onwards you had entered into sexual relations with an especially high level of arousal and anxiety. A prime factor favoring a faster ejaculation. To this, we must add the fact that you had not made love for a long time. Another disadvantageous factor."

"But then what you're saying is that I'm condemned to fail every time with a new partner?"

"First of all, you must understand that rare are the men who effect flawless sexual exploits with a new acquaintance. Men and women need time to learn how to manage together their sexual excitement. And then again, you didn't have all the techniques needed to succeed."

"What you're saying is that I didn't have a chance. That the failure was automatic."

"What I want to say is that you weren't ready yet to obtain a satisfactory result. We can't even call this a failure because the possibility of success was—so to speak—nil."

Michael's hands relaxed. The feeling of failure dwindled at the same time as his rancor vis-à-vis the sex therapist.

"Let's go over the precise elements: Did you decide to effectuate penetration when you really felt ready?"

"Ah, well, not really," admitted Michael. "I let myself be carried…"

"I see. And your pauses, how long did they last?"

"Hard to say. They appeared long enough to me…"

The sex therapist turned silent and watched the second hand on the watch on his left wrist. About 15 seconds later he asked Michael if his pause had covered approximately the same period of time.

"Yes, it was about that long. Even maybe a little shorter than that I think…."

"These breaks are not long enough to really bring down your level of arousal. It's possible your eagerness to satisfy your new conquest had dominated the necessity to control your level of excitation. Am I right?"

Michael took a while to recall that precise moment. "Yes, I wanted to please her. To give her a good time."

Dr. Carter gestured with his hand. "Don't worry. The first tries are rarely successful. Analysis of this recent experience will serve as the basis to help us during the course of treatment. There's a positive point on which you could concentrate. Let's move, on shall we?"

CHAPTER 21

A cold chill hung in the early morning air. Agile as a cheetah, the duty guard approached Vanessa's tent and whispered at her door: "It's three o'clock. Gathering in fifteen minutes."

Tired—having barely slept a wink—and her stomach in knots from apprehension, Vanessa grabbed her backpack and joined the servicemen at the canteen. But, like most of the soldiers, she couldn't bring herself to swallow a bite. The men spoke little or tried without much success to hide their anxiety by swapping dirty jokes.

After breakfast, the camp was transformed into a swarm of silent activity. The noncommissioned officers, nervous and irascible, gave their orders in a low voice and the privates accepted these with a slight nod of the head. The foot soldiers checked the contents of their bags and had a hard time trying to close them because they were so packed. Next, the first quartermaster sergeant in charge of weapons distributed the ammunition with the large, rough hands of a farmer. And for the first time, Vanessa realized this was war.

The column of soldiers finally hit the road at close to five in the morning. It always surprised Vanessa how slow the troops were to get going. The A.I.F.V.—armored infantry fighting vehicles—were leaving even later, and would only catch up to the infantry three and a half miles from the village. Up and about in the briskness of dawn, she scrutinized the men edging their way in silence out of the camp. Greg and William, smiles plastered on their faces at the prospect of witnessing some action, waved goodbye to her excitedly. Suddenly tempted by adventure, she changed her mind about riding in the armored vehicle and decided to join them on foot. Jimmy desperately tried to keep her from going, but he was unsuccessful at holding her back. Lieutenant Demat attempted as well to dissuade her. "Go ahead, follow us. But I want you to know that if you can't keep up with us we will not wait for you. The mission prevails over all other matters. You are solely and entirely responsible for what happens to you. The choice is yours!"

* * *

The last stars faded into the cold light of the early morning hour. A still-shy sun peaked out from behind the distant plateaus, teasing with its first fine rays the mist haunting the tall grass. And then, very quickly, the sun soared into the sky and enveloped the column of soldiers with soft warmth.

The pinkishness of the morning evaporated in a matter of minutes, liberating entrancing scents that permeated through the nostrils of each soldier like a rich, strong perfume. A group of monkeys in the surrounding trees, stopped what they were doing, and with small, bright eyes stared inquisitively below at the strange creatures moving slowly, overloaded with heavy backpacks.

Sambizanian scouts led the formation, dragging their feet through the thick vegetation.

"Lieutenant, have you noticed how our guides are just strolling along? Even on a mission they maintain their African nonchalance," remarked Vanessa.

"It's not out of laziness but caution. They walk like that to chase away snakes, scorpions and spiders."

Vanessa instantly regretted not having stayed on board the armored vehicle. "Why aren't the trucks following us?"

"Because the terrain isn't suitable for tracked vehicles. Also, the Sambizanian forces would see us coming from afar and the trucks are easy targets, offering no protection." The lieutenant was visibly preoccupied. Vanessa didn't dare ask him another question. She followed in forced silence, harassed by a multitude of voracious flies.

The hours flew by and the sun was now beating down mercilessly on the caravan with all of its blazing radiance. The straps on Vanessa's backpack were cutting into her shoulders and the harness belt was irritating her waist. The dust being raised by the soldiers in front of her dried out her nostrils and burned her throat. She tripped on dead acacia branches that littered the ground and her feet ached, but pride prevented her from asking for help. Especially since her two CNN colleagues were marching without complaint despite the camera and telecommunications system they were lugging on top of their military survival equipment.

Vanessa was bitterly regretful for having gotten involved in this so-called adventure. So this was the fascinating life of a reporter! Entire days go by without a single thing happening and you walk for hours under the unbearable rays of the sun to get to who-knows-where! If anyone else was in as much pain as Vanessa no one griped about it, and the troops progressed in silence. Only the lieutenant spoke from time to time with the noncommissioned officers regularly opening and closing a crumpled map of the region.

At around noon, the column finally stopped and everybody gratefully dropped to the ground. Vanessa wanted to take off her ankle boots but the lieutenant stopped her. "If you do that, your feet will swell and you won't be able to put them back on when we start up again." Sighing, she opened her second water flask, only to be reprimanded by the lieutenant. "Stop drinking this instant! We don't know if we'll find water today." Vanessa truly hated this experience and she couldn't stand this military chief who seemed to do nothing but stick his nose into everybody's affairs and bark out orders.

* * *

In a deafening uproar, the lightweight tanks joined the resting column. Jimmy staggered out of the vehicle, his face as white as chalk and dripping with sweat.

"It's pure hell in there! We've been shaking up and down and around like in a washing machine and it's as hot as an oven inside. It's giving me motion sickness."

Vanessa cracked a tiny smile. Jimmy carried on with his tirade. "But seeing the kind of state you're in, I think I'd much rather ride in my stifling chariot than kill myself walking! Do you want to continue with us? Lieutenant Burton told me it's much safer to travel in an armored vehicle—"

At the same moment, gunfire sounded. Jimmy fell to the ground, followed by Vanessa. After a few minutes of agonizing silence, Lieutenant Demat shouted some orders and everybody stood to their feet. It was a false alarm. A nervous soldier had opened fire on a too curious wart hog, an African wild pig, which had unfortunately ventured a little too close to the column.

A long, shrieking howl reverberated in the air immediately after. It was Jimmy. In his haste to take cover, he had landed on an ant's nest. Vanessa and the soldiers burst out laughing at the sight of him. He was smacking, gesticulating, shaking and jumping around with every bite from the frightened insects. "Help me! Somebody help me! I'm being devoured!"

"Take off your clothes!" ordered Sergeant Hermans. "If not, they'll swallow you alive!"

Jimmy executed the command without thinking, exposing a milky white chest that contrasted sharply with the beet red of his face and hands. The soldiers once again broke into a fit of laughter.

This comic relief, at Jimmy's expense, dropped the tension a notch and for those few fleeting minutes the men forgot about the serious nature of their mission.

The strained and spirited conversation being held by a group of officers contrasted sharply with the good humor of the soldiers. It was clear that Lieutenants Demat and Burton and Captain Muller did not share the same opinion. Vanessa couldn't understand what they were saying, but the volume was getting louder by the second. The conversation finally ended when the captain exploded, shook his head and walked away. The officers quickly dispersed and Edouard joined Vanessa.

Furious, the lieutenant vented his anger: "That moron, Muller. You know what he wants to do? He wants to directly occupy the village instead of first settling on the hill overhanging Kiboyo. A ten-year-old child would know that if we control the hill, we control the village. By surrounding the village in the valley we will be trapped in case of an attack. Lieutenant Burton agrees with me but the captain is in command. We don't have a choice—"

Gunfire crackled in the distance. It was coming from the direction of the village. Edouard instantly recognized the sound of rifles fired from the vanguard scouts. Maybe they were in trouble. Lieutenant Burton climbed into his tank, followed by Jimmy, who waved and blew Vanessa a kiss goodbye. She was touched by the young photographer's sweet gesture—in the end, his chronic clumsiness had become charming in her eyes. The vehicles pulled away noisily and quickly took off toward the village to be rejoined with the scouts.

Edouard issued a number of orders to the sergeants surrounding him and the entire platoon started walking again, noticeably picking up the pace. They could not yet see the village that was located at the bottom of a depression in the ground toward where the armored vehicles had rushed.

The men advanced more rapidly, rushing to the aid of their comrades on the front line. There was still no visual sign of how the fighting of the vanguard was taking shape. The one thing that could be clearly picked up was the explosive thunder of machine guns from the Belgian vehicles entering into the action. They also heard the dry, deafening sound of the 20mm cannons blasting from Lieutenant Burton's armored vehicles.

Lieutenant Demat grabbed hold of his radio to be briefed on the current situation. He spoke into the transmitter with a nervous stutter. Vanessa, sick with apprehension at the thought of what could take place, dared not interrupt him. She looked straight ahead and saw that the soldiers were no longer walking in a column one behind the other. They were advancing into battle all at the same time, as a skirmish contingent, in a horizontal line, legs bent, back stooped and finger on the trigger of their rifle. They looked to the left and to the right to maintain the alignment of the formation. If they walked too fast, too slow, or to the side, they risked finding themselves in their fellow companion's line of fire.

Vanessa took her place to the right of the lieutenant. Some one thousand feet ahead they saw the first huts made of dried mud that were bordering the village. The blaring row from the cannons and machine guns had stopped. The journalist turned her head toward Edouard, and in crossing his glance, clearly understood this lull was not good.

CHAPTER 22

M ichael outstretched his arms one by one high above his head and spread his legs in a slow, voluptuous motion. He was wak ing up in an excellent mood. His stay in Florida was working won- ders for him. Not only did his body feel better, so did his mind. A beam of sunshine filtered through the blinds in his hotel room. But since the morning was his to enjoy, Michael decided to laze in bed for a while. Stark naked underneath the light bedsheet, he moved his body languorously. He closed his eyes and a lifelike image of Vanessa appeared vividly before him. The sun was reflecting off her flowing, auburn tresses—forming a fiery halo above her head. Her long, curled eyelashes framed her lustrous eyes, an intense luminous green the color of water in a lake high up in the Rockies on a spring day. She smiled at him and her soft, full lips parted, revealing a set of excep- tionally straight gleaming white teeth. He smiled back at her and pictured her even more vividly in front of him. Vanessa's bountiful breasts instantly bounced before his eyes. She offered her bosom ea- gerly to him to be kissed and fondled. The creamy flesh looked so warm, so soft, and so copious.

His heart was beating harder and he felt his body get tense from desire. But remembering Dr. Carter's advice, he reduced the tension in his muscles and began breathing from his belly. He embraced an open position, and envisaging Vanessa sprawled on top of him, he initiated the pelvic movement he had learned. He curved his lower back as he breathed from the abdomen—his belly swelling as if it was being filled with air—and pulled back his buttocks. Then, he swung his pelvis forward as he exhaled, making sure not to contract the gluteal muscles of his posterior. The exercise required no effort and only his pelvis moved—like the pendulum of a clock.

This backward and forward motion of the pelvic region evoked the movement of intercourse in Michael's mind. It was exactly what he wished to do with Vanessa. All he really wanted right now was to take her, to hold her, to devour her, to penetrate her. He was moving with harmony and suppleness in perfect unison with his breathing. When he effectuated the movement of penetration, he breathed out while projecting his pelvis forward. When he withdrew from his imaginary partner, he breathed in while pulling back his pelvis. He remembered the correction Dr. Carter had made for him. Evidently, Michael had a tendency to move the trunk of his body as a single unit, as if the pelvis and the back were welded together. This increased his muscular tension and prevented his excitation from diffusing throughout his body. The sex therapist had instructed him to isolate the pelvis from the rest of his back. Now, when his pelvis swung behind, he only used his lumbar muscles and the lower part of his back curved. When his pelvis thrust forward only his abdominal muscles contracted. His thighs, buttocks, chest and neck remained relaxed even if he was experiencing intense sexual excitement. He continued this movement for many long minutes and for the first time in his life he took the time to savour the sensations of sexuality.

Michael changed position to carry out an even more stimulating exercise. He lay down on his stomach and cradled the pillow in his arms. His heart began beating faster. He imagined Vanessa sighing with pleasure, abandoned in his arms.

He played along with his own game and whispered into the pillow. "Vanessa, I want to make love to you. You turn me on so much. You're so desirable, so sexy...." His first impulse was to curl up and execute quick and vigorous movements. But he recalled the sex therapist's advice and reduced the speed of his pelvis, while at the same time still continuing to rub his sex against the sheets.

Nevertheless, he felt ejaculation nearing and realized that all of his muscles were contracted. His gluteal muscles, abdominals, the muscles in his arms and legs and even those in his face—were all taut toward discharge! He wasn't breathing any more! He was fully aware that if he executed one more movement it would be too late, he would no longer be able to continue: His excitement would reach the threshold reflex and ejaculation would take place automatically!

Michael immediately made a pause to interrupt the flow of stimulation. He did not try to hold back his ejaculation. On the contrary, he stopped moving and breathed from the mouth slowly, deeply. He relaxed all of his muscles, especially those of his abdomen, chest, shoulders and neck. He spread apart his legs and arms and opened his hands. And in his heart, he thought affectionately about his darling loved one.

Once his sexual excitement dropped by half, he slowly started moving his pelvis again, allowing his breathing to fully occupy the space in his belly. He carried on this experience—mixing fantasy, sexual excitement and technique—for almost an hour. And then finally he decided to leave the woman of his dreams and head for the shower.

Under the water pressure, Michael was still erect. He had been able to consciously dream about making love to a woman without ejaculating. This lengthy sensual experience was a considerable change from the quick masturbation sessions of his adolescence. He no longer viewed his excitement as a tension that he had to frantically relieve but like a succession of sensations that he could savour. He had evolved significantly and this allowed him to realize that sexuality could be positively influenced through learning.

CHAPTER 23

T he tiny blue waves in the hotel's swimming pool made Michael want to plunge right into the water. He quickly slipped on his swimming trunks and gave into his desire. The temperature of the water was ideal. He dove in headfirst.

Michael swam with lots of stamina. Freeing all of the energy in his muscles, he propelled himself at great speed from one end of the pool to the other. There was no doubting he was a very good swimmer. He possessed excellent technique and could have participated at a competitive level. However, he lacked suppleness and gave the impression of fighting against the waves instead of being carried by the water.

Anyone watching Michael would have said that he was a man in complete control and at the peak of his prime. His fast crawl drew attention to his broad shoulders and muscular arms, the blood vessels in them dilated from the effort. This healthy virility certainly did not go unnoticed by the woman sitting poolside. When Michael stopped to recuperate a bit, she asked, flashing him her most seductive smile, "How's the water?"

Michael wiped the water off of his face and took a good look at her. Her very black eyes and hair, tanned flesh and the look of her features led him to guess that she was South American.

"Why don't you jump in? You'll find the water is delicious," he suggested light-heartedly.

The pretty vacationer inched her way into the tepid water with utmost precaution, as if there was a chance of her disfiguring her beautiful body. Once fully immersed in the water, she did a few laps, completely ignoring Michael. But the sexy swimmer was hard to ignore. Michael watched her attentively. And when she got out of the pool, he couldn't help from noticing her barely there bathing suit exposed a perfectly round, sculpted behind.

With the lascivious moves of a salsa dancer, the sultry swimmer took a few steps alongside the pool. And then, like an animal seeking heat, she sat down at the sunny end. She splashed her feet in the water, like a bored child.

Michael's gaze rested on the busty bosom of this ravishing water goddess adorned in a minuscule hot red string bikini. The wet fabric brought into relief two nipples—arrogantly erect from the contact of the water. The young woman was perfectly aware of her charm and she used it without scruples. She raised her arms above her head to lift her thick, frizzy curls away from the nape of her neck. The gesture hoisted up her pear-shaped breasts quite provocatively. And once again, she exposed her chest before Michael's eyes.

"Your swimming technique is quite remarkable," she said, flashing him an even more charming smile.

Michael swam toward the bathing beauty with an energetic crawl. Face trickling with water, he pressed up against the edge of the pool, right next to her. The young woman leaned toward him, baring her titillating cleavage, and declared, "My name is Maria Dominguez. I'm Colombian. And you, what's your name?"

* * *

Lieutenant Demat's men cautiously marched toward the first huts located on the edge of the village. There were huts burning here and there and the villagers were anxiously trying to put out the spreading fires. The soldiers advanced with trigger fingers poised and ready to fire, their facial expressions spelling nervous unease. Vanessa's heart was beating extremely fast and her body was drenched in sweat.

Upon entering the village, she spotted the armored vehicle Jimmy would have been in. It had stopped beside a row of half-demolished huts made of ocher earth. The immobile tracked vehicle showed no signs of combat, but a sinister black cloud of smoke was emanating from it. As she moved toward the vehicle, Vanessa noticed that the troop carrier was in perfect condition, except for a hole—the size of an orange—through its armor plating. As she got closer, the atrocious odor of rubber and burning flesh assaulted her nostrils.

She wanted to get even closer to the vehicle but the lieutenant held her back by the arm. "Don't go near it, there's nothing to see. They're entirely charred. You wouldn't even be able to recognize them anymore. Their bodies are like the ashes of a cigarette." The lieutenant swallowed his saliva and articulated with difficulty, "We now know the bastards have anti-tank weapons."

"Jimmy!" screamed Vanessa, struggling to free herself from Lieutenant Demat's hold. "No, not Jimmy!" she cried out in anguish, hitting and kicking the officer who was trying to calm her down. Vanessa had lost all control. She turned her rage against Edouard who took her blows without any reaction. Finally, she collapsed in tears on the dry Sambizanian soil.

"Lieutenant Burton was my best friend at the Royal Military School," Edouard gently declared, as if to better share the young journalist's pain. But Vanessa, curled up on the ground, crushed by the immense suffering within her, couldn't hear him anymore.

* * *

"Well done, my tropical bird," declared Christopher Clays. "I knew Michael Lancaster would not be able to resist your charm."

Maria Dominguez smiled with smug satisfaction. Seated casually on a large black leather couch, she scanned the modern surroundings of the luxury apartment. It wasn't decorated in poor taste, but on the whole the atmosphere was a shade sinister. The dark rugs, charcoal furniture and the *El Greco* reproductions portraying faces struck by fear or pain would send shivers down anybody's spine.

"I invited him scuba diving tomorrow. We're going to take my boat out for a romantic cruise. But I sure hope poor Michael doesn't end up in a stupid accident. Scuba diving is such a dangerous sport...."

"Exactly, and I'm counting on you to make it look like a real accident."

"Don't sweat it, my handsome Romeo. I know how to handle myself around men. And I know exactly how to seduce them. They're so gullible, especially when guided by what is tucked between their legs."

"You better be careful," replied Christopher Clays, his male pride having just been directed a bruising blow. "Michael Lancaster is no imbecile. And you've got to understand that he's as stubborn as a mule. Even after his boss, under my strict orders, prohibited him from carrying on with his investigation, he still continued to stick his nose where it didn't belong. Fortunately for me, Lancaster wanted to talk to Bilodeau, if not, I would have completely lost trace of the guy. So, I repeat myself—be careful—and don't trust the man. Watch him like a hawk."

Maria got up slowly from the sofa and slithered her way toward Christopher who was leaning against the bar in his living room. She came up so close to the man in the black polo shirt that her chest brushed up against his arm. "I have all the right assets to convince any guy to accompany me wherever I desire, whenever I desire," she whispered sultrily into his ear. Christopher sprung back violently as if the devil had just touched him.

"Does the contact with my breasts scare you, Christopher?"

"You're not my type," he lied to save face.

"Funny how last Friday when you brought me over here, you seemed to find me to your liking…."

"That was a mistake. It was late and I had too much to drink. I'll tell you once again, you're not my type."

"A woman who knows exactly what to do can be any man's type. And just by looking at you, I can guess what kind of female creatures turn you on. You like the very seductive ones. A woman who is willing to participate in the kinky fantasies you have in your head. But she also has to be a nice, submissive girl who won't put your fragile virility into question. That's what you're looking for. And that's why you'll never end up with anything but second-rate, insignificant women."

Christopher didn't reply because he knew that she was more right than wrong. Yet his piercing eyes and his clenched jaw betrayed the anger he was trying to keep from violently erupting. He dug into his pockets and yanked out a crumpled envelope that he threw down on the coffee table with wrath. "It's all in there, just as we discussed.

You'll get the rest of the money at the end of the contract. And don't ever set foot in my apartment again. It's far too dangerous. I told you that the last time. We'll meet again in a week—two o'clock at the Miami Zoo in front of the tiger's cage."

The pretty Colombian nonchalantly scooped up the envelope, casting him a nasty look. She loathed Christopher Clays who treated her like a prostitute. She hated every single man who leered at her like some vile object of consumption. He was going to pay her back for this lack of respect. All men were going to pay for this lack of respect!

Teresa—her real name—pledged inextinguishable enmity for the male species. This rampant hatred was sowed on her fourteenth birthday. Her father, a lousy unemployed man from a shanty town surrounding Cartagena, promised her a very special birthday present. She was so excited, so happy and so full of joy. Usually, he didn't give her a thing. The only thing she got from him regularly was a beating whenever he was drunk and her mother wasn't there to control his violence. On that day, he took her to a bar in the city. For the occasion, she wore the only pretty dress she owned—a short frilly white one with tiny pink roses and a wide satin ribbon around the waistline that had been handed down to her from her Aunt Lucia.

Her big surprise was three fairly plastered men in their early thirties who took turns viciously raping her on the bathroom floor in return for the quick settlement of a card-game debt her father had run up. From that day on, Teresa swore to herself that she would take revenge on all of the dirty bastards in the world.

Maria—or rather Teresa—left Christopher Clay's apartment with the smile of a butcher who had just sold a thin pig for the price of veal.

CHAPTER 24

M ichael walked into Dr. Carter's office full of pep. "I met a super woman, a Colombian with a dream body. I think I'm going
to give it another trial with her."

Dr. Carter moderated his enthusiasm. "I don't want to preach to
you, Michael, because what you do is your business. I am a therapist
and not a minister or a moral advisor. However, I don't think it would
be a good idea. Just because your problem is on the road to recovery
doesn't necessarily mean you have to absolutely sleep with a woman
as soon as you meet her. And by the way, the first time a man has sex
with a new partner, he has a tendency to ejaculate more quickly. You've
already found that out yourself. It's normal.

"You're obviously free to do what you want, but I think it's more
constructive to wait for Vanessa's return. I'm sure you both have strong
feelings for each other. I also believe there exists a rich and meaningful past between the two of you that you're interested in preserving.
Sex isn't the only thing that counts; there are also the feelings and the
commitments we make in life."

Michael politely listened to what Dr. Carter had to say. He then
fired at the therapist a question that had been tormenting him from
the start. "And what if this method doesn't work with Vanessa?"

Dr. Carter replied in his usual calm manner. "It's already working! You're progressing very nicely with the exercises we've been
doing together. If you're able to move and breathe properly in the
office, there is no reason why you can't do this on your own, in private. The only problem that may arise is that during sexual relations
you don't apply the techniques you've learned and end up ejaculat-

ing prematurely. And in this case, the onus will be on you. What you must do is go over the techniques on your own and follow them through at the time of sexual activity. I assure you that the method has worked—obviously with different degrees of success—for more than ninety-five percent of the men who have applied it correctly. For example, I had one client in therapy who was so sensitive that the simple contact of his wife's hand on his thigh made him ejaculate. And he came out of it brilliantly. Now, he decides when he's going to ejaculate. So you—whose difficulties to begin with were less serious—have nothing to worry about.

"I will warn you that you will still experience challenging moments. But don't panic! This happens to everyone. If things don't go that well once or twice, it doesn't mean it's hopeless. In all cases, it's important not to consider these awkward episodes as failures but rather to look at them as learning experiences and occasions to get to know yourself better. It's also a perfect time to ask yourself questions on what might have taken place: Was my breathing thoracic? Was I moving too quickly? Was I aware of the sensations coming from my body—and especially those from my genital organs—which were indicating to me the approach of the ejaculatory reflex? These questions provide you with the answers to what you must do to correct the situation for the next time. I encourage you to observe your body during foreplay and intercourse to study its reactions. This will provide you with the opportunity to analyze the effect of the techniques on your sexual excitation and will help you to acquire, with time, greater control.

"Anyway, if you encounter the slightest difficulty, don't hesitate to give me a call. It's possible that you might need to refresh your memory on a point or two, and the problem will be quickly settled. There is often a loss of control after a prolonged period of abstinence, a change of partner or the nonapplication of the techniques. Since these techniques rest on motor skills, they could easily erode if they aren't applied regularly. A similar phenomenon is present in sports. Think of tennis or golf, for example. If you haven't played either game for six months, you won't serve the ball with the same precision or swing the golf club with as powerful a stroke.

"We've already reached the halfway point of the program. I think this would be a very good time to recap the material to date. Could you summarize for me what you must do to modulate your sexual tension and delay the arrival of ejaculation?"

Michael thought about it for a few seconds, then said, "First of all, and you've mentioned this several times, it's essential to maintain muscular tension at very low levels. I realized while practicing the exercises in my hotel room that in the past, I reacted globally to sexual stimulation. All my muscles became tense, I would stop breathing, I moved my body like a solid block and I raced toward discharge like a starved person fights for a crumb of bread. The exercises taught me to breathe from the belly, to dissociate the pelvis from the back, to move slowly and only to use the muscles I really needed to execute a movement."

"Fantastic! You're on the right track, Michael."

"Thanks. But I have to admit it's not that easy. All my life I've programmed myself to move fast, to use my strength and to push my body to the limit. When I was younger, I played football in college and did a lot of weight training. Today, I still train with free weights and barbells, I play racquetball, I run. Everything I do demands speed and power. Now all of a sudden, you're asking me to master fluidity and sensualness. I'm entering into an entirely different universe!"

"And you're not the only one. The majority of men in our culture have been submitted to the same social conditioning. Our education system emphasizes excellence, performance and power. The development of sensuality, pleasure and refinement is entirely neglected. There are a lot of things we must change in society. But that's not the purpose for your being here. Okay, so what else have you retained?"

"Before starting this program, I had a very low opinion of myself. Because of my problem, I tended to idealize women and put myself down. I was a terrible lover, they were perfect. If they didn't have an orgasm, it was my fault. This led me to become hyper-vigilant and to concentrate uniquely on their pleasure. I stimulated them as much as possible before penetration so that they became extremely excited. And once inside of them, I moved like a rabbit—hoping and praying that they would climax before I ejaculated. Of course, I now understand that by moving at this speed, I made myself ejaculate even more quickly. But you have to realize, I was so afraid they wouldn't orgasm. This is why I didn't carry out a pause. I was telling myself that if I stop moving, her excitement will drop and she'll end up frustrated. I had already tried to take little breaks, but my partner at the time wasn't at all keen about that. She blamed me because I spoiled her pleasure. 'Go on, go on, don't stop…,' she used to say. So I continued and…I'd ejaculate. But I'm still not completely convinced about the pause thing. If we stop the movements of penetration, isn't it awful for the woman?"

"Michael, you have a very narrow vision of female sexuality! For the woman, making love isn't limited to in-and-out movements of the penis inside of the vagina. And her arousal isn't fed solely from genitality. The same goes for a man, by the way. The pause, when used effectively, contributes to enrich and to enlarge excitation, not diminish it. It's as if you'd tell me that a port of call ruins a cruise or that to stop chewing spoils a meal at a restaurant! Imagine for a minute that you're taking a walk in the woods with your lover. Is the afternoon wasted if you stop to look at a squirrel, to inhale the scents of the undergrowth, to admire a tree or to whisk your lover in your arms, whispering the words, 'I love you'? Are you going to tell me that a *real* stroll in the woods consists only of trekking through the trees without slowing down the pace, without marveling at nature, without taking the time to breathe and enjoy the experience? It's the same way when you're making love. If a woman insists that you move continuously from the start of penetration right up until she has an orgasm, then her conception of sexuality is very limited. And if you adhere to her desires, then you are very naïve.

"In reality, the pause embodies more advantages than disadvantages. First, it constitutes a variation in rhythm and breaks the monotony of routine intercourse. The variety of rhythms in sexuality compares to the variety of rhythms in music or dance. It enhances the interaction between you and your partner by expanding the emotional and arousal register that ensues from the variation of sensations. Second, it opens the door to creativity and fantasy, that which favors a woman's sexual excitation. These breaks could make way for tender exchanges, sex play, passionate declarations, erotic improvisations or loving moments of romance and sharing. You can smother your lover with kisses, hold her in your arms, caress her entire body, make a stop just outside of her vagina, penetrate her deeply and remain motionless inside of her, tell her how much you love her, sip on a glass of brandy entwined in one another's arms, talk about nothing, laugh or simply lie there and breathe together. Your partner will be able to feel you inside of her and to sense that you are close to her. She will be sharing a happy moment with you and all of this will make her feel loved, beautiful, desired and every bit a woman."

"What if she continues to move while I'm initiating a pause?"

"You have no choice but to assert yourself and bring her to stop her movements if you don't want to ejaculate prematurely. Male physiology embodies a constraint that you can't get around. If you remember, at the very start of our sessions, I spoke to you about the ejaculatory reflex. This reflex puts a limit on the amount of stimulation that you can receive. When you are too sexually stimulated, your excitation rises to the point where it sets off this reflex and ejaculation occurs automatically. There's nothing we could do to counter this mechanism, unless we resort to chemical means. Consequently, I'd like you to remember the following information until the day you die: If you have to take breaks, it's not because you are a premature ejaculator, it's simply because you are a man. All the men in the world who desire to prolong intercourse for over more than one minute are obliged to effectuate pauses or in the very least, move very slowly. Men who don't suffer from premature ejaculation naturally apply these techniques and that's why they don't suffer from premature ejaculation! They allow for a few moments of respite here and there, they talk to their partner, they stimulate her in various ways, they kiss her, they slow down their movement, they change positions, they take their time, they breathe...

"The responsibility of controlling the moment of your ejaculation comes back to you. Only you know the exact level your excitation has reached at a giving moment during the sexual relation. You're also the only one who knows just how vulnerable you are on that certain day. If you want to remain erect for a reasonably long time so as to give your partner pleasure during intercourse, you alone must determine the rhythm to adopt so as not to ejaculate too quickly. This implies that you will sometimes have to slow down or stop the movement of your pelvis to reduce the amount of stimulation that you receive on your penis. This also means that your partner must adapt to your rhythm. If you require her to reduce the speed of her pelvis or stop moving it, she must accept the drop in stimulation that might follow. This in itself, however, is not catastrophic. Your partner can

215

also learn how to modulate her sexual tension. A woman doesn't have to worry about no longer becoming excited when her arousal diminishes. Yet, if she's very demanding and if she requires you to move fast from the start of intercourse, there are very strong chances that this intense activation will provoke a premature ejaculation.

"There are several ways to bring your partner to a stop. The best one consists of involving her in the process, turning her into a companion and an accomplice in your romantic journey. Carried out in a sensual manner, the pause no longer breaks the flow of sexual activity. It falls right in with the other romantic variations. In fact, it becomes a delight among many other delights."

"I believe you," Michael said sincerely. "Yet I'm still under the impression there are also a lot of women out there who don't accept these pauses."

"Women who don't accept pauses or changes in rhythm generally view their excitation like a climb that should keep rising without interruption until the point of an orgasm. The sexuality of these women is often reduced to its most simple form—a few caresses followed by intense stimulation of the clitoris at the time of foreplay and frenetic stirring of the pelvis during intercourse. Obviously, when the rubbing of the clitoris ceases, stimulation disappears and excitation plummets. Hence they become frustrated. These women experience their excitation in a very narrow corridor. When their clitoris isn't stimulated anymore, they lose the base of their sexual excitation. They would benefit greatly from broadening their horizons, diversifying their forms of stimulation, modulating their sexual excitation and interacting with their partner.

"The main problem is that most men, as a result of their insecurity, take their partner down this very restricted road. Out of the fear of not making them climax, they stimulate their partner's clitoris in a very quick and intense manner so that they may bring her to orgasm. Understandably, this mechanical approach acts to focus the woman's entire attention on the sensations arising from her clitoris. At this point, the pause or any other type of sensual interaction that favors romantic exchanges—and the control of ejaculation—completely cuts off her line of arousal! As you can see, frustration doesn't stem from the pause in itself. It derives from the interruption in the feverish state of excitation into which you have locked your partner by stimulating her in such a mechanical manner. As you make a pause, you suspend this type of heated excitation and she finds herself dangling in a realm of nothingness, totally sexually frustrated.

"If you both enter into sexual activity from a sensual standpoint, the pause doesn't interrupt a thing. It becomes a part of your lovemaking. It gives you access to a universe of emotions, feelings, pleasure and symbols. It opens the doors of communication, romantic complicity and sharing. And all of this benefits your partner as well. Actually, she has opened herself up to you and has received you inside of her. Now, she wants to feel you. She wants to know that you are there with her—both in body and mind—and that you love her. Under these circumstances, the pause is warmly welcomed because it brings you closer together and enables both of you to establish an intimate connection while continuing to be sexually aroused.

"There exist women who aren't interested in this type of a sensual approach or who respond above all to clitoral stimulation. In this case, you can fondle your partner's clitoris with your fingers while keeping your pelvis still. This way, you will be less physically stimulated and she will be more. It is possible as well that she will prefer—like numerous women who know their body well—to touch her clitoris herself. And to finish off, a good way to heighten the pleasure of the female partner consists of combining the stimulation of the clitoris with other erogenous zones like the breasts, neck, lips, sides of the body or anus. This provokes a synergy of nerve impulses and favors the rise of her sexual pleasure.

"Such an approach, more focused, magnifies a woman's sexual excitation and her chances of having an orgasm. But it is interactively, emotionally and symbolically limited. This is due to the convergence of attention and stimulation it induces toward neural endings. In general, women report that clitoral stimulation proves to be more intense and gratifying physiologically but less fulfilling emotionally. Neither approach seems to be better than the other. In this case, the couple must be prepared to identify what they desire and to understand what it entails.

"The man holds the responsibility over the moment of ejaculation. It's up to you to determine the amount of stimulation you're capable of receiving at any given moment during sexual interaction. If your excitation gets too high at the time of intercourse, I suggest you either decelerate or halt the movement of your pelvis. You can also ask your partner to slow down or to stop from moving. As a couple, it would be in your best interest to vary your sexual activities by slowing down and making pauses among other things. On the one hand, this permits you to enrich your erotic life and fully enjoy sexuality. On the other hand, this helps you stay under control by reducing the strong stimulation resulting from the rapid movements of the penis inside of the vagina, which is often the root of rapid ejaculation.

"Nonetheless, you have nothing to worry about. Thanks to the exercises you've learned, your capacity to control yourself has increased. You will be able to support more stimulation and satisfy your partner's needs like never before. But be careful! You'll always be obliged, like all men, to take breaks. Of course, there will be days when no matter what you do, your excitation will seem to rise too fast."

"You've made me feel a lot better," admitted Michael. "I thought I was alone in this ordeal. If you tell me that all men must slow down, it lifts the tremendous weight I've placed on my shoulders. With all the porno films out there and all those stories I heard when I was young, I imagined that a normal man went at it a hundred miles per hour without ever stopping."

Dr. Carter smiled, happy to see that his client had made progress.

Michael continued to summarize what he learned. "You also recommended that I keep my body open: arms and legs spaced out, hands at ease, eyes opened and lips parted. This allows sexual tension to diffuse throughout the body. If not, it converges toward the genital organs, ready to burst.

"You advised me to get myself progressively used to experiencing high levels of excitation at the time of foreplay with the goal of being able to do the same during intercourse. Given that intromission of the penis inside of the vagina heightens excitation, it's essential not to approach intercourse too excited to maintain a margin of maneuver. It's important to keep in mind that the initial thrusting movements are an intense sensorial and symbolic moment. If I'm very sexually aroused, I must allow for my excitement to come down before proceeding to intromission. And at the beginning of intercourse, it's not recommended for either the man or the woman to move too much if they desire to prolong their pleasure."

"I even suggest couples to pause for one minute before initiating in-and-out movements," the sex therapist intervened.

"And if the man loses his erection?"

"It's normal to experience variations in your erection. Women themselves undergo fluctuations in lubrication. These phenomena are perfectly natural. If you feel your erection lessening, it means you're applying your techniques well and that your sexual excitation is diminishing accordingly. And then again, you may simply experience a normal variation and this could be caused by a thousand and one different factors. To regain your rigidity, you only have to affect a few movements of the pelvis to receive more stimulation."

"After all, it's simple," carried on Michael. "You taught me that it's completely useless to try to restrain ejaculation by contracting myself when I approach the ejaculatory reflex. This does nothing but increase muscular tension. And muscular tension favors ejaculation. I remember what I used to do when I felt ejaculation coming on. I used to arch my back, pull in my stomach, lock my jaw, block my breathing and try to hold back my sperm. I would be screaming in my head: 'I must not! I must not!' But even after all of this, I'd still ejaculate. I learned, on the contrary, that the best approach under these circumstances is to effect a pause, to breathe deeply and to relax all of my muscles. My partner and I could then slowly recommence our movements. It's better of course if I keep my excitement a certain distance away from the reflex threshold. This way I won't continually find myself in a state of emergency and I won't always have to jump on the brakes like a madman. A smooth ride, actually!"

"Excellent!"

Michael felt ready to put his knowledge into practice and still very much desired to see Maria again. Dr. Carter seemed a bit too serious. And besides, what was a little boat ride?

CHAPTER 25

T he Sambizanian village was totally silent. After putting out the fires resulting from the skirmish, the local population hid inside the huts that served as their homes. In the middle of the village, a school and a church constituted the only buildings constructed of brick. The soldiers were extremely nervous because they were finding it hard tell an African enemy apart from an African ally. The Sambizanian troops normally wore a khaki uniform distinguished by its drab olive color and its small matching cloth cap. It was an outmoded Russian hat, obtained inexpensively from the immense uniform reserve of the defunct Red Army. But a split second of hesitation could prove fatal. The peacekeepers had been ordered not to shoot first. They could only open fire if they encountered an attack from the enemy. However, they had already been attacked and several of their comrades were dead. They no longer knew exactly what to do.

Soldiers wearing blue peacekeeping berets aren't professionally prepared for humanitarian missions. They are simply men who belong to armies from a number of different countries, drilled for years to fight and to kill within the context of war missions. And then, after a brief period of training, a sky-blue beret is placed on their head. They are told that from that point on they're peacekeeping soldiers whereby their main mission is to observe and to stay in control of the situation without generally being able to retaliate. This type of attitude was standard for peacekeeping missions but went against everything they were taught during their military instruction. Consequently, the soldiers progressing cautiously between the huts felt particularly vulnerable.

Greg and William, taught as journalists to be in the role of non-combatant observers, were more in their element. Nonetheless, it was with a certain amount of apprehension that they arrived on the square of the extremely quiet village. They entered the church and discovered a great many women and children crammed one beside the other, their eyes filled with terror. William filmed the scene, wanting to expose the true horrors of war to the CNN television viewers. Greg attempted, without success, to come into contact with a child by offering him a partially melted chocolate cookie.

Normally, starving children weren't able to resist such a temptation. Greg knew this. But right there and then, it wasn't working. Fear proved to be stronger than hunger. The little boy looked at the cookie intensely, but failed to reach for it. Greg knew that, for the time being, he wasn't going to get anywhere. Stepping back, he tried his best to display a benevolent smile. William continued filming as they backed away.

When they got out of the church, a hail of machine gun fire ripped through the air. William collapsed to the ground and life departed from him instantaneously. Greg bent his body in half. And then a second blast to the chest caused him to suddenly straighten up. He remained standing briefly whereas everyone else was lying flat on the ground or hiding behind the huts. His eyes wide open—showed no sign of fear, no sign of pain. Just amazement. His mouth opened up and his face slowly became rigid. And at that moment, his legs ceased to support him.

Greg was lying down on the ground, his face buried in the dirt. He opened his eyes with much difficulty and realized that he was still alive. He had clearly felt the impact of the bullets however the pain still hadn't fully hit him. He tried to get up, but his legs no longer obeyed him. Panic suddenly seized him. He was paralyzed. The gunfire was intensifying and he couldn't move. He turned toward his friend. William lay motionless on his back, eyes turned toward eternity. A terrible pain gnawed at his gut and he realized then that he had been hit in the stomach.

A new round of gunfire exploded and cries of horror reverberated throughout the village. Lieutenant Demat—crouched behind a small hedge of branches, hurled out to his men, "Where is the fire coming from? Where is the fire coming from?"

In the confusion that followed, the soldiers indicated different directions. Greg, wounds bleeding profusely, tried to pull himself along with his arms. A soldier darted toward the front of the church to his rescue, but he was shot down in full flight by a blast of gunfire. Lying in the middle of the square, he wriggled and wrestled on the ground screaming in pain. The impact of the bullets lifted a cloud of dust all around the body of the unfortunate soldier. The battle increased in ferocity and Vanessa, face to the ground, had no idea what was happening. The lieutenant continued shouting, "Where are the shots coming from? Where are the shots coming from?"

A young man responded in a rasping voice, "From the hill, lieutenant. I saw the smoke from their rifles!"

Edouard muttered under his breath, "Damned hill, I knew it. What a stupid idiot Muller is!" And then he yelled into the radio's telephone, "Squad one-one, squad one-two spray the hill. Over." But the men from both squads were taking cover in the village and their machine guns were not in position.

Greg dragged himself next to the door of the church to seek shelter from the gunfire. He was having difficulty breathing and every movement was causing him excruciating pain. The soldiers crawled toward him, quickly dodging the bullets flying above their head. They grabbed him by the armpits, pushed open the door of the church and pulled him carefully inside the nave.

"Shit, he's badly hurt. Quickly, we mustn't let him go into shock or we'll lose him." The soldier put his hand to Greg's throat and his face to his mouth.

"Okay. He's breathing and his heart is still beating. Oh, there's blood gushing from his stomach.... Shit! We have to stop the damn hemorrhaging or he's going to bleed to death...."

Finally, the platoon's machine gun was heard and the acacias lining the slopes of the hill shot up under the force of the 12.7mm bullets. The gunfire in the direction of the village immediately ceased. A medic equipped with a first aid kit rushed toward the church, accompanied by the lieutenant and the young journalist. As Vanessa approached the nave, she learned William was dead. Greg, stretched out on the floor inside of the church, was still breathing. On the verge of passing out, he asked Vanessa to grab the video camera and begin filming him. Fully aware at this point that his wounds were fatal, Greg wanted the camera to record his agony.

Vanessa mustered up enough courage to keep herself from shedding the tears quickly mounting in her throat. She was incapable of talking and it was only in a zombie-like state that she managed to capture Greg's final moments. The cameraman wanted to express himself for the last time and he wanted the entire world to hear his message. But being so weak, he was hardly able to speak. He managed to articulate a few words directed to his wife: "I'm sorry...Julia...I should have listened to you...." And then his thoughts turned toward his sons: "Never go to war...life is too precious.... Never risk your life...you...." A choked moan escaped from his throat and, too frail, he wasn't able to say another word.

Tears streamed down the corner of Greg's eyes because he would have liked to tell them how much he loved them. He turned his face to Vanessa, trying desperately to transmit a last message to his family, and then slowly, he slipped into an irreversible coma. Vanessa didn't know what else to do. She wanted to throw down the camera, to hold his hand, to talk to him, but Greg had insisted that she film him right up until his last breath and she didn't want to go against his wishes. A medic attempted to revive the cameraman by giving him a cardiac message. However, his efforts were in vain. A few convulsions, each one considerably weaker, twitched the CNN journalist's body and then finally he died, his head pointed toward the camera, his gaze turned toward his family.

Vanessa stood there in a petrified stupor. Everything had happened so quickly. She didn't even have time to absorb the events. Now she was no longer capable of reacting. The sweltering heat, having become unbearable, was overwhelming her. With difficulty, she opened her mouth in search of a bit of oxygen, but only hot and fetid air filled her lungs. She lifted her eyes and observed through the partially destroyed windows of the church, gigantic dark gray cumulus clouds that seemed to be proclaiming the end of the world. And then, like a frightened child, she withdrew deep within herself and closed her eyes in an attempt to escape far, far away. But the exchange of new gunfire brought her back to the horror of this inferno into which she had ventured.

Lieutenant Demat took Vanessa by the hand and led her toward the door. "This church is a perfect target for the enemy. We have to find ourselves a safer shelter." He cautiously approached the exit and whispered to Vanessa, "On my signal, I want you to clear the front of the church square and run as quickly as possible in the direction of that tree, over there to the left. And then, abruptly shift directions and run straight toward that heap of stones. I want you to take cover behind them. All of this should take no more than a few seconds. Are you ready?"

"Yes…"

The platoon's heavy machine guns once again rattled out, obliging the enemy gunners to seek shelter. The lieutenant immediately gave Vanessa the order:

"Go!"

Vanessa tore out of the church, running as fast as her legs could go. She followed the sequence indicated by the lieutenant and plunged headfirst behind the pile of stones.

As soon as he himself had reached safety, the lieutenant yelled out to cease all fire and the crackle of machine guns died out within a matter of seconds. Apparently, the enemy itself wished not to waste all of its ammunition because soon after, a heavy silence settled over Kiboyo. Only the soft flutter of the wings of a lone green parrot flying from one tree to the next disturbed the hot and humid air. Not the slightest sound could be heard over the village.

Fifteen minutes later a violent storm broke, freeing a fierce rain destined, it seemed, to wash away all the blood from the day. The lieutenant rejoined Vanessa and they sought refuge under an old corrugated piece of iron along with the soldier who was in charge of carrying the radio. Edouard tried nervously to catch the messages of the other units. But he could hardly hear them for the static from the radio was terrible.

"One-six here, two-six…one-six here, two-six…one-six here, two-six…. Speak louder, I am hearing you weak and disturb—"

The static from the radio mixed in with the rumble of thunder from the storm rendered communication impossible.

"Yes, nothing good on this end. Connect me to Hermans' section," the lieutenant said, addressing the radio operator.

"...what...you too?.... What's left of Delta-one...No... impossible?... Speak up, Hermans! Shit! I can't hear a thing. Over."

Edouard, sitting cross-legged, leaned forward and covered one ear: "Do you have any casualties?...We'll see later....No?... The others as well...And what about Muller, any word?... No...what, an encounter with one-three? Okay, I'll contact the colonel to warn him.... Roger."

Edouard called Tellier immediately. "Colonel? No? Who am I speaking to? Yes, it's Demat here...radio procedures? I don't give a shit! Pass me the colonel, and quick, we're in trouble over here! Over." Edouard looked in the direction of the hill. "Colonel...? It's Lieutenant Demat.... No word on the captain.... Over. What, you too. No?... Good...Okay...At your command. We'll work things out. Roger."

And with a gesture of disillusion, he hung up the radio receiver and turning to Vanessa said, "We're in deep shit. The Sambizanian forces have us trapped. They destroyed our four armored vehicles with antitank rockets and waited until we had invaded the village to surround us. Trust me, we're in big trouble."

Vanessa leaned against the tree supporting the roof of the iron shelter. She felt her legs giving out.

The lieutenant was still talking: "...In a real fine mess. ...Holy shit! It's impossible for us to withdraw because we're encircled. Thank God, it appears our platoon hasn't suffered many casualties. On the contrary, Lieutenant Burton's armored infantry was almost completely wiped out. Most of the poor boys were burned alive inside of their tanks without even having the chance to fight—another error of command. We should have played it out with a lot more prudence. In short, we must have about forty able men left. With our strength this reduced, we can only assure limited protection of the village, far from what was originally anticipated. We won't hold up like this for much longer because the enemy is ten times more numerous than we are."

"And the reinforcements?"

Edouard replied without looking at her. "I contacted Colonel Tellier. They are at the moment undergoing a serious attack. They can't do anything for us. That bastard El Tabernasti really set us up nicely. While we're stuck here in Kiboyo, they're attacking the camp base we left. We've been well and truly and completely had! Oh, international guarantees are so great! A lot of asinine babble from diplomats stashed away in their cushy consulates. And we're the ones who end up paying for their bloody bullshit stupidities! I knew this would turn out badly. I didn't have a good feeling about this crummy operation from the start!"

The lieutenant thumped the butt of his rifle with his fist. "How on earth do you expect to carry through a humanitarian mission with such limited resources?" He pointed his finger in the direction of the hill. "There are millions of enraged religious extremists out there who want to kill the poor minority. I knew it. I knew it."

Vanessa was sure the lieutenant was about to give up in discouragement. But he surprised her by declaring, "We have one last chance. We're going to wait until dark to attack that wretched hill. This way, we'll stop serving as targets for those bastards hiding up there."

The rain stopped, leaving the savannah reeking of wet soil and the flies renewed their presence. Vanessa regained her calm. She sat with her back to the escarpment and jotted down a summary in her reporter's notebook of the incidents that had just taken place.

The lieutenant was speaking to the sergeant of squad one-two planning for the attack on the hill. "Okay, Hermans, there's no time to issue an order in due form. We must arrange this as quickly as possible. You take on the hill this evening with your men. With the element of surprise, you stand a chance. They must expect that we will keep in line with what peacekeepers generally do: Take the blow without making a move. Check the map for the best path to take, you should—"

At the same moment an explosion went off and then a second and then a third. The roof of the church caved in under a thunderous blast followed by the piercing cries of the women and children crushed by the rubble.

"Mortars, the bastards are shelling us with mortar fire! That's just what we needed. It's going to be a real massacre." Edouard yanked the radio and ordered his men to start digging shelters—fast. He grabbed his own shovel and began frantically hollowing the ground with Vanessa's help, she doing the best she could with her bare hands.

CHAPTER 26

R elaxing on the bed in his hotel room, Michael called his place in Seattle to retrieve his phone messages. He knew he should have done this a lot sooner, but a part of him wanted to just get away from it all. Here in Florida he found much needed solitude. But now it was time to get back to reality. The answering machine reliably repeated his recorded calls. Michael was ecstatic when he heard Vanessa's voice. He now knew that she still loved him. He jumped on the telephone receiver and called *Metropolitan* magazine in Seattle to get a phone number for her in Africa. Vanessa had not left him a number where she could be reached and he was sure the magazine would be able to help him out.

Michael was a little envious of Vanessa, who was living exciting adventures under the African sun at the magazine's expense. While he, on the other hand, had lost his job and had but two short days to convince his boss to take him back along with the idea for the show. But in reality, it was already too late. Michael was sure Tony had found another subject for the program. He would have already started promoting it on PDS. Even if by some miracle he managed to solve the Davidson affair within the next twenty-four hours, it would be too late to deal with the matter on the next show. Anyhow he was far from solving the mystery and right now that was the farthest thing on his mind. The hope that Vanessa still loved him relegated his professional concerns to second place.

"Who may I say is calling?" asked the receptionist at the offices of *Metropolitan* magazine.

"Michael Lancaster from the PDS network."

"Ah! Uh…yes…right away, Mr. Lancaster." The young woman impressed by the caller's fame, stuttered a few more syllables and transferred Michael to the editor-in-chief.

"Hello. Mr. Lancaster, this is Rose Wilcock. What can I do for you?"

"Do you know the telephone number where I could reach Vanessa Andressen in Africa?"

Rose Wilcock's tone of voice dramatically changed. "We no longer have any news of Miss Andressen and—"

"You no longer have any news?"

"It's to say that…I mean…," she hesitated momentarily and then continued, "What I mean to say is that all communication with Sambizania has been cut off since this morning."

"When will we be able to talk to her?"

The editor became more and more distraught. She took a deep breath and in one gulp flatly stated, "We don't know. Rumor has it that the entire population of the UN camp in Sambizania has been massacred, the one in which Miss Andressen was staying. But no one could definitively say what has in fact happened. We no longer have any information on the two CNN journalists, on Jimmy McFarlane, the photographer, or on Vanessa Andressen. We have no idea if they moved to another camp, if they were made prisoners or worse. In the last message she sent us, Miss Andressen said that she was heading for a village with a group of peacekeepers. That's all we know."

Michael was in so much shock he couldn't speak.

Rose Wilcock carried on, this time with a tone of assurance. "But we'll be doing everything we possibly can to get hold of any information on their whereabouts and we most certainly will keep you posted. Should I call you at the TV station?"

"No," replied Michael. "I'm in Florida at the moment. But you could leave me a message at my hotel. It will be faster that way. I'm counting on you to inform me as soon as you hear something."

"Certainly, Mr. Lancaster."

Michael was terribly worried about Vanessa. Was she even still alive? Instantly, a phrase came to his mind: "Last year, sixty-three journalists lost their lives doing their job." He couldn't remember where he had read the harrowing fact, but the number had stuck in his memory: sixty-three! "No, it isn't possible. She's still alive." Michael was certain, he just felt it. But her life was in danger, that was for sure. He had to come to her immediate rescue. "What can I do to save her?" he asked himself nervously. To just get up and take off to Africa would do him no good. Whom would he contact there? He could do nothing except wait all afternoon for his appointment with Dr. Carter.

Suddenly, he remembered his date at the port with the Colombian woman. He would have to cancel. Having a fling with this attractive stranger was now absolutely out of the question: Vanessa still cared for him. Since Maria Dominguez didn't leave him her phone number, Michael was tempted to just let it go without saying a word. But this would be inconsiderate on his part and Michael was in the habit of acting like a gentleman.

He decided to quickly pass by where they had planned to meet and cancel their afternoon rendezvous. He ran out of the hotel and jumped into the first taxi he spotted. "Palm Harbor, please."

The taxi dropped Michael off at the marina where rows of opulent yachts awaited a visit from their millionaire owners who hardly ever enjoyed them. He walked along the dock in search of Maria's boat.

"Michael!" shouted a female voice. "Over here!" Leaning against the railing of a modest-sized sailboat, when compared to all the other floating palaces in the marina, Maria Dominguez gesticulated grandly.

With a few supple strides, Michael reached the side of the boat.

"I wasn't expecting you this early," Maria admitted, raising her eyebrows in a seductive manner, "but that's okay," she was quick to add, "I'm glad to see you."

"In fact, I just swung by to tell you that I can't make our date this afternoon."

A look of pure annoyance crossed Maria's face.

"I'm really sorry. Another time, perhaps. I love scuba diving. Your offer is awfully tempting but something unexpected has come up. Thanks again for the invite."

"You must have at least five minutes to spare?" inquired the pretty Maria, straining her smile. "Come in and have a drink."

Michael glanced at his watch.

"Only five minutes!" insisted Maria. "Then you don't have to feel that you came all the way here for nothing."

Out of politeness, Michael gave in to his hostess' offer. He entered into the sailboat's cabin lowering his head only to discover a magnificent mahogany interior.

"You take ice with your whisky?" asked Maria, heading toward the well-stocked bar. She swayed her hips in a most arousing manner, which made one think of the moves in provocative Latin dances. Finally, she sat down facing Michael and looked at him straight in the eyes. There was something strangely Machiavellian-like to her penetrating stare. Maria must have sensed this because she quickly averted her eyes and adopted a relaxed look. Her goal was certainly not to spook Michael but to seduce him.

As he sat there, Michael was overcome by a troubling uneasiness for which he couldn't quite account. Certainly, the terrible news concerning Vanessa rested heavily on his heart. As it turned out, however, his present anxiety was of a different sort altogether. It stemmed from the troubling attraction he felt for this desirable Colombian. And the prudent resolve he had exercised up to this point was cracking like the facade of a house shaken by a seismic tremor.

The five minutes promised ticked away and then another five minutes went by and Michael no longer seemed to appear to be in a rush to leave. He was listening to Maria's trivial chatter with obvious distraction. Michael couldn't help admire her voluptuous body with lustful desire. His eyes frequently landed on the outline of her breasts, barely concealed by the thin orange cotton T-shirt. Her full breasts, which were very firm and upright, lifted the intentionally too short top Maria wore just enough to reveal a slim, bronzed stomach. As soon as she got up to serve him another drink, Michael's eyes examined her curves and rested lasciviously on her rounded bottom. She had on a pair of jean shorts so tight that he was distinctly able to see the crease marking the limit between her thighs and the beginning of her derriere. When she bent down to reach for the bottle of Johnny Walker, it was clear that she wasn't wearing any underwear.

Michael's hungry looks did not go unnoticed by the young Colombian. The seductive power of her physical charm was starting to work. This was a good sign, but she had yet to succeed in leaving the port and sailing out into the high seas to put her plan into action. And time was ticking.

"What would you say about taking a short boat ride, a very short one," proposed Maria, forming a perfect heart with her fleshy lips the color of blood.

Michael hesitated. His intuition screamed danger. Maria, despite her friendliness and charm, seemed to fall into the category of insects with whom amorous flings constituted a prelude to death. But Michael saw this as a challenge. "Is that really a good idea?" he asked in a suave voice tinged with humor.

"Of course it is." She looked at him languorously and touched his arm lightly with her slender fingers and long red nails. Michael shivered. There was something disturbing about the touch of this woman's hand. Before he had a chance to answer, Maria's face was next to his. Her long black hair tickled his cheek. Traces of her perfume wafted past his nostrils. He felt as if he was about to fall over. And then, in a terribly sexy voice, she whispered into his ear: "We can't stay here at the port. If my husband surprises me dressed like this, in the company of a strange man, on board his boat, he would very likely kill us both. I'm sure you know just how jealous Latino men can get. I promise you, it'll just be a little cruise. But we'll both take back a wonderful memory…."

It would have been wise of Michael to refuse this new offer and to stick to his first decision. But this was way too good to pass up. Standing in front of Michael was an extremely provocative woman who would have corrupted the most pious among men. And, by the looks of it, she appeared ready to show him everything her stunning body had to offer. After all, this presented the perfect opportunity to put Dr. Carter's techniques into good practice. There was really nothing left to stop him from accepting Maria's offer.

The Columbian obviously knew how to navigate a boat, steering them out of the marina with ease. Arriving on the open sea, thanks to a GPS of maritime navigation, she maneuvered the small boat in the direction of a place sometimes frequented by divers. She scanned the area and, seeing that there was no other boat in sight, cut off the motor and dropped the anchor.

"I haven't showed you the entire boat yet. Follow me." She took Michael by the hand and they descended a small winding staircase. They entered into a cramped cabin decorated with tinted mirrors and in which reigned a huge round bed. On the tiny night table lay a pair of shiny steel handcuffs.

The Colombian turned around and looked at Michael, tilting her head slightly and forming a tiny smile. She grabbed the bottom of her T-shirt with the tip of her fingers and began gently pulling it over her head. Her breathing quickened, making her mammary spheres swell as they slowly came into view. She finished taking off the cotton article of clothing and gracefully flung it to the far corner of the room.

Her naked torso revealed two superb breasts shaped like pears and tipped off with large dark brown nipples. Her evenly tanned body reflected beautiful ochre highlights. Then, without saying a word, the audacious young woman pulled down the denim shorts that had been hugging her hips. Michael couldn't believe his eyes. A woman with a breathtaking body was standing naked in front of him. As if to pick a piece of ripe fruit, it would have been simply enough to extend his hand and take possession of this exotic body. But Michael didn't even have to do this. Maria took him by the wrists and pulled his hands toward her exposed breasts.

Just as Michael was about to grab hold of these gems, he pictured Vanessa's face. He took a step back, freeing his arms that Maria attempted to restrain. The Colombian looked at him in utter shock, the way one would if a man refused a $10 million lottery jackpot. Nonetheless, convinced of her charm, she once again approached him.

"Maria, I'm sorry. I just can't..."

"I understand...," she hissed between her teeth.

The Colombian—livid and her pride bruised—got dressed calmly without uttering a word. Dressed, she returned to the bar, opening a compartment that held ice and lemon slices. She removed an automatic Walter P38 pistol and turned nonchalantly around to Michael, running her hand through her thick mane. "It's too bad," she said in a soft voice, "I would have preferred to have arrived at this point some other way. It would have been a lot more enjoyable. However, you leave me no other choice but to use more drastic means to get you to undress."

"You have a very strange way of treating your guests, Maria. Are you going to rape me?" he asked sarcastically.

"Have you not noticed that I am already dressed? How unfortunate for you, you blew a really great opportunity. Now it's too late; I already altered my plans." Maria's tone of voice became abruptly authoritarian. "Take off your clothes! Then put this on!" she said, throwing a wet suit on the bed. "Finally, you'll put on the handcuffs over there on the night table…"

Michael, sitting at the edge of the bed, watched Maria, half smiling. "Well there you have it. You plan on getting me into these handcuffs and throwing me overboard. And as soon as I drown to death, you'll dive in to recover your precious handcuffs. Not seen, not known, no traces of violence. The police investigation will conclude that it was an accidental drowning. Bravo! But how are you going to convince me to jump into the water with my hands tied behind my back?"

"You almost have a point there. Not bad. But I had only intended on using the handcuffs until the sleeping pills you swallowed with your whisky started to produce its effect. They were just to keep you under control. But that might not even be necessary. The effect of the pills should be kicking in anytime now," she added, casting a glance at her watch.

A shudder of fear ran through Michael. He had been trapped. He would have to act quickly.

"Listen, Maria," he said slowly, "I had my doubts from the beginning that your interest in me was uniquely as a result of my charm and—"

"That's where you're mistaken," interrupted Maria. "You're a very attractive man and the prospect of being the last woman to make love to the famous Michael Lancaster turned me on. But we've wasted enough time already. Come on, put on the wet suit!"

"Yelling at me is useless, because there is no way in hell I'm going to wear this." Michael could tell Maria was starting to get nervous. She was stuck. If she wanted to camouflage her murder as a drowning, she couldn't pull the trigger. And how else was she going to be able to force him to get into the scuba gear? Michael had the upper hand and this would buy him some time. But how much time? There was no real way of knowing that if Maria went into panic, she wouldn't suddenly turn the gun on him. And what about the sleeping pills that were continuing their progression through his system?

"In the meantime, just in case this might be of interest to you, I would like you to take a look at a nifty little gadget." Michael showed Maria his watch. "This is a tiny transmitter comparable to what is used by pilots in the U.S. Air Force. When a plane is hit, it enables search and rescue teams to locate them. But this miniature model includes its own special features. First of all, it's equipped with a heart monitor. As soon as my heart stops beating, it immediately sends out a distress signal. The same system is automatically triggered if someone tries to rip the watch off of my arm. Obviously, I could also set off the alarm myself and in less than ten minutes an FBI helicopter will be hovering right above this splendid sailboat. I'm sure you wouldn't want our charming get-together to be interrupted by a couple of law enforcement agents. Good, neither would I, because I think you can help me out."

Maria burst out into hysterical laughter: "Help you! That's a good one. My job is to kill you! Do you honestly think I believed one word of your farfetched gibberish?" She loaded the revolver with a sudden, sharp gesture.

Michael began to feel the effects of the narcotic. An insidious sleepiness was taking hold of him. He had to make a conscious effort to continue to talk and play his bluff.

"Of course, you can always kill me. But I guarantee you within minutes following my death, you will be apprehended by the FBI. And if memory serves me correctly, Florida is one of the states where the death penalty is applied...." But Michael knew this particular argument had never before stopped a criminal, so he quickly changed his approach. "You're an awesome woman, Maria, without a doubt the most attractive woman I've ever met. And I would have likely given into your charm if you were just a little more patient. What a horrible waste for such a gorgeous body to rot away in prison...."

"But I don't intend to end up in there!" The beautiful temptress shot back, showing obvious signs of nervousness. "By the time they learn of your death, I will already be relaxing comfortably on a pretty patio overlooking the ocean, somewhere in Colombia."

"You'll never have the time. And besides, my death will signify the end of your very own existence. Listen to me!" exclaimed Michael, trying desperately to fight the fatigue attacking him. "I have a deal for you. Your freedom in exchange for testimony affirming that Jack Kotten is your employer. You'll benefit from the same protection and advantages as the repentants of the mafia."

"I don't know this guy Kotten. He's not the one who pays me."

"It's one of his men, then. Christopher Clays?"

Maria hesitated briefly, and then looked directly into Michael's sleepy eyes. "I have no idea who you're talking about."

Michael's eyelids were getting heavy and he was having a hard time holding his head up straight. "You love your country, Maria, this is obvious from the way you speak. And yet Jack Kotten wants the American military to intervene in Colombia. It'll take too long too explain, but it's all outlined in his anti-drug program. You're working for racists who want to destroy the country of your family and friends."

"Shut up," hurled the Colombian.

"No! I will not shut up!" Michael tried to yell. But his voice was getting weaker and weaker and his body parts were getting heavier with each passing second. "They tricked you, Maria. They correctly suspected that I would protect myself. They knew you would be arrested right after my death and…" He could barely speak…. "And that's why…" Michael struggled to stay awake…. "And that's why…," he repeated with much difficulty and strain, "…that's why they chose you, a Colombian…." His head bobbed forward. "To link my murder to the Colombian drug cartel…You…you will never touch the money they promised you…."

Those were his last words before he fell into a deep sleep.

CHAPTER 27

"To die for nothing! To die foolishly in some hole in the middle of Africa. To die in a war that doesn't even concern me and one I don't even understand." These were Vanessa's exact thoughts. She tossed and turned, unable to fall asleep in spite of her immense fatigue. The moonless night was streaked by flashes of light generated by the explosions from the mortar shells. Every explosion caused her to jump. At this very moment, she was no longer thinking about her article, the Pulitzer Prize or the condition of women in Sambizania. She was tormented by the fear eating away at her gut, obsessed by the thirst drying out her throat and tortured by the cuts formed from the blisters on her feet. Confined in the hollow shelter hastily dug out by the lieutenant, her shoulders touched the sides of the hole, her legs were crushed against those of Edouard and her back rested uncomfortably on a bag filled with video material. A suffocating feeling of claustrophobia was coming over Vanessa. She could barely breathe. The hole felt like it was already her grave.

Vanessa's lips wouldn't stop trembling and then her entire body started. She was breathing more and more from the top of her rib cage and gradually beginning to lose complete control of herself. Lieutenant Demat, who was studying a map with the beam of his flashlight, looked up haphazardly only to realize that Vanessa was on the verge of a fit. He grabbed her by the arm and in a firm voice said, "I need you for tonight's operation." Edouard knew it was important for Vanessa to keep her mind focused on something so she wouldn't go into panic if a traumatic situation should present itself. He began to explain the details of the mission to her: "Our last chance is the conquest of the hill from where the mortar fire is coming. That's where we should have started off, by the way. We can no longer find Captain Muller. I have taken command over the platoon. You will set up your video camera facing the direction of the hill and will commence filming at one o'clock in the morning. Don' be alarmed if you hear gunfire from the opposite direction ten minutes before; it will be a diversionary tactic on our part."

Edouard showed her a military map at a scale of 1/25,000. "This here, you see, is the village of Kiboyo," he circled the area with his index finger. "Our platoon is divided into three infantry squads and one command squad of which we are both a part. On this line, east of the village, we find the men of squad one-one; they are also in charge of protecting the south. On the west side, we find squad one-two and at the north end, squad one-three. As for ourselves, the command squad, we are here, right next to the church, in the center of the village. Evidently, Captain Muller was the one who chose this theoretically perfect plan of action. But in reality, it's completely insane. Kiboyo is far too vast for the number of men at our disposal. In fact, we're incapable of protecting the entire village. The distance between each team is too great. Not only can they not communicate between each other, but the enemy has the freedom to infiltrate inside these unoccupied areas. We were obliged to make the painful decision to consolidate our defensive position solely around the center of the village. We've abandoned the civilians who are hiding on the periphery of Kiboyo.

After the diversionary maneuver, I will dispatch the men from squad one-two to attack the hill that you can see here on the map, to the north. I know it's pure folly to launch an attack with a single squad but this position has to be controlled, if not, the entire village will be massacred. The darkness and the effect of surprise will assist the operation. Even if only two among them reach the top of the hill, they'll still be able to position our machine gun. I'll then send them backups. This way we'll reverse the situation and from the first rays of sunlight we will dominate the whole plain. The sacrifice of squad one-two will save the rest of the platoon as well as the inhabitants of Kiboyo."

Edouard's plan restored Vanessa's hopes somewhat and she managed a weak smile. She then turned toward the church whose jagged silhouette rested in misery against the dark sky. "Please, get me out of this horrible hell," she implored to God in her prayer. At the same moment, a man with a blackened face appeared at the edge of the trench. Vanessa jumped back violently.

"Don't be afraid, it's only Sergeant Hermans," said Edouard. "He's wearing night camouflage. He's the one leading the attack on the hill; he has come for his final instructions."

The lieutenant and the sergeant briefly exchanged a few words in Flemish. Marc Hermans then turned toward Vanessa, a huge adolescent smile plastered on his face. Vanessa immediately recognized him as the guitarist with the great voice. The glow from the flashlight revealed big, clear blue eyes. Behind the war makeup, fatigue and anxiety, Vanessa guessed that the purity and innocence of the features belonged to a young man who was no more than twenty-one years old. The young sergeant looked at her without saying a word. Edouard in the end simply spoke for him: "Sergeant Hermans would like you to wish him good luck."

Vanessa didn't know what to say. "G-g-g-good…good luck, sergeant," she stuttered.

Edouard approached Vanessa and whispered into her ear. "He's leaving on a very risky mission. He might not return. I think it would give him courage if he received a kiss from a pretty young lady."

Vanessa didn't hesitate for an instant. She quickly took Marc Hermans' face in between her hands and placed a delicate kiss on his chapped lips. A broad smile lit up the young sergeant's face. He stammered a thank you and then, filled with renewed fervor, disappeared into the night in a flash.

The wait seemed interminable to Vanessa who, eye glued to the video camera, was monitoring the hill. At the expected hour, a round of gunfire exploded at the south end of the village to divert the enemy's attention. At this time, Sergeant Hermans and his men climbed the slope of the hill. Minutes later, a brilliant white light suddenly appeared in the sky and lit up the entire village. It lasted a few seconds, gradually becoming blurred as the tiny beads containing the phosphorous charges drew closer to the ground. Darkness had barely reclaimed the night sky when another illumination materialized.

"Shit! They have mortar rocket flares!" exclaimed Lieutenant Demat. "They're going to spot our men."

Within a few minutes, the firing ceased and once again obscurity reigned over the plain of Kiboyo. Vanessa glanced at her watch and used the gleam of a passing flashlight to make out the time. It was 1:13 A.M. and nothing had happened yet. What were the men from squad one-two doing? Where were they?

Suddenly, the silence enclosing the hill was pierced by the frantic exchange of gunfire. The UN soldiers had become engaged in combat with the enemy. The short blasts characteristic of FNC rifles used by the Belgian soldiers could be distinguished from the more powerful crackling coming from the AK47 assault rifles held by the Sambizanian forces. With her eye stuck to the camera, Vanessa could see nothing of the battle except for the flames bursting from the assault rifles and the explosions from the grenades. At times everything returned to calm. And then all hell would break loose, and each time the exchange of deadly flares got closer to the top of the hill.

Full of enthusiasm, the lieutenant declared to Vanessa in a convincing voice, "It's amazing, squad one-two will dislodge these bastards! I knew Hermans was capable! Another hundred meters or so and they'll make it."

Vanessa rejoiced. She was starting to believe that she was actually going to escape from this living nightmare. She could return to thinking about the future, about returning to the United States, about reuniting with Michael.... Her mind was no longer in Sambizania but already in the comfort and security of her native country.

The rockets lighting up the landscape gave the overall impression of its being the end of the world. A scramble of shadows could be seen at the top of the hill running in all directions. The automatic assault weapons didn't stop crackling. All over the bottom of the hill hundreds of luminous spots appeared briefly, time enough to launch a deadly blast. But as the battle progressed, the sound of AK47 assault rifles dominated the din of the combat.

"Shit, there are too many of them. Our boys will never make it. They must withdraw immediately!" The lieutenant rushed toward his rocket launcher pistol, opened it and feverishly fed it a cartridge. A green rocket rose into the air, ordering the squad to retreat. But the gunfire continued in full force. A second green rocket wandered the sky without any better results.

Vanessa's hopes faded in an instant. She turned toward Edouard, her eyes tormented with worry: "What are we going to do now?"

The lieutenant replied flatly, "I have no idea. All we can do is wait for the survivors of squad one-two to return to us."

* * *

"Wake up! Wake up," Maria shouted, slapping Michael across the face.

He coughed and sneezed several times. Both his throat and nose were burning sharply. With great strain, he pried open his eyes and observed above him a dark shadow shrieking. For a moment, he thought it was a flock of cawing crows hovering over his carcass. He saw himself dead, washed up on a beach. It took him a few minutes to stand up and get a grip on reality. He coughed again and sniffed a few more times. And then he felt strangely energized even though his legs barely seemed to be able to support him.

"What did you give me?" he articulated with difficulty.

"I helped you snort a bit of coke. To wake you up," calmly replied the Colombian who was now dressed in a crimson leather outfit.

"What? You gave me that crap!"

"Calm down, *mi amor*. It's the only way to keep you awake. You're not happy? You are nevertheless still alive. I thought over your proposition and I'm ready to give you a hand in exchange for my freedom. But don't count on me to testify before the courts. I don't want any more problems. I've already taken enough risks as it is."

Michael was still drifting in and out of the fogginess of sleep when he realized that he was stark naked. He looked at Maria in astonishment. She threw some clothes at him that were not his own.

"Here. These belong to Gilles Tremblay, the owner of the boat. Get dressed quickly. Put on his hat and glasses as well so that no one will recognize you. Let the rumors of your death circulate for a couple of days. This way you'll have peace and so will I. *Adios!*"

Michael struggled his way into the clothes and then sluggishly walked over to Maria. "We have to find the guy who hired you. The lives of many people depend on it."

"Are you mad? Do you want to throw yourself into the jaws of the lion? You already got very lucky today. Don't push it."

"You obviously don't understand, Maria. We won't have peace until the head of this organization is put behind bars. Come on, we're taking your car." He took her by the arm and pulled her toward the gangplank. Maria let herself be dragged along without resistance, even though she didn't usually take kindly to orders from men.

Maria stopped her car a few houses away from Christopher Clay's apartment. She had lost her smile and her face looked very pale beneath the tan. Michael followed the Colombian as they walked around the building to get to the backyard.

"What floor?" he whispered.

The young Colombian didn't reply. She looked terrified.

"What floor?" Michael asked again. Every one of his words caused a crippling pain that went straight to his sore head.

"Third," Maria said tightly.

Michael scaled the building and landed with a bit of trouble onto the balcony of the apartment where Christopher Clays lived. Night had fallen and there were no lights shining from inside. Michael decided to risk it and he forced open the sliding glass patio door. He breathed in relief: No alarm system had gone off.

He entered the premises and flicked on the light switch. A bright light pierced into his brain and he brought his hands to his temples, holding back a howl. After having opened his eyelids with painful dread, he noticed packed cardboard cartons strewn all over the place. Aware that Maria knew his address, Michael guessed that the man in the black polo was about to move. He rummaged quickly through each box without finding anything of real interest. Finally, he came across a box with a bunch of photographs. But nothing too revealing—a few family portraits, a graduating class photo, baseball team pictures. Michael slipped a couple of them into his pocket and continued on. But his search got him nowhere. Completely drained, he sunk onto the sofa, his body dripping in sweat. He slowly scanned the walls of the apartment on which *El Greco* reproductions remained intact. A few seconds later he heard footsteps coming down the corridor.

Hoping it was just the neighbors, Michael leaned on the edge of the sofa and held his breath so he could better hear. But when the footsteps stopped in front of the door, it was clear the apartment's owner was back. He heard the sound of the key in the lock and crept toward the balcony. On his way out he tripped over a box and landed smack in the middle of the living room just as Christopher Clays opened the door.

Face contorted in surprise, the man in the black polo remained frozen for a fraction of a second. Taking advantage of this momentary lapse, Michael got up and ran toward the balcony. But Christopher Clays hardly gave him enough time to move. He quickly removed a nickel Colt Anaconda from a holster attached to the inside of his jacket. With his thumb, he clicked back the hammer of his enormous revolver and pointed it toward his target. Michael climbed over the balcony railing and looked down. It was too high to jump. He turned back toward Christopher who was ready to shoot. He had no other choice.

A gunshot blast rang out just as Michael plunged into the open. He landed on the lawn and rolled like a parachutist. But as he got up, a sharp pain ripped through his left ankle. He took a few paces, limping, and fell back onto the grass while Christopher Clays continued firing shots at him from the balcony. Luckily, the gunfire lacked precision due to the darkness in the garden.

Michael hoisted himself up and started hopping away on one foot. He was completely out of breath by the time he made it to the corner of the street where he had arranged to meet Maria. But the Colombian's red Pontiac had of course vacated the spot a long while ago. Christopher Clays, by this time, had bolted down the stairs of his apartment and was running toward the sidewalk in hot pursuit of his victim.

Michael waved wildly at the cars going by on Montgomery Street but no one stopped. Living in perpetual fear of attack, none of the Miami drivers risked picking up the stranger. Michael knew it. He also knew that Christopher Clays could kill him on the street corner without anyone even batting an eye. The residents of this region were far too accustomed to violence to be moved. Michael turned around and caught a glimpse of his aggressor's silhouette approaching at a quick pace. Christopher Clays wasn't even running anymore, so convinced was he that his prey could not escape him.

With a last painful hurdle, Michael attempted to cross the street. But his wounded leg refused to endure the stretch and he only managed to move forward a couple of steps. The man in the black polo was clearly catching up to him. Just then, an old beat-up Chevrolet stopped in front of Michael and a door opened. Michael jumped in and the car sped away, leaving behind a most flabbergasted Christopher Clays.

"You hurt?" asked a voice laced with a heavy Spanish accent. Michael lifted his head to get a good look at the face of his savior. A woman of mixed race, probably of Cuban origin, took up the entire space between the seat and the steering wheel. She may have been fifty or sixty years old. It was hard to tell—her age was disguised in layers of fat.

"You shouldn't be wandering the streets alone at night like that, it's dangerous. You never know what could happen to you over here. By the way, Maria said she'll hold fond memories of you."

"Maria? Where is she?"

"She's the one who sent me to pick you up. She didn't want Christopher Clays to find out. She fears for her family in Colombia. Over there they assassinate people like having a cup of coffee. She phoned me. I'm sorry, it took me a while to get here, I don't know this neighborhood very well."

Michael, still out of breath, declared, "This neighborhood isn't worth getting to know. I could have been gunned down and nobody would have given a damn...."

"Not as bad as in Colombia..."

"You're Colombian? I figured you for Cuban."

"Bah, Latinos, we all look the same to strangers. Me, I come from Medellin, the second largest city in the country," she said with pride, grabbing open a pack of cigarettes with her great big pudgy fingers. "You smoke?"

"No."

"Does it bother you?"

"It's your car. You're the boss."

"I swear you sounded exactly like my late husband just then....
When I lived in Medellin, my husband and I taught in a high school.
Jorge, was his name, he dabbled in a little politics. He wanted to fight
against drug trafficking and corruption. He was assassinated in broad
daylight right smack in the middle of the street."

"I'm sorry."

"There's no reason to be sorry, that sort of thing takes place daily
over there. I immigrated to the United States in 1996. That year, over
five thousand people died violently in Medellin alone. Something
like an average of fourteen murders a day. The number shook me up.
Did you know that Colombia holds the world record for the most
violence? Jorge was honest and courageous, but poor. Not like those
who killed him. Rich guys. Rich and powerful. Do you know what I
think? Drugs aren't the real evil. The real evil is easy money."

"Do you know what kind of people your friend Maria works for?"

"I have my suspicions but it's none of my business, really. I'm
not like my husband. She helps me out; I help her out. In our case,
money has nothing to do with it. That's all that counts for me. I'm a
natural chatterbox, but I do know when to shut up."

"Very wise."

"This might come as a surprise to you but I'm quite attached to
my old and cumbersome carcass. Shall I drop you off at a hospital?
Your leg seems to be causing you great pain."

"That would be great, although preferably not in the area."

"I understand. You come across as a nice, friendly guy. It doesn't
bother me in the least to travel some ways with you. This reminds me
of the time when I hitchhiked from Cartagena to Baranquilla."

The obese Colombian casually carried on the conversation, re-
counting every minute detail of her past and present life. She drove
Michael to Fort Lauderdale where she dropped him off in front of a
remote private clinic that offered night services. Before closing the
car door, she leaned forward and said, "Don't forget to forget Maria..."

"She has nothing to fear. I'm a man of my word: my life in exchange for her freedom. I didn't lie. Thanks for everything."

"Don't even mention it.... And by the way, I like your show a lot,
Mr. Lancaster," she said, with the wink of her heavy eyelid.

CHAPTER 28

T he first glimmer of dawn broke over Kiboyo and not a single man from squad one-two had yet returned. It seemed clear they had all been killed or taken prisoner.

"It would be best for us to surrender," Vanessa said to Lieutenant Demat, with obvious anguish in her voice.

"There is no question of doing so! Never! And besides, it would be a crazy thing to do. General El Tabernasti's troops are pitiless. You saw what they did to the civilians. Don't think you'll be protected or spared just because you're a journalist. Anyway, they haven't made us any offer of surrender. And even if they would make us one, I'd refuse it. I haven't forgotten what happened years ago to ten Belgian soldiers on a humanitarian mission in Rwanda. After putting down their weapons and being taken as prisoners, they were butchered with machetes by the enemy soldiers. I don't want the same thing to happen to us. We will either leave here with weapons in hand or we will perish. But I refuse for us to be exterminated like defenseless animals."

The chill of his words caused Vanessa to freeze up from terror.

The lieutenant once again began sending out calls for help using the radio system. But communication with the UN base camp was cut off and only a single sinister hissing was coming through on the receiver. Edouard realized then that the camp had been attacked and, without a doubt, destroyed. His thoughts turned to Yasmine and he couldn't help feeling sick with worry: What had become of her if the UN camp had indeed fallen into the hands of the Sambizanian army?

Did they spare her? Was she raped, tortured or murdered like other Sambizanian women had been?

"Lieutenant, the warrant officer has sent me." An outpost soldier had appeared suddenly inside the shelter seeking new instructions.

Edouard pulled himself together. He quit being Yasmine's desperate fiancé and returned to his responsibilities as the marine infantry lieutenant. "Listen carefully to what I'm about to tell you, and you will then report it back to the warrant officer. We will take advantage of this lull to reinforce our position and secure our defense zone. You will dig a second trench in back of the first. It will serve as a retreat shelter. I want nice deep holes, and make them good and solid with an evacuation shaft for the grenades. Fire only at sure shots, every bullet must meet its mark. Yesterday, in the confusion, I'm sure that at least two of our men were hit by our own bullets as well as several civilians whom we are supposed to be protecting. This must never happen again. I want each one of you to kill at least ten of these worthless vermin point blank. I know you are all capable of this. You must also always remain at your post. While your team member sleeps, you must survey the area nonstop. They must not take us by surprise. Don't move from where you are. My squad will take care of the water supply. There will be no additional supplies of food or ammunition; you must make do with what remains. Be sparing, reinforcements will be arriving shortly. You must hold on until then. I have confidence in you. We are Marines! Remember our motto: *Courage to the last!*

When the soldier left to relay the orders, Vanessa asked Edouard, "Why did you tell them reinforcements would be arriving when you know very well this isn't true?"

"You must never destroy hope. There is no way for us to escape since the village is surrounded. And besides, we simply can't abandon the inhabitants when a systematic massacre awaits them. We can no longer retreat, either. Every soldier must fight or perish in his trench alongside his team member. The men will continue fighting if they believe a few among us will manage to stay alive. That's why I spoke of backups. I don't like lying to my men. In fact, there's still a possibility the UN has taken heed of our situation and is sending troops to our rescue. But this could take several days..."

Suddenly, the thunderous sound of explosions resounded around them. Mortar fire action had resumed. A shell exploded close to the only existing well, literally blowing apart the bodies of the women which had come to gather water. The force of the explosion was such that it caved in a section of the well that from then on became unusable.

* * *

"Doctor, thanks again for your understanding. As I mentioned over the phone, due to very serious reasons, it would have been impossible for me to remain at the same hotel or to continue our meetings at your office. It was a matter of safety...."

"I understand completely. It isn't my first time holding a therapy session in a hotel suite. But generally, it's for reasons of discretion. Some of my clients include showbiz celebrities and politicians. They ask me to meet them in undisclosed locations to escape from the paparazzi."

"I'm glad we were able to work things out. I would have hated to end our sessions."

"Good." The sex therapist removed Michael's file from his briefcase and started the session. "Today we'll be dealing with the subject of receptivity. However, before we begin, I'd like to obtain more information on how you behave during sexual relations."

Michael explained at length how he conducted himself during sex. Like many men who ejaculate quickly, he avoided as much as possible to be caressed by his partner during foreplay. He feared becoming overexcited and ejaculating prematurely. Sex play was a one-way exercise. He expertly stimulated his partner and when she was ready, he moved on to intercourse. He shunned all stimulation, whether it was simple hand caresses, contact of their bodies or kisses on his penis. To become even less aroused, he tried thinking about something else or closed his eyes.

"Yes, I understand. This approach was in a way a form of compromise, given the limited methods of control you possessed at the time," noted Dr. Carter. "However, you have to agree with me that there are many disadvantages to these types of avoidance behaviors.

247

Let me explain. First, it's not especially gratifying to take part in sex without really becoming engaged in it yourself, that is to say by receiving nothing and thinking about something else. Second, it's not very satisfying for your partner either. She's forced to repress her tenderness and her sexual fantasies. Moreover, when her partner is thinking about something else during sex, she probably and most likely does feel neglected, undesirable, rejected and even abandoned. And she has every good reason to feel this way because you're there neither mentally nor emotionally! In the third place, thinking about something else during sex prevents you from observing your corporal reactions and from applying the appropriate techniques. In other words, thinking about something else cuts you off from the actual means that would enable you to control yourself. Finally, by preventing yourself from being stimulated physically and by thinking about something else during sex, you risk facing erectile difficulties after a certain age.

"With all the techniques you now master, you and your partner will be able to let yourselves go a lot more freely during sexual relations. You'll both have time to be receptive to what is taking place during foreplay as well as intercourse. It will be possible for you to be fondled, hugged, kissed and stimulated without the fear of provoking ejaculation unexpectedly.

"Receptivity to sexual stimuli comprises several advantages for both the man and woman. First of all, perceiving touches leads, in a paradoxical way, to a release of tension as well as an increase of sexual excitation. You will be both aroused and relaxed, which will allow you to remain below the point of no return. Second, you will experience pleasure—an advantage in itself! Third, sex with your partner will be reciprocal and not one-sided. This will provide both of you with wonderful moments of sharing and partnership. Fourth, being receptive provides the essential basis of erectile capacity. If you let yourself be touched and if you're in tune with what is happening during lovemaking, then you enable the psycho neurophysiological sex processes to become activated and provoke an erection. After age forty-five, this condition becomes more and more necessary in sustaining sexual potency."

"Doctor, can I offer you something to drink?"

"Gladly. It being a scorcher out there, I'm feeling dehydrated."

Michael got up quickly and headed toward the mini-bar in his room. "I have coolers, beer, crème de menthe, or…"

"No alcohol, thank you. I never drink while I'm working. Juice or mineral water will do."

The sex therapist accepted the bottle of cranberry juice Michael handed him and continued on with the session: "We still have some time left. Before leaving you, I'd like to touch on the question of the frequency of ejaculatory discharges. To do this, we'll be comparing the sex drive—or libido or sexual appetite—to the appetite for food. The comparisons with food or the action of eating are always full of imagery and allow us to fully understand the phenomenon of sexuality.

"As time goes by our appetite for food increases. As soon as we eat something, this appetite is satisfied and we are no longer hungry. The same goes for our sexual appetite. With time, man's sexual appetite increases. When he experiences an ejaculatory discharge, this appetite decreases considerably. Now, if the frequency of the appetite for food varies in general anywhere from two to four full meals a day depending on the person, then the frequency of the appetite for sexual activity presents greater variations. It could be two times a day, three times a week, one time every two weeks and so on, according to the individual.

"What happens when time goes by and we don't eat? In general, our appetite increases. When we finally do get to eat, chances are we gobble our food down quickly. The same applies for the sexual appetite. If a man goes a long time without having an ejaculatory discharge, there are huge possibilities he'll ejaculate quickly at the time of his next sexual encounter.

It is important you respect your ejaculatory frequency and that you act while taking into account your physiological needs of discharge. If your frequency is greater than that of your partner, you can always resort to masturbation. This sexual practice, which is used by many men and is altogether normal, becomes a good way of controlling your sexual appetite. Once your sexual appetite is regularized, it'll be much easier for you to apply the techniques of control that I have taught you. You and your partner will benefit in the end."

Michael cut in, "Do you think it's normal for a married man to masturbate?"

"Statistics show that seventy-six percent of married men masturbate. They do it for all sorts of reasons—because their spouse is ill, because she's not in the mood, because her sex drive is weaker or simply because they want to get rid of some tension without involving her. I know that for a number of reasons, many men feel guilty for giving into such an activity. However, it's better that you resort to masturbation rather than forcing your wife into unwanted sexual relations or going to bed sexually famished and as a result ejaculating prematurely.

"Let's move on to our exercises. You have reached an advanced level. Up to this point, you've learned how to breathe from the abdomen; you're able to dissociate the top of the body from the bottom part of the body; you're capable of varying the speed and extent of your movements; you no longer use your buttocks to move your pelvis; and you no longer needlessly contract the uninvolved muscles when it comes to maintaining different positions. Very good. You've made considerable progress.

"We'll be tackling a very difficult stage today. There exists a very small muscle, but one that plays a very big role in controlling the moment of the appearance of ejaculation, called the pubococcygeal muscle. This muscle is situated at the base of the penis, inside of the body. It contracts involuntarily when you get sexually excited. However, these contractions are barely perceptible and it takes training to be able to perceive them during sex. As soon as you can identify the pubococcygeal muscle and relax it at will, you'll have excellent control over the moment of your ejaculation.

"The following information will help you discover its exact position. The pubococcygeal muscle is the muscle that you use to give tiny thrusts with the penis when you are erect. It's also the muscle that voluntarily cuts off your stream of urine. Finally, if you have difficulty finding it, you'll notice that when the anus is contracted, this muscle is also tense. So you just have to contract the anus and you'll immediately perceive the pubococcygeal muscle.

"Sitting comfortably on your chair, I want you to try to discover where the pubococcygeal muscle is located."

"Yes, I feel something moving in the crotch area, just below the testicles," said Michael.

"Good, this very thing that's moving is precisely the pubococcygeal muscle. In order for you to really feel it, I want you to contract and relax it twenty times right now...."

Michael complied. While breathing deeply from the abdomen, he slowly contracted and relaxed his pubococcygeal. As he tensed the muscle, he sensed his crotch getting tighter and his penis retracting. When he relaxed it, he felt that his breathing had become deeper and his entire body was less tense.

After Michael had finished his series of repetitions, Dr. Carter continued with his explanation. "The pubococcygeal muscle is more difficult to find while engaging in sexual activity than when you do these exercises. A trick that will help you a great deal during sex consists of contracting the muscle deliberately and then relaxing it right away. This voluntary contraction will allow you to better feel the muscle and to better relax it. To master this technique, you will now do the following exercise twenty times. You contract the pubococcygeal. Don't forget to breathe...." The sex therapist paused between each of his instructions so that Michael could really feel his body. "Contract it a little more...relax it completely...breathe from the stomach...repeat the exercise...."

CHAPTER 29

T he sun was now high in the sky and the heat was becoming suffocating. Thousands of flies attracted by the pungent odor of blood buzzed above the corpses. Vanessa, buried in her hole, could not find the courage within her to get out and film the death of the village. Her knees were scraped, her lips dry and cracked, her dirty clothes clinging to her skin. She fumbled in her backpack for a piece of fruit because her water flask had been empty for a long time now and she was extremely thirsty. But there was no more fruit left.

"You could always suck on a tiny pebble. This will keep your mouth from drying out completely. A little piece of wisdom passed along to me by a veteran from Algeria."

"That's all you have to offer me?"

"Yes, that's all. We'll see tonight whether it will be possible to recover the water flasks of the dead or if we'll be able to have them replenished by the villagers. In the meantime, we keep cover."

"But we're going to die of thirst here, let's leave."

"No, a human being can usually last forty-eight hours without drinking, if he doesn't move too much."

"You have an answer for everything," groaned Vanessa. Oppressive heat, acute thirst and fear were making the young woman exceptionally irritable.

"At this moment, I assure you that I would very much like to have an answer for everything. Unfortunately, this isn't the case. However, let me tell you this: You and I, we chose to come here. We knew the risks involved with our respective jobs. But the children of this village, they didn't have that choice. So as long as I am in command of this detachment, we will not abandon them."

"You're right. I'm sorry…I guess I was feeling a bit discouraged…."

"You're entirely excused," the lieutenant gently replied. "It's perfectly understandable. It could happen to me."

"You think so? You seem so together."

The lieutenant brushed off an ant that had been crawling up his arm with the flick of his hand. "In a crisis situation we never know at what point a human being will lose it. There are a lot of tough soldiers who pee on themselves from fear at the time of bombardments. We've already witnessed veteran officers crying like babies in front of their astounded men. Sometimes, certain disciplined soldiers transform into sadistic torturers. Do you remember the humanitarian operation carried out in Somalia following a horrifying famine?"

"Yes, it dates back several years."

"Well, during this operation—paradoxically called Restore Hope—several peacekeepers were accused of severely mistreating the Somalian prisoners, made up mostly of young adolescents. Some Belgian, Italian and Canadian paratroopers, among others, committed cruel, barbaric acts that were clearly racist. Do you understand, as a consequence, why your presence here as a journalist is important?"

"It's true, you know. We, journalists, are privileged witnesses. However, servicemen don't usually like us much."

"Servicemen don't like you because they're often ashamed of the fact that the world ends up seeing what really goes on inside the military. Yet, I must say journalists often broadcast images out of context purely for reasons of sensationalism. If you film one of my soldiers shooting a Sambizanian assailant, the television viewers will simply see a white guy shooting a black guy. Without the appropriate commentary, they won't understand the situation."

"Don't you worry one bit, I will faithfully report what really went on here. If…" Vanessa added, swallowing what little saliva she had left within her, "…if we make it out of here alive."

* * *

Michael turned toward Dr. Carter. "Do you remember Vanessa, the woman I spoke to you about?"

"Yes?"

"Well it seems as if I've known her forever. Almost as if we were childhood friends. But I really only met her a few months ago. The more I think about her, the more I realize that I want to get better for her."

"You love her a lot, don't you?"

Michael lowered his head and didn't say a word.

Dr. Carter had touched a sensitive nerve. Out of respect for Michael, he remained silent.

A few seconds later, Michael started to talk. "It's not easy, you know. At first I was drawn to her beauty. I only truly became attached to her after we began spending a lot of time together. If I was told today that we would never get to see each other again, I don't know what I would do."

"If you would allow me to intervene…You do have feelings for Vanessa. And they are real and sincere. However, and you tell me if I'm right or wrong about this, I get the impression that you're 'fusioning' with her and that you're falling out of touch with your-self. Emotionally, you no longer differentiate yourself from her. This is undoubtedly intensified because of her absence—one knows that absence makes the heart grow fonder and that it inflates the amorous dream. And the amorous dream, simply because it has no bounds, promotes emotional fusion. On top of that, your current state of lone-liness in West Palm Beach doesn't help either."

"I get the feeling that I've become one with her. But what you've just said to me has somehow opened my eyes. If I understand you correctly, what this means is that it would be better for me to come back down to earth. And that ultimately, I could continue to love her without losing touch with myself."

"Exactly! And this observation leads us to consider another cause of premature ejaculation: anxiety. The fear of ejaculating too fast and the apprehension associated with it—for example, the concern that once again you won't be able to satisfy your partner, the assumption that you will be laughed at, the dread of being humiliated, the an-guish of being rejected—could all accelerate the arrival of ejaculation.

Actually, Michael, anxiety, like sexual excitation, activates the autonomic nervous system. When the autonomic nervous system is sufficiently activated, it precipitates ejaculation. Consequently, a man who's anxious about ejaculating prematurely risks ejaculating even if he's not that sexually aroused because of this double activation of the autonomic nervous system. In addition, not being entirely sexually stimulated means that he doesn't have access to all the corporal signals indicating the rise of sexual excitation and as a result, has no further reference points to enable him to control himself."

"So what can we do to control anxiety apart from taking medication?"

"Well, we have several physical means and psychological methods at our disposal. The physical means include abdominal breathing and diminishing the tension of all the muscles in the body. Lucky for us, the physical behavior we employ to moderate our level of sexual excitation also acts to reduce anxiety. There are no other techniques to learn! If you breathe deeply, if you refrain from using the muscles you don't need when executing your movements, if you move in a fluid manner, if your body expands instead of curling up, your anxiety will decrease accordingly.

"As for the psychological methods, they're endless. That's why I'll only be revealing a few. First of all, there's something I call the utilization of the 'limits of the field of consciousness' or you could call it 'perceptual limits' or still 'cognitive limits.' Let me explain: When you're focused on things that please you sexually, when you pay attention to your level of sexual excitation and when you apply the techniques of modulation, there's not much room left in your mind for distressful and defeatist thoughts. In other words, since the field of consciousness contains a limited scope, while you think about sex you don't think about anything else. So by following the program, one, you have pleasure; two, you lessen your anxiety; and three, you prolong the duration of intercourse.

"Another way to offset your anxiety is by not overdramatizing the fact that your partner might be experiencing frustration and disappointment during lovemaking. It's obviously unpleasant for a woman to have her sexual excitement interrupted by her partner's ejaculating prematurely. But it's not the end of the world. She won't die. She won't break apart. Consequently, if you don't turn the irritation your partner is feeling into a calamity, chances are you'll be far less stressed and you'll have an easier time staying under control. And because of this, your chances of giving her more pleasure will increase. The same applies if your partner leaves you because of your lousy sexual performance. Sure, you'll suffer. Sure, you'll have a rough time with it. And yes, you'll feel demoralized. But once again, it's not the end of the world. You won't die. Women won't despise you forever. All the doors of opportunity won't shut in your face. The entire universe will not reject you! It's essential not to create a catastrophe out of the hard times in your sex life and relationship. This way, you won't be as distressed over the thought of a failure. Your autonomic nervous system will be less activated and you'll be able to control yourself more easily.

"Finally, it's important not to set unrealistic standards of success for yourself. If you manage to prolong the length of penetration six to eight times out of ten, that's excellent. If you demand perfection, you'll become apprehensive and will have more difficulty delaying the arrival of your ejaculation."

"I'm sure that's true, but I'm a perfectionist. I don't deal well with failure. I've always worked extremely hard at whatever I do, and I think it would be very difficult for me to act otherwise."

"You could most certainly keep up this attitude in your everyday life and you'll continue to benefit from it. But the mistake you're making, just like a great many Westerners, consists of turning sex into an activity where you have to perform at all costs..."

"...Rather than an occasion of discovery and mutual pleasure," continued Michael. "That's really true. My sex life is not like my television show. I'm not obliged to act a hundred percent professionally. I should be able to be what I am: a fallible and imperfect human being."

"That's a very good way of looking at it, Michael. And don't forget: *Errare humanum est*, to err is human. It's best to accept this reality.

"I'd like to add a final word about the field of consciousness. The more sexual excitation rises, the more the field of consciousness shrinks. A man closes himself off to everything around him except for his partner. He no longer hears the street noises, he pays no attention to the decor, he doesn't feel the cool breeze coming in from the open window. This reduction of lucidity toward his surroundings, luckily, exercises no influence over his capacity to control himself. On the other hand, the perception of what is taking place inside of him is also weakened. And this is where the problem arises. From his internal environment, he no longer concentrates on anything except feelings of pleasure. He forgets about checking his level of sexual excitation and applying the techniques of control. He heads toward ejaculation without thinking. It's only after he's ejaculated that he remembers he could have modulated his sexual tension.

"When we think about it, the human species is very well programmed for reproduction. When a male becomes aroused, his muscular tension rises, his breathing becomes more thoracic, he moves faster, his pleasure grows and he's less aware of what's going on. He doesn't think about the consequences of his actions. He advances naturally toward ejaculation…and toward reproduction. If things would take place differently. If making love were painful and unpleasant, the problem associated with control wouldn't even be an issue. Just imagine—and I'm joking here—that whenever sexual excitation increased, we would start getting cramps in our legs. Nausea would come over us. As sexual stimulation continued to climb, suddenly smoke and hideous odors would be emitted from our body. Well, we would have closed up shop a long time ago and the human species would no longer exist! But that's not the case at all. Sex is an enjoyable act. We derive pleasure from it. We make love and forget about everything else! And we forget all about the techniques of control! In this case, if you desire to postpone the arrival of your ejaculation, you must maintain your pleasure within certain limits. Your field of consciousness will not be as diminished and you won't forget to modulate your sexual excitation."

Michael broke in, "Finally, if I understand you correctly, ejaculating quickly is a natural act oriented toward reproduction, an ancestral behavior stemming from the animal nature of humans and motivated by the instinct of survival. The desire to make intercourse last longer and the whole act of modulating sexual excitement is a cultural acquisition. Through the desire to prolong pleasure, we express the refined nature of civilized man."

"Yes, indeed, we could say that. We have now come to the end of our program. Michael, I appreciated working with you. You have been very motivated and committed. The way in which you have mastered the exercises and the results you have obtained during your own private sessions indicate that your chances of succeeding are very high. I'm convinced that everything will go well for you. However, don't hesitate to contact me if you should experience even the slightest difficulty."

"Thank you so much for everything, doctor. Because of you, I finally understand what premature ejaculation is and I now know what to do to control my sexual excitement. This program has really been enlightening for me. Thanks again!" Michael rose from his armchair and offered a warm hand to the sex therapist.

CHAPTER 30

C omfortably settled onboard an American Airlines plane, Michael distractedly took the glass of orange juice the flight attendant handed him. His complete concentration was devoted to the photographs spread out on the flight table in front of him. He looked attentively at a group photo of graduates from Christopher Clays' high school year. A student taller than all the others grabbed his attention. He looked familiar, but Michael couldn't quite place him. He then diverted his thoughts to Vanessa. How could he come to her rescue? Here too, he found himself at a personal deadlock. Michael adjusted his seat and took a break from thinking.

He turned on the radio and put on his headphones. But instead of hearing relaxing music, he got an earful of the daily news: "...the worst flood in the history of China.... And now for the latest development in the Candy Kopersky scandal. A college friend of U.S. President Jeffrey Grant claims that the president came on to her and later attempted to take her bra off without her consent.... The incident allegedly took place in a drive-in theatre in Ventura, California when they were both twenty-one years old. Candy Kopersky maintains that the president's actions, which arose from his uncontrollable sex drive, have left her permanently traumatized. The woman, now in her mid-fifties, says she is planning to file a complaint. The vice president has responded on behalf of the White House stating that the matter is under investigation...."

"Henry Hurst, the vice president of the United States!" exclaimed Michael. "Now there's a man who would be able to do something for Vanessa." Michael had his wife as a guest on his program once and they had hit it off really well. What is her name, he racked his brain. Of course, Barbara...Barbara Hurst. That's it! Just like Barbara Rowland, the former mistress of the late Senator Davidson. Barbara Rowland? Wait a minute.... "Johnny Silver!" Michael yelled out, startling his seat mate. He was the tall guy in the picture. Johnny Silver, who just so happened to be Barbara Rowland's new lover. That explained everything! He knew Christopher Clays since high school. How could I not have pieced that together earlier? He's the one who murdered Davidson, Michael said to himself. Finally he held the missing link!

Using Christopher Clays would have presented risks. Somebody might have discovered his connection to Jack Kotten. But with Johnny Silver, it was easy. No one knew him. The only thing he had to do was seduce the senator's former mistress. Once he had succeeded, he stole her handgun, her keys and the code for the alarm system to the old senator's mansion. After that point, the affair was in the bag. Before setting off to commit his crime he most likely sniffed some coke for courage. But undoubtedly a little too much, which would justify the imprecision of his shots. The senator's murder was clearly not the job of a professional hit man, as deduced from the shoddy manner in which the operation was carried out. Johnny Silver had even lamely attempted to mask the real motive of his crime by stealing a couple of valuable objects from the senator's house. As for Barbara, she must have known he was responsible for the crime, but didn't dare say a word. And so when she found Johnny hanged, she correctly presumed that he had been executed. Consequently, her only chance of staying alive was to keep mum, even if the cops pinned the senator's murder on her back.

Thoughts continued pouring into his head in a dizzying stream. The Davidson affair was finally solved. But this didn't do him much good. His television program would not be dealing with the topic as previously planned. And besides, he was missing the most important pieces of proof needed to incriminate those who were guilty. For one thing, the accounting documents that proved Jack Kotten was embezzling funds had been destroyed by Dave's widow. And the videocassette where Jack Kotten was seen ordering Davidson's assassination had also been destroyed. The elation resulting from his findings was clouded by the impossibility of putting them into effective use. As for Vanessa, the situation she was in demanded immediate action on his part.

* * *

The minute he got home, Michael tried contacting Vice President Henry Hurst by telephone. The vice president was unable to be reached although Michael was able to talk to his administrative assistant. She, like all other high-profile aides, was considering whether it would be wiser to simply brush him off or actually refer him to the right person. Michael, exercising his customary powers of persuasion, was successful in convincing her to put him through to the vice president's wife.

"Mr. Lancaster, I remember you very well," Mrs. Hurst declared in a friendly voice. "I watch every single one of your shows, by the way, with much interest. They've been announcing on television that you won't be hosting *It Concerns Us* tonight. Have you resigned?"

"Not exactly, Mrs. Vice President, but I am calling you concerning a matter of utmost importance." Michael went on to explain Vanessa's situation so that Barbara Hurst could ask her husband to negotiate with the Sambizanian government. He then added that he possessed exclusive information concerning Jack Kotten, the U.S. presidential candidate. Mrs. Hurst promised to tell her husband immediately and to keep him informed of any news.

* * *

Michael took a cab to Audrey's place. When he arrived there at around noon, Audrey answered the door in horror: "Michael, what happened to you? You look awful! And what's with this limping? Did you have an accident?"

"Yes, and I will tell you all about it later. But before anything else, I want you to answer this question: "What did you do with the top-secret video cassette Dave had on Jack Kotten? Please don't tell me you burned that too?"

"I...I don't know what you're talking about," she stammered, playing nervously with her fingers.

"Audrey, this is a very serious matter. My life will be in danger for as long as I am without any concrete evidence."

"Michael, Michael did you bring me a present?" asked Janet, the eldest of Dave's daughters.

"Stop bothering him," Audrey chided her daughter sternly. And then she turned to Michael. " I didn't burn the documents. I told you I did hoping that you would just forget about this sordid affair that had already cost the life of the father of my children. I didn't want the same thing to happen to you. But if as you say these documents can save you, then they are at your full disposal."

Michael heaved a great big sigh of relief as Audrey continued. "But I have absolutely no idea where Dave would have hidden this videocassette."

"Could I sit on your lap?" begged Janet.

"Leave Michael alone, sweetheart," repeated her mother.

"I've got to find that videocassette," insisted Michael.

"You're looking for a videocassette?" Janet stared at Michael, quite taken in by the topic of conversation.

"Yes, princess."

"I have lots of Walt Disney videos," she continued with a big smile.

"Unfortunately, that's not what I'm looking for."

"Oh! I also have another one, but it's really boring. It's like the news on television. There are only men talking on it. You wouldn't like it, I'm sure. But I can get it for you if you want." With these words, Janet ran and got her Alladin video, opened the case, and slipped the tape into the VCR. In place of cartoon characters, appeared Jack Kotten's face. The picture was fuzzy and the quality of the sound wasn't very good, but the individuals were completely recognizable.

* * *

Michael was now talking directly on the phone with the vice president of the United States of America.

"My wife told me that you wish to discuss a matter of the highest order with me."

"That's correct, Mr. Vice President. And since my conversation with your wife, I have managed to get my hands on the proof I was looking for. But because what we're dealing with here is top secret information that will directly impact the course of the presidential election campaign, I cannot speak to you about it over the phone."

"I understand," replied Henry Hurst.

"Furthermore, I would like to appeal for your help in settling a very urgent situation."

"I can see that you're also a businessman, Mr. Lancaster. You play the game of give and take very well.

Michael explained to him the critical situation Vanessa was in.

"Sambizania unfortunately does not have very good political or economic relations with the United States," the vice president stated bluntly. "It is impossible to use traditional diplomatic channels. Likewise, a recent report by the CIA has brought to my attention that the UN camp you spoke about has been entirely ravaged by the Sambizanian soldiers. But this same report also mentions that fighting between a certain peacekeeping detachment and General El Tabernasti's troops persists in the village of Kiboyo. We know that the American journalists, your girlfriend included, are with this detachment. But we have not received any word on them since. However, the Belgian soldiers with the UN have transmitted a number of desperate messages demanding immediate reinforcements."

"Can't NATO intervene quickly? From what I know, the Belgian soldiers are part of the organization, right?"

"Most certainly," Henry Hurst calmly replied. "But they are under a UN mandate. We can't do a thing without backing from the UN and that always takes a long time."

"Can't the CIA or the American army carry out a commando operation? You could ask the president to give his approval."

"I would do that most willingly to help you and to save the lives of our American citizens. But with the election fast approaching, there is no way the president will ever give his blessing to a foreign operation. Polls indicate that public opinion at the moment is hostile toward any type of military intervention outside of our country."

"So what can we do for them?" Michael persisted.

"I'm afraid, Mr. Lancaster, that at this time we can't do anything for them."

* * *

"I can't see what else we can do." Lieutenant Demat looked at Vanessa, his eyes glazed over with culpability. "And this is all my fault. I should not have allowed you to come along on this badly organized expedition. I should never have followed Captain Muller's senseless orders. As a result of my weakness, men with unwavering faith and confidence in me will be killed for nothing. I repeat, for nothing, because no matter how you look at it, sooner or later the village will be attacked. It will take weeks for the UN bureaucrats to make a decision. They are so afraid of offending each other's feelings that we will all be long dead before they finally agree to something. Besides, they might assume we're all already dead by now. The batteries for the radio are very weak. The base is no longer responding to our calls and this leaves us virtually cut off from the outside world."

"No!" Vanessa interjected excitedly. "We still have the CNN transmitter! I should have thought about that sooner! We could communicate directly with the United States, thanks to this super transmitter. I can even send them the images I filmed yesterday. My friend, Michael, is a famous television broadcaster. He could plead our cause and speed up the dispatch of backups!"

Vanessa immediately put her thoughts into action. She recovered the transmitter from under an old piece of corrugated iron. The batteries were still charged. After several futile attempts, she finally established communication with the United States.

The sharp sound of the CNN correspondent's clear voice caused Vanessa to jump for joy. She summarized the situation in Kiboyo and offered startling video footage of the conflict on condition that CNN accept to collaborate with the show *It Concerns Us*, hosted by Michael Lancaster. The CNN correspondent promised a swift response.

CHAPTER 31

M ichael dove for the telephone and practically exploded with euphoria upon learning that Vanessa was still alive. The ex ecutive director of the PDS network told Michael he was being re-hired—with a promotion. And that he was going to host that evening's special edition of *It Concerns Us*. The originally scheduled program would be canceled and replaced by a special live report on the incidents in Sambizania. There were only eight hours to prepare for the broadcast. He had to view the images provided by CNN, speak to the special guests and become informed on the subject. This gripping show would be a first in the history of PDS as it was going to be broadcast live and simultaneously on CNN. Michael would have the opportunity of reaching a more extensive audience.

At six o'clock sharp, in Seattle, Michael began the two-hour special *Journalism: The Deadly Quest for Information*. He presented the political and economic problems facing Sambizania with additional commentary and insight by a number of specialists in the field. Images from the UN refugee camp as well as the village of Kiboyo accompanied their remarks. Michael later drew the television viewers' attention to the dangerous lives that journalists lead in the name of better informing the public. At this point, the graphic images of Greg Bryan's pain and agony flashed onto the television screen. "He was working for CNN when he was taken away in the prime of his life," reported Michael, his voice charged with emotion. "Greg was fatally shot while filming a group of African refugee children seeking shelter in the church of Kiboyo. He died so that the entire world could witness the suffering of these children who are involved in a war they don't even understand." Millions of Americans witnessed the thirty-nine-year-old reporter's final moments.

Michael then shifted the focus to the UN soldiers who were so valiantly fighting even with the despair of knowing that the enemy was a hundred times their size. The television audience then watched the footage of the night attack carried out by the courageous squad one-two. A close-up shot of Vanessa, filmed by Edouard, surfaced on television screens across the country. Her face was aged from fatigue and her expression was grim. Michael, extremely moved, concluded the program with a poignant appeal to the viewing public: "The UN soldiers who are fighting at this moment are neither colonizers nor mercenaries. They are fighting because they want other human beings, from another race, from another culture, who speak another language to also have the right to live in peace. They simply want to protect the women and children of Kiboyo from a horrible massacre. For this totally impartial cause, they have put their lives in the hands of destiny. Are we going to just stay put and let them die, the same way we saw Greg Bryan die? Could we really accept—sitting comfortably in front of our television sets—that children from the south of Sambizania be slaughtered only because they have been unfortunate enough to belong to another ethnic group?

"I, Michael Lancaster, as a Christian and as a citizen of the nation that has come to symbolize justice and freedom, I insist we intervene in this crisis. I ask...I implore UN officials and representatives of the American government to respond immediately to save these innocent men and women from all crimes of humanity."

Softening his tone of voice, Michael added: "The only female American journalist you saw during our report is twenty-eight-years-old. She is there because she believes in an ideal: improving the lives of Sambizanian women by informing you about their situation. She strongly believes that freedom for women is worth taking risks for. You—citizens of America—will you let her die? No, I can't believe that!

"Please, pressure our government into acting without the slightest delay. Tomorrow will be too late. Once again, she is only twenty-eight. She's a wonderful woman...a close friend...What I want to say...She's my girlfriend and I...I love her."

CHAPTER 32

T he dark, somber night enveloped the entire village of Kiboyo, which lay upon the hill like a foal at the flank of its mare. This particular elevation rose a little above the other high plateaus, standing out over the rather mundane relief that characterized this region of Sambizania. From afar the village looked like any other poor and peaceful eastern African community. Hundreds of small huts arranged in disorderly fashion around the main square took on the appearance of haystacks in a field of rye after the harvest. Small enclosures confining a meager livestock surrounded each dwelling. Despite its modest size, the church clearly overshadowed all the other buildings made of packed mud and straw.

Overcome by lack of sleep, Edouard and Vanessa collapsed in their trench. The shelling had ceased and only the painful moans of the wounded disturbed the silence of the night.

At around three o'clock in the morning, they awoke to gunfire and the radio began crackling weakly. The men from squad one-one were signaling a massive assault of the village. The enemy was trying to infiltrate into Kiboyo. All the remaining able-bodied peacekeepers rushed to their arms. The men tucked away in shelters to the north, east and to the west couldn't move from their post because their sector could be attacked at any moment. The soldiers were forced to wait in their trench, seething with rage. And each one of them was suffering from the terrible frustration of feeling useless, incapable of fighting alongside their brothers in arms.

"It's quite clear that squad one-one will be quickly overpowered," Edouard conceded to Vanessa. "You can already hear the gunfire getting closer to the center of the village. The final bloodbath is about to begin."

The lieutenant now seemed resigned to this lamentable fact. Regardless, he continued to act with care and meticulousness. He gathered a few soldiers from the command squad and provided them with final instructions. He then dug his hand into his knapsack, withdrew a GP pistol and handed it to Vanessa: "It's a 9mm; the magazine contains ten bullets. It could very well hold more, but I don't like forcing the spring. It has three safety-catches—the only one you have to concern yourself with is that of the small lever on the side. You see the one here on the left. There aren't any bullets in the barrel. Don't forget to load it before firing."

Vanessa knew all of this. She remembered her days from shooting practice very well, but the lieutenant's detached tone still sent shivers up and down her spine. And sheer terror struck her when he added, "Shoot the Sambizanian soldiers at point-blank range, only when they're less than ten feet from the shelter. Beyond that, in the dark, you could miss them. And, believe me, they won't miss you. Make sure you keep count of your shots. You have ten cartridges, that's it. Fire no more than nine times—save the last bullet for yourself. They must not take you alive. I shudder to think about the sort of thing they would have reserved for a young white woman like you. Your status as a journalist will not protect you any more than our status as a peacekeeper. And, worse, they hate Americans. Anyway, in the heat of battle, they won't bother making a distinction. All they'll see is a female prisoner—just good to rape and slit the throat of after the entire regiment has had its helping...."

The lieutenant looked Vanessa directly in the eyes. She could see that he was extremely sorry. He went on in an unsteady voice, "Please excuse this sinister talk. I would never want anything of that sort to happen to you. But I'm leaving you here alone to try something out. Don't move from the shelter. Don't let anybody come close to you even if they speak English. Only reply if you are given the password with a Flemish or French accent. The password is 'Brugge.' You will answer 'Brigit.' In all other cases, you will shoot without hesitation. To hesitate is to die! Understand?"

Vanessa replied with a strangled "yes."

The lieutenant once again dug his hands into the bag and took out a pair of strange night vision goggles. He adjusted them on his face blackened by night makeup and tied a camouflage net around his head, like a pirate. The greenish light from the light intensifiers invaded his eyes. He looked up at the sky and the twinkle of the stars had suddenly become blinding. He shot a glance around the village and reflected back at him was a hazy image akin to that from an old black and white television. He grabbed his short MINIMI submachine gun along with four magazines holding thirty cartridges each, and slipped out of the hole without a word.

Edouard crawled in the direction of squad one-one. The dry African soil scraped his elbows, making them bleed. But he didn't feel a thing; his body charged by a powerful surge of adrenaline. He had covered only ninety feet when he was forced to stop for his breathing had become too noisy. Apart from some sporadic gunfire, a deadly silence reigned over the village. The soldiers from both camps were trying to track down their adversaries with the slightest noise. Edouard took shelter for a few seconds behind a clay hut so that he could catch his breath. Through his light intensifiers, he suddenly spotted two men walking cautiously along a fold enclosing goats. His heart started beating faster. But he had to control his breathing so as not to make a sound. For the first time, the silhouettes of soldiers came into view. He couldn't quite distinguish their features because the image remained blurred. He also had trouble making out their weapons: The curved magazine of the AK47 could be easily confused with that of the FNC used by the Belgian soldiers. The last thing Edouard wanted to do was open fire on his own men. And so, extremely slowly, he attempted to adjust the luminosity of his special goggles. But the two men had already disappeared.

"Shit! Where did they go?" he asked himself. "They might spot me if I move."

The high-pitched cries of children put an end to his questions. Gunfire shots exploded inside of a hut and howls of terror burst forth from all directions. The Sambizanian soldiers were methodically executing the inhabitants of the village, hut by hut. A shadow dashed out of one of the huts. Edouard positioned his weapon on his bipod and adjusted it against his shoulder, heart racing.

"Don't shoot yet," he told himself. "They have villagers with them!" True enough the Sambizanian soldiers were kicking and shoving several women in front of them. Seconds later they turned around and threw a grenade into the crowded hut. A streak of light, amplified by the night vision goggles he was wearing, blinded Edouard. For a few critical seconds his eyes remained dazzled. By the time they regained their acuity, the enemy had slipped away.

The lieutenant was raging. He wanted to rush in pursuit of them, but that would be a crazy thing to do. Beyond the pen of goats, he was entering into the firing zone of Warrant Officer Depraeter and risked being blown away by his own man. In fact, in the instant that followed, he heard the familiar sudden short blast from the FNC assault rifle, followed by intense cries.

"That good old Depraeter just killed the two bastards. Our plan of action is working!" thought Edouard. He stayed put—weapon aimed toward a path of sorts where a row of silent huts stood aligned on each side. Many long minutes passed by without anything else happening in his sector whereas to the left and right of him, several confrontations were in progress. The enemy was now everywhere....

* * *

With his features strained, Michael looked outside the window of his living room at the lights of Seattle. He couldn't sleep. Tormented by worry and pumped up by his special program on the plight of journalists, ideas were swirling around inside his head like bats in a cave. Was Vanessa still alive? Was the American government willing to take immediate action? And if yes was the answer, would things move fast enough to save her, to rescue the UN soldiers and to protect the population of the South? Far off in the distance, he caught sight of several cranes in the port that seemed to resemble dinosaur skeletons set in contorted shapes. Despite his mind-set, it reminded him of his session with Dr. Carter on sexual positions.

He tried to calm his racing mind, and inevitably, his thoughts drifted back to what Dr. Carter had said. The sex therapist had explained to him that there were certain positions that contributed to ejaculation more than others. "The basic principle is as follows: The more effort a position demands to be maintained, the more it favors ejaculation," he said. "The reason for this phenomenon is that as an individual exerts physical effort, he contracts different muscles. And as mentioned in our first session, the contraction of muscles facilitates the arrival of ejaculation.

"The position most susceptible to induce ejaculation is the one where the man is on top of the woman, leaning on his hands and knees. In this position, the muscles in back of the arms, the pectorals and the abdominals are contracted. And we know that it leads to a substantial elevation of muscular tension. Moreover, as the abdominal muscles tense up, it is almost impossible to breathe from the diaphragm. Consequently, this makes it very difficult to use your breathing to lower muscular tension brought on by sexual excitation. Finally, it's hard to effectuate the forward-backward movement of the pelvis in this position because of the limits imposed by the coxo-femoral joint. This causes a man to render the in-and-out motion of penetration by contracting the gluteus muscles and by moving the back and the pelvis as a single unit. It follows, therefore, a series of major muscular contractions hastens the arrival of ejaculation.

"The following position is a variant of the first. The man is still on top of the woman, propped up on his knees, but this time he supports himself with his elbows rather than with his hands. The advantage of this position over the latter is that the triceps don't have to contract for you to hold yourself up. Also, if you rest your stomach and your chest on your partner, your pectoral and abdominal muscles will have less work to do. But this still isn't the best position.

"These two positions were analyzed in detail because they are the most commonly used by couples. What's important for you to retain from all of this is that as soon as a position demands a certain degree of muscular effort, it prompts ejaculation. Tell me then, what positions would allow for greater control over the moment of the arrival of ejaculation?"

"Well, if I base my answer upon the principles you have just laid out, I suppose the best position would be the one where the man lies on his back and the woman sits on top of him," replied Michael. "Lateral positions should also produce excellent results."

"You're absolutely correct. And I also strongly recommend that you use these positions at the beginning as a way to learn the skills and gain confidence. However, I must remind you that even if your partner is on the top, it is preferable that, at the start, you initiate the rhythm of the movements. But without yourself moving your body! In fact, you can control your partner's speed with your hands or with words. For it should not be forgotten, that you're the only one who is able to judge your level of excitation and your need to slow down or stop to prevent ejaculation.

"Now, most couples quite like and appreciate the man to be on top of the woman during intercourse. A position does luckily exist where the man could be on top of the woman without too much effort. In this position, which I call latero-superior, the man is on his side, between the female's legs. She's lying on her back, pelvis turned toward her partner. The man embraces the woman's upper body with his arms and his chest. In this position, you don't have to exert any effort to support your weight. You can also breathe from your belly and move your pelvis with ease. In addition, the fact that you are cradling your partner's upper body with your arms and chest procures the symbolic and emotional benefits of the position where the man is completely on top of the woman."

* * *

Alone in her shelter, Vanessa had rediscovered a religious fervor long forgotten. She prayed with conviction, committing herself to myriad promises if God spared her life. The hole she was in seemed even smaller than usual. She had the impression that slowly it was closing in on her. Vanessa felt totally alone and afraid. The gunfire was relentlessly getting closer to where she was positioned. The image of her dead father came to mind. Tears blurred her eyes and she began to sob softly.

A sinister lull replaced the exchange of automatic gunfire. The sound of footsteps seemed to be moving in on her trench. Vanessa stopped breathing. Her hands tightly clutched the handgun that Lieutenant Demat had given her. A hush of whispers reached her ears. The men were not Belgian soldiers. She felt her heartbeat hammering her temples. The footsteps got even closer, they had to be only a few feet from her. Vanessa loaded the pistol with a trembling hand.

She then pivoted the GP's safety catch and delicately slid her finger on the trigger. The men stopped whispering. They had heard the click of the mobile pieces of the breech introducing the bullet into the barrel. They didn't move, trying desperately to pinpoint the precise origin of the metallic sound.

Vanessa was also trying to guess the exact location of her enemies. Curled up in her trench, she saw nothing above her but a cloudless, starlit sky. Her entire body was tense; her eyes were wide open and intensely scrutinizing the dark. She didn't dare move a muscle. At any given moment the men could discover where she was hidden. Suddenly, she heard from behind her the faint hiss of the pin being taken out of a grenade by one of the soldiers. It sounded just like a can of beer being opened. She then heard the grenade rolling into her shelter and the hurried steps of the enemy getting away. Vanessa was paralyzed with terror. The deadly device was going to explode in exactly three seconds. Her childhood flashed before her eyes. She then saw an image of her dad and finally, Michael's face....

CHAPTER 33

E douard was continually asking himself if he was in the right place and whether he should move or not. His motionless body was growing progressively numb. Physical and mental exhaustion was compelling him to close his eyes. The light intensifiers were too tight. They dug into his forehead and gave him a terrible headache.

Suddenly, he saw a group of five men crouched down close to the ground, heading toward the marketplace inside of his firing zone. Edouard immediately identified them as Sambizanian soldiers by the small Russian military cap one of them was wearing. They were fairly far away from him but still within his weapon's range. A blood-thirsty excitement came over him. He removed the safety catch and put his weapon into automatic rate of fire position. The men were cautiously feeling their way around, stuck together. It was obvious that they weren't wearing any night vision goggles. Edouard knew he could very well hit them with a single blast.

The lieutenant secured his weapon against his shoulder, restricted his breathing and pressed his finger slowly down on the trigger. The MINIMI jolted between his hands firing off a long, bright blast. He heard instant howls of pain and shouts of horror. The bullet had hit them.

As the acrid odor of the burnt gunpowder perforated his nostrils, the smell of victory rushed over him. But there was no time for him to confirm the gravity of injury or total number of losses he had inflicted on the enemy. He was forced to quickly find himself a new location because the smoke and flames released from his submachine gun had betrayed his present position.

Edouard had two possibilities—spring back onto his feet and run out of the area as fast as possible, or crawl sideways and try to get away without being noticed. He hesitated. "To hesitate is to die," he yelled to himself. Quickly he folded up the bipod of his submachine gun, pulled back the lever to its safety position and strapped the weapon against his chest. Without wasting a second, he rolled over to the right. A fence made of cut branches obstructed his movement. He crawled forward very fast, trying to stay as low as possible. The whistle of bullets streaked the air above his head.

By this time the night vision goggles he was wearing had slid down to his nose. He couldn't see a thing. His black leather gloves were virtually shredded from the acacia thorns covering the ground. Jaw locked, he furtively edged his way through the dust amid the malodorous trash surrounding the clay huts. He finally emerged behind a hencoop that looked out onto an open path. At this point, he was far enough from his old location so as not to feel threatened by the risk of enemy fire. Exhausted, Edouard's face dropped to the ground. He couldn't catch his breath and sweat was trickling steadily down his face. He stopped for a few seconds and closed his eyes in desperate search of a brief period of respite.

* * *

Tucked away in fetal position, Vanessa didn't dare to move. She knew she was alive, but what was left of her body? Gently, she brought her left hand to her face and spread apart her fingers. All five were intact. She did the same thing with her other hand. Nothing missing. She felt her legs with a trembling hand—they were still there. She reached for her shoes and realized that her feet had not been blown off either. Suddenly, her entire body came back to life and started to shake. She then began to cry uncontrollably. The young journalist wanted so much to thank God for this miracle, but she didn't have the strength.

At the same moment, approximately six hundred feet from her position, Lieutenant Demat was readjusting the light intensifiers on his eyes. He scanned the path in front of him and spotted a few soldiers proceeding vigilantly alongside a row of trees. He placed his weapon in shooting position and freed the safety catch. He held back his breathing and pushed down on the trigger. The shot didn't fire.

"Jammed! The damn thing is jammed!" Edouard swore in silence. He grabbed the cocking tenon and pulled the mobile pieces back roughly. A case popped out. He quickly let go of the cocking tenon and a loud metallic *click* resounded in the night. He once again aimed the submachine gun, but the enemy had disappeared. The sound of footsteps could be heard approaching him from behind. "Shit! They heard me! I've been located. I have to clear this place as fast as possible."

A few seconds later, he heard the sound of crunching branches to his left. "My retreat is blocked off. I'm going to have to fire frantically into the open and take off, it's my only chance." Edouard turned around and pressed his back up against the dried mud wall of a deserted hut. He was in a pitch-dark area and knew the enemy could not see him. With his night vision goggles, he was able to clearly see the soldier who was walking toward him. He aimed his submachine gun at the enemy. There was no way he could miss him. The soldier was merely seventy-five feet away. His target continued to move toward him—a little more than fifty feet away now. Don't shoot, yet. Wait. He was now at thirty feet. Wait some more.

Edouard turned off his light intensifiers knowing that the little green light emitted from the goggles could cause him to be spotted. He was now plunged into darkness. Without a sound, he raised his weapon and shouldered it. The enemy continued his advance, his shadow slivered under the starry sky. Edouard could hear the soldier's intermittent breathing getting closer and louder.

"Now!" He pressed down on the trigger, but the detonation didn't go off. Edouard felt his blood running cold through his veins. His weapon was still jammed and the enemy was now less than ten feet away from him. He knew the soldier couldn't see him, but the slightest gesture or sound would easily give away his presence. If he moved, he was dead.

Edouard tried hard not to look directly at the foot soldier who moved toward him. Humans instinctively sense when someone is watching them. Therefore, he wrenched his glance a little to the left of his enemy.

The lieutenant also concentrated on his body. "I am a pile of dead branches, I am a pile of dead branches," he repeated this again and again inside of his head to induce a state of total stillness.

The enemy put his foot down two feet away from that of Edouard's, passed by directly in front of him, and advanced some more. He was now standing with his back to the lieutenant, scrutinizing the entrance of the hut, AK47 in hand. Edouard felt his hunter's instinct coming back to him. A rare opportunity to regain a weapon lay before him. He brought his hand to his belt and, with infinite care, detached the leather tongue that kept his knife in the sheath. Next, he slowly took out the old Kabarr from its case. The Belgian lieutenant gripped the long marine knife in his right hand. All that was left for him to do was assume the position of a tiger ready to pounce on his prey. He would surprise the enemy soldier from behind, stop him from screaming with one hand and with the other slice open his throat with the sharp blade.

The Sambizanian soldier was still, clearly looking for a way out of there. While stepping back for speed, Edouard unintentionally landed on a brittle twig and snapped it. At the same moment, by sheer luck, a series of gunfire shots grabbed the soldier's attention. It was now or never. The lieutenant propelled himself forward and grabbed the soldier by the face. But the adversary reacted more swiftly than expected. He struck Edouard in the stomach with the butt of his rifle and with a solid kick to the shins, sent him flying to the ground. Then, he aimed his assault rifle at the lieutenant. Edouard, lying on the ground, grasped the barrel of the Sambizanian soldier's weapon with one hand and with the other hand stabbed him in the thigh with his knife. The soldier cried out in excruciating pain and attempted to pull out the Kabarr firmly jabbed into his leg. With all his might, Edouard tugged at the AK47 and snatched it away from the injured soldier. He leapt back onto his feet like a wild cat, shot the soldier with malevolence and sprinted away in three quick strides toward the closest hut.

Heart beating violently, Edouard hid behind a wheelbarrow and turned his light intensifiers back on. He could see about a dozen men rushing to the quick rescue of their wounded army mate. The lieutenant crouched down and rested the AK47 against the handle of the wheelbarrow. When all of the Sambizanian combats had huddled closely around the fallen soldier, Edouard opened fire. He was taken aback by the powerful recoil of the AK47 and his first shot completely missed its target. A blind fury seized him. He gripped the rifle tighter between his hands and fired one shot at a time. This time, the bullets accomplished their objective. Excitement and sadistic satisfaction overwhelmed the lieutenant. But the thrill of the kill was short-lived for his weapon suddenly stopped firing. The magazine was empty.

Once again Edouard found himself unarmed. He had to escape. The idea of being taken prisoner made him tremble in horror. "I'm unarmed, they could take me alive. They'll torture me before hacking me to death with their machetes. I have to get out of here!"

Edouard sprung up from his hiding place and ran like mad toward another group of huts. A hail of bullets trailed behind him. He automatically threw himself to the ground and his head struck on old, rusted spade. The shock practically knocked him out. Painfully, he gathered his strength and managed to advance another thirty feet forward. He rested a few seconds beside a nondescript hut and tried to find his bearings. He had no idea where he was any more. "Goddamn it! All these huts look the same. I must try to locate the church bell," he cursed to himself. But the batteries in his light intensifiers had died.

* * *

The gunfire ceased at the daybreak and, almost instantly, the fowl resumed their cackling. When daylight streamed into her trench, Vanessa knew it was a miracle she was still alive. The grenade had rolled right to the bottom of the deep sump inside of the trench that had been dug out by Lieutenant Demat for this very purpose. It had exploded down there, damaging only the things placed closest to the opening of this providential hole. Among these objects, unfortunately, was the CNN transmitter—found in an irreparable state and beyond use. They were now really and truly isolated from the rest of the world.

Vanessa slumped down against the dirt wall and let out a discouraged sigh. The lieutenant had promised to return before dawn. If he was still not here, it meant that he had been killed. She wondered what was going to happen to her from this point on. Several more questions rushed into her mind: "How did last night's battle end? Is the Sambizanian army in control of the village? Why is it so quiet out there? What should I do if the enemy soldiers find me here?"

Vanessa glanced at the pistol she still held tightly in her hand: "I don't think I could ever find the courage to kill myself. But the lieutenant had a point: They would have no pity. They would torture and rape me." Vanessa shuddered at the thought. She imagined the army mob pouncing on her, ruthlessly ripping off her clothes, lecherously groping her body with their rough hands, soiling her lips with their slobbering mouths and brutally thrusting their dirty and stinking penises inside of her. She became nauseous.

Suddenly, she heard some faint rustling close by her shelter. Literally crammed inside of her hole, Vanessa couldn't see what was happening around her outside. She aimed her pistol in the direction from where the sound was coming. She swore she'd start shooting as soon as she caught a glimpse of her intruders. If she killed several of them, maybe they would kill her on the spot instead of taking her alive. Her heart began to beat recklessly and her hands got all sweaty. The soft rustling noise was almost directly above her. She then heard a feeble whisper. "Brugge?"

Vanessa's eyes brimmed with tears of relieved joy and she replied with trembling lips, "Brigit!"

At the sight of Lieutenant Demat, she uttered a shriek of horror. His face was caked in blood and his clothes were torn and tattered.

"It's nothing," he assured her. "My head banged on a spade and I bled a bit from my forehead. I was very lucky. I am still alive and I'm not wounded. I'm also very happy to see that you too are alive." Edouard attempted a tiny smile and gave her a friendly squeeze on the shoulder. Vanessa held him tightly, wanting badly to cry.

The lieutenant, unaccustomed to such a demonstration of tenderness in the context of combat, gently released her hold and handed her a water flask recovered from the enemy: "Here's some water."

Vanessa raised it to her mouth and swallowed several gulps with thirsty eagerness.

"Do you still have the pistol?"

"Here," she said and handed him the gun. "I didn't have to use it, thank God. And what about you, how did things go?"

"It was the longest night of my life. There was chaos and confusion everywhere. The Sambizanian army invaded the village and began to coldly murder countless innocent civilians. But we didn't make the job easy for them. On my way back, I saw the bodies of many enemy soldiers who had been killed by my men. The rest of them fled from the village at the first sight of the sun's rays. The night, as a result of the light intensifiers, gave us an advantage over them. But daytime has returned. I don't know how many able men we have left and if they still have any ammunition."

Edouard was exhausted and desperately needed to rest. He took off his torn black leather gloves. His hands were covered with scratches and the several thorns embedded underneath his skin were causing him severe pain. Vanessa fumbled through the contents of her backpack and found a pair of tweezers. As she removed the needles from his flesh, Edouard began thinking out loud: "We must reorganize our defensive position. We will then take care of our wounded and if possible, bury our dead. We have to round up a team of volunteers to clear the well—we need water. We must also divide and distribute among ourselves what little ammunition remains." He paused, turned toward Vanessa who was pulling out the last thorn and declared reluctantly, "I'm going to leave you here again. I have to get informed on the latest developments as well as try to recover a more powerful weapon than this pistol."

"No way," objected Vanessa. "I would much rather be instantly shot and killed in the middle of the village than slowly torture myself waiting for my death in this horrible hole."

"All right then, follow me!"

Edouard climbed out of the trench with tremendous physical difficulty. Every muscle in his body protested in painful resistance against this extra effort. He had not eaten for over twenty-four hours and the night's weighty ordeal had consumed all of his energy. He felt as if he were lugging around the body of an old man beaten and battered by the hardships of life. But the chivalry exhibited by a poised European gentleman was still very present. He helped Vanessa hoist herself out of her refuge and led her along from one shelter to the next always making sure they were protected from possible gunfire.

They moved away from the center of the village in this manner so as to reach the outposts and become informed about the situation among the men.

The impact of the shells had hollowed out dangerous craters here and there. The village of Kiboyo looked like an open mass grave. The dogs and vultures were fighting over the rotting remains of the mutilated bodies that had been blown to pieces by the bombardments. No one dared step outside to bury the unfortunate victims.

Edouard spotted an overturned mound of dirt close to where he had been fighting the night before and pointed it out to Vanessa: "Look. It's Warrant Officer Depraeter's trench. I'm sure he'll be able to tell us how things went." The lieutenant moved with caution toward the hole and whispered, "Brugge." There was no response. He repeated the password without success. Figuring that his whispers might be going unheard, he yelled loudly almost directly over the hole: "Warrant Officer! It's Lieutenant Demat. Do you recognize my voice? Don't shoot! I have the journalist with me!" But no sound escaped from the underground shelter.

Edouard and Vanessa moved closer and heard the resonating sound of buzzing flies. They then saw Warrant Officer Depraeter slumped on his back, mouth open and eyes looking to the sky. His khaki shirt, soaked with coagulated blood, had turned brown down the front of his chest. A circle of black flies buzzed around his neck, all along the gaping slit in his throat.

Vanessa suppressed a cry of horror and averted her eyes from the mangled body. Observing the gruesome scene, Edouard concluded, "He fought right up until his last cartridge. The battle then ended hand-to-hand. Poor Depraeter, he was really a very courageous guy. He was like..." The lieutenant's voice broke. He covered his face with his right hand to hide his emotion. "...a big brother to me...." He quickly composed himself: "Let's go. We'll see if there are any survivors elsewhere."

The young woman followed the lieutenant as he headed toward another trench. The sun had quickly gained in intensity and was literally cooking the village with its burning rays. Vanessa was dripping in sweat. Her perspiration had intermixed with the dust on her clothing and formed a muddy film on her skin the color of ochre. As they walked among the dead, she asked herself repeatedly if she and the lieutenant were the only survivors of the UN contingent.

Without warning, the terrifying whistle of a shell sliced through the air, quickly followed by a deafening explosion. The blast hurled Vanessa to the ground. The lieutenant, lying down, turned toward her. "Are you okay?"

Vanessa could barely hear him. She felt as if her eardrums had burst from the piercing noise of the explosion.

"Run to the hole next to the tree!" yelled Edouard.

Other mortar shells were already falling around them. Vanessa plunged headfirst into the abandoned hole hastily dug out by soldiers who had obviously been in a rush. Edouard didn't even have time to join her when another shell exploded right next to the trench. The thunderous explosion filled the shelter Vanessa was in with dirt.

When he opened his eyes, Edouard realized that the American journalist had disappeared under the dirt embankment. "She's buried!" he gasped. "Buried alive!"

CHAPTER 34

Michael jumped at the sound of clanging interspersed among a tussle of sinister hisses. A pair of feuding stray cats had turned over a tin can on his terrace. The ruckus had abruptly shaken him out of a horrible nightmare: Christopher Clays was strangling Vanessa while he, powerless, was sinking in a pool of quicksand. He opened his eyes and thought for a split second he was still in Florida. No, it was definitely the familiar furniture of his Seattle bedroom that stood out in the darkness. Thirsty, he got up and walked to the kitchen in search of a bottle of mineral water. He glanced at the clock on the wall and grumbled: "It's too early to get up; too soon to get information on Vanessa. And with this lousy jet lag, I have no idea if I should wake up or hop back into bed."

A glass of water in hand, Michael sat down on the leather chair in his office. He outstretched his left arm and turned the rheostat switch around. A warm light lit up the room. Hanging on the wall in front of him was a small seventeenth-century Dutch painting. He was very familiar with the unidentified seascape he had purchased from a dealer at Le Louvre des Antiquaires six years before. Tonight, however, he looked at the painting with different eyes. The elegant sails of the Dutch trader boats and the gentle undulating waves of the North Sea brought him back to the notions of voyage, duration and alternation.

As he rediscovered the painting, his mind drifted back to one of his sex therapy sessions with Dr. Carter. "The journey is as interesting as the destination," stated Dr. Carter. "The process we engage in offers us as much appeal as the end result. For example, you can always gulp down a glass of ice-cold orange juice in one sip to quench your thirst and it's over. Or you can take the time to savour at length what you are drinking.

"I'll give you another example. You can get to the beach by jumping on the expressway, driving 250 miles in four hours and then diving straight into the water when you arrive there. Or, you can opt to take the longer country route. You enjoy the scenery. You make a stop alongside a lake to take in the peaceful sight of colorful sailboats drifting in the light summer breeze. You feast on some of the region's culinary specialities. You chat with the locals. You admire the architecture. And by four in the afternoon, you make it to the beach. You walk along the fine, white sand and slowly enter into the warm water. After you come out of the ocean, you rest along the shoreline and watch the sun set. You go to a restaurant and dine on fresh seafood while sipping slowly on a good bottle of white wine. At the end of the day, you would have had just as much fun and pleasure traveling as you would have had rushing to the beach and jumping into the water. But for a much longer time!"

"I can certainly relate to what you're saying. In life, I'm more of a go-getter, a fighter. It's time for me to learn how to live for and appreciate the present moment," Michael had replied.

"To follow up on my previous example, the same thing goes for sex. An individual can either forge ahead toward the intense sensations of an orgasm or take the time to fully experience and appreciate all the subtleties of intercourse. I admit that we live in a consumer society based on high efficiency and immediate returns. But you could liberate yourself from this social conditioning and, while still remaining productive in your career, begin to really enjoy what sex and life have to offer.

"In the beginning you might be faced with a few difficulties. In fact, when you will modulate your sexual excitation for five, ten or fifteen minutes, you won't experience the same sensations as when you head toward ejaculation in thirty seconds. These sensations are not as strong for the simple reason that your excitation is not as high at that moment. Consequently, when you control your sexual excitation, you shouldn't expect to feel the same types of pleasures as when you allow it to soar."

"Does this mean I'll derive less pleasure?"

"No. These pleasures are just more subtle. To fully appreciate them, you must refine your capacity to perceive them and to distinguish their various qualities. This will require a certain amount of time and learning. Initially, you might consider these pleasures to be dull and not very stimulating. But in the long run, you'll get to relish them to the fullest."

"If I understand you correctly, this comes back to the idea of adopting a more sensual attitude as you mentioned at the beginning of this program."

"Exactly! Another useful detail for you to remember is that, physiologically, a man can't cultivate the intense feelings of pre-ejaculation and hope to last a long time. This is wishful thinking. There is no question that very high levels of sexual excitation are extremely pleasant. But inevitably they lead to discharge. If you want to delay ejaculation, you must accept not to be continually at very high levels of sexual excitation. You must endure putting off the strong sensations that precede ejaculation until later. Your best bet is to learn how to physically and mentally savour the subtle pleasures associated with the modulation of excitation as a way to achieve prolonged intercourse."

Dr. Carter's explanations made sense to Michael and they were logical. But at the moment, in the quiet haven of his own office, he couldn't help thinking, "What good will all of this do for me if I don't ever see Vanessa again?"

* * *

Lieutenant Demat dragged himself all the way to the heap of dirt that had entombed Vanessa, and began frantically clearing the ground with his fingers. As he dug, more dirt fell back into the hole. He would need a tool of some sort to work faster, anything would do— a helmet, a billy-can, a scrap of metal. He scanned the area for something: nothing. He would have to continue with his bare hands. The seconds ticked away. Despite his effort, he wasn't able to reach Vanessa's body. He kept on digging with determined fury. The muscles in his arms burned from the violent effort. He was losing oxygen. Sweat poured down his back. An arm appeared. Then a shoulder. And finally the head.

Vanessa no longer was moving and her eyes remained closed. He put his ear to her nose. She wasn't breathing. He pressed his thumb against her carotid—there was no sign of a heartbeat. "My God, my dear God," repeated Edouard, "It isn't possible, it isn't possible...."

He desperately removed the dirt from Vanessa's mouth, tilted her head back lightly and blew two breaths into her. He then cleared her chest and pushed down on it firmly five times. He came back to her mouth, blew into it again, and resumed the cardiac massage. Vanessa was still not responding. The lieutenant counted out his moves like a robot. "You must not give up. You must not give up."

Shortly after, he heard a deep coughing and Vanessa started breathing again. Joyful tears gushed from the lieutenant's eyes. "Thank you, God. She's alive."

Edouard moved closer to her ear: "Miss Andressen!" He shook her gently, but she didn't react. She wasn't regaining consciousness. "I hope she doesn't fall into a coma," worried Edouard. "Maybe she was left without oxygen for too long? Was her brain affected?"

He quickly came back to reality. Right now their lives weren't worth much for shells continued falling all around them. He had to move Vanessa to another shelter fast.

The lieutenant attempted to lift Vanessa, but a sharp pain cramped his thigh. He suddenly became aware of his own wounds. Fragments of shrapnel had pierced through his left leg, obviously fracturing it because he could no longer move it. Yet, he had to urgently seek shelter—no matter how much pain he was in.

Using his good leg, Edouard dragged himself toward the closest depression in the ground, pulling Vanessa by her shirt. With every movement, he felt as if a scalpel was clawing into his thigh. He bit down hard on his lips to stop himself from screaming out in pain.

Finally, they collapsed inside of a crater formed by an explosion. The hole wasn't very deep, but it offered them a relatively safe shelter—it being rare for two shells to fall in exactly the same spot. Heart speeding and short of breath, the lieutenant placed Vanessa, who was still unconscious, down as best as he could. He then took out a Swiss army knife from his pocket and cut his pants around the gaping gash. Blood was coming out in small, steady spurts. "An artery must have been punctured," Edouard thought to himself. "At this rate, I'm going to lose all my blood in a few minutes."

He pulled out a packet of sterile compresses from his pocket, ripped open the protective package and firmly applied the gauze on his wound. The force of this action caused him to yelp in pain, but he knew that the application of strong pressure was the only way to stop the hemorrhage.

Within seconds, the entire compress was soaked in blood and Edouard could feel his strength diminishing. His vision was becoming blurry, a cold sweat covered his brow and his breathing got heavier. The sensations in his body were gradually getting numb, his eyelids closed and he felt himself getting lighter and lighter. Edouard only wanted to do one thing: sleep. He knew, however, that if he allowed himself to fall asleep he would never wake up.

In a last attempt at survival, he pressed down harder on the gauze and the pain jolted him. But the insidious torpor quickly returned. Death was no longer a stranger to him. She appeared rather like a friend who accompanies you on a trip. And Edouard already wanted to leave, on this final upward journey. He felt so drained—so exhausted. The moment had come. He opened his eyes to contemplate the African sky one last time. This clear blue sky released such a wonderful gentleness, an infinite peace.

The mortar fire had ceased. The Sambizanian infantry would soon seize the village without much difficulty, for there weren't many more peacekeepers left to stop them. It was over and Edouard knew it. He felt relieved; his suffering would also be ending soon. To bleed to death or to die from enemy fire—it really didn't matter anymore.

Edouard eased the pressure of the compress and the pain dissipated. Eyes wide open, he continued to stare into the azure sky. He slowly detached himself from the world, oblivious even of the Sambizanian soldiers who were cautiously moving toward his shelter. He closed his eyelids and his ears began lightly buzzing. He was on the verge of fainting. His breaths were getting further apart, shallower. His heartbeat was declining gradually. "How easy it is to die," thought the lieutenant, drifting in and out of a delirious state of consciousness.

The sound in his ears grew more and more acute. Far from diminishing, it increased with persistence. It seemed to Edouard that the droning was louder and coming toward him. Confused, he opened his eyes and spotted enormous engines above.

American helicopters! His heart instantly accelerated and a powerful vital force bolstered his entire body back to life. At the same time, the pain once again ripped through his thigh with dire potency. Edouard let out a cry of pure joy mixed with pain.

The helicopters continued to hover over the village. Every pilot knew exactly what he was supposed to do. Using the information Vanessa had provided in her message; some bombarded the hill while others marked the landing zone with colored smoke. The U.S. troops proceeded with extreme prudence, since they couldn't suffer the slightest loss. In fact, under pressure from the public, the American army was supposed to carry out their military operation without losing a single man.

Fortunately, the speed of the attack and the intensity of the gunfire frightened the Sambizanian soldiers so much so that they didn't even attempt to retaliate. The northern troops dispersed in all different directions. Some of them fled away staggering, loaded with worthless loot stolen from the villagers. Others dropped their guns to run faster. Then there were those who surrendered, yelling and waving their hands frantically in the air.

The soldiers carried out their orders to the letter. They jumped out of the helicopters, immediately establishing a defensive position on the dropping zone. The U.S. Marines aimed their weapons in all directions while the medics followed them with stretchers and first-aid kits. In a few minutes, they had taken control over the west extremity of the periphery of Kiboyo. More to the north, Apache AH-64 helicopters sprayed the hill with rocket fire. In a few seconds, the entire hill was transformed into a blazing inferno.

The helicopters had landed in the open zone on the west periphery. Lieutenant Demat—completely immobilized and away from the defensive perimeter—witnessed from afar this unexpected military intervention. By his side, Vanessa had still not regained consciousness and he was not physically able to carry her.

Minutes passed by and Edouard's enthusiasm began to wane. "To die at this moment would really be too stupid. No, no, no...," he repeated again and again to chase away the heavy wave of lethargy once again washing over his body. He no longer accepted his end, or that of Vanessa. But death wasn't ready to let go of its prey that easily and Edouard's life was fleeing from him at the same rate as the blood flowing from his leg.

"A tourniquet, I have to make a tourniquet." Edouard took off his shirt and tightly wrapped a sleeve around his thigh. At the same time, he saw in the distance the first medical helicopter—a *Pave Hawk HH-60G* with Red Cross insignias flanking its sides—taking off in a whirlwind of dust. The second rescue helicopter hovered at low altitude and got ready to land. And within a few minutes, it too would take off. Without them.

"No way. It can't be possible! They're going to leave without us!" exclaimed Edouard, his eyes brimming with tears of rage. "And I can't even alert them that we are here. I left my rocket-launcher pistol in the middle of the village." He turned around with distress deeply etched on his face and looked at Vanessa. The young journalist was still unconscious. Uncontrollable sobs began shaking the lieutenant's body. He looked at his thigh. His shirt was already drenched in blood, just like Warrant Officer Depraeter's. "Depraeter! As a warrant officer of the platoon, he also would have had a rocket-launcher pistol!"

In a last burst of energy, Edouard crawled through the dirt on the strength of his arms—more dead than alive—right up to the nearby hole occupied by the corpse of the ill-fated Depraeter. Fumbling through the dead officer's bag, he discovered the rocket-launcher pistol. With difficulty, he fed it a cartridge and fired it above his head. The rocket produced an enormous colored arch before it fell behind a thorny grove. He reloaded the gun and fired again. Then he pulled off the water flask attached to the corpse's belt and painfully exited the tomb.

Back at the shelter, Edouard uncapped the water flask and moistened Vanessa's lips. She still didn't respond. This time around, he tried to take a sip. But he barely brought the bottle to his mouth when his head started to spin. What little strength he had, finally left him and he collapsed on his back.

A few minutes later, a huge U.S. marine sergeant appeared above the shelter and yelled with a thick Alabama accent, "Are you okay?" But he got no reply. Edouard and Vanessa were both unconscious.

CHAPTER 35

"I'm so glad to see you!" Henry Hurst declared loudly as he greeted Michael. "Forgive me for not receiving you at the White House, but it was wiser to meet with you here."

"I fully understand, Mr. Vice President." Michael let his eyes rove around the small office at the Washington U.S. Naval Station.

"Your girlfriend is safe. The helicopter rescue operation led by Colonel Ziegler was a total success. I must tell you that your performance on television along with the spontaneous public demonstrations that followed the program persuaded the president to take immediate action. My most sincere congratulations, Mr. Lancaster!"

"Thank you. I must emphasize that the success of this humanitarian operation will have a positive effect on the president's popularity ratings." Michael lay down a heavy brown leather briefcase on the polished surface of the solid cherry table. "Mr. Vice President, here are all the documents that will allow for the arrest of presidential candidate Jack Kotten. You will find substantive proof of his implication in the assassination of Senator Davidson as well as his involvement in diverse criminal operations." Michael smiled slightly. "I won't hide my great relief at finally divesting myself of these burdensome papers. Tonight, I'll sleep a lot more peacefully—particularly, if I am assured of your utmost discretion as to the origin of these revelations."

"You most certainly can be assured of that, Mr. Lancaster. Only the president will be informed of your contribution in settling this affair. Be equally convinced that everything will be put in place to punish the perpetrators of this odious crime. I will see to it personally." The vice president took the briefcase and held out a hand to Michael. "I regret, but I must leave you." He turned around briskly, and disappeared into the hallway accompanied by two U.S. Navy officers.

* * *

Vanessa was slowly recuperating at the Bethesda Naval Hospital in Maryland. When she regained consciousness, a nurse explained that U.S. Marine helicopters had rescued her: "As a result of intense public pressure following a special report on *It Concerns Us*, the U.S. government acted very quickly. A unit of Marines was immediately deployed to Sambizania. They saved you, the peacekeepers and the inhabitants who had survived the massacre. You were very lucky!"

Vanessa asked in a frail voice, "And the lieutenant…is he alive?"

"Yes," replied the nurse. "They told me that the Belgian lieutenant who was with you survived. But since he is not an American citizen, he was hospitalized in Kenya."

Vanessa's thoughts naturally drifted to Michael. "Why isn't he at my bedside at this very moment? Does he still want me? Is he still in love with me even after our breakup? Did he meet another woman?" The pain in her head intensified such that it became unbearable. Vanessa willingly accepted the painkiller the nurse offered her and fell asleep.

* * *

Michael finally stepped into the vast entrance hall of the hospital. He moved quickly toward the information desk. The attendant told him what floor Vanessa was on. He was so anxious to see Vanessa again that he had to hold himself back from running down the hallway leading to her room. The hospital staff had told him that she had regained consciousness without any major after-effects. However, she was suffering from partial amnesia—the most recent events in her life, including the harrowing incidents in Sambizania, were a virtual blank in her memory. Michael was feeling nervous and apprehensive: "Will she remember me? Will I recognize her? Will she have any recollection of our love affair?"

Heart racing, and a bouquet of white calla lilies in hand, Michael pushed open the door to the room where Vanessa was recovering. She had dark circles under her eyes and her face displayed the traces of several bruises. But to Michael she was the most beautiful sight. He looked at her with eyes of love. Vanessa smiled and gave him a look that was worth all the declarations of love in the world.

"Michael...oh, Michael! I...I thought I'd never see you again...I...I..." She wanted to go on, but the words lingered on the tip of her tongue, unable to be vocalized. Her eyes misted and tears ran down her pale cheeks.

Michael relinquished the flowers on the bedsheet and grasped her hands ardently. "Vanessa, I'm so happy to see you."

He leaned forward, wanting badly to give her a kiss. But he held back. Wrung by emotion, he didn't quite know what stance to take. He, like she, was at a loss for words. "Where can I put the flowers?" he asked.

"They're beautiful," declared Vanessa, her voice a mix of tears and joy. "I think there's a vase on the bottom shelf of the white closet."

Michael was about to head for the closet when Vanessa lightly grabbed him by the arm.

"Oh, Michael, stay here. Hold me tight." He leaned toward her and they embraced for several enduring minutes.

CHAPTER 36

In the enchanted kingdom of Disneyland where Michael and Vanessa were walking, everything looked fine to the naked eye. Despite the late hour, hordes of chubby-cheeked children were devouring jumbo ice cream cones. The whole scene was in sharp contrast to the vivid pictures of the African villages still etched in Vanessa's mind. Unfortunately, part of her experience in Sambizania had completely disappeared from her memory. Her brain had also erased the most traumatic images of the battle and bloodshed in Kiboyo. The memories before her departure to Africa, however, were exactly in place.

She perfectly recalled the time she spent with Michael and the reason for their separation. Both of them avoided the subject of their breakup, preferring to hold onto the illusion that it was nothing more than a brief interlude in their relationship. But in reality, they had changed a lot since then. Vanessa had experienced firsthand the fragility of life. Michael had learned that social success had its pitfalls and had shifted his thoughts toward more human values.

The time apart and what they went through had in fact brought them closer together. Vanessa was far less egocentric. She now shared Michael's ideals of justice. And he had become more in tune with his sensitive side, less driven by politics and the hustle and bustle of everyday events. He was now able to share with Vanessa his fears and weaknesses as well as his worries and feelings. They spoke in this manner, both candidly and from the heart, along the lush, animated paths of Disneyland.

"You know, I was really lucky to have made it out of there alive," said Vanessa.

"I know."

"Twice I saw death staring me in the face. But I guess it wasn't my time—it's as if I still had something important to accomplish on this earth."

"What you just said to me is really strange, because I had the exact same feeling."

"Maybe we'll do these important things together?" She looked at him with a smile.

"I would like that a lot."

They continued to walk and talk right until the moment when the sun, in all its blazing glory, disappeared from the horizon.

Nightfall marked the start of the fireworks display. The first colorful pyrotechnics to explode into the night sky made Vanessa jump and she began to shake. "I'm sorry, Michael.... This is so silly...I know it's nothing more than harmless fireworks, but I—"

"No, I understand." Michael put a protective arm around Vanessa's shoulders. "Let's go. It's already late." They headed leisurely toward the exit of the amusement park, totally in sync with one another.

On the way back from Disneyland, Vanessa took the wheel of the car. Michael still hadn't got back his driver's license. They rode safely all the way to their ocean front hotel. Before going inside, the couple took a stroll along the sandy shores of the Pacific Ocean.

The starry California sky brought Vanessa back to Africa. Bits and pieces of her memory were beginning to come back to her. And for the first time, she talked about the positive moments she had experienced on the faraway continent. She described the beautiful yet humbling grandeur of the wild landscape, the shy yet friendly smiles of the women, both young and old, and the overall strength and courage of the local population. She remarked on how much the elders were listened to as well as the great degree to which the children were full of life despite all of their deprivations. Michael's attentive ear helped Vanessa recount her memories. The events she lived through, both good and bad, were fueled with emotion and she still felt vulnerable when she spoke of them.

They sat down on a huge rock beside the roaring waves and Michael took Vanessa's hand in his own. "I missed you a lot, you know. I thought about you all the time. I was very worried—worried about losing you, worried that something horrible might happen to you."

Vanessa was moved by Michael's words. It was the first time he was actually opening up to her. She now found him beautiful not only on the outside but on the inside. Like every other woman in the world, she dreamt of a man who was able to communicate his feelings. And such a man was sitting by her side—vibrant and charming, spellbinding and incredibly attractive.

Vanessa was in love. She even felt herself getting sexually aroused. But she was nervously anticipating the moment when Michael would once again express his desire for her. She wished he would demonstrate his passion but she was afraid of reliving all the frustration related to his premature ejaculation. And that thought was enough to extinguish her desire to make love. Certainly, there was no longer any question of ever leaving him. But how meaningful was a romantic relationship amputated from its sexual dimension? Would she have to forever forsake this very important part of pleasure? Was this the price to pay to be with such a wonderful man? Her brush with death did teach her just how precious the joys of life were. But did this mean sexual satisfaction was now suddenly less important? Should she renounce it, like certain religions encouraged? No. Romantic and sexual ecstasy seemed far too beautiful to her, far too powerful and far too magnificent to be regarded as anything other than a divine creation. It was clearly the work of God—His masterpiece.

* * *

Back at the hotel Vanessa asked Michael if he wouldn't mind if she spent the night in the same room as him because she was afraid of sleeping alone.

Since her return to the States, Michael had been very careful to respect Vanessa's privacy for she was still shaken by the disturbing events she had been through. He went so far as to book separate rooms for their first trip together since their reunion. But deep within, he was questioning his true motives: Am I demonstrating such respect and physical restraint to delay making love to her? Or am I just afraid of not being able to control myself? Dr. Carter was very considerate when he told me that making love was about pleasure and not about performance. But I know that if I fail sexually with Vanessa it will be extremely disappointing. A mix of pride and discretion stopped him from sharing his therapy sessions with Vanessa. He accepted with mild enthusiasm that Vanessa share his bed.

They stayed on top of the covers without taking off their clothes and didn't say a word to each other. Michael felt his stomach tense up at the thought of putting his new sexual knowledge into practice. He was sure that as far as sex went, it would be a traumatic night. He regretted having not gone over his exercises after his therapy sessions had ended. But it was too late now. He would have to confront the situation with what he remembered.

Vanessa lay her head down securely on the shoulder of her reunited lover and fell asleep amazingly quick. Michael heaved a sigh of relief. He had been granted a new delay before the final hour of truth. He would take advantage of this respite to recall what the sex therapist had taught him. Slowly, he breathed from his diaphragm and one by one his muscles relaxed. He went over in his mind all of the exercises he had practiced. With their simple evocation, he felt himself regaining confidence. But the confidence was limited to that of being able to successfully carry out his exercises well, not yet that of being able to make love well. In order for this to happen, he would have to test his sex techniques in real life. And the opportunity for him to be able to prove himself was imminent. "Let's hope it works out," he thought to himself. He turned over on his side and allowed sleep to win him over.

In the middle of the night, the backfire from a Harley-Davidson motorcycle startled Vanessa, awakening her full of anguish. Michael comforted her by rocking her tightly in his arms. And to relax her, he cracked a joke: "Really, 'Davidson' is following us everywhere!"

Vanessa managed a tiny smile and little by little calmed down. "I think I'm going to think about Africa for a long time. Thanks for your patience and support, Michael. It's been a real help so far." She snuggled up to Michael and took refuge at the hollow of his shoulder. In an instant, she plunged back into the land of dreams.

Feeling Vanessa's warm body brushing lightly up against his own, Michael was greatly turned on and instantly overwhelmed by erotic thoughts. He desired to press himself close to her body, to cup her plentiful breasts in his hands, to make love to her. Violent urges stormed inside of him. But he didn't move for fear of disturbing her sleep. All he did was watch and admire his sleeping beauty. Sometimes Vanessa moved in her sleep and her legs grazed those of Michael. One particular moment, she flipped over on her side and her buttocks pressed against Michael's penis. Again, he didn't dare move.

For a good part of the night, Michael just couldn't fall asleep. The warm proximity of Vanessa's body and her involuntary contact with his own aroused a hungry desire within him and a rather frustrating anxiety. It was finally around five in the morning when fatigue got the better of him. Only then did he close his eyes and put his mind to bed.

* * *

Lieutenant Demat glanced at the empty seats on the plane heading for Europe. An old Belgian Air Force Hercule C130 was flying back the peacekeepers who had survived the bloody conflict in Sambizania. The plane was almost empty, the unoccupied seats were a painful reminder of the men he had lost. *Lost.* The word haunted his mind incessantly. Every single young man who had died on African soil had put his faith and confidence in him. As head officer, he was their guide, the shepherd responsible for his flock. And he had lost them.... He couldn't help judge every one of the decisions he had made. Many now appeared to him to be errors of command. No one blamed him; he himself knew the truth. He, alone, carried the heavy burden of regret.

The soldiers on the plane were silent, each one absorbed in his own thoughts. They all looked ten years older. Six months earlier they had left full of verve, with the unconcern and temerity typical of youth. The sudden and brutal confrontation with suffering and death had made old men out of them. Nothing in their education or training had prepared them for this cruel encounter. And the Gulf War had given them the false illusion that it was somehow possible to fight a technological war, a so-called video game war, almost without the loss of human lives. But precisely, the technological means were simply not on hand for this particularly gruesome battle. The somewhat ambiguous nature of the UN mission had sent them out on the battlefield without the sufficient military resources. Upon arrival at the Melsbroek military airport, the soldiers, seething with rage, ripped apart their blue berets—a symbolic gesture signifying the fact that the UN had abandoned them. The peacekeepers knew they owed their lives to rapid intervention by the Americans. As a sign of gratitude, many among them were wearing on their uniforms the insignia of the U.S. Marines who had saved them.

The gray Belgian sky spat out cold, fine drizzle, drenching the tarmac on the runway. Lieutenant Demat spotted the throng of parents and journalists who were waiting for them behind the base's gates. But the closer he got to the crowd, the farther his thoughts drifted—they wandered over and beyond toward distant horizons. Yasmine...his beloved Yasmine had disappeared during the annihilation of the UN camp in Sambizania. Was she dead or alive? He couldn't go on living without knowing this. Nothing else mattered; nothing else was important. All that counted from this day forward was the hope of seeing Yasmine again.

Journalists, his friends and his parents surrounded him on all sides. They were asking him dozens of questions, but Edouard didn't reply. Trickles of water ran down his impassive face and no one could say for sure if they consisted of rain or tears. Edouard seemed absent; a vital part of him was already long gone. His soul was lost somewhere in Africa, searching for the one he loved.

CHAPTER 37

V anessa woke up late in the morning feeling all energized. "What a gorgeous day! Wake up, sleepy head! Come play tennis with me! I'll be ready in five minutes."

Michael, still trapped within the snare of sleep, muttered a jumbled, unintelligible reply. A cheerful Vanessa ignored him and slipped into the bathroom to get ready. He promptly fell back to sleep.

The rich aroma of coffee finally cranked open his eyelids and Vanessa motioned for him to come and join her on the terrace. Michael got up like a sleepwalker and resumed his awakening process under the pressure of a cool shower. When he finally made it outside, Vanessa was just sinking her teeth into a warm croissant. The view was spectacular. The terrace overlooked the ocean and in the distance, sea otters could be seen breaking open shells on their stomach with the help of pebbles. Michael felt like he was alone on a deserted island with his lover.

Vanessa looked radiant in an adorable tennis outfit—the bright white fabric a flattering contrast against her tanned skin. She was in an excellent mood and amused herself by kidding around with Michael who was still not totally awake. The young woman dipped her croissant into his cup of hot chocolate, saying that it was surely better than her own cup of coffee. But the croissant slipped from her hands and fell into the mug, spattering Michael with the hot chocolate drink. Michael's sports shirt was spotted with brown splotches. Vanessa burst out laughing and Michael himself couldn't help finding his girlfriend's clumsiness funny. Happiness made them both feel incredibly care-free.

Vanessa got up and sat down on Michael's knees to better rub out the stains. As Michael ran his hands through her long auburn locks, she looked at him with love in her eyes. She wrapped her arms affectionately around his neck and nestled against his chest, feeling safe. Nothing else in the world mattered. Vanessa lifted her head and once again looked Michael in the eyes, this time with lust. She placed a kiss on his forehead, then on his nose, then on his lips. Her body crushed itself against his and she began kissing him more intensely.

The night before, Vanessa had subtly tried to rev up Michael's sex drive by making what she wanted to have him believe was involuntary contact with his body. But he had not reacted. She decided that he would make love to her now or she would have to rape him. This wasn't going to be necessary because already Michael was reciprocating her passionate kisses. He caressed her arms and ran his hands up and down her back ravenously.

Vanessa encouraged Michael with a long, lustful sigh. Still sitting on his knees, she slid her hands underneath his shirt to better feel his chest. In the end she took it off completely, dropping innumerable impassioned kisses all over his coppery, sun-soaked skin.

Michael indulged in Vanessa's ardent passion. He let his hands explore the length of her silky thighs. He was finally able to freely touch the woman he had been waiting for these past interminable weeks. He would have wanted ten hands to be able to fondle his partner everywhere at the same time.

Vanessa's overexcitement was contagious. Michael realize he had become just as emotionally feverish as he was sexually excited. If he carried on like this, he wouldn't get too far. He straightened himself out and breathed deeply from his belly, as if the oxygen was reaching his crotch. He loosened his tight muscles while exhaling. After a few breaths, he became calmer and more sensual. He applauded himself for having repeated his exercises on the shores of Palm Beach. In practice, the breathing technique really wasn't as complicated as he had imagined. And it didn't prevent him from being perfectly in tune with Vanessa.

Michael began provocatively exploring Vanessa's voluptuous body. His fingers slowly slipped underneath her T-shirt and walked up and down her bare back and sexy curves. Every now and then he stopped momentarily to let the palms of his hands soak up the heat escaping from the young woman's vivacious body. He then resumed his seductive climb—making sure that every square inch of Vanessa's flesh had received a visit from his fingers.

A barrier was obstructing him from sliding his hands down his partner's back unimpeded. So with an experienced hand, Michael unfastened her bra clasp. Vanessa let out a sensual moan as she felt her breasts being liberated from the hold of the cotton support, ready at last to be offered into her lover's hands. She propelled her bust forward inviting Michael to greater venture toward the velvety skin of her bosom. She could feel the tips of her nipples hardening, almost painfully. Fortunately, Michael's sexually scalding hands fingered her firm curves with a lot of tenderness. It seemed to the young woman that her breasts had become even more sensitive during the time away from her lover.

Vanessa succumbed to the delicious caresses without moving. Michael had succeeded to regulate the rhythm of their exchanges. With slow and gentle touches, he had established a languorous tempo favorable to controlling his sexual excitement. In addition, he had reached a new stage where he could enjoy his partner and become moved by her reactions. He was regaining his confidence and for the first time in what seemed like forever, he eagerly anticipated what was to come.

Despite how fantastically good Michael was making her feel, the position on his knees was becoming less comfortable. Vanessa took him by the wrists and obliged him to follow her into the bedroom. She shoved him against the wall and proceeded to passionately attack him. She kissed him again and again, full on the mouth, boldly caressing the inside of his thighs. Vanessa was in an anxious rush to feel her man's hard penis in her hand. But out of pure capriciousness, she wanted him to be the first one to touch her between her legs. So she avoided directly touching his penis and satisfied herself with stroking the bottom of his stomach.

Michael, for his part, feared that his own pleasure combined with Vanessa's voracious appetite would make him lose control. Backed up against the wall, he sucked in the inebriating feminine scent of his mate who was leaning suggestively against him. He could feel her hot breath against his neck as his fingers reached the top of her thighs. He felt a powerful surge of sexual excitement rush through him as she put his hand under her short white skirt. Vanessa's muffled murmurs ultimately turned into clear howls of pleasure when Michael slid an audacious finger between her scandalously round buttocks.

Consumed by his partner's racy reactions, Michael lost track of the course of his own excitement. He suddenly realized that his entire body was tense with pleasure. He understood that it was absolutely crucial to start thinking about his diaphragmatic breathing if he desired to prolong his pleasure. By doing so, he would shift to a more sensual mode, one that was more diffused, and this would allow him to benefit more from the sexual encounter. He took all the time in the world to explore Vanessa's sexy derriere and the lower part of her stomach, avoiding directly touching her genitals so as not to stimulate her too fast.

Vanessa strongly desired Michael's hands to venture farther. So every time he lightly grazed the fine red mane of her pubis, she let out a little groan of encouragement. But this sexual appeal didn't quite provoke the response she had wished. She opened her legs slightly so that Michael's fingers would have greater room for maneuver. This move actually heightened her desire—for the more her thighs spread apart, the more the lips of her sex swelled with pleasure.

Intimate sap began to form on the edge of her vulva, moistening her underwear. To push Michael into more sexual audacity, she whispered into his ear, "Take off my panties..."

He replied in a single breath, "How do you want me to take them off? With my fingers or with my teeth?"

"It doesn't matter. Just take them off quickly, they're already very wet..."

This erotic exchange enabled Michael not only to take part in a fantasy, but also to catch his breath. He executed Vanessa's sexual request by grasping the elastic on her white thong with his teeth. And then with the help of his hands, he slid the cotton article down the length of his lover's long, shapely legs. Next, he scooped her up in his arms and spread her out on the bed. He lay down beside her and smiled broadly knowing how happy he was making her. Michael was extremely turned on and wanted Vanessa so badly, but just thinking about the imminence of penetration caused him to doubt if Dr. Carter's technique really worked. A shudder of dread shot down his spine at the thought of failing in his effort to win back Vanessa. But he reassured himself with a dose of reason: "Whatever the case may be, I don't have a choice. So it's best that I apply what I learned well and whatever happens, happens." Once again he concentrated on his breathing and on relaxing his muscles. Little by little his excitement diminished and his body turned more fluid. He even felt his erection becoming less rigid. But he knew it was perfectly normal so he didn't worry. He told himself that there was no need to rush, their lovemaking was just beginning.

Michael walked over to the table and brought back with him a bunch of green grapes that he offered to Vanessa's full, pink lips. This sensual diversion allowed him to expand his erotism as well as control his sexual excitement. Vanessa bit down firmly into the grapes which, upon bursting, spattered all over her body. Michael leaned over her and sucked up, one by one, the clear droplets of juice from the various parts of her anatomy. As his lips made their way to the inside of her thighs, Vanessa tilted her head back. And as if she were in a slow motion film, she stretched out on her back, her legs spreading apart instinctively. Michael's mouth approached her vulva excruciatingly slowly. And when he finally touched the edge of her clitoris, she bit down on her lip to keep from screaming out in pleasure.

Michael was perfectly aware of the emotion he was causing Vanessa. He was thrilled at the wild pleasure he was giving her but he no longer considered this luscious delectation the final frontier. This was not the end; this was only the beginning. No longer did he feel limited to satisfy his partner uniquely by stimulating her clitoris. It was but one stage of mutual pleasure. And he was secretly hoping to satiate her in another way. But would he be able to pull it off the first time with Vanessa with so little practice? Even Dr. Carter had warned him about possible problems. "Don't expect miracles when you get back with your girlfriend. You will need a period of adjustment before you are able to master the techniques and fully control your excitation."

Michael distanced his mouth from her clitoris, which was taut from excitement. He knew that from now on it was preferable to bring about different sensations in Vanessa, ones that were more diffuse, more internal. He gently inserted his middle finger inside of her opened vagina. It was so welcoming and so lubricated that he didn't hesitate to introduce another finger into it. He then effectuated pushes against the vaginal wall toward her stomach, prompting a series of voluptuous sighs from his partner. While his fingers pursued their internal pressures, his other hand was pressing down on her warm and soft lower abdomen.

Vanessa simply adored the entire gamut of stimulation that she was receiving from Michael's hands. The pleasure was so strong and so delicious that she had an orgasm. But it didn't completely satiate her. She was waiting for something else: the moment when Michael's phallus would fill her body. She desired to feel his hard penis vibrating inside her belly. She dreamt of sucking in all of her lover's maleness deep within her. At the same time she feared this embrace would once again be too brief. The memory of Michael's rapid ejaculations entered her mind. These thoughts perturbed her a little, but did not discourage her from really wanting to be penetrated.

Vanessa quickly and insatiably removed Michael's white shorts. She couldn't hold off for another second longer. She took her lover's erect sex organ between her hands and started lightly stroking it up and down with her fingers. Michael let himself fully enjoy the pleasure she was giving him while still paying close attention to his own corporal reactions. When Vanessa accelerated the up and down movement on the shaft of his penis, he felt his abdominals and buttocks strongly contract. Without panicking, he relaxed his muscles and returned to breathing slowly and deeply. For once in his life, he took the time to savor the pleasure his body was experiencing. Intensely powerful erotic sensations germinated in his phallus. They spread to his stomach and then to his chest, which formed an arc. They then continued their course right up to his throat, screaming their way to the edge of his half-opened mouth.

When he realized Vanessa's hand caresses were progressively drawing him toward ejaculation, he feared for a second that it would bring an abrupt end to their pleasure. He delicately freed her hand from its hold and kissed it affectionately.

Vanessa got the message and once again surrendered herself to Michael. Lying flat on her stomach, she felt his masterly fingers caressing her back under the T-shirt she was still wearing. Michael's hands eventually made their way down to her hips and lingered on the back of her legs. Vanessa then felt her lover's palms wander underneath her skirt and lightly brush the very fine and sensitive flesh on her thighs.

Michael chose this very moment to initiate the next part of their romantic journey. He knew Vanessa was now ready to receive him inside of her. For his part, he had voluntarily brought down his sexual excitement to a safe level by applying the techniques. His erection was still very present although not one hundred percent hard. He took Vanessa in his arms and turned her over. She was now lying on her back and staring at him with eager eyes. He lifted her short tennis skirt and slowly spread apart her legs.

Michael knew that Vanessa had been anticipating this moment for a long time. She gently grabbed his penis between her fingers and pulled it into her. Without panicking, Michael thrust his sexual organ into Vanessa's warm vagina with extraordinary sensual slowness. This languorous penetration roused up within him particularly scintillating emotions and fantasies. Just to be on the safe side, he effectuated a long pause that enabled him to considerably reduce the amount of physical stimulation he was receiving.

He took advantage of this respite to look deeply into Vanessa's eyes and declare, "You are a wonderfully desirable woman. Making love to you is amazing. Our bodies are the perfect match. I love being inside of you so much and I wish this moment to last forever."

Vanessa replied with a lustful look. He felt the muscles at the entrance of her vagina contracting, summoning more sensations. Michael, less stimulated but still very worried, answered this call with an ample and harmonious movement from the pelvis. Leaning on his forearms, he realized that he didn't have to contract the muscles in his crotch or buttocks to become aroused and to maintain his erection. Also, more at ease, he gradually let go of the tension in all the muscles he didn't need to support his position or to execute the movement from the pelvis.

Michael swayed his hips with suppleness and without hurry. After a few movements, he felt his erection intensifying to an alarming degree. "No!" he spoke sharply to himself. "It would be stupid to ejaculate now!" He wanted to tighten his entire body to restrain his ejaculation from occurring as it was about to any second now. But he recalled Dr. Carter's words: "Breathe amply and slowly right to the bottom of your belly, relax your muscles and let your sexual excitation diffuse throughout your body." Just narrowly, he interrupted his movements and successfully applied the sex therapist's advice. He breathed deeply and relaxed his muscles, especially those in his crotch. When he regained his composure, Michael acknowledged that the hurried pause he had just made was far from graceful. It would be wise in the future for him to pay closer attention to his level of arousal.

Happy that he had triumphed at keeping his sexual excitement below the threshold of the ejaculatory reflex, Michael prolonged the pause by tenderly caressing Vanessa's hair. He inhaled her perfume, felt the heat of her vagina around his penis and saw her quivering in his arms. Michael was discovering love. He was no longer simply an excited sexual creature. He had become an erotic man—capable of being moved by the female mystique, capable of sipping her sweetness and her sensuality, capable of harmonizing with her multiplicity.

Enraptured by the presence of the woman he loved so dearly, Michael recommenced the movements of penetration. He once again let himself be swept along by the sea of pleasure, forgetting all about technique and breathing. Ready to explode, his hard phallus entered into Vanessa's hot and muggy abyss. Michael's excitement was reaching dangerously high levels. Vanessa, sensing that he was going to ejaculate very soon, quickened the movements of her pelvis in hopes of bringing herself to orgasm before him.

Noticing his partner speeding up, Michael realized how sexually stirred up he was himself. His gluteus muscles were contracting spasmodically so as to push his penis into rapid forward movements. He was panting at the top of his thoracic cage. Every single muscle in his body became tense in a final effort toward the redemptive discharge.

His penis suddenly got extremely hard and was becoming more sensitive along its entire length—the telling sign that his ejaculation was imminent.

"I'm gonna come! One more move and that will be it. I have to stop immediately! And what about Vanessa? She's going to be so disappointed. She's so turned on, so hot, so very aroused! But I have no other choice. I have to stop now!"

Michael pulled out and let himself drop over Vanessa's stomach, his penis tucked between her legs. He relaxed his gluteus muscles, his thighs, his crotch and his stomach. He then began breathing deeply and slowly all over again.

Vanessa was sure Michael had ejaculated. Having herself soared to very high levels of sexual excitement she had not felt a thing. Once again she experienced maddening frustration. Even more than in the past. Because this time around, their lovemaking had lasted longer than ever before and she had climbed to very steep heights of sexual pleasure. Right up until everything was so moronically stopped. She would have to start all over again. It was back to square one, when she was now very aroused and close to orgasm. Her heart was beating wildly and her stomach was burning with desire. She wanted so desperately to be penetrated, to be consumed and tortured with pleasure. But it was all over; her poor lover's sexual organ would now be out of commission for an indefinite period of time.

As for Michael, he was feeling a lot more serene. He had succeeded in controlling himself a second time and his excitement had diminished substantially during this last prolonged pause. He was very aware that he had totally frustrated Vanessa. But, proud of his success, he forgave himself for having not played out everything to perfection. He also accepted the fact that he still had lots to learn. And it was also despite this that he had finally gained the certitude that Dr. Carter's technique worked.

Still, things weren't exactly going wonderfully well. Vanessa had turned her head and appeared more and more distant. Michael had to act quickly.

There wasn't much he could do. In fact, he only saw two alternatives. He could call it quits, end sexual activity and then try to explain later. Or he could resume their lovemaking and risk that Vanessa was no longer in the mood.

Michael chose the second option. He glided to the side and skilfully removed Vanessa's last articles of clothing. He moved toward her shoulders and held them delicately. Then he went down to her fabulous breasts, which offered themselves like succulent fruit to his mouth.

Vanessa, still full of desire, surrendered to the scrumptious caresses without the slightest reluctance. A sweet feeling of pleasure flowed into the firm extremity of her breasts and diffused across her chest. Then, the delectable simmering radiated toward her stomach and blew over the still piping hot embers of her genitals.

In an explosion of passion, Vanessa drew her lover's face to her. Their mouths met in an impetuous kiss. Their lips locked with the voracity of a predator devouring its prey. Their tongues clashed in a duel of lust. They rushed, touched and twirled in a frenzied dance. Impulsively, Vanessa clutched the nape of her lover's neck and her fingernails dug into his damp flesh like *banderillas*. Michael firmly grabbed Vanessa's shapely waist, slipped his sizzling hands on her hips, and groped her sultry feminine curves with brazen robustness. He relinquished his partner's intoxicating lips and fervently tore into the delicate skin of her neck. Vanessa released tiny plaintive cries of pleasure broken by short breaths. Her pelvis flung forward and her legs spread apart in a feral call for the fusion of their bodies.

Michael slammed down against her hot stomach and she once again felt, like in a dream, the exquisite sensation of penetration. With surprise and rapture, she realized that her lover was still erect and was resuming possession of her.

Michael was much more confident now. Although he kept on proceeding in a chaotic manner, he was able to modulate his sexual excitement. And this had enabled him to avoid ejaculating quickly two times. The sensations of thrusting appeared less intense than at the beginning of intercourse. His penis was accustomed to Vanessa's vagina. However, being cautious, he carried on with exceptional slowness.

These slow penetrations allowed Vanessa to appreciate each sensual stage of the progression of her lover's penis within her. She felt her sex opening like a shell rocked by the ocean. She eagerly grasped

Michael's behind with her hands and drew him deeper inside of her. And then she wrapped her legs securely around his waist so that he wouldn't escape again. It was too good to be true. Vanessa had a hard time believing it—he had not ejaculated! He continued to love her, to enjoy her and to appreciate this beautiful innermost act. She didn't want to let him go; she wanted to totally possess him. She immensely desired for him to come inside of her, to inundate her with his semen.

Michael felt that his penis was prisoner of Vanessa's ardent hold. To release himself from this loving grip, he initiated with dexterity a circular movement from the hips. Free, he slowly thrust into his partner's warm and inviting valley. The young woman, drunk from pleasure, let out many provocative moans. Turned on by her sighs, Michael seized both of Vanessa's wrists and pinned her down on the bed. He had the firm intention of making her orgasm with the quiet force of his movements.

He pursued this languorous in and out motion without accelerating the rhythm. His arms, shoulders, neck, buttocks, nor legs showed any signs of superfluous muscular tension. Only his abdominals and his dorsals contracted regularly to sway his pelvis with the elegant suppleness of a lambada dancer. His languid thrusts contrasted with the virile grip he was using to keep his lover seductively bolted to the mattress.

Vanessa, conquered by Michael's manly force, delightfully withstood his repeated assaults. The young woman felt as if her lover's slow yet at the same time strong sexual blows would go on forever. Her euphoria had an eternal fragrance to it. The moment seemed timeless.

Feeling his companion tormented by the desire to scream out her pleasure, Michael finally unleashed all of the savage energy he had channeled and restrained to this point. Vanessa, wrists captive to her partner's grip, was experiencing a crazy and wild sexual excitement. She was now vibrating in unison with Michael's movements, feeling his phallus penetrating her more and more fervently. With the muscles located at the entrance of her vagina, she clutched his hard member while fervidly projecting her pubis forward. Her excitement reached a painfully exquisite point until she felt a series of uncontrollable spasms shake her entire body. She heaved loud, ecstatic moans and totally surrendered to his sexual hold.

Michael stopped thrusting and gently pulled out. He then rested his head next to Vanessa's and held her lovingly in his arms. Cheeks flushed and eyes closed, Vanessa slowly caught her breath. Her arms were over her head and she was no longer moving—drained by the orgasmic waves that had engulfed her.

And then, without a word, she spontaneously embraced Michael tightly with her long graceful arms and pulled him toward her feverish body. Her flesh was still searing from the pleasure she had just experienced.

She was happy.

Very happy.

Vanessa opened her eyelids and looked into his eyes. A deep, intimate bond was formed between them.

Vanessa pulled Michael closer to her. She didn't want to lose a morsel of the man she adored. She still wanted to listen to him breathe, to indulge in the heat of his epidermis and to inhale the scent of his skin.

The young woman let out a short cry of surprise, tinged with delight, as she felt her lover's sex organ prying open the petals of her vulva. Michael entered her with extreme delicateness. But he didn't hold back for long. This time, he knew their union was to develop under the seal of complete unbridled love. After a few supple movements, he drove his sex in with a new kind of passion marked with power and amorous furor.

Vanessa raised her legs higher to accommodate his penis more profoundly. She desired for her man to be as deep inside of her as he could get. She wanted to monopolize him, to immerse him within her. She wanted them to form a single fused union, a true communion of the heart and the soul.

They were looking into each other's eyes.

Michael increased the speed of his movements. Vanessa screamed in ecstasy. She wanted him to ejaculate inside of her, to flood her with his source of manliness.

Michael completely let go and felt the imminent arrival of liberating climax. His pleasure suddenly exploded and the orgasm shot through his entire body in a sequence of violent spasms.

Vanessa, feeling this lightning-speed masculine vibration in the deepest hollows of her stomach, experienced a second wave of pleasure—this time even more internal, more muted. And the happiness that engulfed her was so intense that it left her gasping for her breath and in tears on the edge of the bed.

* * *

Lying on her back, conquered and without strength, Vanessa kept her eyes shut. She reached out for Michael's hand, the last concrete link with reality following the ecstasy she had just experienced. But already the physical sensations were fading, inexorably. Only the last vapors emanating from the storm of sensual delight reached her nostrils.

Michael placed a kiss on her forehead and slowly got up. Their fingers separated and Vanessa suddenly felt very alone. She was thirsty. Her throat was totally dry. It surprised her that she had not noticed earlier. "I would really like to drink something," she dreamt. But this would require moving, opening her eyes, getting up and ultimately spoiling the mood.

Vanessa once again felt Michael's presence before her. "How long had he been gone?" she asked herself. "A minute? An hour? A century?" She finally opened her eyes and smiled at her lover.

Michael held out a large glass of pineapple juice to her. "I had a feeling this would make you happy." The young woman brought the refreshing drink to her lips. Michael watched Vanessa for a long time as she took little sips, without rushing, appreciating every mouthful. Then, he took her by the shoulder and gave her an affectionate kiss on the cheek. Vanessa nuzzled up against Michael. They smiled and together turned their eyes toward the ocean voluptuously caressing the Californian shore. Sun rays danced on the waves. And then Michael began to recite Vanessa a line from the *Divine Comedy*: "Love that moves the sun and the other stars…"

New York Institute of Sexology

Individual Consultation

If you want to consult Dr. Frank Carr or Dr. Patrick Sutter, call their New York office toll free at: 1-866-222-4442.

Professional Training

Drs. Carr and Sutter are offering training seminars and supervision in sex therapy for health professionals. For more information, call the New York Institute of Sexology toll free: 1-866-222-4442.

Give the Gift of

CONFIDENTIAL FILE 101

to Your Friends and Colleagues

CHECK YOUR LEADING BOOKSTORE OR ORDER HERE

❑ YES, I want ____copies of *Confidential File 101* at $24.95 U.S. or $35.95 Canadian, plus $3 shipping per book (New York residents please add $2.12 sales tax per book. Allow 15 days for delivery.

My check or money order for $_____ is enclosed.
Please charge my: ❑ Visa   ❑ MasterCard

Name _____

Organization _____

Address _____

City/State/Zip _____

Phone _____   E-mail _____

Card No. _____

Exp. Date _____   Signature _____

Please make your check payable and return to:
ANGLEHART PRESS
244 Fifth Avenue, Suite D243, New York, NY 10001-7604

Call your credit card order toll free to: (800) 953-0038